*Where The Time Goes*

*Also in the Western Lights series*

DARK SLEEPER
THE HOUSE IN THE HIGH WOOD
STRANGE CARGO
BERTRAM OF BUTTER CROSS
ANCHORWICK
A TANGLE IN SLOPS
WHAT I FOUND AT HOOLE
THE COBBLER OF RIDINGHAM

A WESTERN LIGHTS BOOK

# *Where The Time Goes*

JEFFREY E. BARLOUGH

GRESHAM & DOYLE
PUBLISHERS

A Western Lights Book™

Copyright © 2016 by Jeffrey E. Barlough

All rights reserved. No part of this book may be
reproduced, stored in a retrieval system, or transmitted
in any form or by any means, except in the case of
brief passages quoted in critical articles and reviews,
without the prior written permission of the publisher.

This is a work of fiction. Names, characters, places, and incidents
are the products of the author's imagination or are used fictitiously.
Any similarity to actual persons, living or dead, or to actual firms,
events, or locales is purely coincidental.

WHERE THE TIME GOES
First Edition / October 2016

Published by Gresham & Doyle
Los Angeles, California

Cover: *A Garden in Shoreham*, c. 1830 (w/c) by Samuel Palmer (1805-81)
Victoria & Albert Museum, London, UK / De Agostini Picture Library /
Bridgeman Images

To learn more about the Western Lights series visit
www.westernlightsbooks.com

Library of Congress Control Number: 2016904522

ISBN: 978-0-9787634-5-9

Text set in Garamond Antiqua
with decorations in Edwardian Medium
Printed in the United States of America
on acid-free paper

*To serendipity*

And lo! I have thee by the hands,
and will not let thee go.

ROBERT BRIDGES

## Chapter One

**F**OR as long as most anyone can remember, there has been a monster in Eldritch's Cupboard.

Just who is this Eldritch, you may ask, and where is his Cupboard? And why does he keep a monster in it?

Eldritch's Cupboard — so named because a bestial giant called Eldritch in days of yore is supposed to have cached his victims there — is a cavern or grotto of considerable extent, which lies at the base of the Graystone Crags, a few miles from Dithering, in Lingonshire.

The Crags and their companion scarps are honeycombed with tin mines of old, now long played out, for Dithering and its neighboring hamlets once were renowned for them. But the tin is gone, and the miners too, although some there are who remember them. But there be many who remember Eldritch.

Down in Lingonshire there dwells a host of Cornish folk — that is, people descended from the ancient families of Cornwall, in Old Britain — among whom tales of giants have long loomed large, so to speak. Indeed our Cornish ancestors were rather big on giants. Giant Blunderbore, Giant Bolster, Cormoran, Wrath, Rebecks, Giant Eldritch — all figure in the traditions of those of Cornish lineage whose forebears had braved the sundering down in these Lingonshire dales, many miles inland from the long coast.

My own heritage is mixed — Lowland Scots on my father's side, but my mother among her predecessors numbered many Cornish of old who could trace their roots to St. Ives. But of course St. Ives and Cornwall and the Lowlands of Scotland and Old Britain itself long years agone had been erased from the earth — the sundering had seen to that.

Dickie Fish, who had been accounted a bully since that day in his cradle he had poked his doting grandfather a good one, and who always had bullied me, and delighted in chaffing me for my studious habits, is thought to have gone into Eldritch's Cupboard and never come out again. The person who thought this — about the only one in Dithering who did think it — was myself. Most believed he had scorned his family and, having looked out for his chance, had seized it and run away up the country to Medlow or Chedder.

"He is in a bad course, and will meet with a bad end," had been the prediction of the old quiz of a landlady at the Pack Horse Inn. For Dickie Fish had fallen into just about every sort of mischief that a boy of his years can fall into. Well, it's not every stone that is capable of polishing, and Dickie Fish was just such a hard one. After day-down and he hadn't returned, people began to talk. Perhaps he had missed his way home, some suggested, and been drowned in the stream. Or perhaps he had been murdered. For years folks at Dithering kept a lookout for him, not so much because they hoped to find him, some day, but to confirm the old quiz's assertion that he'd met with his bad end.

Although he had bullied me, Dickie Fish had been the best friend I ever had. This is a paradox not unknown among children. Though he fumed, fretted, commanded, and was obeyed, it was difficult for me to bear him the least ill will. Anyhow, the little swaggerer vanished; it all happened a long time ago now. Although most thought he had run off to escape the drudgery of his life in Dithering, I think he returned to the Cupboard for another go at the monster, and there was taken. Leastwise he never was heard of again.

If indeed the monster had got him, then it had served him right, was the view of most in the town. For Dickie Fish had been a heller — a scamp — a troublesome lad. For those who thought he had been killed, there was no paucity of suspects: saber-cats, short-faced bears, dire wolves, teratorns. Of these you may take your choice, for all can be found haunting the wildways of our Lingonshire dales.

At intervals over the years, calves, sheep, goats, and other small animals, often in bunches at a stretch, now and then had gone missing from the fields and barnyards of Dithering. It was as if a gang of poachers or stock thieves would appear and remain awhile, living off the country, before breaking camp and moving on. Perhaps Dickie Fish had moved on with them, some suggested. But I knew better.

I knew Dickie hadn't run off with any poachers or stock thieves. I knew he hadn't run away to Medlow or Chedder. I should have bet my soul against a horseshoe it was the monster in the Cupboard had got him.

Be that as it may, I for one had not grieved for Dickie, despite his having been my best friend. I expect his family must have done so, in their way; but to boys of our age the disappearance of one of our number had been an exciting point of gossip, rather than a cause for sadness. Lucky fellows we were to have had youth on our side, although we didn't know it at the time.

In my mind's eye I can see the little swaggerer before me, bent upon some new mischief. With a quid in his cheek and hands clenched into fists at his sides, he would strut up and down, one moment smirking, the next snuffing the air with a truculent aspect, and bristling like a butcher's dog. I dare say when his pluck was up the little bantam was about as stout a lad as any dalesman who trod the wildways of Lingonshire.

Ah, well, it's a done thing. Poor Dickie has been gone these many years now. It was only afterwards that I learned to miss him, and to mourn his passing, as I have mourned the passing of my youth. Of course it all happened so long ago, before I had grown to manhood and left Dithering and the farm for Maunder College.

In the years since, some few others had vanished from Dithering with not a trace of them ever being found, as had been the case with Dickie. Little Fanny Meadows, Harry Smelt the old tinker, Bridgit Gooderly — they couldn't all have run off. And all those many miles away, at my studies in college at Penhaligon, I felt certain I knew the truth of it. I knew that Dickie had gotten no farther up the country than the Cupboard. As for Fanny, Harry, Bridgit . . . well, enough said.

Monster or no, something was living in Eldritch's Cupboard — to this both Dickie and I could have attested. For this *mounster,* as it's commonly termed, is a very real thing. From across the years a childhood memory, awful in the recollection, beckons as though in a dream, or more properly a nightmare. It is a memory of the events of a certain summer's morning, which to this day still has power to chill me to the quick.

It was the day the two of us, Dickie and I, had set out from town on our ponies for Eldritch's Cupboard. Both Dickie's parents and my father expressly had forbidden it; but we were boys and found the proscription all the more irresistible, arising as it did from figures of authority. Certainly it should have drawn my father's ire down upon me, had he been conscious of our intent.

Having crossed the bridge at the side of the Pack Horse Inn, over the hurrying stream, we swung into the old cart-track which winds northeastwards into the hills. Trees stretched their shaggy limbs over the gully through which our road lay, along the skirts of a silent wood. It was a dank, cold morning, but every now and again, as we jogged along, a stray sunbeam would pierce the mist that had chilled the air around us. A couple of miles farther on we reined down and led our ponies into a lonely by-path, through the dark pines and firs into the loom of the Graystone Crags.

And there at the foot of the Crags, in a quiet, out-of-the-way corner of the world, the opening to Eldritch's Cupboard gaped sinister and dark as a wolf's mouth.

No tin mine was this Cupboard of Eldritch's, but a cavern where in former times — warmer times, long before the sundering — a river once had coursed, that had spread flowing fingers through all these dales of Lingonshire, before retreating under the onslaught of the glaciers. Throughout untold eons the river's steady current had worked to hollow out this and the other like tunnels which were to be found in the neighborhood, or so my researches in the coming years would show.

Even on the brightest of mornings the Cupboard entrance admitted only a dim and uncertain light. Given the conspicuous gloom by which we were surrounded, there was hardly any useful light at all. It was for this reason we had brought with us a lantern from Dickie's father's shop. For we had come that morning to ferret out the monster, or the tricksy goblin, or the gang of thieves, or whoever it was who was using the Cupboard for a headquarters.

*Better look long before you leap in the dark.* So runs an old saying, but we were boys and paid it no heed. In those days most ordinary folk wouldn't go near the Cupboard, as most won't go near it still today. To challenge the unknown always has been the special province of invincible youth. To Dickie and me it was an enterprise that held promise of fun and adventure; but it in no wise diminished the danger.

Our voices, as we spoke to each other there in the cave entrance, awoke whispering echoes that went muttering off into the impenetrable dark. Eerie and ominous were the glimpses we had of the interior, as the lantern's pale beams chased back the encroaching shadows that rushed upon us on every side. A vaulted chamber of substantial dimensions, its ceiling supported by slime-encrusted pillars, its walls built from tier upon tier of sculpted shelves of rock, its floor littered with man-sized boulders and heaps of fallen debris, behind which almost anything, human or monster, might be hiding — well, it was no cheerful prospect. And we had only barely set foot inside Giant Eldritch's vast domain, which stretched for an all but unknowable distance ahead!

As we crept along our eyes scanned the shadows, slanting keen looks into this dark corner and into that one, with a wary scrutiny. The irregular masses and soaring formations of stone that towered up all around us were like natural statuary in some ghostly sculptor's workshop.

All at once I swung sharply about.

"Hallo! Did you hear that — ?"

My ears, awake to the slightest sound, had been alerted by something that had sped past my head in the dark.

"Wasson?" said Dickie, glancing round.

For he'd heard it too — a queer sort of whirring or droning noise, as of wings in rapid motion. Could it be a teratorn, I wondered with some anxiety, one that had nested inside the Cupboard? But this unpleasant idea was quickly dismissed, in view of the fact that the lazy, stroking wings of the vulture-like birds of prey most assuredly did not *whirr*.

My first impulse, I am ashamed to admit, was to hie home just as fast as my pony could carry me, and some whispered words to this effect must have escaped my lips.

Dickie, stopping short, shifted the quid in his mouth and squirted out the juice in his best coachman-like fashion.

"My ivers! You'm not afeard, are 'ee, boy?" he demanded, thrusting his chin in my face.

Dickie Fish had always called me boy, though he was but scarcely a month older than myself, and some two inches shorter.

"I shud whack 'ee for a coward, boy," he went on, and for a moment he appeared to be considering it. Then all at once the whirring noise went rushing past us again, and a stray beam from the lantern caught something in the air overhead — a shimmer of wings of a metallic glint, beating fast — that just as suddenly vanished again in the black dark.

There were some folks in Dithering who had seen it — the droning, whirring thing. A *piskie* they called it, making use of an old Cornish term. For really, what else was one to call it? It was as good a name as another. However it was not a piskie we were hunting that day in the Cupboard.

Some in town there were who blamed the Woldfolk, who believed it was they who were the source of the evil in the Cupboard. Not that the Woldfolk were held to be evil, necessarily; so little is known about them, you see. But what connection if any the Woldfolk might have to the *mounster* had long been a subject for debate.

By now the droning had faded and a silence deep and strange lay all about us. As we made our careful way along, some words of doggerel I knew well began running through my head. Mordaunt's Refrain, the piece was called.

Who Mordaunt had been nobody knew, but his composition had been of sufficient import as to have been immortalized on a board in the taproom of the Pack Horse Inn —

*Where The Time Goes*

*Hickory, dickory, dare.*
*The piskie flew up in the air.*
*The man in the Cupboard*
*Hisself is no sluggard.*
*Hickory, dickory, dare.*

Maybe Mordaunt had been a poacher, in days of yore, and his refrain had been intended to keep Dithering's angry landowners away from his hiding-place in the Cupboard. This thought occurred to me now as Dickie and I found ourselves in a much larger chamber which had opened up before us, a huge, wide room, dimly lighted by a tiny air shaft in the hollows of its high ceiling. What we discovered in this room was to prove instructive.

Only the day before a calf had gone missing from Colley's farm, just along the stream from my father's; and there it was now before us — or, more precisely, what was left of it. We saw the hole in the ground in which the fire had been prepared, and the greasy spit on which the carcass had been roasted. Portions of the animal's gnawed remains lay strewn about the area.

Someone had cooked the animal over a fire and eaten it there — an entire calf — and been none too neat about it, either. Indeed there was almost a flavor of savagery in it.

"'Twas a braggaty (or spotted) calf as was taken — wasn't it?" said I.

"So 'twas," nodded Dickie. With the toe of his boot he had been idly turning over a scrap of hide that lay at his feet — a buff-colored scrap with dark, irregular markings. "An' this do be 'e, by the look of 'e. Do 'ee see the spots there?"

There was little doubt about it. It *was* Colley's calf. Or had been.

We still were weighing the significance of our find, when a beam of light — narrow, green, and piercing — abruptly shot forth into the hushed gloom of the Cupboard. With lightning strokes the brilliant emerald ray darted about the chamber — now here, now there, now this way, now that — as though searching for something.

As though searching for intruders, perhaps.

As though searching for *us* . . .

Instantly Dickie and I hurled ourselves behind the nearest pile of fallen rock and lay still. Breathless, we saw the light go raking over the terraced shelves behind us.

"What *is* that?" said I, in a panicked whisper. But Dickie made no answer; for once the little swaggerer was at a loss for words.

Eventually the light went out, having failed perhaps in its search. Next moment there appeared a soft orange glow, which arose from behind a level slab of rock at the far edge of the chamber. Flowing up as if from underground, this subterranean effluvium was attended by a disagreeable noise — a kind of skittery, dry, rattling or crackling sound, as of joints creaking, a host of them and all at the same time, as though by a being in motion.

The noise reverberated throughout the chamber; then, as Dickie and I watched from behind our screen of boulders, we had our first glimpse of it — of the monster, that is.

To my very great surprise, not to mention alarm, Dickie abruptly called out to it, in a voice of a thousand echoes —

"Who's that, you?"

A bully though Dickie Fish might have been, unlike myself he was no coward, but had heaps of pluck. It is this which convinces me that he must have returned to the Cupboard, soon after our adventure there. For it was only a short while later that he went missing, like Colley's calf.

No coward was Dickie, but most definitely a fool, thought I, for having betrayed our presence to the creature. You'll note I call it a creature, for despite the testimony of the celebrated Mordaunt a *man* in the Cupboard it most certainly was not.

No piskie was it either, whose shadow grew large upon the Cupboard walls as it rose from behind the slab, as though from a cleft in the earth. We watched in awe as its gaunt figure mounted higher and higher, blackly silhouetted against the orange light.

I confess, the events described here occurred so long ago that I retain but a confused impression of them, and of the creature. But oh, what a creature it was — hideous — malignant — misshapen — a tall, thin, gruesome, ungainly scarecrow of a thing, supported by a pair of spidery stalks, with forelimbs dangling so low they nearly touched the ground on which it stood on clawed, bird-like feet. Worst of all was the grisly, swollen head, unholy and evil, which topped it . . .

No, no man was this that stood before us. The disagreeable noise it made, we realized, was caused by the action of the great, knobbed joints punctuating its stalk-like limbs. So like a thing from another world it was, this scarecrow, rising as if from the very fires of hell —

Why, were else to find such a creature but in hell? Where else to find a creature so entirely deserving of the term *mounster?*

Was this the fierce Giant Eldritch of yore? Could it be that the monster in Eldritch's Cupboard was Eldritch himself?

Having lifted itself to its full, awful height, which was some seven feet or more, the thing stood awhile silent and motionless, staring, it seemed, in our direction, and likely listening too. As yet I could discern nothing of its face, silhouetted as it was against the hellish glow. The glow appeared to emanate from the same cleft in the earth from which the scarecrow had emerged, as though lighting its way.

This monster in the Cupboard was a nightmare of a sort as might have been dreamed upon some fevered night, never to be forgotten. It made the sweat come out all over my brow and turned my knees to jelly. I felt an odd pulsing in my throat and ears, and gave thanks to God its face was hidden from me, or I believe I should have gone mad.

"Holy m-murder," I heard Dickie gasp. There was a sickly tremor in his voice such as I'd never heard from his bullying lips.

We hesitated for only an instant, however, as there was but little doubt what our course should be.

Up we got, on Dickie's signal, and, flinging aside any and all vestiges of caution, took to our heels. In blind unthinking terror we fled in the direction of the cave entrance and our ponies and salvation.

It was a close-run thing — too close. A glance behind showed that the monster had sprung lightly down from its slab and was racing after us. On its quick, bird-like feet it swiftly closed the gap, its forelimbs and grasping claws held out before it like the spiny appendages of a mantis, poised as if to strike. Faint-hearted coward that I was, I stumbled at the sheer horror of the thing, tottered, and caught at a ledge for support. Dickie already had vanished ahead of me. I never saw him again.

My ears rang with the sharp clatter of its feet on the rocky floor as the scarecrow bounded up.

As I struggled to get away, bony claws — or were they fingers? — gripped me by the shoulder and spun me around, hard.

It was then I screamed.

## Chapter Two

RECOILING from the shock of it, I started from my seat. For some moments I was unable to recall exactly the circumstances which had brought me to this pass. Quoth then the monster in the Cupboard —

"Beg 'ee pardon, sir . . . Mr. Earnscliff, sir . . . but Sir Lancelot he did come last hour from Medlow town, and be a-waitin' on 'ee."

Evidently it was the touch of Stokes's hand on my shoulder that had jarred me from my dream. I sank down again, rubbing my eyes and groaning. And what a whopper of a dream it had been — whopper of a nightmare, more like! Thank heavens it had been no more than that.

The abrupt appearance of Stokes, Dr. Callander's household manservant, had recalled me to myself. Still but half-awake, I was unable to suppress a yawn. My stars, this is bad form — shape up, Earnscliff! What would Mr. Bladdergowl say?

My glance strayed to the law-papers spread before me on the table. I had been reviewing them here in the doctor's small study, with the aid of a little food and a glass of sherry, when a tremendous wave of sleep had washed over me. It seemed I had barely put cup to lip when I had nodded off. In my defense I dare say I must've been more tired from my long journey than I had imagined.

So the eminent Sir Lancelot Wale at last had come.

"Very good, Stokes. Is Sir Lancelot with the doctor now?" I inquired, gathering up the papers and ordering them in preparation for their return to my blue bag.

The doctor's man Stokes was a middle-sized, oldish sort of fellow, loosely jointed, with a cheerful eye, a rumpled face, and a thatch of dusty locks.

"Ess, Mr. Earnscliff. You'm to go up to 'em, sir."

"How does he seem? Any improvement?" I asked as I rose from my chair.

"No better'n some hours ago, sir, by the look o't. I bain't ashamed to own it, Mr. Earnscliff, but I do much fear for the master's life. For he was ever a fit man, and able-bodied, but the apoplopsy — 'tis a hard thing to bear. I'm much afeard he may never agen be right." And he wrung his head sadly.

"Then I shall go up at once."

My way led through a rustic gallery hung with old family portraits, then up a flight of stairs. Somewhere a clock had begun chiming. On the landing I turned into a passage, at the end of which the doctor's bedroom-door stood ajar.

I tapped lightly on the panel then pushed the door in, after being invited to enter. Sir Lancelot Wale, deep in his examination of his patient, signed for me to approach.

Sir Lancelot was a big, angular kind of man, with a close-cropped head of hair splashed with gray, as if by droplets of time, and a bold pair of mustaches neatly trimmed and brushed. He was accounted the finest medical practitioner in Lingonshire, and had long been a friend of Dr. Callander's.

"Ah, Mr. Earnscliff," he murmured as I drew near. His manner was dignified yet benevolent.

Philip Earnscliff is my name — solicitor, a junior in the firm of Bagwash and Bladdergowl, Bodmin Square, Hoggard. I had been called to Dithering to the home of one of our clients, Dr. Hugh Callander. Well, to his farm, actually; though to be precise it no longer was a real, working farm. It had been known as Callander farm, however, since the days of the doctor's grandsires, who had been hardy tillers of the soil.

I had been summoned by Stokes, after he had first sent for the local medic, a stringy, spindle-shanked little jasper who had held out no hope for the doctor's revival, collected his fee, then gone away again. Once I arrived from Hoggard and had observed the doctor's condition, I sent word by express messenger to Medlow for Sir Lancelot to come at once to the bedside of his old friend. The great man's arrival by post-chaise, after a day's rattling on the roads, had coincided with my embarrassing doze in the study.

I stepped to the head of the bed, where Sir Lancelot sat crouched over his patient. I looked into the face of Dr. Callander, who lay upon his back, eyes closed, lips still, his respiration scarcely perceptible. His hand which was resting on the coverlet did not move. Indeed the poor man had but rarely stirred since his attack. He looked as if he simply had fallen asleep; the trouble was that no one could wake him.

There was no palpable sign of any disease. He lay with his head cradled on a pillow, his expression impassive, I might even say placid, his flowing silvery hair smooth-combed back from his distinguished brow. Indeed he looked almost serene in the midst of his affliction; for afflicted the doctor most certainly was. He had fallen into a coma and Sir Lancelot was worried that he might not long survive it. The doctor had passed the day as he had passed the previous three — insensible and inert, save for the faint rise and fall of his chest beneath the blankets.

"We do not know he suffers," had been Sir Lancelot's consolatory word on the subject.

But it had eased the grief and anxiety of those at the farm not a jot. Stokes, despite his cheery eye, internally was fearful and uneasy. He thought of his wife, who was herself an invalid in the house. Mrs. Stokes had been a maidservant once, but now she could serve no one, owing to a crippling illness which had come upon her many years ago. It was Stokes himself now who acted as cook and housekeeper at the farm, with the assistance of a lone housemaid, a dejected-looking girl named Annie, who sat quietly in a corner of the room wringing her hands and weeping.

And lately there had been Miss Carswell, who was standing at the side of Sir Lancelot with an aspect of the deepest concern. Miss Carswell was a veterinary's daughter, and an acquaintance of Dr. Callander's. A good-looking young woman, she had been visiting from St. Bees when the doctor's fit had struck him. It was she who had assumed the management of his care, with Stokes and Annie acting as her deputies. The three of them had been taking it in turns to watch over him, though the better part of the vigil by far had fallen to Miss Carswell.

As I've related the Dithering physician had first been sent for, but he had offered no hope. And so the call had gone out to Sir Lancelot Wale, that we might have the very best advice for the doctor's case. Sir Lancelot was possessed of a big name and a ditto reputation, and had a very exclusive practice; for he was one of the great medical baronets in the county, if not the realm. Nor did it hurt that he had been a college chum of the doctor's.

Uncorking a vial of salts, he waved it under the patient's nostrils — to no effect. It seemed there was nothing in the modern medical armamentarium that might rouse the stricken man from his slumber.

The physician's expression was grave as he rose from the bedside. In a sober tone he explained that his examination had shown his suspicions to be well-founded, that his patient was in a most unfavorable state.

"I fear the worst. It is looking very bad for him. He is sunk in a heavy coma."

"A stroke then, was it, sir?" I asked.

"Very likely, Mr. Earnscliff. As matters stand he looks to be holding his own at present. But I fear there is little chance of his rallying, or of anything like a final recovery. I grieve to say it, but my old friend may be lost beyond recall."

"Do you mean he'll not awaken from it?"

"He may do so, or he well may not; it's impossible in such cases to tell. He clings to his life by the merest thread. He and I were undergraduates together at Maunder, and like myself he is no longer a young man. Tell me, were there any premonitory signs, anything out of the ordinary before his collapse? Had he seemed forgetful of late or confused in his mind? Had he spoken strangely — uttered meaningless phrases, or made up words — slurred his speech — anything to suggest an impending attack? Had he had difficulty remembering facts or faces? Had he complained of any physical weakness?"

"Not that anyone had observed," was our joint reply.

According to all reports the doctor on the day of his collapse had seemed perfectly himself while at breakfast, and in his usual tranquil good humor. He had then gone for his morning's ride into town, to the Pack Horse Inn and the stationer's, but had returned a changed man. He had staggered indoors, as Miss Carswell related, and with a sudden lurch had fallen to his knees. She had been unable to support him entirely, but he had retained sufficient strength and awareness and she had helped him upstairs to his bed. Trusting him to the care of Annie, she then had gone off in search of Stokes, whom she found in the lower wood cutting timber.

The next that she and Stokes knew, the doctor had lapsed into that unfavorable state in which they and the rest of us now saw him. Annie for her part testified that the doctor had asked her for a sip of the cordial which he kept at his bedside, and that after taking a swallow of it he had fallen asleep. The maid had thought this a good sign; as it turned out it had been a very bad one.

Miss Carswell and the others had ministered to him to the best of their abilities, but they had been unable to rouse him. Evidently he had suffered a second attack, one more severe than the first. For some four days now he had lain in his bed, scarcely breathing, scarcely alive.

I had driven down from Hoggard, which is the nearest borough-town to these remote dales of Lingonshire, as swiftly as I was able. Now as I gazed at the doctor's still-living face — an intelligent, handsome, stubbornly vigorous face — my faith in the healing arts, and in the essential goodness of that higher power which orders all, was receiving one of its sternest tests. One moment the doctor had been warm with life, health, and humor; the next he had become a mannequin of his former self — a waxwork figure — the effigy, perhaps, on his own grave-slab.

"How long will you give him?" I asked.

"I should not like to say exactly to the day," Sir Lancelot replied, with some delicacy, "but not long. There is very great cause for fear. The brain, you see — well, it may be gone."

Stokes drew a handkerchief from his pocket and blew his nose into it a time or three, in mournful rhythm. "The master," he lamented between blasts, "was ever of a strong constitution. But now, by the look o't, I do b'lieve 'tis the end of an era at the farm."

A strangled sob from Annie contributed an exclamation mark to his sad pronouncement.

Dropping my voice to a whisper, I put to Sir Lancelot the terrible question that was in the minds of us all.

"Will he last the night, do you think?"

The physician stroked his chin in sober reflection.

"We'll see, Mr. Earnscliff. But I don't like it — don't like it at all. My old friend! We were youngsters then, in college at Maunder. We lived on the same staircase. But when men of our age have a stroke of apoplexy, it seldom comes lightly. How well I remember the joys of those early days! Our endless talks together over buttery beer in our rooms, over meals in hall, and our later discussions when oft our paths have crossed in the succeeding years. I delighted in hearing him speak of his beloved geology, for he was quite the rising star. Then, inexplicably, he gave it all up." He shook his head and sighed. "Now I fear he'll never speak again."

## Chapter Three

It was tear-stricken Annie who had been detailed to sit awhile with the patient.

"Such a fine, good gentleman the master was," she cried, dabbing at her eyes and sniffling. "'Tis heaven only knaws how we'm to repair his loss."

"You must not speak in such a fashion, Annie, while there is still hope," Miss Carswell reminded her. "The doctor is not lost to us just yet."

"But miss," objected the maid, endeavoring to understand, "axin' yer pardon, miss, but 'tis Sir Lancelot hisself says there be no hope, an' old Dr. Wambly, too. The master he be but clingin' to his life-strings."

"We musn't throw up the cards while we have a chance of the game," Miss Carswell said firmly.

*My dear girl — how foolish you sound* was Sir Lancelot's thought as he stepped from the room. *Recovery is all but impossible. Well, she is young, and you can't put an old head on youthful shoulders. A pretty head, though. And pretty shoulders.*

Sir Lancelot apprehended only too well the gravity of his patient's condition, but in his depiction of it he had softened its crueller edges, so as not to cause greater distress to the household. In his career the physician had seen too much, had had too much experience of such cases, to be blinding himself to the truth. There was little chance that his old friend would recover his senses, should he by some miracle manage to survive — that was the truth of it, cold and unvarnished. The only question remaining was whether he would die sooner, or later. Whether he might be restored to himself, so far as to be conscious of his state and of the people around him — well, those were very long odds indeed. Their little talks together over buttery beer, or claret, or old port, Sir Lancelot reflected, never would come again this side of the Styx.

Sir Lancelot thus found himself in entire agreement with the verdict of the Dithering physician, Dr. Wambly, who had come, made his examination, and gone away again. The vicar too had come and gone at the farm. Mr. Croakstone, although no graduated physician, seems to have concurred in the general view that the doctor was himself a goner. Having spoken some prayerful verses over the unconscious man, and offered words of consolation to the household, he had left the farm gravely shaking his head and shovel hat.

It seemed that no one had given the doctor so much as a tinker's chance of survival, and — truth be told — I could not have disagreed with them.

It had been decided that Sir Lancelot should establish his quarters at the Pack Horse Inn, the only hostelry of note in Dithering, down at the bridge-end beside the stream. It was a house with which he had become familiar over the years, from his frequent travels in the area, and he was known there. We were pretty cramped for space at the farm, with Miss Carswell occupying the guest room, and I the couch in the doctor's study. The farmhouse was no very large abode, and a squeezing of the eminent medical baronet into its available volume — as into a truckle-bed in the kitchen, for example — was not to be thought on. Because the inn was not far off, its atmosphere more congenial than that of the farm, and its larder and cellar more generously supplied, its choice as a bivouac was obvious.

There was little more to be done now respecting his patient, but to watch, to wait, to hope, and to pray; and so it was agreed that Sir Lancelot might as well retire to the inn for his supper and a smoke. In his directions to us he offered some few suggestions how we might enhance the comfort of his old friend. Importantly, water alone was to be given him for the present, and nothing stronger.

For a number of years now, Dr. Callander's legal affairs had been attended to by our Mr. Bladdergowl. However, as Mr. Bladdergowl was himself in ill health — although not so badly off as old Mr. Bagwash, certainly — this responsibility had devolved upon me as his junior. In the event that the doctor should recover sufficient of his wits, and have aught of significance to impart respecting his will or other instruments, I had been authorized to act on his behalf. It was some of these very papers that I had been reviewing when I had nodded off in the study.

I had been introduced to Dr. Callander about a year ago, not long after I had joined the firm in Bodmin Square. As it had been explained to me, he was formerly a University don, and Fellow of Maunder College, Penhaligon, his *alma mater*. The doctor had been accustomed to discuss with Mr. Bladdergowl any and all business pertaining to Callander farm; now it was I who was to be his adviser. On two occasions since, the doctor had called on me in Bodmin Square to attend to matters arising. The present was my first experience of Dithering and the farm; it was regrettable it was under circumstances so unfortunate.

A tutor and lecturer at Maunder, and considered a rising man in his field, the doctor unexpectedly had resigned his post — thrown it right up — after the death of his father, and returned home to assume command of the family holdings. That had been almost twenty years ago. More than this I didn't know, as the doctor in our talks had volunteered nothing further.

The afternoon was growing late, an afternoon of shadowless muted grays that accorded well with the somber atmosphere at the farm. As I stood gazing out at a window my eyes traveled to an old, moss-grown pile, a sprawling mansion topped by red tiles and lofty chimney-stacks, that was visible amidst some patchy greenery beyond the lower wood. The house lay down the road a space, above the stream bank at the foot of the slope. I had observed it earlier while on an errand in town, but had not thought to inquire about it.

"Ess, 'tis the Moorings, sir," Stokes informed me. He related that he and his "ould woman" well remembered the good old days of the Squire, whose home the mansion had been. Squire Fetching had been his name, and like Dr. Callander's father he had been a widower. He had lived at the Moorings with his daughter, but she had passed away suddenly — this was years agone now — and for the remainder of his days the Squire had been a broken man.

The house had been closed for some while, ever since the Squire's death. Tussles amongst the various heirs, all of them distant, had produced a good deal of activity in the law-courts, and a comfortable living for the attorneys concerned. I recollected something of this now, having heard talk of it in the office amongst the other juniors. Bagwash and Bladdergowl at one point had been involved, in some small capacity. It had been the province of Mr. Bagwash, before the latter's several ailments had overwhelmed him.

"But none do live there now," Stokes concluded with a sigh, "not for many a day. How quick the time have gone, to be sure."

As Sir Lancelot was about to depart for the inn, he was reminded of something while being tendered his coat and hat by Stokes.

"And how is your wife? Any better? No? Ah, well, perhaps I should step in and see her . . ."

We were conducted by Stokes to the tiny sitting-room where his "ould woman" was wont to be found of an afternoon.

A slight, feeble-looking lady, she sat alone before an old-fashioned casement that looked out upon the fields, which formed a charming vista in its leaded panes. It was only as one got near her one observed that, like her husband, Mrs. Stokes was not so elderly as she at first appeared. In the case of Stokes, it was his rumpled physiognomy that aged him; in hers it was her hair — shockingly, savagely white hair, like a ghost's — which made her seem older than her years.

Sir Lancelot drew a chair up to hers and seated himself. Putting on his best genial manner, he began, amiably enough — "And how are you today?"

She turned to him a face lined with care, eyes meeting his with a dazed, distant look. To his question she made no reply.

The physician took her hand gently, with an almost exaggerated courtesy.

"May I know your name?" he asked.

Slowly her eyebrows crept up her forehead; but a minute passed and again no answer was returned.

Frowning, Sir Lancelot studied her face long and closely. It was a face that, like her hands, was of a dead pale cast, as if all the blood had been chased from it. Her eyes had a faded look — still they were kindly eyes for all that — and round them time and trouble had hollowed out deep cavities.

"Do you know who I am?" the physician asked.

By degrees her expression changed from one of vacancy to one of confusion, anxiety, fear. Haltingly she met his gaze; then, trembling, she shrank from it like a frightened hare.

"Do you know this good man?" Sir Lancelot went on, indicating Stokes.

Her glance shifted to her husband. It was a frail glance, as frail as she herself, and was attended by a ruffling of her brow, and a quiver of her eyelids, as if she were summoning all that remained of her wits in her struggle to understand.

*Who are you? Where am I? Who am I? What has become of me?* — all this and more could be read in the eyes straining in their cavernous sockets. Such an effort she was making to remember!

Ultimately it was unsuccessful. Wringing her head in a bewildered way, she let go Sir Lancelot's hand and drew back into the safety of her cushion, as though into her shell, where no harm could come to her.

The physician sat for a few minutes in thoughtful silence.

"What a queer thing the mind is," he murmured.

Stokes nodded sadly. "Ess, no better, sir. My ould woman, she be nowt but a cheeld now."

And so had she been for these many years — nothing but a child, and an awful weight at his heart. His wife no longer could speak, no longer could read, or write; indeed it was debatable how much of the talk going on around her she fully comprehended.

"A lamentable case. There's no help for it; she is as mute as a fish. Try as hard as you might, you cannot make her speak. I doubt if she knows what we say. Indeed," the physician sighed, "this has become a lamentable house. I remember when it was otherwise. Sunny moments on the pilgrimage of life's way have left traces of their passing . . ."

I believe Sir Lancelot felt the same as had the rest of us since the doctor had been struck down — that something was fading and vanishing from the world that never would return.

We quitted the room, leaving the invalid to her leaded panes and their view of the waning day.

In the hall Sir Lancelot took his coat, his gloves, his hat, his cane, his bag, and his leave. He had driven the chaise and pair up the farm road from town, and I proposed to accompany him on his return. Sir Lancelot Wale is not a tall man, indeed his legs are rather short, and though angular enough in his limbs his mid-person does tend towards a certain fleshy roundness. But he walks with an easy step, and an air of authority in his gait. He is supremely self-assured, as befits a great medical baronet. Thus he was entirely capable of managing his cattle and chaise himself, having left the postilion to his devices at the inn.

Much of the way, which descends towards the stream and town, we drove in the company of our own thoughts. Scarcely a word passed between us. The skies had been craggy and lowering all day, and the atmosphere oozed a chilly damp. At one point a glimpse of a red-tiled roof, gables, and chimney-stacks spurred a question of my companion.

"Did you know the old Squire, sir? He who lived there at the Moorings?"

"Squire Fetching do you mean? Oh, indeed. Capital fellow. Had a wooden leg. It was little Hankey who sawed it off for him. He was ever so obliged to him afterwards."

"Little Hankey?"

"Sorry — the late Dr. Willis Hankey. No disrespect towards a fellow practitioner intended, I assure you. Hankey was long the physician and surgeon in these parts, before Wambly."

"I see. And Squire Fetching of the Moorings — he had a daughter, as I understand it?"

A shadow fell across the brow of Sir Lancelot, and for a moment his eyes touched again the manse that was peeping through the trees.

"Ah, yes. A shame. A lovely girl she was, lovely. Yes, another lamentable house. I hear tell the lawyers still are picking over the carcass, all these years on . . . oh, sorry . . . forgot you were a . . ."

He said no more about it — I could see the subject troubled him. A further quarter-mile's rumble down the slope placed us in the yard of the venerable establishment where the physician was to lodge for the duration.

The Pack Horse Inn at Dithering is a neat and comfortable, old-fashioned house. Like the Moorings, it is situated adjacent to the hurrying stream which flows the length of the town. Thatched and latticed, its walls amber-washed and timber-striped, it is a house rich in picturesque detail and appointments. With the old pack-horse bridge beside it spanning the stream, and the hills like slumbering giants rising up behind, it has one of the most enviable situations in the dales. Boasting "good attendance and good cheer, at moderate rates", it is home not only to its keepers and staff, but to a host of retainers and regulars, neighborhood visitors, and guests, many of them attached to fishing in the stream. Its welcoming fireside, with its light pouring warm and yellow from deep bay windows, and its generous tap make it a heartening destination for many a weary laborer at the end of a long day. For company and conversation are never lacking at an inn, and that of the Pack Horse was no exception.

I left Sir Lancelot at the arched entry being greeted by the proprietor, Asa Mundey, by Mrs. Mundey, and by the ostler, young John Cornish, who took the horses in hand and removed the chaise down the yard. In the morning, in the comfort of the dining parlor, the physician could have himself a proper breakfast — certainly better than any we could muster up for him — and return refreshed to the farm.

Feeling the need of refreshment myself, in the shape of some air, I set off on an invigorating stroll back up the road to the farmhouse. As I walked along, in the little cobbled lane that serves as the chief thoroughfare of Dithering, I glanced admiringly at the color-washed cottages in their neat rows which graced it on either side, and about which something of another era seemed still to cling. After crossing the town — it was no great distance — I emerged at the foot of the slope that led to the farm. Instead of proceeding that way, however, I directed my steps to the eastwards, into the path that runs above and alongside the stream. This I followed for a short time before arriving at a dilapidated quay, a crumbling mass of fieldstone and brick. Round the shingle at its base the stream waters flowed mumbling and chattering on their course to Dithering.

A distance above me, the Moorings stood amidst its wilderness of fir-trees and bramble. Like the Pack Horse Inn it was a two-storied, rambling affair; but there all resemblance between the houses ended. Whereas the inn was bustling with activity, this house of the Moorings showed only too well how much time had passed since its Squire or anyone else had lived there. No curls of smoke rose jovially from its several chimneys, no welcoming firelight gleamed in its shuttered windows. Lonely, long neglected, its tiles stained with moss, its walls mildewed and discolored with age, it was a picture of sad decay, melancholy and dreary.

And yet there hung about it an air of mystery, somehow — an air of romance! What had happened in this house, I wondered, behind those sagging gates? There had been the Squire — a widower, with a wooden leg — and his child, a daughter, who had died young. Well, I reflected, it was an all-too-common tragedy. For did not tragedies happen to somebody somewhere every day? Besides, I argued, it was nothing to the purpose; it had no relation to the business which had called me to the farm. It had nothing to do with Dr. Callander's sudden incapacitation, with Bagwash and Bladdergowl, or with me.

I returned to the road and commenced my uphill slog. As I drew near the farm, I can't deny but that it gave me a sickish feeling to see it. The gloomy atmosphere, the disheartening scene, had begun to tell on my spirits. But it was only to be expected, I imagine, in a house where death seemed to be hovering in the air.

When I went inside I learned that the doctor, fortunately, was no worse, his condition unaltered. Annie still was sitting with him when

I entered. As I did so my eyes lighted on a tiny creature that, snuggling on the doctor's pillow, had secured him by the ear and was pawing at his cheek.

## Chapter Four

WHEN the first moment of surprise was over — "My stars!" had been my involuntary exclamation — I fell back a step, a trifle sheepishly, to collect myself. For as it happened what had excited my alarm was nothing more sinister than — a kitten.

A mackerel tabby, it was lounging on the pillow beside the doctor's ear, batting playfully at his head.

Annie, sniffling, turned in her seat. "Mr. Earnscliff, sir?" she inquired, in some confusion.

Embarrassed, I stammered out a reply.

"For an instant I had a foolish fancy it was a — a — oh, an I don't know what — a piskie, perhaps — assaulting the doctor. I can't think what made me imagine anything so — so outlandish — so ghoulish. For I see now it's only the kitten . . ."

"A p-piskie, sir?" Annie quavered, glancing nervously round. Her eyes darted to the casement, to assure herself it was firmly shut and latched. "No piskies h'yur, sir — pray heaven it bain't so — not at the farm — "

At that instant a low knock was heard — fortunately it came not from the window. My nerves nonetheless were tingling as I whisked round to behold Miss Carswell's trim figure in the doorway.

"There is no need for concern, Mr. Earnscliff," she said brightly. "I can guarantee you Figgie is no piskie, nor for that matter am I. I brought him up to see Dr. Callander, as I thought there a chance it might help to restore him. The doctor is dearly devoted to cats."

Her abrupt entrance had startled me. *Don't be a goose, Earnscliff!* My nerves certainly were on edge today.

"Figgie" was the mackerel tabby kitten, who had been discovered by the doctor one morning in the barn. A poor homeless motherless thing, half-starved, and mewing piteously, it had won his heart in an instant. He had always been very fond of cats, as it had been told to me, and had had several such companions in his lifetime. It was barely a fortnight ago he had acquired this new one.

Young women too are much given to the cultivation of pets, and Miss Carswell was no exception. She gathered the kitten, a tiny ball of fluff, into her arms and kissed it, and hugged it to her breast with much warmth and affection. The kitten responded at once — whiskers fluttering, it mewed its contentment in a soft, small voice, and gazed upon her with eyes soulful and serene.

"He had only just recovered his strength again," Miss Carswell related, "when the doctor was struck down. Poor little vagabond," she murmured into one furry ear, "poor little lost one . . ."

This latest of the doctor's string of cats he had christened Figgie — for *figgie hobbin*, that delightful dish which the little vagabond had shown a taste for in the kitchen.

Meanwhile Annie had resumed her watch over the patient, who remained senseless of the kitten's presence. Miss Carswell, undaunted, returned the animal to the doctor's pillow. Without hesitation the little lost one snuggled up to his stricken master and, reclining against his cheek, settled in for a comfortable doze.

And the doctor too slumbered on.

Downstairs, as I passed through the little rustic gallery, I felt, or fancied that I felt, the eyes of the Callander ancestors watching me from out of their pictures. Unnerved by the sensation, I traversed the chamber with a quickened step.

In the hall I was approached by Stokes, who had been attending to his wife.

"The doctor appears to be no worse," I reported. "I suppose that is something. Sir Lancelot will examine him again in the morning."

It seemed that Stokes in his turn had some intelligence to convey as well.

"There be summat 'ee ought to knaw, sir," he began, hesitatingly I thought.

"Yes? What is it?"

"I do b'lieve the master he did fear that summat o' the like might happen to 'en."

"By this do you mean his illness?"

"Azackly."

"How so? I understood he had been in admirable health, and had expressed no such concern to anyone."

Stokes bent thoughtful brows. "So 'e did appear to us, sir, at the time. Nary a word of 't did escape his lips. He'd a-led his life as ever he'd done. Hows'ever . . ."

"Yes?"

"About a week agone, sir, he did draw me aside, and we did talk privily togither, sir, the master and I. P'raps 'twas nowt, sir, but summat o' which he spoke did puzzle me, as now I do think on't."

"And what did he tell you?"

"The master he did say that ef aught shud happen to 'en — ef on a suddenty he shud lose his wits, or be ta'en ill, such that he cudna speak, or ef he shud be struck down cold — that I was to send for 'ee at once, sir, at Hoggard."

"Well, it seems a wise precaution. Perhaps he did indeed have a hint of his impending attack, for such things are not unknown. Perhaps he had been feeling unwell but had not cared to burden anyone. You'll recollect Sir Lancelot inquired if there had been any premonitory signs."

The servant rumpled his face and frowned. For a long minute he remained thus; then he shook his head, his doubts unresolved. "'E do be possible, sir, I s'pose, but — thankin' 'ee kindly — I don't b'lieve so. For I've knawn the doctor an' his ways a good many year now, an' he weren't unwell."

"Yes, as I recollect you were a young man when you were hired on here at the farm. That was in the time of the doctor's late father?"

"And his granfer, sir. 'Twere dree of 'em in those years — dree Callanders, and o' course the women folk."

Again a pause of thought, again a skeptical turn of his head. He did not know what to make of the doctor's instruction to him, or why it should be troubling him so.

"Perhaps he intended to alter a provision of his will, should some misfortune befall him?" I suggested.

"Savin' pardon, sir, but I don't b'lieve so."

"No?"

"Nay, sir."

"Then what can the doctor have meant?"

"Belike, sir, he simply wished 'ee h'yur — in case he had need of 'ee."

"His affairs seem to be entirely in order. I have been looking over copies of the deeds and his will and testament today. If he had desired any changes he had not communicated them to Bodmin Square. How else might I have been of help to him? For the rest is Sir Lancelot's province."

The poor fellow shook his head in a baffled way. Meantime a different thought had occurred to me.

"What about Miss Carswell? Might it have had something to do with her?"

"Ess, 'e may have done, sir, 'er bein' a friend and all . . ." Then a new idea struck him. He seemed about to give utterance to it, but thought over it again and held his tongue. Still . . .

"Yes? Was there something more, Stokes?"

Hesitantly he volunteered the information that some few months ago, well before the doctor had been taken ill, the thievery had started up again.

"What thievery is that?" I asked.

It turned out that a number of animals — livestock mostly, calves, goats, sheep, an occasional dog — had gone missing from some of the neighboring farms, that indeed Callander farm itself had lost a lamb from its barn. These occurrences had seemed to trouble the doctor greatly.

"Perhaps the poachers have returned," I suggested.

Stokes's brow folded into a net of wrinkles, and he eyed me curiously. "And how might 'ee knaw o' the poachers, sir?"

His question stopped me short, and for the moment I was uncertain how to respond.

How *did* I know about the poachers, I asked myself? Why did the idea of poachers and stock thieves suddenly come into my head? The head of a stranger and townsman unschooled in such matters?

Stokes went on to describe how, backalong in the days of the old Squire — Squire Fetching, he of the wooden leg — the Squire himself had been wont to blame the losses on poachers. Others however had not been so certain, and over the years no poachers had been apprehended. The losses occurred at intervals, separated by long stretches of time. Over several weeks numbers of animals would vanish, without explanation; years then would pass with naught but the occasional disappearance, attributable to one or more natural causes.

As well there had been periodic reports of individuals who had gone missing. Strange reports were they that would circulate about town, and the most absurd rumors, heard in broken hints and dark mutterings over cider and spruce at the Pack Horse Inn. But nothing ever came of them.

Dr. Callander had seemed particularly troubled by this new series of losses. Even as he was relating the circumstances to me, however, I had a vague impression that Stokes knew something more about the business than he felt comfortable disclosing; although for the life of me I could not fathom what connection it might have to the doctor's illness.

More ominously, uneasy reflections of another sort had begun to stir within me while Stokes was speaking. The thoughts now were coming thick and fast into my brain, images in familiar shapes were gathering apace. A memory of my nightmare had returned — nightmare, dream, vision, infernal illusion, whichever you choose.

Disappearances. Livestock gone missing, vanished, and more. My best friend, Dickie Fish — little Fanny Meadows — old Harry Smelt — Bridgit Gooderly — why should these names be known to me? To me, Philip Earnscliff, a stranger in these parts, who never had had a friend called Dickie Fish?

A grim scene took vivid form in my mind. A roasting-spit — Colley's calf — a *whirr* of wings — and last but hardly least the monster in the Cupboard, and my own self within inches of destruction, as its vile, bony claws seized me by the shoulder — the manacle grip, the sudden wrench, the spin round to face —

But what had these things to do with me? How had I known of them — I, who had never before visited this remote corner? Where had I gained my knowledge of them?

That is, assuming they were not mere inventions of my imagination.

"Where is Eldritch's Cupboard?" I asked Stokes on a whim.

## Chapter Five

THE poor fellow seemed taken aback by the question — rather say startled by it. His eyes narrowed and he scratched his jaw uneasily. How had I known of the Cupboard, he asked me in return?

How indeed? So it was true — there *was* a place called Eldritch's Cupboard!

"Well, it's hard to say," I told him, "for I had a dream today — a nightmare, more like, while dozing in the study — you'll recollect, you woke me in my chair — and it had to do with Eldritch's Cupboard, at the foot of the Graystone Crags. It's the place where the Giant Eldritch is said to have lodged his victims, is it not? What can you tell me of it?"

"Nowt, sir, 'bout Eldritch's Cupboard," he replied — evasively, I thought — "exceptin' 'e be a place not to be visited, ef a man can help it. Pass it by, folks do say. I shudn't go a-nigh the spot, sir, and I bain't ashamed to own it. Backalong the doctor he was wont to carry out his researches there . . . but no more, sir . . . not for some time . . ."

"Have you ever heard that there was a monster living in it?"

Stokes positively froze at the suggestion. His face was a study in blank amazement; then —

"A mounster, sir?" he said haltingly.

But I learned no more, for it was at this juncture that Miss Carswell appeared. Looking crisply alert, she beckoned to Stokes and issued him a few words of instruction, which sent him off upon a household errand.

Miss Violet Carswell was a good-looking young woman, as I have said, and a well-made. Light blue eyes and an abundance of fair hair, cherry cheeks, a figure trim and neat — as attractions in a young woman they are beyond dispute. And yet for all this she seemed rather an ordinary sort of girl, her beauty lying in the very simplicity of her manner and dress. Her charms were of a natural order, her features untouched by any artifice, her demeanor lacking the conceit so prevalent in her town-bred cousins. For Miss Carswell was country-bred and country-born; beyond this, blue eyes and a cherry cheek in a country maid have a way of communicating that seems proof against resistance.

As a consequence I found myself telling her of my dream, or my nightmare, every detail of it, after we had adjourned to the doctor's study. Throughout she regarded me with polite attention, responding to its more sensational elements with little gasps of surprise.

"That is a most interesting tale, Mr. Earnscliff — a singular dream indeed. What does it mean, do you think?" she asked.

Sensible of her gaze, I could feel the touch of her blue eyes drive the color deep into my face. She smiled prettily; this mingled kindness and frankness of her manner was another of her charms.

"They seem like the broken fragments of some evil memory," I told her. "It's as if I were Dr. Callander and it were his dream I was experiencing, viewed from his perspective. For the person I seemed to be in my nightmare had been raised upon a farm in Dithering, had gone up to Maunder College, and there had made geology his study."

"Certainly it sounds much like the doctor," Miss Carswell allowed, "but I've not heard him relate such a tale from his childhood as you describe. Perhaps it embarrassed him? At any rate, no one visits the Cupboard any more."

"Ah, so you know something of it?"

"Very little, actually. I believe it lies a few miles from town. Rumor has given the place a bad sort of name. But surely an aireymouse — a bat — is more likely than a piskie to be flitting about in a cave?"

It seemed past understanding, at least for the moment. For as the mind of a child fashions terror from the harmless and familiar, so too must I have done, in those shadowy realms of the unconscious while skating on the fringes of sleep.

Stokes, acting as butler, housekeeper, groom, gardener, and cook, returned to inform us that dinner would be delayed, and so I might remain awhile until called. Miss Carswell meantime went off to lend a hand in the kitchen. Amongst her good gifts she was a fair cook in her own right, and had been of much assistance to the household.

Reaching for my blue bag, I withdrew the documents I had been reviewing and fell to studying them again. The sherry still was there, that portion I had not drunk, and I finished it off in a couple of swallows. There is nothing like a glass of sherry — or half a glass — before dinner for clearing the ideas. After a few minutes however I put the papers by, and for a time sat thinking and musing over my empty glass through half-closed lids. A sharp frost wind, which made itself heard from time to time, was singing amongst the trees outside and muttering around the edges of the lattice.

*It's an ill wind blows nobody good . . .*

I took out my watch and looked at it, then stopped. Such miserable slaves of time are we! Here in this remote corner of the realm, in this countryside so scarcely peopled and scant of borough-towns like Hoggard, to escape the tedium and confinement of office quarters was a wonder and a revelation indeed. There was freedom here in these dales of Lingonshire, far removed from the ceaseless press of business in Bodmin Square . . .

In these dales of Lingonshire, in this legended land echoing with its stories of ogres and piskies and giants sporting seven-league boots . . .

Giant Eldritch — real or imagined? How had I heard of him, and why should I have dreamed such a dream? And what of this monster of his that had risen from behind the slab? A frightener told by arrant yokels and nurserymaids? A bugbear to haunt country imaginations?

I fell then to wondering about the inscrutability of fate, and what it held in store for Dr. Callander — indeed for us all — and whether the doctor should last out the night . . . whether perhaps this was to be his final night on earth . . .

Ordinarily I am not of a somber, meditative sort of habit, but the atmosphere at the farm positively seemed to be affecting me — how else to explain my evil dream? I made a mental note of it, that I must resist these impulses of the imagination and not give way to wild fancies.

No sooner had I dropped my chin upon my hand in thought than I felt myself nodding. Then the shadows tiptoed softly in, the lamp on the table dimmed, and a wave of sleep rolled over me.

## Chapter Six

**M**Y mother died when I was quite young. But for a faint impression of laughing dark eyes and the scent of rose water, I have no memory of her. But her death broke my poor father's heart, and in after days he never was the same — or so others have told me, for of course I had scarcely known him ere then.

My father, like my grandfather and great-grandfather Callander before him, was a dalesman and a farmer, a tireless tiller of the soil. Yet from the outset he had espoused the view that his son should go to college. In this opinion he may have been influenced by my mother, whose brother, my Uncle Jory, had been a college man. To my father the advantages to his son of a University education were clear, and he held firm in his belief that I should possess something which had been beyond both him and his forebears — the stamp of a college degree. I myself was of two minds about it, for I loved the countryside and the people of these Lingonshire dales, and had no desire to leave them. But in the end I relented, thanks in part to a timely legacy from Uncle Jory. Unbeknownst to my father, however, it remained always in the back of my mind that one day I should return to Dithering and Callander farm.

And so in the autumn I went up to Penhaligon, and was enrolled at Maunder College, of which my Uncle Jory had been a member.

Our set of rooms was nearly the oldest in the college, and one of the most secluded, with pleasant views of the garden and of the cloisters beyond. There were three of us undergraduates on the stair, one on each floor. The ground-floor rooms were occupied by our tutor, who, coincidentally, was of Cornish ancestry. His name was Alastair Vivian — later Sir Alastair. The dread which Mr. Vivian's tall, stately presence inspired in a poor freshman from the dales was, in retrospect, ludicrous; but at the time he was a bugbear to us all. He was an imposing figure, a man of signal authority in his field. As it turned out, however, he and I got along rather well, particularly after he learned that I had had a Cornish mother and that I hailed from Lingonshire. Later he proved to be of material assistance to me in the furtherance of my graduate career, after he was unanimously chosen Master of the college.

I recollect my fellow undergraduates on the staircase. On the top floor was Jellipot, a bore of the first water — he was going in for the law. Above me, on the second floor, was a pleasant chap called Wale — Lancelot Wale — who was inclining towards medicine. He and I quickly became friends — we both disliked Jellipot. In due course he completed his studies at the Hospital of St. Peter Palsey and was entered on the list of physicians. Eventually he too would be made a knight of the sundered realm.

As for myself, once the preliminaries were over I undertook to read geology, inspired by my explorations of the countryside round Dithering and my fascination with the ancient history of the district. From the beginning my progress was rapid, for I was keenly interested in my subject and had a natural aptitude for it. Indeed I worked to such good purpose as to obtain First Class Honors in the Tripos. And so at long last, after three years of unremitting labor, I donned my B.A. gown. After an additional year I took my M.A., and finally the Doctor of Philosophy, and after a further period of study was appointed tutor and lecturer in the Natural Sciences at Maunder. My researches, which lay in the field of *diluvium,* or drift, terminal moraines, and theories of the advance and retreat of glaciers, were well received, and I was generally acclaimed a rising man.

It was then that the unseen hand which rules the game of life intervened to work a great change. One day from Dithering came the sorrowful news that my father had passed away at the farm. His span had not been long — scarcely more than my Uncle Jory's — although it had been far longer than that accorded my poor mother. Sadly, my father already was dead and buried by the time the news reached me. I had been away on a fortnight's researches in the field, and upon my return had discovered the vicar's letter awaiting me.

In the succeeding weeks I was to be faced with a considerable dilemma. What was I to do? How was I to proceed? For in the years since my appointment as tutor and lecturer, the chasm that exists between the life one leads as an undergraduate, and that of a busy University don, had become only too clear to me. As the time passed, my college duties — apart from my researches — had grown ever more burdensome. The routine of lectures, occupying at times seven or eight hours a day, the private instruction of pupils, the examination papers, college committees — it was with no light heart that I endured it all. And recently, additional obligations had been imposed on me, owing to the retirement of Professor Snufflegreek. These new responsibilities, coupled with the lecture- and committee-work, had left me with precious little time for my researches, which were, and ever have been, the chief pleasure of my days. As for the rare blessing of leisure — well, it was a thing unknown to me.

My circle of acquaintance in college was not numerous. I was not an overly sociable fellow, never one for taking the readiest road to popularity. I suppose that over the years I had remained at heart a countryman, and a dalesman, through and through.

I was conscious as well that general opinion amongst the undergraduates did not set me very high. As had been overheard from time to time, my lectures had been pronounced "dull as ditch water," "unspeakably tedious," and my manner of instruction "singularly dry and perfunctory." Well, such may well have been the case. But who amongst us is perfect?

I thought of my Uncle Jory and of the legacy that had made my education possible, and for which I had had no opportunity to thank him. What would my uncle have wanted? What would my poor dear mother have wanted, she of the laughing dark eyes and rose water? What would my father have wanted?

What choice had I? How could I ignore my family's farm — the work of generations of Callanders, but with no Callander now to till it — in selfish furtherance of my career? What indeed would my father have wanted?

After exhausting a week of sleepless nights in meditating over it, in rolling it over in my mind and debating its merits *pro* and *con*, my course at last became clear — the only course, indeed, that seemed open to me. The wisdom of it — or lack of same — I would trust to time.

It was shortly afterwards that I resigned my position at Maunder and returned to the farm, at Dithering in the dales. Well, it was over shoes, over boots with me now; there would be no going back, no second guesses.

"On my soul, this really is too bad," wrote my friend Wale, an accomplished physician at Medlow, on receiving the news. "Whoever heard the like? Relinquish your post? Become an agriculturist, a clod-breaker? Next you'll be turning *horse*-breaker or whipper-in! My dear Callander — what has come over you?"

What indeed? For I am myself often surprised at the turn things take in this world. Take Callander farm for instance.

It seems that my father, unbeknownst to me, had accumulated a number of debts, of rather an usurious character, to settle certain accounts pertaining to the farm. Over the years he had become sorely pinched for money, the knowledge of which he had kept from me. As a result, he had been selling off whole tracts of land, and clearing off encumbrances, so that by the time I took possession of it very little of "Callander farm" remained. Indeed it was no longer an actual, working farm, but had been transformed into what might be termed a hobby farm, well suited to a retired collegian seeking solitude and reflection. Despite it all, however, my father had been rather shrewd in a way, for he had kept his timbered acreage — especially the lower wood and the older plantings — as few crops are so profitable as timber, for those who have the patience to await its growth.

I took up my new endeavor with an energy that had been flagging at Maunder. I was not so swell-headed to think that I, a scholar and academician with few practical skills beyond my area of study, could make the farm once more into a genuine, working enterprise. Rather,

I wanted simply to keep it as it now was, as my father, otherwise a confidant, capable man, to the best of his ability had left it. I wanted to keep it from diminishing further, bit by bit, until no trace of it and the acres that had been tilled by generations of our family was left.

It was my intent that there always should be a Callander farm at Dithering, even if its master did no real farming. A few cattle, perhaps, some sheep and goats, some chickens, turkeys, a modest plot of garden — this was all that would be needed to sustain us. My father's and my grandfather's world may have passed away, but I was determined that their farm should not.

Of course every path has its puddle, as the saying is. Wrong roads there are many, and are most easily taken when we are unsure of our way. But I was not unsure — I was rock-steady in my purpose. And living on a farm in the midst of these dales, where my interest in geology had been born, I could put the gift of leisure time to excellent use. For it was geology that would be my hobby now, and maintaining the farm my vocation.

Before leaving Maunder I had resolved that I should bring Stinker to Dithering to assist me. Stinker had been the "gyp" on our staircase when I was an undergraduate. The gyp, as he is popularly termed, is a species of college servant, who looks after the rooms of the young men, lays their breakfast and puts the kettle on the fire, brushes up their coats and hats and blacks their boots, fetches jugs of beer and other necessities from the buttery, and in general is the nearest thing to a confidant — at times co-conspirator — that an undergraduate enjoys.

At Penhaligon these servants are called gyps because Penhaligon had been founded by Cambridge men, and at Cambridge University in Old Britain, before the sundering, such servants had been so termed. In a Salthead college — Salthead University having been established by Oxonians — they are called "scouts", because this had been the tradition at Oxford.

Stinker had been my servant afterwards as well, for when I had taken rooms as tutor and lecturer I had asked that he be assigned to me. The request had been very kindly granted by the new Master, Mr. Vivian, my former tutor.

For Stinker it had represented a promotion, from playing nursemaid to a clutch of undergraduates always hard up for ready dibs, to life in service to a college don. Indeed his view of the matter might be summarized by the celebrated lines —

> *Be it better, be it worse,*
> *Be ruled by him that has the purse.*

And to Dithering I brought Flounce as well. Flounce was a calico cat — a big, showy girl, with a wavy coat sporting lots of white, and a great long plume of a tail. She had come to me when I was an undergraduate, in my second year. I had found her on the stair outside my door, and as no one claimed her I adopted her as my own. From the outset we were fast friends, and she quickly became an intimate of my small circle of acquaintance.

It was a dodgy thing at first, however, for undergraduates, as you know, are partial to dogs. Indeed the possession of a little something in the terrier line is considered absolutely essential to a college man's existence. Terriers are good ones for the vermin, and indispensable for sport and show. To keep a beast is a virtual *sine qua non* for any undergraduate worthy of the name.

Flounce had been little more than a kitten when she came to me, and adjusted remarkably well to her new life and surroundings. She soon became the envy of every dog in our set for her outgoing ways, for her shrewd judge of character, and for her talent as a mouser, which matched or exceeded that of the best ratters on our court. In brief, she was as much a terrier in her way as any showy calico could be.

Flounce was unusual as well in being an expert traveler, for from the start I took her everywhere with me. Her first experience of the wider world she gained from the pocket of my coat, then from the rucksack in which I carried my tool-kit for use on field excursions. In time she became as well known to the community of undergraduates and out-college men as were the stately dons themselves. Flounce knew nothing of Lingonshire, but once I had decided to return home there was no question but that she should accompany me.

And last there was Bob Cob.

A bay gelding, Bob might not have been able to clear a five-barred gate with ease, but he was an active cob nevertheless, on whom I had trotted briskly through the lanes and byways of Penhaligon. My father, who had known how to take a fence, had always been judge of a good horse, and I daresay I had inherited some small portion of his horse sense. (And some of his farm sense too, I trusted.) Ere we left Penhaligon I took Bob to the farrier's to be rough-shod for the journey, which was to be made in conjunction with a mastodon train. For while Stinker, Flounce, and I would be snugly ensconced in a passenger-cab, poor Bob would be following on a lead.

I had not seen Dithering for a couple of summers, what with the arrears of work which had occupied so much of my time. Now all this was changed; now there would be no more arrears of work, for I was going home.

The passing years had passed so very fast. I knew that I should be retiring to a life of quiet loneliness there at the farm — loneliness, because of the absence of my father who had died and been laid to rest ere I had known anything of it. Because I little recalled my mother, her presence I should not miss so much. Her small portrait which hangs in the rustic gallery at the farmhouse was my sole connection to her. This painting I remember from my earliest childhood, and the reverential way my father would take it from the wall and hold it in his big hands, and smile again upon those laughing dark eyes as if no time whatever had passed. I remember his telling me so much about her, over the years, that it seemed she and I had known each other after all.

There would be no corresponding portrait of my father to fill up the blank; I don't recall his ever having sat for one. There would be only memories, and the few lines he had jotted down for me the day he died. My father had never been the man for writing, but what he wrote me that day I carry with me always in my heart, as I carry the note always on my person.

A more honest, upright man than my father never had graced the dales of Lingonshire. I suppose I always have been envious of those fortunates amongst my friends with both parents living. For me there had been only my father, who had done his best in raising me. He himself had not been highly educated, and had wanted better for his son and heir. Evidently this had been a wish my mother had shared, one that later was granted by her brother Jory's having died at an opportune moment.

On the road home I had the curious sense that the shades of my parents and my uncle were hovering about me, keeping me company. I knew that they should very much like Flounce and Bob, and would welcome them at the farm. As for Stinker, well . . . they should have to get used to Stinker.

A young man named Stokes from the town had been my father's chief servant. He had been hired, while still a tousled youth, in the last days of my grandfather. Of course he was older now, but otherwise he was the same cheery-eyed, rumple-faced, indifferently-attired, entirely trustworthy Stokes whom I had known. "Natty" had been the ironical nickname given him by my grandfather, and he still often was so addressed. He was a free-and-easy young spark, who enjoyed the bachelor estate as much as did I. Assisting him at the farm were a cook and housekeeper, Mrs. Peters, and a maid-of-all-work, both of them somewhat advanced in years. Thus was constituted the household to which Stinker, Flounce, Bob Cob, and I retired after leaving Penhaligon.

A shivery sun was trembling in a frigid sky, on that chill day in June that witnessed our arrival in Dithering. We had parted from the train at the Sugar Loaf, the chief inn and posting-house at Dozmary. For the trains no longer proceeded so far as out-of-the-way Dithering, leaving it to coaches and chaises to carry travelers the remaining distance. At the Sugar Loaf a fly was hired for Stinker, Flounce, and the luggage, while I mounted to the saddle on Bob Cob. As for the rest of our belongings, which included some items of furniture from my rooms at Maunder, they had been dispatched by carrier and would reach us in a few days.

And so we pushed on at a steady pace through the wildways from Dozmary to Dithering, and in due course hauled up in the yard of the Pack Horse Inn, for a spot of refreshment, before entering into our new life at Callander farm.

## Chapter Seven

W E had been several days at the farm and were settling in nicely, when Stinker, Stokes and I went for a ramble into town with Bob Cob. For the first time I permitted young Natty to sit his saddle and to have the reins of Bob, while Stinker and I trod alongside at a brisk pace. We stopped awhile at the shoeing-smith's, now that the road journey was done, to have fresh iron applied to Bob's feet. This accomplished, we made convenient use of the gray day to avail ourselves of the warmth and hospitality of the Pack Horse Inn.

That house of good repute and old standing had not seen us again since our brief halt on arriving in town. We entered to find a splendid fire in the chimney, and a buzz of conversation in the air. The landlord, drying his hands on his apron, stepped forward and bowed us a cordial welcome. He then ushered us to the oak bar, where some of the regulars had established themselves. Others were making use of the chairs and tables which were disposed at intervals about the floor.

Mr. Readymoney, the landlord, was of that blustery species of publican who favors clean chins, pencil-thin mustaches, and bow-ties. He it was who had charge of the house now, having received it as an inheritance from a maiden aunt, a regular old quiz called Elva Blossom. Old quiz — or old crab-fish, as some preferred — Miss Blossom had ruled with undisputed sway over all matters at the inn until her death some years ago, caused by choking on a rissole.

I recalled the formidable Miss Blossom from days agone, posted there at the bar at the head of her household troops. It is in fact one of my most cherished memories. For of late my thoughts, stimulated by old associations, had turned to former scenes and times. Many were the hours I had passed in this same taproom in the company of my father, and it was with regret I had accepted the fact that he and I never more would visit here together. Never again would we come striding in at the door, the two of us, to be greeted by the proprietor and the regulars and the household staff. Never again would I hear my father return their welcome, his familiar voice having been stilled now and forever more.

Mr. Readymoney pointed out to me a line of envelopes that were ranged on a shelf behind the bar. This being the posting-house of the town, the landlord amongst his other duties served as postmaster for the district. He indicated there were no letters awaiting us at present, but reminded me it was there on the shelf that in future any would turn up. I responded by saying I should have Stokes collect them for me. It was a commission the young fellow had taken very kindly to, as indeed most any excuse to be calling at the inn would have been agreeable to him.

Stinker, hearing of the arrangement, speedily protested.

"What's this? Here now, sir, that's to be me own job, ain't it?" he grumbled, rubbing his little bald head in confusion.

"On the contrary," I told him, "for as Natty here has performed this same service for my father these past few years, I see no cause to be relieving him of the responsibility."

"But bother it, sir — " spluttered Stinker.

"However you are free to accompany him if you so desire, whenever it is convenient."

The toothy smile that flashed from Stinker's grizzled chops might have lighted the room.

"Thank ye, sir, thank ye. Ye're a gentleman as ever, Dr. Callander, sir, if not so much the scholar as afore."

"An' so 'tis true then, is't, 'ee've thrown up yer ould job, ay, Mr. Callander?" the landlord remarked.

No one in Dithering ever had addressed me as *Doctor* Callander, for I was no physician, and no one in these dales ever had heard of a doctor who was no physician. Nor did they always call every physician *Doctor*, unless it be from respect and long usage, as it was for little Dr. Hankey. To these honest rustic folk I simply had "gone up the country" for my schooling, and now had come home again.

"Indeed I have, sir. It's my pleasure now to enjoy myself here in these dales where my ancestors were born and bred."

"An' the farm? How do 'ee find the farm, sir?"

"We shall make do, Mr. Readymoney, with what we have. For I intend that there always shall be a Callander farm at Dithering. I believe — I dare say I know — it is as my father would have wished." As I spoke I was thinking of his letter to me, which resided in an inner pocket of my coat.

"And how is business, Mr. Readymoney?" I said.

The landlord tossed up his hands. "'Thankin' 'ee kindly, sir, for axin'. Well, 'tis much like yer own case, sir, out o' doubt. We make do wi' what we have."

My eyes traveled to a familiar notice-board which hung inside the door, and which proclaimed to all and sundry that —

Every comfort and convenience is offered to visitors, anglers, &c., and the prime fishing-grounds being found dreckly across the bridge, the necessity of a lengthy walk is avoided.

J. READYMONEY, *Proprietor*

A further line communicated to the brethren of the angle that the fishing-tackle and other implements displayed on the walls were available for rental, at modest rates.

"Your guests, they have had good sport this season?"

"More so than the fish," the landlord noted, brightening. "An' so what can I do 'ee for, Mr. Callander? Natty? An' yer small friend there? Ale, thick an' muddy? A Fenshire gray, or nappy brown? Or honest spruce-beer?" he said, bustling round behind the engine.

Young Stokes's face folded into a smile; Stinker grinned until his eyes nearly disappeared into his head. Both looked at the engine with keen expectancy as we tendered our requests.

The landlord, making a swift calculation of the reckoning, shifted the quid in his cheek and drew the liquor from the engine. The pewters being set before us, I told down the coins, which he gathered up with practiced fingers.

"Thank 'ee for yer custom, sir."

"Not at all, landlord."

At that moment a door opened and an aproned belly walked in, joined to a lumpish, pudgy-faced youth. His circular eyes, round and staring, and vivid thatch of curly red hair gave him the look of a startled carrot.

"Gilbert!"

It was Mr. Readymoney, demanding to know why the pot-boy — a painfully apt designation — had absented himself from the taproom for the last half-hour.

The youth, swabbing a greasy chin, stammered out a reply which communicated his entire desire to avoid answering.

"Gilbert!" the landlord said again.

"Blimey, nuncle," the youth exclaimed, evasion having failed, "but I likes a nice capon leg, an' I likes pretty Maizie o' the upstairs too. So when I see'd the chicky-sweets a-kissin' o' the ostler i' the kitchen, I did keep a-watch of 'em from the scullery, till Mrs. Pottle she did deliver me a boot in me fundaments." Despite this embarrassment a sly grin stole across his lips, from which he had yet to remove the grease from the capon leg. "But I did see 'en a-kissin' of 'er, a-kissin' o' pretty Maizie," and his cheeks flushed a molten red near as shocking as his hair.

"Ess, an' bain't it 'nough to make a man's flesh creep?" the landlord sighed, to no one in particular. Having instructed the youth to resume his duties, he leaned across the bar and in a hushed tone explained to us that he had had a number of complaints respecting the delinquent Gilbert, whom he accused of being a shirker, and a layabout, but against whom he was incapable of acting, the delinquent being in fact his sister's only child and his godson.

"For we must make do wi' what we have, sir," he nodded glumly.

As we stood there washing our livers — a favorite phrase of Stinker's — we were approached by another of the patrons ranged at the bar. He was a moldy-looking little man with a large, discolored nose, to which something other than exercise had communicated an inflamed appearance. The upper half of him seemed fixed in a permanent half-turn, in relation to his lower half, as if he had been screwed into his trousers. A battered Scots tam hung on the side of his head; fluffy white side-whiskers, a rheumy eye, a blubbery lip, and a dingy plaid and tweeds completed his *tout ensemble*.

For a time he stood regarding us expectantly, as if waiting for one or another of us to speak. At length he seemed to tire of the effort, and, choosing Stinker, he addressed him thus —

"I hae kend him these thirty year, yer friend the young Callander laird there, an auld acquaintance, as was his father afore him. But I dinna believe I ken yer fizzogg."

Stinker stared open-mouthed. "Me what?"

"It gars me grue tae look upon ye, man, for 'tis an unco dowdy aspect ye wear as ever I hae set een on. Wha are ye, then? How shall I ca' ye?"

Another dubious glance from Stinker.

"He wants to know your name," I explained, "as he doesn't know your face."

"Well, why don't he say it? Stinker's me moniker. What's yers, then, eh?" he demanded of the other.

"Toad Henry," replied the Scot, mechanically extending his hand, only to withdraw it as fast. One rheumy eye narrowed suspiciously. "Stinker, is't? And wha' for do they ca' ye that, man?"

"Why, 'twas the young college gents, as did always call me Stinker since the old times."

"Sure ye hae the fizzogg for it, by ma certie, Maister Stinker. But 'Stinker' I dinna care for at a', ony mair than a bad smell. And deil a drap o' yill hae ye offered me."

Stinker looked his befuddlement. Quite at a loss, he applied to me again for a translation.

"It seems he's disappointed you haven't bought him a drink."

"Ooh, is he, just?" Stinker retorted. He eyed the other stonily; then, drawing himself up — the distance was not far — he challenged the moldy Scot: "And so why do they call ye Toad, eh? What's the meaning o' *that?* For 'tis a fine moniker for a galoot with a clock like yers on him."

It seems it had been Stinker's turn to be offended, by the other's presumption that the gift of a dram was expected.

This Toad Henry had been a *jowster* — an itinerant pedlar — of some renown in the district, who had retired in favor of a more settled existence. Always short of funds, he was a familiar sight in Dithering, and it was of some amusement to young Natty and myself to observe Stinker's reaction to his quips and quignogs.

Far from taking offense himself, the jowster smiled and wrung his head. "Aweel," he sighed, with a tolerant air, "I judged as muckle. Dinna pit yersell into a kippage, Maister Stinker. I see's ye hae been at the wee cappie there, and as ma puir mither used aye tae tell me, ill I shouldna say o' him as speaks frae liquor. Fash yer pate nae mair aboot it; I do forgie ye. Maister Callander, sir — " he went on, transferring his attention to me, "and is it yersell as may offer yer auld acquaintance and friend o' yer dear father's a drap brandy-wine to haud his puir heart up?"

*Toadying* was the origin of his nickname — insinuating himself into the good graces of others, that they might feel disposed to relieve his thirst. No sooner had I sent the jowster off with his dram, than a second familiar visage, belonging to another of our town characters, loomed up on the other side of me to take his place.

Wrapped in a haze of vapors thrown off by his old briar pipe, he resembled a sort of traveling cloud of tobacco smoke. Nor was it just any kind of smoke either, but that rankest species of mundungus, as would clear the senses of less hardy individuals than our Lingonshire dalesmen.

"Who's this one, then?" Stinker muttered, holding his nose. "For he looks a bird as me own moniker might fit to a partickler T, now's I've had a whiff of him."

The chimney's name was Cedar Jack. He was a leathery-faced old veteran, a woodsman of prowess some fifty years old, who gained his living transforming the mighty giants of the woodland into fuel for cottage hearths.

He stood awhile in silence with his arms folded, calmly surveying us and smoking. A wide-awake hat the size of the moon shaded his head. His other integuments consisted of a fleecy jerkin, much sullied, made of the hide of some forest creature; a weathered baldric that crossed his torso from shoulder to hip, and from which a cutlass depended; frayed but serviceable corduroys; and knee-boots.

At length he spoke. "Callander," he nodded, touching a confidential finger to his hat-brim.

"Mr. Jack," said I, returning the greeting.

Of course the woodsman knew young Natty, but my man Stinker was a stranger to him; accordingly I introduced them.

"Stinker," nodded Jack, eyeing him gravely.

"Mr. — er — Jack," said Stinker.

The forester took another whiff at his briar.

"Stinker," he said again, after a moment's deliberation.

"Mr. Jack?"

Perplexed, the woodsman knotted his brow under the eaves of his hat as big as the moon.

"Why Stinker?" he asked.

"Why *not* Stinker?" returned the other.

Again the veteran deliberated for a moment; again a blue cloud of mundungus rose to engulf him. His thinking done, he appeared satisfied with the result. Stinker had passed muster, if I read his leathery countenance aright.

"I'll have 'ee knaw, Mr. Stinker," he remarked, "that ould Jack is one o' the maddest boys in these dales as ever slept out o' straw, or went loose under the stars, is ould Jack." And directly another volley of smoke was discharged to the atmosphere.

"And who said ye wasn't?" was Stinker's considerate reply.

"I dinna misdoubt ye, Maister Jack, sir," said Toad Henry, cutting in — he had finished his dram — "but an ever should ye feel it in yer heart to be commiseratin' of a puir jowster body, blythe will I be o' yer ain company mysell," saying which he doffed his tam and smilingly bowed his head, at the same time pushing forward his empty glass.

"Toad Henry," grunted Jack.

"Aye, sir," said the jowster, lifting his eyes.

A rigid jaw and a steely look confronted them. It was the sort of look that gets into a man who has seen most all there is to see in this world.

"Go drown yerself in a puddle," was the forester's gentle reproof. For emphasis he jerked his head in the direction of a stout wooden pole, some eight feet in length — a quarterstaff — that was leaning against the wall behind him. The ancient game of quarterstaff was as out of date, perhaps, as was old Jack himself; but the veteran was a skilled master of the sport, and widely renowned in the dales.

Altogether it did little to quell the spirits of the jowster, who was heard muttering "Flatterer!" as he sidled away.

Meanwhile Stinker's attention had been arrested by an object that hung on the wall near the staff.

"What's that, then, eh?" he asked, tapping me on the sleeve. "For of all clocks, there's one as 'tis the worst o' the lot, I'll be bound."

"It's a vizard — a mask — popularly called the 'Eye of Days'."

"Ooh, it's horrible. I don't care for it at all," Stinker said, making a wry face not far different from that represented on the mask.

With its single, goggle-eye and primitive features, it was an ugly little thing — the mask, I mean. It was carved from pumpkin-wood — the wood of a pumpkin oak — and had graced the wall of the tap-room for ages, if tradition is to be believed. It was rather unpleasant and a bit frightening to look at, with its leering grin, jagged rows of teeth like a jack-a-lent's, and staring eye-hole. Nonetheless it was such a fixture of the place that I had scarcely given it any notice.

"What's it for? And what lunatic made it?" Stinker asked.

They were reasonable questions. For whom indeed would a one-eyed mask have been fashioned?

"It's thought to have been made by the Woldfolk," I told him.

Stinker first looked blank, then mildly insulted. He scratched his chin, conscious of its grizzle, and narrowed his eyes at me. "Made by old folks? Whose old folks?"

"Not old folks — *Woldfolk*. They are but one of the many folk legends of the dales. To some they are malign or capricious entities, who are thought to haunt these hills of Lingonshire. Of course in so remote a district as ours there are many such stories. Some believe it to be the cold air on the wolds, and the periods of stringent isolation, that have contributed to these fanciful tales told over a winter's ingle."

Stinker's face was concerned.

"Tales, did ye say, sir?" he muttered, eyeing the mask darkly. "It ain't tales alone as made a horrid thing like that."

"'Tis for safety's sake — a charm to protect the wearer," the landlord explained, "or so my aunt Elva Blossom used to tell it. But my auntie she cud be some great buster of a liar at times."

"Protect him from what?" Stinker wanted to know.

Ere the landlord could answer, his chubby nephew, the pot-boy Gilbert, lumbering by with a fistful of pewters, blurted out — "Piskies! I knaws 'tis piskies, nuncle! And I see'd one, too" — before vanishing in the direction of the scullery.

## Chapter Eight

**S**TINKER reflected a blank slate. "Piskies? And what's piskies now?"

"Piskies," volunteered Cedar Jack, with a long roll of his head, "is things not to be thought on, nor looked into. 'Ee've had it now from Jack o'the wolds. *Not to be thought on — nor looked into.*"

It was believed by some that piskies — mischievous sprites of local legend — were possessed of but a single eye, the object of the vizard-mask being to shield the wearer from their antics by mimicking their appearance. So much I communicated to Stinker.

"And 'twas these here Woldfolks did make the mask as is to protect against piskies?"

"So tradition holds."

"And where be these Woldfolks now?"

"A-standin' aside 'ee p'rhaps, just — *there,*" the landlord suggested, giving a sudden poke at Stinker's ribs. Considerable and rare was the amusement engendered by Stinker's startled leap some inches out of his boots.

Once he had collected himself, I explained to Stinker that these Woldfolk were believed to have mastered the art of invisibility owing to their discovery of a species of fern-seed, the wearing of which enabled them to walk amongst human beings unobserved.

This last unfortunately acted only to magnify Stinker's concern. "Ain't these Woldfolks human?" he asked.

"Not human," intoned Cedar Jack, with another roll of his head. "Not human — *not right!*"

In fact the Woldfolk were discouraged from mingling with human beings, or so it was thought, although the reason for this proscription was unclear. And yet legend supported the idea that they *did* mingle on occasion, at times in their visible form — which otherwise is indistinguishable from our own — or invisibly, by gliding amongst us unsensed and unseen.

And as Mr. Readymoney had intimated by his poke at Stinker's side, one of these Woldfolk even now might be there at his elbow, attending to his every word.

Invisible Woldfolk, piskies, a goggle-eyed vizard-mask — it was getting to be too much for Stinker.

"'Tis a good job then, Mr. Stinker, 'ee haven't heard tell of Obadiah Outland," the landlord remarked.

Given his present state of mind, Stinker was feeling disinclined to inquire into this; but Mr. Readymoney, unprompted, answered him anyway.

"Ess, the ould man o' the waterways — a fiend of a bargeman and creature o' the Woldfolk, as does ply the streams an' rivers o' Lingonshire. For a fee 'ee may go aboard his craft, and be ta'en where none else may go — to call on the ancient dead an' buried — over the water — and ef 'ee be lucky," the landlord hinted, "'ee may be returned to tell of't."

Already Stinker had heard rather enough of the folk traditions of Lingonshire. It was just possible he may have been reconsidering his philosophy — being ruled by him that has the purse — but I should doubt it. Fleetingly he may have longed for a return to the comforts of Maunder, but for the jingle of coins in his pocket he longed even more.

But such concerns abruptly were swept from my mind, when Mr. Readymoney addressed me by asking —

"An' what o' the Squire an' Miss Dora, Mr. Callander? Have 'ee called yet at the Moorings? For I s'pose they'll be keen to see 'ee."

I answered him by stating that I had received an invitation to dine at the Moorings, and that I had accepted. In replying to him I made particular note of the fact that the invitation had come from the Squire directly, and not from Miss Fetching.

Already, however, a contagion of roguish smiles and winks, and knowing nods and chuckles, had broken out amongst the company.

"For sarten 'ee knaws, Mr. Callander, sir," the landlord drawled, "that our Miss Dora be still the 'andsomest maid in these dales, just-about."

"A dazzler!" "A charmer!" "A peach!" "To Miss Dora!" was the ardent chorus that arose.

"Tell me, sir, and is she still upset with 'ee? Or have 'ee two made it up?" Mr. Readymoney inquired.

Perhaps it was the twinge of conscience I felt, perhaps it was simply embarrassment, perhaps it was something else, that caused me to lapse into the vernacular in chiding him —

"Giss on, landlord! Don't 'ee be spoutin' such talk now."

Toad Henry, still seeking a patron, gave a waggish laugh. "No yet paid yer addresses tae the young leddy? Aweel, sir, ye do pit a gude face on't, Maister Callander, by ma certie, ye do."

An enraptured Gilbert, who had reappeared and been eagerly attending to the discussion, all at once was seized by a violent fit of industry — prompted no doubt by the stern glance of his uncle — and lumbered off again in search of pewters.

"I dislike the cut o' that boy's bib, I do," the landlord was heard grumbling to himself.

It was at this point that the topic under discussion changed again, when a heavy, unadorned block of a man, entering at the door with a pair of companions, loudly announced to one and all —

"Drabbet it, naybors, ef the thievin' poachers bain't returned agen to flummox us!"

## Chapter Nine

THE unadorned block of a man was Mr. Tristan Colley, our neighbor just along the stream from the farm, and his proclamation created something of a stir. His companions were his sons, Quince and Kale, and the story the three of them had to relate ignited a fever of interest among the listeners.

It was his daughter Lettice who, not many hours ago, had advised her father that a brawny young calf, and one of their best ewes, a favorite of her sister Olive's, had vanished from their pens. The losses had occurred overnight, but in this instance the scoundrels had left traces of their activity — footprints in the slush and snow leading to and from the yard-gate. In this brazen act of thievery the animals had been snatched cleanly from their straw, and not, as was the more usual case, while on pasture.

"So it bain't saber-cats or teratorns as be back of it," the landlord concluded, "but desperate men."

"Azackly," nodded Colley. "For there be the tracks, Mr. Readymoney — one bleddy villain's at least — and there be another's, too — tracks of a kind as bain't familiar to me, but as wud set any decent heart to tremblin' to look on. 'Twas some proper job, hows'ever, for none heard a sound i' the night."

"What of these other tracks?" I asked him. "What were they like? Can you describe them?"

The farmer massaged his stubbled chin. "Queer sort o' shoon the villain wore, Mr. Callander — soft shoon, belike, as be my suppose. 'Twas a biggish man as wore 'em, but his toes they all was splayed, on both his feet. Queerer still, hows'ever, was the number o' toes as was splayed."

"The number? How so?"

"Dree toes, Mr. Callander — dree toes was splayed."

"The man had three toes? And on each foot the same?"

"Ess. An' queerer e'en than that," said Colley, his audience straining like one collective ear to catch the rest — "was the fourth toe, as did stick out behind t'others, backwards, like a bird's foot. More'n this I cudn' tell 'ee."

Audible gasps were heard, prompting a renewed buzz of discussion in the room.

"Fourth toe behind," murmured Cedar Jack, nodding sagaciously; and taking a monstrous whiff at his pipe he quickly lost himself in a rank blue haze of concentration.

It had been some half-score years since the last incidents occurred. Since that time, almost like clockwork, an interval of quiet had prevailed, with no activity. But now, as it seemed they always did, and always would, the thieves had returned. Small livestock had begun to disappear. Tristan Colley it was, our neighbor, who had been victimized when I was a lad; I remembered it well — Colley's braggaty calf, or what was left of it, which Dickie Fish and I had discovered at the roasting-spit. So too had other farmers, men like Sweezy and Kneebone, lost animals to the rascally beggars, as indeed had my father. Now it looked as if the miscreants had started in again afresh.

And always some half-score years would intervene between episodes. It had struck me as odd when I was a boy, and it struck me as odd again now. *Why the appearance of clockwork?*

"Ess, hows'ever, naybors, there be a further point," Colley went on, silencing the throng, "for 'ee knaw, the boys h'yur and I did trail the villains a fair way upside the stream and clean into the trees. An' where do 'ee suppose their tracks did lead? Well — away off towards Bothack's mansion."

"Mawgan Bothack! That rude churl?" said one of his hearers.

"Mansion, indeed! Hovel, more like," scoffed another.

"Ess, his sylvan lodge," reflected a third, "that queer contrap of a bunkhouse as the megalops men from Slopshire did laive ahind."

Farmer Colley drew up his stout square substance, and indicated it was his intention now and that of his sons to proceed at once to

Bothack's manse and confront him over the business. They had first stopped at the inn, however, to apprize as many of their neighbors as possible of the trouble that had returned to Dithering.

Then the name Harry Smelt came up, and I was reminded it was not only livestock which had gone missing. Old Harry was a tinker who had vanished some years back, during another rash of disappearances. It was thought a saber-cat might have gotten him, in which event his end would have been no pretty story. But there was something else as well, for Harry Smelt, a reclusive sort, was known to have established his camp in the area of the Graystone Crags.

"Fourth toe behind — Eldritch's Cupboard," were Cedar Jack's words upon emerging from his reverie.

My ears pricked up at this, and on a hunch I asked him —

"Have you seen something out there, Mr. Jack?"

The veteran's eye glanced wildfire. "Seen something? Indeed, sir, I have. For in his time ould Jack has seen *plenty.*"

"Tell us of it," I urged him.

"Do 'ee, ef 'ee please, Mr. Jack," seconded the landlord.

The woodsman considered a moment, working his briar in silence and thinking. The room had fallen deathly quiet in anticipation. No one moved, no one breathed. The utterances of Cedar Jack were few and often cryptic, but his authority was such that all stopped to listen.

"The Cupboard," the forester answered at length, "it does lie out o' Jack's ordinary road. But he bein' of a wanderin' mood of a marnin', was ould Jack, by cart-track and by-path he did find hisself i'the nayborhood o' the Crags. 'Twasn't far off from the spot where ould Helyer was gibbeted on a post, years agone, in the grand ould days. O' course he was on his guard, was Jack — ears alert, and eyes ditto. And 'twas well with him that it were so, for 'twas a lurker there in the gloom o' the gully alongside.

"'Twas a foggy mist i' the air, and a brooding silence over all. The daylight, well, it cud hardly fill a peascod; consequent the figure o' the lurker 'twas darksome at best. A great long, gangly, ghastly sort o' figure 'twas, a-prowlin' and a-skulkin' there, and a-peepin' from the brush, an' for no good purpose I dessay. But then the rascal he spies ould Jack wi' his quarterstaff at the ready, to whack 'en, and of an instant does up an' scuttle off into the fog, as much like a beast as any man. 'Twas a queer, creepin' manner o' gait he had — but fast as lightnin'! He did lead Jack a proper chase, he did, straight to the Crags, and as he bounded along he rattled as he ran."

"Sure 'ee don't say so, Mr. Jack?"

"Rattled? What, his brains in his head?"

"Ess — but who with a brain in his head wud go a-nigh the Cupboard?"

Responded Jack, continuing in his same tone — "But 'twasn't all, for the rascal did escape ould Jack there at the Crags, by fleein' into the Cupboard an' so was gone."

A chorus of voices rose in noisy protest.

"The deil ye say, Maister Jack," exclaimed Toad Henry.

"My ivers! Escaped *into* the Cupboard?" another asked.

"The doited fule!" said the jowster.

"Some chawbacon stranger more like, some great dobeck as don't knaw the Cupboard from his ear-hole. No brains at all."

"Or some chawbacon jowster, p'rhaps. The rattlin' was the trifles in his sack," suggested a third. "'Tis plain as a pigstaff."

"Or chawbacon poacher, p'rhaps," dittoed Mr. Readymoney.

At these words all looked to the woodsman, who had been studying the ceiling and musing.

"There be more, Mr. Jack — ay?" the landlord hinted.

The wide-awake as big as the moon rocked back and forth, slowly. When the veteran's reply emerged from its shadow, smoke flowed out with it.

"Footprints," said Jack. "Footprints — dead straight into the Cupboard . . ."

Ere he had time to speak them, I had divined his next words.

"Dree toes," he nodded grimly, "and a fourth behind."

All this held a special interest for me — or should I say a special horror? I shivered inwardly at the woodsman's report of the rattling sound, made by the ghastly, gangly figure as it scurried off. What a nuisance it all was, these unexplained raids at six-year intervals, Eldritch's Cupboard and the monster lodged in its bowels! Had it really happened the way I remembered it, or thought it had happened, or had it all been a dream? Had the experience been nothing more than a nightmare — or was it indeed a memory of a real event? For it was no ordinary species of poacher that Dickie Fish and I had run upon in the Cupboard. The *whirr* of the piskie, the roasting-spit, the horrid picture of deformity rearing up from behind the slab, the skittery crackling and rattling of joints as it sped after us, the clatter of birdlike feet, the awful grip of bony claws deep in my shoulder, the spin round to face it —

Meanwhile heads were put together and looks exchanged as a babble of excitement swept the company. From their talk I learned that there had been more of these disappearances than I had heretofore been privy to. Of Harry Smelt, Bridgit Gooderly, and Fanny Meadows I had heard. But what of Jocund Josie the little milkmaid, who in May month twelve years agone had been snatched from her cot in Sweezy's barn? A search had been mounted but no trace of her ever was found. She had vanished as completely as if the earth had opened up and swallowed her.

And there was one who had disappeared and come back, but had had precious little say about it. Six years had passed since Davy Zoze, Dr. Hankey's man at the time, returning from an errand in the village of St. Neot's, had failed to appear. His saddled horse, however, had been found drinking at the doctor's trough. A while later searchers discovered Davy himself, slashed and bloodied, and cowering in a tree, where evidently he had fled to escape an assailant. In all likelihood the villain had been frightened off by the arrival of the search party. As for Davy — stout, sturdy, dependable Davy, a youth in the pink of condition — he had been unable to communicate to his employer, or to anyone else for that matter, what had happened to him. Indeed he seemed unwilling to communicate anything at all, on any topic. From that day forward there had been a fearful, haunted look in his eyes, and a stopper in his throat. He never spoke of his experience — never spoke of anything again. Some said the look in his eyes was that of one who had gazed upon a basilisk. Many, Dr. Hankey included, reckoned the poor fellow had been driven out of his mind. Tragically he did not long survive his ordeal, but died in a headlong leap from his mother's second-floor window.

"Who amongst us is safe?"

The question could be heard circulating through the crowd. Some ventured to suggest that the Woldfolk, undetected by our eyes, might be amongst us at this very minute, might even be behind the business of the disappearances.

"You'm not wanted h'yur!" someone gritted out, to any invisibles within hearing.

The memory of my childhood experience in the Cupboard had crystallized itself into clarity in my mind. Then, all in a flash, an idea came to me — an explanation for the clockwork. I dare say my expression must have altered rather a lot, for it caused the landlord and some of the regulars to fall silent and to turn expectant eyes on me, as though awaiting my solution to the mystery.

How was I to tell them that the monster in Eldritch's Cupboard in all likelihood was awake again, and had begun — feeding?

It was this I knew in my heart to be the true source of the evil. Poachers? Stock thieves? I did not believe in them. But I did believe in my childhood experience, and in Dickie Fish — Dickie Fish, who himself had vanished and never been heard of again. *Had he gone back into the Cupboard and been roasted on the spit?*

No poachers or stock thieves, not by a long chalk, but a ravenous beast.

All these years on, my memory of that sinister, dreadful thing in the Cupboard still had power to chill me. Now the creature had displayed a willingness to venture forth from its lair in search of prey. More abominable even than this, it seemed to have gained an accomplice.

*Who indeed amongst us was safe?*

In view of the circumstances I chose to hold my tongue. The rest meanwhile had taken to stroking their chins and trading thoughtful glances, the play of their features a study in suppressed emotion. Cedar Jack had resumed his smoking; perhaps behind his cloud of vile mundungus he was back again at the foot of the Graystone Crags.

Some peculiar, and possibly dangerous, researches would have to be made. My eyes circled the room, lighting on the many varied and familiar objects on show there. On one object in particular my glance settled, then sharpened.

It was a signboard, inscribed with the verses of the immortal Mordaunt, whoever he had been —

> *Hickory, dickory, dare.*
> *The piskie flew up in the air.*
>    *The man in the Cupboard*
>    *Hisself is no sluggard.*
> *Hickory, dickory, dare.*

A goblin tale which had thrilled through many a Dithering bosom in its time was that of the monster in Eldritch's Cupboard. But more than a goblin tale, I believed, it was the truth.

This monster I had swept from my mind years agone, and now back it had come. One can't ignore the past, I reflected, without the past having its revenge.

I turned with a start as the long-case clock in the corner, a gruff old giant with a domed hood and copper-plated face, chose that moment to begin sounding.

## Chapter Ten

MID-AFTERNOON, two days on, saw Bob Cob harnessed and in the shafts of the weathered gig that my father had kept. Beside me on the cushion, her furry head and ears poking out of the club bag that had become her favorite for adventuring, was Flounce. Eagerly her green eyes darted this way and that — "Where are we off to now, Callander? Some exotic place, is it?" — as I switched the reins in my hand and lightly touched them to Bob to start him going.

"Walk on, Bob. There's a good lad."

Flounce seconded the command with an authoritative *meow* — in the event Bob had not gotten the hint — and settled down in her bag for a comfortable excursion, however brief it might be.

We proceeded down the hill at a leisurely pace. Beyond the lower wood, near the outskirts of town, we swung left into the drive that crossed the heights above the stream. A few minutes' further travel brought us to the Moorings.

Long, rambling, rustic, partly of plaster and timber framing, partly of fieldstone, with a red-tiled roof, it was a pleasant, sprawling manse — a mansion indeed compared to our little hutch of a farmhouse — and as familiar to me as my watch's dial, from the number of times I had called there. In its setting of fir-trees atop the slope, on a goodly space of ground, it presented a delightful picture. Down at the stream a small skiff lay ashore by the quay, the tranquil sounds of the water flowing past it a joy to hear.

As it always had been, and seemingly always would be, all looked to be in good order, with an air of comfort pervading the scene. For I had received my invitation to dinner, and now here I was calling at the house I knew so well but had not visited in some long while.

For a minute or two I sat at gaze, taking it in. Then I gathered up

Flounce, tossed the reins to the lad who had come out to receive me, and mounted the steps to the door.

I was ushered into the snug, comfortable parlor — I remembered it well. On the sofa near the fire sat the Squire at his ease. He struggled to his feet to welcome me. Struggled to his *foot*, rather, as he had but one that he might call his own. The other was an impostor, a forgery — for Squire Fetching, you see, had a wooden leg.

He greeted me with his usual courtesy, and we shook hands. His eyes opened when he saw Flounce spring nimbly from her club bag.

"I thought Dora would like to meet her," I explained.

"By thunder," the Squire murmured in some surprise, "I dare say she will."

"And as Flounce is a regular traveler, the drive from the farm was a simple one. She goes almost anywhere with me. Has done so since she was a kitten."

The Squire's bushy eyebrows lifted. "Has she, now? Well, Dora's mad over these little creatures, as she calls 'em. Found herself a new one just this week."

Squire Fetching was a tall, upright old dalesman, of an aspect that might be termed iron-gray. Despite the occasional outburst to protest this or that damnable enormity which the world of late had thrust upon him, his manners were easy, blended with a kind of frank and forthright good nature.

As for Flounce, she accepted the introduction with her customary grace. *He seems a pleasant old duck* she mused, while searching round her for a convenient place to settle. She found it on the hearthrug. There she stretched herself to her full, luxurious length, and purring her pleasure soon was enjoying its lazy warmth, with eyes half-shut but ears alert to all that went on around her.

Meantime the Squire waved me to a chair, then stumped back to the sofa, his wooden leg creaking.

"Keep intending to oil the damned thing," he explained. "Can't get about so much now, you know. Need this blighter too, so I don't make a damfool o' myself," and he tapped the floor with his walking-stick, which had been propped against the arm of the sofa. He sighed and shook his head regretfully. "What a damned blasted thing it is to be old."

"I should hardly call you old, sir," I told him, putting on my best encouraging face. "Distinguished, certainly."

He eyed me sharply for a moment. "You always were exceedingly polite. Dora says so, too."

He took up his pipe and tamped it calmly, then spent several seconds setting fire to its contents. This accomplished, he stuck it in his teeth, under as imposing a pair of mustaches as were to be found in the dales, laced his fingers together in his lap, and stretched his long legs — the flesh and blood, and the impostor too — towards the fender.

"Ah, well," he sighed, gazing on the flames and Flounce and musing, "*tempus fugit*, you know. To you young people life is a dream. Age, well it turns a man to stone. Or in my case — cork," he grunted, giving his leg (the false one) a rap with a bony knuckle.

The Squire was a man who loved good wines and good measure, and ringing for a servant he ordered a bottle of sherry be conveyed to the drinks station. The wine was superb, naturally, and we passed the ensuing minutes in small talk, the Squire speaking at some length about his son Robert, a year younger than Dora, whose career had taken him a world away to Newmarsh in the north of Fenshire.

"Laboring in the mines of Plutus," he explained.

"Sir?"

"Some hard-nosed banker by the name of Stubbs lured him from us. Why not Medlow, I said to Rob, or why not Hoggard? Why not Lingonshire at least? But no — 'I must get on', says Rob, 'and besides I want to see something of the world'. What! Newmarsh the world? Offered to give him the run of my holding, but it wasn't on. The difficulty is that we've no commerce in Dithering — well, none that my son would view as commerce. We've agriculture, but Rob's no farmer — never was. So there he sits, toiling away in Threadneedle Street — in Fenshire, no less! Well, he has determination, I'll say that for him. Knows what he wants, and goes after it." Then of a sudden the Squire's gaze dimmed and grew distant, a tide of melancholy sweeping him into its flow. "Of course, he'll have his share of the Moorings — in time — nothing else for it — he and Dora — after — "

His reverie was interrupted by a tread of footfalls in the passage. He turned his eyes to the door and a light like the sun on a dewy morning went on in them, banishing the tide.

"Ah, here she is now — Dora, my dear," he exclaimed, levering himself up with his stick, "come along in and have a chat with an old friend."

"Hallo, Dad." The young woman, smiling, rushed to her father and greeted him sweetly.

"Tell me, do I look nice?" she asked, taking his hand in hers.

"You look a treat, dear."

"How are you feeling?"

"Better, now that you're here. And sentimental. For look now — here is your old friend, Mr. Callander, come to dinner. James Callander's boy."

Her eyes shifted from her father's to mine. What would I see in them, I wondered?

"Good afternoon, Mr. Callander."

Her glance was less enthusiastic — but I had expected that — and her voice level.

"Hallo, Dora. It has been some time."

"Yes, hasn't it?"

A set of light, intelligent features — sparkling eyes with a trace of impudence in their depths — a face full of liveliness and animation, a smile that was eloquence itself — hair of a rich, chestnut hue, worn short — they could belong to no other than Dora. Who else in Dithering — indeed in all the dales — was there to match her?

The "some time" that had intervened had left its traces — to this I was not blind — but otherwise she was the same Dora Fetching I had known of old. Only a trifle cool, a trifle reticent, and, I fancied, a trifle unsure how to proceed.

I quickly put her at her ease by introducing her to Flounce.

It required no urging on my part for Flounce to spring into her arms. Dora was, I think, a little startled by her forwardness. But such was the way of Flounce, a friend of everyone who would be a friend to her.

"She's a dear. I do believe she has taken a liking to me," Dora exclaimed.

"Flounce is a shrewd judge of character," I observed.

Flounce snuggled closer. Dora passed loving hands over her, and scratched her furry ears and chin. An outburst of purring was her reward, or as Flounce might have phrased it —

*Hallo! She's a charmer, this one is, and uncommonly handsome. Well done, Callander.*

"Like takes to like," I noted.

"What was that?" said Dora.

"I meant to say that Flounce appreciates being accorded such a reception."

"How green her eyes are! How beautiful her coat!"

"She's no stick-at-home either. She can be very adventurous."

"I see. And did she drive you from the farm in a dog-cart, or was it vice versa?"

"Vice versa, of course. And it's my father's old gig — never a *dog-cart* for Flounce."

Dora's response to our gentle banter — her artless smile, blushing cheek, her sparkling gaze — was my reward, however undeserved it might be. Despite all that had passed between us, I found it hard to take my eyes from her.

The Squire, knowing the beauty of his daughter was everywhere admired, said — "Well, there are plenty of young chaps in these dales, Mr. Callander, but none of them I dare say has the advantage of your Flounce there. Is that the secret, eh?" His brows rose and he eyed his daughter meaningfully.

"Oh, Dad," she sighed, but in a smiling way, "whenever will you understand me?"

"Probably never," her father grunted — also in a smiling way. He twinkled at her, then glanced at me with a helpless shrug. "Daughters!"

"Fathers!" was Dora's good-humored retort.

Restoring Flounce to her place at the fireside, Dora turned to me, hands on hips, and said —

"I'll see you one showy calico cat, *Doctor* Callander" — it was all right, Dora was one of the few in Dithering who understood the title — "and I'll raise you one whatsit from out of time."

Ringing for a domestic, she gave orders to "have Mattie bring in our new addition."

The servant promptly dropped a curtsy and vanished on her errand.

I caught the Squire's eye, but he was impervious; and so I was left hanging in expectation of some erudite mystery that was about to be revealed.

A *whatsit from out of time* — now what could that be?

Minutes went by. Then a rustling was heard in the corridor, and another of the domestic retinue appeared, bearing in hand a wire cage about the size and shape of a bread-bin. The floor of it was covered with straw, but it was the odd-looking small creature reclining there that drew my attention.

The servant — a mild, dark girl, docile and neat, and not unpretty herself — advanced and presented the cage to her mistress.

"H'yur he be, Miss Dora."

"Thank you, Mattie."

Dora peered through the open-work at the curious, turtle-like little animal, which met her gaze with bashful eyes. "And how is Edmund this afternoon?"

"Edmund?" I repeated.

"Here you are, doctor — for your inspection," Dora invited, placing the cage on a convenient side-table, then stepping away. "Edmund is my whatsit from out of time. What would *you* call him?"

The inspection required but a moment, for Dora's "whatsit" was so unusual an animal — one so unequivocally a specimen of its type — that it could hardly be mistaken for anything other than what it was. The species is uncommon, true, although not exactly rare. I had seen but two of the creatures in my lifetime; here now, in the parlor at the Moorings, was the third.

I bent for a closer look. The animal peeped shyly from behind the wires, sniffing the air and blinking.

"Hallo there, Edmund. My, aren't we a handsome little man? By the way, my name is Callander," I said, introducing myself. Then I straightened and proceeded to render my verdict. Well, not so much a verdict, perhaps, as a plain statement of fact.

"*Glyptodontus minutus* — the lesser glyptodont — often referred to as a 'pocket glypt'. A toy version of the rather larger *Glyptodontus* species."

"Correct!" Dora announced.

"This is the pet you acquired this week? For your father made mention of it."

"It is. What do you think of him?"

"He looks to be in fine shape, from all I can see of him."

Edmund proved quite tractable when removed from his cage, instinctively curling himself into a ball in Dora's arms.

"He really is a tiny thing, in comparison to his giant cousins," she said. "And he won't grow any larger — the shopman in Medlow gave us his assurance. Pocket glypts can live for ages, as do their full-sized relatives. Edmund could well be above a hundred; it's difficult to tell. To me he seems ageless — frozen in time, as it were — which is why I call him my 'whatsit from out of time'. And besides, hardly anyone can say 'glyptodont'."

"As a species as well they're very old. Their fossilized ancestors are recorded in the geological record. What do you feed him?"

Dora consulted her maid. "What did he have for breakfast today, Mattie?"

"Lettuce, a carrot, some celery — oh, and a stewed tomato, miss," the girl replied.

"The tomato was from your own breakfast, I shouldn't wonder — eh, Mattie?"

"Ess, miss. He did seem to enjoy it, right 'nough."

"We must place it on his menu going forward. I'll instruct Cook to prepare him a stewed tomato every morning, so you'll not have to sacrifice."

"Ess, miss. Thank 'ee, miss."

Dora maneuvered the glypt in her arms, that I might better observe its distinctive features — the shell of bony armor, or *carapace*, which enclosed the body and much of the limbs; the furry snout, and velvet ears like a beaver's; the four squat, stumpy legs; the bony rings encircling the tail, the tip of which was provided with an enlarged, bluntly-rounded knob of bone.

Edmund, ignominiously cradled in his mistress's grasp, squinted at me from under his bony head-shield. *Kind sir,* his timid little eyes spoke in earnest appeal, *as I am no human infant, please ask this nice young woman to return me to my quarters.*

"Glypts are found naturally in the far south, in the rainy lagoons that border upon the sundering zone," I explained, "though of course in captivity they may be bred anywhere. The thickened shell is made of interlocking plates of bone called *scutes*. These scutes are like armor — indeed they are armor, in their way — and it's rather hard to damage them. But they differ from the shell material of a turtle, for turtles are reptiles — cold-blooded — whereas glypts are warm-blooded mammals. The composition of glyptodont scutes has been extensively studied and shown to be unique to the species."

The Squire nodded thoughtfully. "And what of its tail there? For it looks a formidable weapon."

"That it can be, sir. A pocket glypt's bony knob can deliver quite the wallop if one isn't careful. She can wield it with daunting efficiency, I'm sure, although with nothing near the ferocity of her giant cousins. The tail knob is her chief means of defending herself."

There was an abrupt pause of silence; then —

"Herself?" echoed Dora. "Why, Mr. Callander, what are you saying?"

"What I am saying is that your shopman in Medlow town either purposely led you astray, or neglected to mention that Edmund here is a female representative of the species."

Again the hush fell like a stone.

"La you there now! Sure you don't mean it, Mr. Callander?" Dora exclaimed.

"Ah, but I do mean it."

Mystified, Dora and her maid turned their backs and, putting together their heads, undertook a careful examination of the erstwhile Edmund. An interval of fevered whispering ensued. At length, satisfied of the result, they pivoted round again, smiling at one another and trading sheepish glances.

"What are you two giggling about?" the Squire demanded.

"Our Edmund — he's a she," his daughter explained.

"Ess, miss," Mattie agreed.

"Even better, don't you think, Mattie?"

"Better, miss. He'm a wonder — bain't she, miss?"

A fit of laughter convulsed the pair. But it was quite lost on the Squire.

"I dare say this is all very wondrous and very fine," he noted dryly, limping back to his seat, "though I for one should be knocked to smash to find my sturdy buck turned to a doe."

"Oh, Dad," Dora sighed.

She was on the point of returning the glypt to its cage, when an eruption of throaty growling stayed her hand. It came from the area of the hearthrug. Flounce, sniffing battle, had risen up onto stealthy paws, her back arched as high as it could possibly stretch, eyes slitted and whiskers bristling.

"She's got her fluff up. Now Flounce — behave. It's only a glypt," I told her. "Just because you've never seen one before is no cause to be rude."

Naturally she ignored me. The object of Flounce's ire — the erstwhile Edmund — had assumed a crouch at the door of its cage. The animal's timid little eyes, timid no longer, blazed up into flame, and its tail-armor began swishing to and fro, to and fro, slowly. A plucky little creature, it was not about to be intimidated by an adversary so commonplace as a cat.

I could see that a certain someone on the hearthrug was readying herself for a spring — a protective instinctive I believe — and so Dora hurried the glypt into its cage and secured the latch.

"Dodgy business," the Squire remarked from his ease on the sofa. The smirk behind his mustaches was ill-concealed.

"I think we had better keep her away from Flounce," Dora suggested.

"I agree. I shouldn't care to see Flounce walloped," I told her.

Directly Dora excused herself, and she and Mattie retired with the glypt. A triumphant Flounce settled herself again and resumed her doze, the incident having been resolved to her entire satisfaction.

"Dodgy business, daughters," the Squire remarked, with a baffled turn of his head. "The prettiest girl in our dales, and she cares not a bean about it."

"How do you mean, sir?" I asked.

"Unmarried — and at her age! What the devil is she waiting for? Is matrimony so terrible a bugbear? It was a good enough thing for her mother and me, God rest her. Have you ever heard the like?"

"It would appear she has other interests. She's most inquisitive."

The Squire grunted. "Always has been."

"Likely she prefers her independence. For you have always given her a free hand."

The Squire, after a moment's reflection, was forced to concede the point.

"But she has the Moorings, for with Rob in Fenshire now I've practically thrown her the reins. And do you know what? Damned if she isn't twice — three times — the farm manager Rob ever could be. She's got a knack for it. And it's many a time and oft she's told me she never could leave the Moorings."

He smoked awhile in silence, then cocked an eye at me and suggested, in all seriousness, that "perhaps you might talk some sense into her, Mr. Callander, as you're old friends. But be warned — for she has acquired some decided opinions, and is a damned free-spoken young woman."

For some moments I made no answer — couldn't have fabricated one had I tried.

It was clear the Squire knew nothing of what had passed between

Dora and myself all those years ago. He was ignorant of our disagreements, in particular of that which had resulted in a parting of the ways. Imagine Dora not telling him! Now why should so free-spoken a young woman have behaved in such a manner?

It rose up to my conscience then, and stung me to the quick, that the chief cause of the unhappiness had lain so heavily on my side.

## Chapter Eleven

SOME time was spent then in reminiscence of my parents, whom Squire Fetching had known well, and of my Uncle Jory, who by his death had made my University education possible, but whom the Squire had known hardly at all.

"Your father," the old dalesman mused, a retrospective look in his eyes, "was no fool. It was bad luck that precipitated the trouble. An honester man than James Callander never stood on his own shanks; I was proud to call him my neighbor. And as for your dear mother Susan . . ."

I confess I had always been a trifle jealous of the Squire, for I had never known my mother — save for that faint memory of laughing dark eyes and the scent of rose water — and here was the Squire who had been her friend since they were children together.

"My Uncle Jory, her brother, had realized some property by business and had become a moneyed man. It was a legacy in his will that allowed me to attend Maunder College. Now, with the sum put by from my stipend, I have cleared off the remaining debts my father incurred. I wish he had communicated to me something of the straits he was in, for then he should not have undertaken certain loans that became burdensome to him. But all this is in the past, and I mean to guide Callander farm into the future."

The Squire nodded his approval. "Damned glad to hear it," he responded, with a long draw at his pipe. "It's a duty, as you see it, to your father, this reclamation of your patrimonial acres. By thunder, I wish every man jack had your sense of heritage and responsibility! By the by, how did that schoolmaster's post at — how d'you call it again? Maunder? — how did that turn out for you? No great shakes, eh? Ah, well, I expect it's for the best. Their loss is our gain."

It was at this juncture that Dr. Hankey, the Squire's other guest for dinner, was announced. He was a fussy, dressy little man, with a lively cast of features. Although conscientious and kind-hearted, he was not insensible of his standing as the only "qualified" physician in the neighborhood. There was nothing the least bit mild or hesitating in his manner, as the doctor was too confident of his own merits — and too acquainted with them — to abide any doubting of his abilities. Like the Squire he was not averse to a little refreshment before dinner, and soon was complimenting his host on the excellence of his sherry.

Dora had reappeared when the dinner bell sounded. Mechanically Dr. Hankey took out his pocket-watch and looked at it, not from an implied criticism of the dinner hour, but from his habit of regularly checking the time while on his rounds.

As we went in to dinner I offered Dora my arm, which I was surprised — pleasantly — to find she accepted.

"Thank you, Mr. Callander. It has been some time, hasn't it?"

The windows, which stretched along one wall of the dining-room, offered splendid views of the stream waters flowing past below, and of the lofty woodlands — the wolds — rising on the opposite shore. From his seat of state the Squire presided over the meal with considerable joy and hospitality. Although subject at times to fits of gloom, the old dalesman was unfailingly cordial when entertaining guests at his board. Venison pasties, some collops of veal, a bottom-pie, and some little fishes in a row were amongst the delectables on offer.

"I'm as hungry as a hawk," he exclaimed, rubbing his hands in anticipation, "and I'll give odds Hankey there can't outpace me."

The physician, although diminutive of frame, had something of a reputation as a gourmand. Rising to the challenge, he clucked his tongue and snorted, declining a reply in favor of action, action.

"I believe he'll be taking you up on that, Dad," Dora interpreted.

The food was superb, the company rare, and as a result the time passed unnoticed. The table wine, like the sherry, was, in Dr. Hankey's view, exceedingly palatable, and the conversation drifted from one everyday subject to the next. Dora's laugh tinkled lightly every now and again, in response to some witticism. It was all so familiar that I soon began to feel rather comfortable. It was as if the intervening years had, like the stream waters, sped past us and been washed away.

Flounce, meanwhile, had been accorded pride of place for dining at the foot of my chair. Toasted cheese being one of her favorites, toasted cheese was set before her. She was not long in the disposing of it, and signaled her entire approval by a zealous licking of her chops with a pink tongue.

"I expect Flounce's favorite Bible story is the multiplication of the fishes," Dora remarked. And suiting the action to the word, she laid one of the little fishes in a row on Flounce's plate. It quickly went the way of the cheese.

"Scones, too," I added, "and most any kind of pastry, are irresistible to her. She really is the most uncommon of cats in this regard."

The Squire eased himself back in his chair. He was enjoying it all immensely. Flounce, her hunger assuaged, lay a dozing lump at my feet. Presently the cloth was removed and the claret and coffee made their appearance. It was then that the old dalesman, a trifle belatedly, broached a subject which had been on his mind throughout the meal, but which he had found too distasteful to speak of while dining.

"Damned poachers are back," he grumbled, striving to conceal his indignation. "Blasted beggars — thieves — band of villains — no respect for the laws of property — great sticks alive!"

His effort failing, he smote the table with such energy that some of the coffee in his cup jumped into his saucer.

"And it isn't only livestock," Dr. Hankey put in, "for sure you'll recollect my man Davy Zoze. A pathetic case. You remember him, don't you, Dora? I feel he had a very real experience, one so shattering that it quelled his speech. Something he encountered there on the road from St. Neot's frightened him almost to death. Ultimately he ended up taking his own life, so far as could be determined." And he clucked his tongue and shook his head regretfully.

"But what has that to do with poachers?" Dora asked.

"Well, they go hand in hand, don't you see? Each time the stock begin to go missing, there are one or two disappearances — of people, I mean. Davy survived — they found him stiff and staring in a tree — but others haven't been so fortunate. Josie from Sweezy's, for example."

"Oh, yes. The little milkmaid. I remember her."

"And there was Harry Smelt, the tinker."

"Old Harry? But all this was years ago."

"Twelve years, to be precise. And what of Bridgit Gooderly and Fanny Meadows . . ." Of a sudden and without warning the doctor blinked very rapidly, produced a handkerchief and blew his nose into it, in one short, explosive burst. "And in each instance," he continued, unfazed, "the thieves were in the neighborhood at the time."

"Bloody beggars!" fumed the Squire.

"But what would thieves want with people?" Dora said.

Her query brought the roasting-spit to my mind; but I dared not venture a guess aloud.

"Are we all right, Dad? Here at the Moorings?" she asked.

The Squire laughed shortly. "The villains — wouldn't dare — the Moorings — cutlasses abounding — by thunder!"

"Why did you say the poachers were here again? Has something happened?"

"There's a calf been lifted from Tristan Colley's."

"And a ewe," I added, and proceeded to relate all that I had learned at the inn.

"My five-times great-grandfather knew how to manage poachers," the Squire said ominously. "Stiffen 'em from the toes upwards!"

"Dad! I never saw you in a state of mind so unchristian," Dora chided him.

"The vicar's not to dinner, so I'll have my say out as I like," he retorted, sticking his pipe in his mouth, like a bung in a bung-hole, with grim ferocity.

It was years agone that the Squire had lost his leg to injury. He'd been thrown from his horse Gallivanter while chasing after someone who had made off with a calf from his south pasture. The villain had got clean away, but the Squire's leg had been so badly mangled that Dr. Hankey had been forced to amputate.

"Awfully decent of you," the Squire remarked, thinking back on it. "Much obliged to you, Hankey."

"Simply a physician doing his job," the other replied, tsking and pshawing his humility.

"Afraid I must have been in a shocking state. I should have had to call Mixit if you hadn't happened by."

At this mention of the town's other practitioner — an apothecary — the doctor snorted and looked sour.

"Mixit! Apothecaries — always thinking of their cash-box. Would he have cut off your leg for a simple fee? No, sir, he would not have done. No regular diploma — not a real medical man — selling medicine, like a pedlar hawking his wares." And the doctor clucked loudly and long his disapproval.

For a minute the Squire allowed himself to look slightly amused. Then he grunted out — "Wish I'd been riding Dapple at the time. *He* wouldn't have thrown me. Damned cowardly villains! And on my own land. But the blighter was too fast for me."

"So for how long now have these raids been going on?" Dora asked. "I remember Gallivanter. That was — let me see now — eighteen years ago, Dad, that you lost your leg."

"They seem to occur every half-dozen years or so," I told her, "almost like clockwork."

"Indeed," Dr. Hankey nodded, mechanically consulting his watch. "And there's the puzzle of it. And now these rumors!"

"Is it Mawgan Bothack d'you mean?" queried the Squire. He gave a hardened laugh. "A bad lot *that* fellow is — a raff — a shammick. I shouldn't wonder if he were involved. But how has he disposed of the meat? Of the hides? He must have them cached in that low hovel of his. It will be interesting to see what Colley found out there."

"Not so much as a sausage," the physician said, "for I heard it this morning at the inn. Bothack proclaimed his entire innocence, but I'll wager he has a role in the business. But who are his confederates, and where are they? For few there are who pass that way, lying as it does on the road to the Cupboard."

"The old tinker, Smelt, often camped in those parts, as I recall."

"Now that you mention it, he did." The physician shook his head gravely. "And there's more yet I learned at Readymoney's. Sweezy lost another last night."

"What! Another milkmaid?"

"No, a fine ewe. It's put his beard in a blaze, I can tell you."

"As well it should — damn and blast!"

The Squire snorted and adjusted his leg under the table, causing it to creak — the leg, not the table.

"You'd best oil it," the physician advised him.

"Ah, well," the old dalesman glided on, oblivious, "so wags the world, as somebody once said in a play somewhere," and then declared that all things might now go to the devil in their own way, for he was tired and would trouble himself no more about them.

"I believe I know why Colley found nothing at the hermit's," I offered.

"And why is that, Mr. Callander?" Dora asked.

"Because the answer lies farther along the road there."

"Great sticks alive," said the Squire, after a moment's reflection, "you don't mean the Cupboard?"

"I mean the Cupboard, sir."

"What? Eldritch's Sideboard?" Dora exclaimed.

"Sideboard?" echoed Dr. Hankey.

"Well, it's where the Giant Eldritch is said to have laid out his grub, is it not?"

Dora I thought was treating the subject a bit lightly, although of course she had not had the same experience of the Cupboard as had I. Nor had anyone else for that matter, apart from Dickie Fish.

"I think somebody should go out there," I said.

The doctor, clucking his disapproval, inquired if I had any particular somebody in mind?

I considered a moment.

"Stinker and I will look into it," I told him.

"Will you, in very deed? I didn't think such an assignment was in your line, Mr. Callander," the Squire remarked. Plainly he meant the *schoolmaster* line.

"I feel it's my duty, should this prove but a blink before a storm. For I've some experience of Eldritch's Cupboard. In my undergraduate years I conducted some researches there while home for the Long Vacation. It's an interesting place, geologically. Some of the flow formations are quite spectacular."

My purpose now had been fixed: I would to get to the bottom of the mystery. These disappearances which had perplexed the dalesmen for so long — could they be explained at last? To me, the monster in the Cupboard was no fiction, no distorted dream that over time had grown in shape and substance in my mind. Of this I now was certain — certain that there indeed was a monster, a hideous, malignant, misshapen, rattling, tall scarecrow of an abomination, which had sprung from a cleft in the earth as though from the fires of hell.

*Three toes, and a fourth behind . . .*

"What do you make of the footprints?" I asked Dr. Hankey.

He shrugged his shoulders. "I make nothing of them," he replied, "simply because I've not seen them."

"Perhaps it's the Woldfolk," Dora suggested, "playing us a trick."

"I don't believe in Woldfolk," I told her gently. "Nor do I believe in these poachers. There is something else afoot here."

"Have you never noticed, Mr. Callander, how an animal oft will freeze in its tracks, and stare unaccountably at something that isn't there? Perhaps it's one of these Woldfolk it has spied, one of these invisibles who are said to walk amongst us. Oh, I know it's claimed it is forbidden, this mixing of Woldfolk and human folk. But who's to say what is true?"

Her father lifted his eyes to the ceiling. "Woldfolk — lot o' damfool nonsense! Where have you heard such things, Dora? It seems we must have some of the talkingest gossips this side of Slopshire."

"I've read it in books, Dad."

"And do you believe all that you read in books?"

"Not everything. But enough to know that the Woldfolk are said to have a special relationship with animals, who can see them while we cannot. Perhaps it is this property which makes it easier for the Woldfolk to gain their trust?"

"Next you'll be telling us it's Obadiah Outland who is behind it, shepherding our livestock away in his barge upon the stream — great sticks alive!"

"And they are capital mischief-makers, opening and closing doors, and knocking at windows, and making ghostly footsteps in the dead of night. It is the fern-seed they wear which renders them invisible. When they do permit themselves to be seen, they are thought to be indistinguishable from ourselves in appearance. This is how they may mingle amongst us undetected."

The talk continued in this vein for some little while. But throughout, it was the testimony of Colley and Cedar Jack that I was revolving in my mind. For whoever had heard of one of these Woldfolk — indistinguishable from ourselves, supposedly — having three toes on each foot and a fourth toe behind?

## Chapter Twelve

**M**Y imagination in my childhood had been fired by the Cupboard, and my intellectual curiosity had led me to return there, while an undergraduate, to make a study of its rarities. Fortunately the "poachers" had not been active in those years, and my researches had proceeded without incident.

Often now have my thoughts flown back to Maunder College and Penhaligon. Had I erred, I wondered, in resigning my post and going home to the farm, that place where I had been so happy as a child? But my childhood had ended long ago, and there are those who tell us one's childhood never can be revisited, nor should be. For it is — and was — of another time.

There are those as well who say that time is immutable — implacable — inscrutable. But what *is* time, come to that? Is it a river flowing endlessly onward, like the waters through Dithering? Or is it a lazy circle, forever repeating? Or is it something else?

And what of Dora? What was Dora to me, exactly — then as well as now? For she too was of another time. Dora could never leave the Moorings, and in those long-ago days I could not stay here. The impasse had been complete. And yet the Squire her father had been told nothing of it!

These, and others of a like nature, were among the stray musings I was turning over in my mind, the day Stinker and Bob Cob and I journeyed the few miles out from Dithering to the Cupboard. Our excursion was the result of my having volunteered us for the task, over claret and coffee at the Moorings. (But of course Stinker had not volunteered himself, as he had not hesitated to remind me.) Flounce we had left with Dora, so that the two might spend some added time together and become better acquainted. It had been Dora's idea, and as she and Flounce had hit it off rather well at dinner, it was promptly agreed to.

*The girl's a trump, Callander. Don't make a hash of it a second time* had been Flounce's charge to me, as she and her club bag were handed in to Mattie at the door.

The sunshine had routed the gloomy mists that so often envelop the dales of a morning. The wildways we tackled in my father's old shay-cart, which I had adapted for use in hauling my cases and toolkit for field work. As we rumbled along our eyes and ears were busy, for to relax one's vigilance so much as a jot in these solitudes is to invite disaster.

At one point a distant habitation came within our view. Long and low-built, and at a little height above the trees, it stood about a meadow's breadth from the road. This was Bothack's retreat — his hovel — his "sylvan lodge", where Tristan Colley and his sons had gone to question the recluse. By Dr. Hankey's account they had returned disappointed men.

Then the Graystone Crags hove into sight, and all at once a bank of clouds came across the sun — almost as if they had been summoned there — and a wind came up that whispered in my ear *Dickie Fish*. Coming here was a risky enterprise, now that the poachers, so-called, had returned. Ahead of us the Cupboard beckoned, dark as a wolf's mouth. Here of yore had dwelt the Giant Eldritch; here of yore had he laid out his victims. Was this same cycle now being repeated? Or was our expedition today a wild-goose errand?

As we drew near our destination Stinker and I alighted and guided Bob and the cart through the narrow by-path. It was quiet now — no ringing notes of birdsong, no rustlings in the branches, not so much as a flutter — here amongst these outland hills. Were these lofty fastnesses really the domain of a people known as the Woldfolk? Or was it all just so much nonsense?

Though a hush had fallen over the area, I had an obscure impression we were not alone. I strained to catch sight or sound of anyone lurking in the vicinity, but saw and heard nothing, nor did Bob's delicate senses betray any alarm.

To guard against danger we had come well-prepared — *numquam non paratus* — I with my traveling-cutlass and Stinker with his small-sword. We had unsheathed them now, and with every faculty on the alert were awaiting some response to our presence. Stinker, I noticed, seemed particularly on edge, ready to spring like a jack-rabbit at the first hint of — anything.

Then of a sudden the ground before me caught my eye, for there in the soft earth were visible the marks of a man's shoe — a broad, flat-soled boot.

And there — and there — and over there — were other marks as well, of a kind made by no known human dweller upon this earth. In general they resembled bird-tracks, but were rather larger than the man's prints, and entirely naked, showing three lengthy toes spread before, and a fourth, smaller toe behind.

Stinker's brow darkened. "Say, what's the score — ?"

No wild-goose errand this!

My thoughts flashed back to my childhood, to a certain summer's morning when Dickie Fish and I had journeyed to the Cupboard to call out the *mounster*, and it had answered — had risen up like another Lazarus from under its slab of stone and come rattling and clattering after us.

It had been no dream, no distorted recollection of events, no trick of the imagination; in my child's waking eyes I had seen it only too plainly. Now here was I again in the domain of Eldritch, who had stowed his victims in his Sideboard, as Dora liked to call it, that he might devour them at a more convenient hour.

Imagine my surprise then to see a figure take shape in the cavern's mouth, and into the light stepped as singular a specimen of humanity as might be found in a month of Sundays.

Thickset and heavy, and near as broad as he was tall, he was a remarkable-looking character for a monster. For such at first glance I had taken him to be, given his deformities — his one shoulder riding higher than the other, his crooked back, his arms hanging unnaturally long and ape-like at his sides. But almost as quickly I recognized he was not half so tall as the malignant, misshapen devil of a nightmare that had chased me down in the Cupboard. No, this was no hideous dream made true.

Moreover, unlike that beast, this one was clad in sober garb — a shabby, dark coat with a collar that may once have been black velvet, coarse-striped waistcoat, drab breeches, leggings, and capacious boots. On his head sat a tall, high-crowned hat of the chimney-pot variety, much battered and worn, and turned up at the sides. A crab-tree club gripped in one muscular paw served him for a walking-stick.

He had not as yet seen us — doubtless he was not expecting visitors — so that when I called out to him he froze where he stood.

Plainly he was surprised to find us there, and thrust out a glance that can only be described as hostile. Then like a specter of ill omen he came lunging towards us.

As he drew near his lowness of stature became more conspicuous. He can have been no more than four feet high, although his head, resembling in its general configuration a pumpkin, was of a size as to have rivaled that of Eldritch himself. His features were rough-hewn, his complexion unhealthy. His brow, bulging and prominent, shaded a pair of hard black eyes, of sinister aspect. His chin bristled with the stubble of a coarse beard as dark as his hair. His mouth was a thin, cruel gash, punctuated by the stump of a cigar clamped in his lips.

So singular and disagreeable a figure can have belonged only to one man — to Mawgan Bothack, the recluse. To Mawgan Bothack, the outcast. To Mawgan Bothack — the poacher?

Stinker from the first did not care for his looks. "This one's a bad lot — been knocked about some," he remarked.

But the bad lot heard him, and his expression hardened — if such were possible. Defiantly he posted himself between us and the cave entrance, his club (which looked more suited to cracking skulls than to aiding his gait) planted on the ground, as if staking a claim to the spot.

For many heartbeats no one said a word. The apparition that was Bothack eyed us accusingly. In the end it was he who broke the spell, by demanding that we remove ourselves, posthaste and double-quick, from the area.

"For the place 'e do have a bad name," he tossed out gruffly. "But I bain't one to palavery, so begone, an' laive me in peace. Off wi' 'ee now! I'll waste no more words on 'ee."

But Stinker and I too held our ground. I introduced myself — unnecessary, as it turned out, for he knew me already — and my compatriot, but the hunchback blithely ignored the gesture, for he understood only too well our purpose.

"I'd not go in there, ef I were 'ee," he advised us, with a jerk of his thumb towards the Cupboard.

"Well, you yourself were in there, weren't you? You're not a man to follow your own advice, then?" I countered.

His look was scowling, arrogant. "Azackly. For 'ee knaw that Bothack bain't be formed as other men, an' that none do give ear to Bothack the wretched, to Bothack the miserable — not e'en Bothack hisself. So push off now, you, an' relieve me o' thy presence, for 'tis hateful to me," he finished with a sneer.

The manners of the man were rude and unsociable — this everybody knew. Some in Dithering considered him an insolent, ill-conditioned churl; others shunned him from superstition. Formerly he had lived in town, in Hog Gut Lane, but had made himself so obnoxious to his neighbors that his landlord had been obliged to evict him from the premises. Nowise slack in taking offense, Bothack's contempt for Dithering folk gnawed at him like a consuming canker. Internally he bristled at the thousand-and-one slights, real or imagined, that he had suffered at the hands of his fellow citizens. He had few worldly possessions, so far as anyone knew, and his source of income was a mystery. It was his hovel on the road to the Cupboard, far from Hog Gut Lane, that served him now for a dwelling-place.

At the moment something seemed to be puzzling him, and thrusting his eyes at Stinker he exclaimed —

"Ees fie, ef this bain't a dainty one! An' why for do they call 'ee Stinker, then?"

"'Cause I'm a right stinker. There! What d'ye think o' that, eh?" hurled back Stinker, flinging out his chin.

"Ess, I reckoned it be short for stinkpot. But I bain't one to gossipy, granfer," returned the hermit with a leer, displaying in the process a very capable set of yellow fangs. He had not forgotten Stinker's remark about being knocked about some.

Stinker turned to me, grumbling under his breath — "What d'ye make o' Mawgan Crookback? For here's a clock as would stop time hisself, and a sizable noggin to boot."

"Far be it from me to trust him. He has some role to play in this, I dare say, for I believe the footprints we observed — those of the man, at any rate — were made by his boots there."

"A pox on his granfer — bother him! — and on his old lady, too. If there's to be a scrap, I've a figo for him at the ready," Stinker muttered, his hand dropping to his small-sword.

"Steady on — we'll not want to provoke him. We're here to gather evidence, not to gratify any particular spleen either you or he may harbor. And those boots and those marks, and his very presence here this morning, are evidence. Now we must find what he has reason to conceal from us in the Cupboard."

"Hides an' meat, d'ye reckon? For the feller Colley and his lads found none at the beggar's hut."

"Perhaps."

Stinker looked his surprise. "Perhaps, is it? What's this? And what else might the creature have in there but hides an' meat?"

Again Bothack heard him, and again he did not like it.

"Bain't this a proper stank," he threw out. We had not heeded his warning, and now Stinker had insulted him again. His eyes, sly and restless, darted over us. They looked to be weighing the utility of his crab-tree club against my cutlass and Stinker's blade.

"I shud give 'ee a round knock, a proper thwack, I shud, the both of 'ee — *for I bain't a creature!*" Bothack glowered wrathfully.

Then he appeared to change his mind, as a more pleasant thought crossed it. He flung away the remnant of his cigar. His lips thinned, his pupils dilated and darkened, and he stared us up and down with cold distaste.

"A pair o' japes 'ee be — idiots — spankin' great dobecks — ef 'ee mean to try the Cupboard."

"We mean to do exactly that," I informed him.

One of his huge fists clenched itself into a ball; the other so tightened its grip on his club that the two seemed melded together.

"Bleddy fools are 'ee," he rasped out, "to be mixin' in business as don't concern 'ee. 'Ee do tread on thin ice, friends. On pain o' doom I'd advise 'ee to clear off, an' keep thy distance from the Cupboard of Eldritch. Begone! Ah, but then why for shud Bothack aid others, when none ever aided Bothack?"

His scowl by degrees had twisted itself into a grin, laying bare his frightful set of teeth. A ghastly, dry, creaking laugh welled from the depths of his gullet.

"Make thy minds easy, friends," he chuckled, "for a hellish scrape do await 'ee ef 'ee durst challenge the Cupboard. But 'ee'll tumble to 'un dreckly — I wish 'ee joy of't — an' may heaven help 'ee when 'ee do!"

## Chapter Thirteen

**D**ISDAINING further talk, Bothack the outcast — Bothack the self-professed wretched and miserable — having conveyed his warning to us, of a sudden took his leave and plunged off.

"There be better dogs bred in a kennel," Stinker muttered, looking after him, an angry spot still showing on his cheek. It was only by a very considerable effort, he informed me, that he had restrained himself. "I'd like to see that flat-face in the Poaching Court. Plaguy villain! A bold bearing for so miserable an object."

"I'll venture that 'miserable object', despite his deformity, has the strength of twenty devils in those arms of his. I admit I really know nothing positively *bad* of him, but his presence here today is incriminating. Likely he's familiar with each track and alley in these woods, and has some knowledge of these disappearances. However, there is one way to resolve the question."

So saying I took an old stable lantern from the cart and prepared to light it.

"Sure ye're not about to go in there, sir? Not now?" said Stinker, with a worried face.

"Of course I am."

"But the crookback — hides an' meat — so much as dared ye, sir, to prove him wrong — footprints — ain't that enough for eveydence — three toes — "

I believe Stinker would have liked nothing better than to return to the farm — for he'd not volunteered for the expedition, you'll remember — and although he disliked the hermit it seemed he disliked the Cupboard more. Like many, he had heard the rampant rumors; and like many he had believed them. No good, in his view, would be accomplished by "challenging the Cupboard". Better to leave it to the thieves, now that Bothack had all but admitted his connection to them. The mystery had been solved; it was time to go home.

"You needn't join me if you don't care to," I said. "I'm familiar with the Cupboard and am prepared to tackle it alone, for I must see what is in there. So if go you must . . ."

I saw his conscience was pricking him. Stinker had not served me for so long that he would abandon me to the Cupboard and whatever unpleasantness it contained. He made no reply, but by his very silence he communicated his answer. It was rather brave of him, I reflected; but I knew my Stinker of old and had not chosen in error.

"If anything should go awry," I instructed him, "if I should be incapacitated in some way, you are to take Bob and ride instantly for the Pack Horse Inn. Alert the men there — tell them what has occurred — and leave it in their hands."

Stinker, after a wary look round, nodded glumly and followed me into the Cupboard.

There night dropped swiftly upon us. Shadows looming ominous and huge upon the walls fled before the lantern's rays. On every side sculpted terraces of rock towered up, in whose varied layers could be read the long history of the abode of Eldritch. It was my considered view, after much study, that the Cupboard and other like hollows in the region had been formed, at least in part, by the action of flowing water — *i.e.*, by a mighty river. Later, with the advance of the glaciers, the water had receded. The stream that today hurries through Dithering is a vestige of that river, which once had filled the entire dale.

Damp and uninhabitable is the Cupboard of Eldritch. Yet despite its inhospitality, it possesses one radiant feature — cascading sheets or "draperies" of flowstone, adorning many of the walls, and in layered deposits upon the floor and in corners. Throwing my light before us and behind, its beams illuminated clearly these wonders, in which nature's paintbrush, as I like to call it, had blended together minerals and running water to produce a tapestry of glittering shades. Weird and strange, but beautiful too, the glorious crystalline arrays shimmered like ghosts in the chilly dark.

As we worked our way round the litter of boulders and heaps of fallen debris, now and again a footprint or other sign of recent activity was disclosed to view. In some cases the mark was that of a flat-soled boot, in others the three-toed enigma with the fourth toe behind.

Presently we reached the expansive inner chamber wherein Dickie Fish and I had seen the brilliant emerald ray dart about. Here too, at its farther edge, was the level slab of rock from behind which the monster had arisen and given chase of us.

"This is the place — the inner sanctum — the lair of the creature," I whispered to Stinker.

"Creature?" he gulped.

"Hush! What was that? Did you hear it?"

We glanced about, eyes wide and ears on the stretch; but the noise was not repeated.

In my undergraduate years I had explored this region of the Cupboard quite thoroughly. The slab had been merely a slab; there had been no orange light, no scarecrow emerging from a cleft in the earth — indeed there was no cleft — no emerald ray darting forth into the gloom. The chamber itself, in geological terms, showed evidence of subsidence. Something had happened here that had precipitated an extraordinary movement of the ground. Perhaps an earthquake had jarred it; for such events are not unusual in the dales. But the evidence indicated it had been no ordinary tremor which had shaken the Cupboard, *for it had affected only this single chamber.* Perhaps it had been the Giant Eldritch himself, rummaging about amongst his cache of victims.

To this point we had found no sure sign of human occupancy — no camp site, no hides, no butchered meat — that is, until we came across a hollow in the ground directly beneath the air shaft, and discovered there a few scattered clues.

"Here are bones," I told Stinker as I knelt to examine them, "and the earth here is charred. It's just as Dickie Fish and I found it years agone. Although the roasting-spit has been removed . . ."

The soil exuded a dank, unpleasant odor, and as I craned over it an evil thought suddenly struck me. Had anyone in Dithering gone missing of late? I was myself unaware of any such incident, but that was hardly conclusive. Likely these were the bones of either a calf or ewe that had been taken. However . . .

I gathered up a few fragments and deposited them in my sample pouch. "I'll ask Hankey to look at them, to ascertain whether they are of human or animal origin."

Stinker's eyes bulged. "Here, what's this? Human d'ye mean, sir — as in folks? As in eaten? Jiminy," he shuddered.

"We cannot exclude any possibility," I told him.

That awkward, unmannerly churl, Bothack — had it been his grisly fangs that had gnawed the flesh from these bones? Or had he conveyed the meat to another who had feasted here?

Might the Woldfolk be utilizing the Cupboard? There were many who believed in the reality of this strange race that lived apart, that once had roamed these lonely hills — and perhaps might roam them still. Most however thought them merely a legend, but one of many brought to this land centuries ago by our ancestors. Once there had been tin mines in the dales, much as in ancient Cornwall. It was the mines which had drawn many of the Cornish to the area. The giants, piskies, spriggans, and knockers of Cornish folklore had been variants on a theme; somehow in these dales the notion of Woldfolk had become entangled in this complicated web of mythology, legend, and superstition.

But of course the Woldfolk were unreal — in this enlightened age how could they be otherwise? I myself had never given the tales any credence, nor had my father, nor Squire Fetching. But Dora — dear, inimitable Dora — ever true to her nature, Dora was another story. I hesitated to think what my colleagues at Maunder would have made of Woldfolk, piskies, and scarecrows in Cupboards.

*We must look at legend and belief with other eyes*, in order to get at the truth of a thing; or so I had read somewhere once in a book. In fact it is was in this same volume that —

There it was again!

I turned to Stinker. "Do you hear it now? A droning noise, there — up there in that splash of shadows — "

We strained our ears to catch it. Through the black vault there sped a curious sort of whirring sound, which in the next instant grew loud as something passed swiftly by in the light. I hoisted the lantern and discovered there a face confronting me from a distance of little more than inches. Egg-shaped, of a silvery, metallic cast, it was featureless but for the single large, protruding eye, velvety and honeycombed like an insect's, with which it was studying me. From the head depended a small trunk bearing six delicate, crab-like limbs, each with fingered ends that were less like claws than like tiny hands for grasping. At its back a pair of wings was beating so rapidly they were a mere blur against the dark.

The sight of the creature hovering there chilled me to the quick. The last I recall was Stinker's blade swishing through the air to smite its goggle-eye; then the light went out and I knew no more.

## Chapter Fourteen

THE grip upon my arm was firm, the speaker's tone insistent.

"Mr. Earnscliff! Please — wake up, sir! Mr. Earnscliff!"

The words were like air to a drowning man, recalling me from the abyss. Gradually, awareness returned, and I straightened in my seat, glancing round me in a kind of dull wonder.

I put a hand to my eyes, thinking that perhaps some mystic spell had been laid on me. But it was only too plain what the cause had been — I had nodded off again after drinking the sherry.

The doctor's wine had proved an effective soporific. *I believe that in future I shall stick to mild tea.*

But my dream — nightmare — Eldritch's Cupboard — the *whirr* of the piskie, the *whish* of Stinker's blade — visions of a day that had long since passed, or that never had happened at all — what did they mean?

I shifted again in my chair. From the land of dreams I had returned to the land of here and now — the abode of the living. For to me, the land of dreams always had seemed too much like the abode of the dead.

In these visions of mine I seemed to be living another man's life — or was I dreaming another man's life, or dreaming his dreams? For was not the man I claimed to be in my nightmare Dr. Hugh Callander, formerly of Maunder College, he whose house this was, whose farm this was, and who, after suffering a stroke of apoplexy, was lying near death in his bed upstairs?

It was Miss Carswell who had awakened me — Miss Violet Carswell, the veterinary's daughter from St. Bees, who had been superintending the doctor's household since his attack. Her fingers still were closed about my arm. She had had difficulty, she said, in rousing me; indeed it had seemed almost as if I had not wanted to return to the here and now. For my head still was in a groggy whirl, my scattered wits having yet to collect themselves.

Miss Carswell regarded me curiously and asked how I had slept, in view of the trouble she had had in waking me. I stared impassively, the shaded lamp throwing a gloomy light on the table like the sun on a pallid day. It was there and then that I told her of this new dream of mine.

In outline I ran over for her the adventures in which I had taken part, or seemed to have taken part, and the phantoms which, one by one, had paraded themselves before me. Even as I spoke I found myself marveling that I recollected so much of my vision, and in such detail. So often, on breaking the bonds of sleep, do our dreams melt from us, like frost-work on a warming casement. Strangely this new one, like the last, refused to melt.

Miss Carswell listened with polite interest showing in her lovely face and tranquil blue eyes.

Did she think me mad, I wondered? For this was the second time now that she had been subjected to one of my wild tales. She smiled at me prettily, as she had done before, and was most sympathetic, thinking it rather odd indeed that I should be dreaming of Dr. Callander. Oh, not so much that I should be dreaming of him, but that I should be dreaming of him *as though I myself were he.*

The entire affair seemed quite beyond the bourne of rational explanation.

"I'm sure I've never heard the like," Miss Carswell said.

Then a fortuitous thought occurred to me.

"Doubtless Sir Lancelot has heard the like, at one time or another, in his practice. He is one of the finest medical baronets in the realm; surely he has run across cases such as this. He has a wealth of experience and may be able to advise me."

But Miss Carswell was skeptical. "Oh, Mr. Earnscliff, I shouldn't trouble Sir Lancelot if I were you. Really, they are only dreams. And moreover Sir Lancelot's plate is quite full in looking after Dr. Callander."

"But Sir Lancelot is a highly qualified physician, is he not? And I shall of course tender him his usual fee for his service. Why should he not accord me the benefit of his advice?"

Truth be told, I suspected that Miss Carswell was right. The stress of recent events, the gloomy atmosphere and unfamiliar surroundings so far from home — likely these things in the aggregate had begun to tell upon my nerves. Indeed they were only dreams we were speaking of here, silly things in and of themselves, entirely meaningless. Why bother Sir Lancelot over them?

To alleviate my mood Miss Carswell suggested that I put aside my work for a time and give my thoughts a rest. Dinner would be served presently, she informed me, before adding that — "I really must dash upstairs now and see about the ladies."

Whatever did she mean by *that*?

I sat for a time gazing at the papers in front of me, which I had been reviewing ere the sherry had set me dreaming. These little lapses of mine were nothing if not embarrassing; I hoped that word of them would not find its way back to Bodmin Square, or my reputation for industry might suffer a comedown. For I was but a junior in conveyancing with the firm, and this my first significant commission, acting on behalf of Mr. Bladdergowl himself.

Directly I heard talking and a tread of feet in the corridor above. Quitting the room I arrived to see a pair of squeaking little old ladies in crinoline being shepherded down the stairs by Stokes. Despite the gloomy setting the ladies' voices had a cheerful ring, and it was with a breath of relief, providing as it did a welcome change of scene, that I was introduced to the visitors.

Rustic characters both — Miss Bingham and Mrs. Lindsay-Woolsey were their names — they were neighbors of the doctor's, and had called round to see how he was faring. The pair were sisters, the elder of whom had been long a widow. In spite of their years they were pleasant and chatty companions, charmingly quaint and kind, with eyes twinkling and alert, and noses for all that went on in the neighborhood. They had arrived while I was asleep in the study, having been driven from their doorstep to the doctor's by an ancient retainer.

From the corner of my eye I saw the invalid Mrs. Stokes, her hair as white as a ghost's, regarding us from her place in the sitting-room. Her frightened glance reached out to me from about the saddest face I think I have ever beheld, one which for an instant stirred a curious echo in my brain. Of course the poor woman said nothing, and her husband, seeing her there, went to her at once, leaving me in the care of the ladies.

"No worse news, I trust?" I asked them, respecting the doctor's condition.

"No change I'm afraid, Mr. Earnscliff, not the slightest," reported Miss Bingham.

"Sadly he remains unconscious, although he looks very peaceful," said Mrs. Lindsay-Woolsey. "Dear Miss Carswell is with him now."

"If there is a man on this earth can do aught for him," Miss Bingham declared, "it is Sir Lancelot Wale can do it."

"I am certain all that human skill can do is being done," I assured her. "It is simply that there is so little *to* be done in such cases, as Sir Lancelot has informed us."

"Ah," sighed Mrs. Lindsay-Woolsey, shaking her head, "it was just the same with poor Greville."

"Oh, very much so," her sister agreed.

"Greville too was bred and born on a farm, like Mr. Callander."

"Oh, yes, indeed. A countryman all his life."

"And he lingered in a similar fashion for weeks. It was most distressing, his lying there inert like any squash or turnip, and nothing to be done about it. And then — and then — " Her lips quivered, and the widow seemed on the point of tears.

"Do brace up, Amelia," said her sister. "One simply must *not* cry, you know. One must be strong. It's a good job you didn't blubber when we saw Mr. Callander. For it should only have gloomed him up, had he been sensible of it."

"Forgive me but you're right, of course. But poor Greville! I still can see him, Letitia, curled up there in his bed, his brave little heart valiantly beating, his lungs fitfully drawing air . . . oh, I'll never forget it . . . and now poor Mr. Callander . . ."

Again she could speak no more.

I waited with polite expectation — a fruitless exercise, as it turned out. "You speak of your husband, I assume, Mrs. Lindsay-Woolsey?" I ventured at length.

"Her husband? Hardly," said Miss Bingham. "It's Greville Tidmarsh she means."

"He was like a brother to us, Mr. Earnscliff," her sister explained.

"Ah, I see. A friend of yours, then?"

The widow nodded sadly. "Like a brother indeed, Mr. Earnscliff, and our dearest friend. Greville Tidmarsh was our prized terrier, you know. Such a happy-go-lucky sportsman — one of the best who ever barked, brave and generous to a fault. And so much the little gentleman in his private life."

"And a finer ratter you couldn't find in Lingonshire in a twelvemonth," said Miss Bingham. "But he went pale in his gums and faded before our eyes. At the end he had no more blood in him as would supper a hungry flea. Amelia in particular took it very hard. Surely you know how dogs are, Mr. Earnscliff? For dogs are people just as are you and we, only littler."

"Poor Greville — we loved him very much," said her sister, sighing and sniffling. "He shared our lives for but a mere nine years — it's all that was accorded us — and we were privileged to have known him. Weren't we so, Letitia? Every day I give thanks to Providence for having blessed us with the gift of his friendship, for however brief a period. Well, it was a kind of miracle, it seems to me. And the service was very comforting."

"The vicar spoke most highly of Greville. Mr. Callander attended, as did Natty and Miss Carswell. A very singular young person, Miss Carswell. She is devoted to Mr. Callander, as of course are we. She is always at his side now," said Miss Bingham, "except when Annie or Natty is with him."

The visit concluded, the ladies prepared to take their leave. They drew on their cloaks and shawls and settled their bonnet-strings, and gathered up their reticules.

"Not to worry, Amelia — Jakes will have us home and dry before you can say dumpling," Miss Bingham said snugly.

The two then sallied forth into the sharp frost wind, to be helped into their carriage by the ancient retainer Jakes. The carriage too was ancient — positively antediluvian — being of that species of vehicle, now scarcely ever glimpsed, that is termed a *whisky*. It was slung very low, like a child's cart, on two tiny, old-fashioned wheels, and in its shafts stood a bangtail pony upholstered in dun, whose age looked to rival Methusaleh's. In place of a hood it was furnished with an upright umbrella spread wide over the small seat. The entire effect was ludicrous in the extreme, the vehicle creating a sizable stir whenever it was seen rattling through the streets of Dithering. I've heard such equipage was fashionable once, back when the world was new. Looking as though it at one time had had aspirations to be a gig, nowadays it served only as a cause for giggling.

The servant Jakes, older even than the ladies themselves, and who doubled as their gardener, gallantly but haltingly escorted them, one by one, to their chariot, wheezing out a brief "whoops-a-daisy, mum" as each was launched onto the cushion. Then slanting me a glance he winked, snapped a brisk salute, and taking the pony by the reins led it and the carriage off at a leisurely pace, to the tinkle of tiny wheels.

After dinner I returned to the study and resumed my perusal of the documents I had brought with me, in particular my copy of the doctor's last will and testament, to familiarize myself again with its provisions. For it was possible I should be needing to refer to them in no very long time.

Having again read it all through, I settled back in my chair and, steepling my fingers, gazed at them for a time in sober reflection. My thoughts drifted back to my first meeting with the doctor, round a year ago it was now, in Bodmin Square. I had been in the employ of Bagwash and Bladdergowl for only a few months, and Mr. Bladdergowl, who had been attending to the doctor's interests, of late had become too ill to continue in that capacity.

A cold, gray day it was in Hoggard, when the doctor and I were introduced and sat down together in chambers. What an impressive figure he must have cut in the halls of Maunder, I remember thinking. The doctor was — is — a tall, slim, distinguished-looking gentleman. His hair was thick and smooth but entirely silvered, his chin clean-shaven, his eyes quick with intelligence, his temperament remarkably easy for a former college don's.

After conducting our business we chatted awhile, and in time the conversation got round to the doctor's field of study, which was geology. Ere long he was waxing positively scholarly over it, telling me of his theories of unexplained phenomena which had excited such interest amongst his colleagues, his ideas regarding the so-called drift deposits, "erratics", boulder clays, and the movements of glacial ice. Frankly I understood very little of it. But the doctor's enthusiasm for his subject was undiminished, despite his having left Maunder College years before. It was his later researches, carried out around Dithering — the study of his home fields, as it were — which fired his imagination now and kept him in trim.

"For we in Lingonshire were fortunate when the sundering came. In this part of the realm, eastwards of the fen country, we're less susceptible to the frequent snows and heavy winters endured by those dwelling in the north. I dare say it's but another advantage in having been graduated an Haligonian. For the Saltonians as I hear do freeze amazingly in their dreaming spires there on their headland above the sea. What a dismal climate a Salthead man must bear, whereas we at Penhaligon by comparison . . ."

With a jerk I started from my reverie, and sat bolt upright in my chair.

Was it Dr. Callander I had heard speaking, I wondered, or had it been I? Incredibly, it seemed I might be in danger of dreaming again . . .

My glance crossed the papers before me — the doctor's will and testament — and I thought of the two little old sister-ladies and their remarks concerning the doctor and how very peaceful he looked, as if they had been viewing him in his coffin. But was it not likely that such would be the case before long?

Banishing this gloomy picture I rose from my seat, thinking that I should go upstairs and see how the doctor was faring. The door of his sick-room I found slightly ajar. Still a trifle disoriented I neglected to knock and, pushing it open, stepped inside.

"My stars!" I exclaimed.

There was an audible gasp from Miss Carswell, shock and surprise writ large in her eyes. My unannounced entrance had caused her to freeze in place, bent over the doctor with one hand propping up his head on his pillow. With her other hand she had been pouring a quantity of a dark-colored fluid from a vial into his mouth.

I recalled that Sir Lancelot had left instructions nothing should be given to the patient but water, that in fact there was nothing at present that would be of material benefit to his condition.

Of even greater importance, I had seen the doctor's eyelids flutter as the vial was applied to his lips, had seen him swallow as the liquid was poured down. For a fleeting instant his eyes met mine, and for a moment more he fixed his gaze on me, before sinking back again onto his pillow.

*The doctor conscious and moving!*

Miss Carswell's glance was desperate, stricken. A warm flush began crawling up her throat, deepening the color in her cheeks perceptibly. At last her smothered emotions burst forth. She wasn't crying, yet there were tears in her voice as she raised her eyes to me — imploring eyes, richly expressive in their blue depths — and exclaimed —

"Oh, Mr. Earnscliff — dear Mr. Earnscliff — not a word to the others — please — please, you must help us . . ."

Somehow or other I found breath enough to reply.

"Miss Carswell," I stammered out, "what is the meaning of this?"

## Chapter Fifteen

A RUSH of wild thoughts came crowding into my head at the turn events had taken.

Miss Carswell rose. There was in her manner a degree of flutter I had not before seen. Yet she was calm again in an instant — trim, assured, resolute.

"This is not what it may at first appear," she said.

My glance touched the vial in her hand.

"What is that you have given him? For Sir Lancelot left instructions that only water was permitted. Or do I find myself mistaken?"

"This is per Dr. Callander's own direction."

"I'm afraid I am at a loss there. I haven't the pleasure of understanding you."

The girl bent over the patient again to be certain that all was well. Skeptical, I followed her example and observed that his breathing, although shallow, was regular. He was once more his insensible, comatose self. Little Figgie, who had been dozing by the doctor's pillow, opened his eyes and regarded me sleepily.

"May I take you into my confidence, Mr. Earnscliff? For — I fear now that I must," Miss Carswell said.

"Indeed I fear you haven't a choice."

Yet for all this I had the distinct impression she was not so upset or so unhappy at having been found out; but that in fact my sudden appearance, far from being unwelcome, had been anticipated, and that Miss Carswell was affecting a surprise she did not altogether feel.

I was determined not to be hoodwinked by this "singular young person" — an apt description, now I thought on it. Singular — perhaps even a trifle odd? But then many excellent people are peculiar.

"I am listening," I said.

It was then she told me the truth of the matter, or as much of the truth perhaps as she felt comfortable disclosing. It was she who referred to it as the truth; I intended to withhold judgment.

And the truth, as she called it, was this —

That Dr. Callander had suffered no stroke, no fit of apoplexy, but that it all was a sham of the doctor's own devising. At periodic intervals, on his instruction, she had been dosing him with the dark-colored fluid, which acted as a kind of sleeping draft. The doctor had placed himself under its spell voluntarily, said Miss Carswell, and it was this, and this alone, which was responsible for his present condition.

"And for what reason has the doctor done this to himself?" I inquired.

The doubt in my voice was palpable — in short, I was aghast. Despite her long acquaintance with him, it was altogether possible that this young woman had some unscrupulous design on my client, and was attempting to fob me off with a sham of *her* own devising.

"His purpose is so that he may dream a fateful dream," Miss Carswell explained, "that in this dream he may revisit certain past events, and by so doing correct a terrible wrong that was done many years ago. It is a wrong for which he has held himself at fault — a mishap, an accident, resulting from negligence on his part. It is a thing which ought never to have happened, and which has caused much suffering to himself and others. For these long years the knowledge of it has haunted him. But now, after much research, he has found a means to put right this wrong for which he has blamed himself."

This I didn't understand at all. Not only was I at a dead loss, but I was at sea as well.

Hang it, this singular young person certainly had some queer notions! For of all the many whoppers told to me in my life, this of Miss Carswell's was the most flagrant, the most shameless.

She seemed to be reading my mind, for it was then she handed me the vial in which resided a quantity of the dark-colored fluid, and invited me to smell of its contents.

"Does the odor of the cordial strike you as familiar?" she asked.

"It's rather strong, I dare say — pungent I should call it. In fact it reminds me of the sherry in the doctor's study . . ."

All at once my heart stood still, my marrow froze in my bones.

"It was I who placed a small amount — a *very* small amount — of the cordial in your glass," Miss Carswell said.

And following which, on each occasion I had tasted it, I had nodded off and dreamed a dream as vivid and horrible as any I had ever experienced in my life. Such dreams — such nightmares! And this after imbibing only a small measure of the stuff!

At the very least I had now an explanation — an excuse — for my embarrassing lapses in the study. But what possible reason could this young woman have had for drugging me? To discover it, however, might prove difficult. For though fair play is always presumed among gentlemen, among members of the "fair" sex — so-called — there are other rules may apply.

Did she take me for an idiot? Already she'd practiced on me one deception, while another, more gargantuan humbug had been foisted upon the entire household and on Sir Lancelot, ostensibly at the doctor's instruction.

"You told me today of the dreams you experienced after drinking the sherry. And in these dreams, Mr. Earnscliff," said Miss Carswell, "who did you believe yourself to be?"

The answer of course was that I believed myself to be Dr. Callander, who in the dreams seemed to be recalling particular episodes in his life. It was as though I'd lost all sense of my own identity, while dreaming, and assumed another's.

"That is because you were sharing his dream," Miss Carswell explained. "But it is a dream only in a very limited sense. In actual fact it is no dream at all, but an accurate and vivid re-enactment of times gone by."

I had to confess, these "dreams" had seemed very real to me. It was if I had myself lived these past experiences in the life of another man.

"And it is this cordial, as you term it, that is responsible for it?"

"The cordial," Miss Carswell said, taking the vial in hand and gazing reverently at the mystical dark fluid, "is the gift of the Woldfolk. Likely you have heard of the Woldfolk?"

Indeed, I had heard of them — in my dreams. Or were they the doctor's dreams, strictly speaking? But again I did not entirely follow her.

"For the last few years the doctor has devoted himself to a study of the Woldfolk, and has become rather knowledgeable on the topic. These Woldfolk are supposed immortals who live apart from humankind, with whom they are disinclined to mix. Members of an ancient race, in outward appearance they are the same as ourselves. And yet they are entirely different, and are able to make themselves invisible — "

"It is the fern-seed they wear," I broke in, recollecting the details, "a particular variety that grows upon the wolds."

"It seems the cordial indeed has worked its magic on you," Miss Carswell smiled. "This is most encouraging."

"It was Dr. Callander himself from whom I learned it. Er — that is to say — it was I who recollected it — that is, recollected it as Dr. Callander had recollected it . . . and explained it to Stinker . . ."

"And it is on account of the fern-seed that the Woldfolk like specters may glide about us undetected."

"But the doctor, as I recollect, didn't believe in the Woldfolk."

"Circumstances change, Mr. Earnscliff, as do minds. I can assure you, the doctor very much believes in the Woldfolk now. The cordial he procured from them himself; although how he managed it he has not been at liberty to say. For the cordial is a secret of the Woldfolk, and a gift of their own giving. Rarely will they offer it to human folk who are in difficulty, or otherwise have urgent need of it, and only under the most extraordinary circumstances, when one considers that intermingling is discouraged."

"But why did you not tell us of this? Stokes, Annie, myself, not to mention Sir Lancelot — his valuable time — calling him all this way from Medlow — giving him to believe his old friend had suffered a stroke — "

The doctor's attack had been a complete fabrication. He had not staggered in at the door after his morning's ride, as Miss Carswell had testified. Together they had made everyone — the doctor's friends and acquaintances, even Sir Lancelot Wale — believe a lie.

"I can assure you it was for a noble purpose — a better purpose," Miss Carswell related. "For the doctor wishes only to do good in the world. He means to *better* the world, by putting right an innocent wrong that never should have occurred. He could not chance having word of his scheme come to light. The Woldfolk, Mr. Earnscliff! Do you know what meaning the term has for us in these parts? Do you know how much they are despised, and what consequences might ensue if it became known the doctor had had dealings with them? Well, I tremble to think of it."

"But Miss Carswell," I protested, shaking my head, "you foist upon me and on the rest of the household lie upon lie — and now this wild tale! For you must admit, this story of yours is altogether too absurd."

"You are a hard-headed city man, I know, Mr. Earnscliff. You are from Hoggard — from Bodmin Square, no less — where country folk and our country ways count for little. Oh, you needn't deny it, it's only too plain. You city folk cannot understand us."

She was resolute and entirely in earnest, having regained the quiet dignity of her manner.

"All of this, I assure you, is as the doctor intended. The Woldfolk have had the keeping of the cordial; its origin lies shrouded in their history in these dales. I gave you but a minuscule sample of it, mixed with your wine, hoping that you would share the doctor's dream — or, say rather, his re-enactment of events. And indeed you did share it, that dream he still is dreaming now. You viewed it from his perspective, because it is *his* dream. But tell me, if you had not tasted the cordial — if you had not lived the dream yourself — seen what you have seen — would you have believed me now?"

For some minutes I paced up and down at the bedside, every now and again glancing at the doctor's still form beneath the coverlet, at the handsome face, distinguished brow, the flowing silver hair, at the gentle rise and fall of his breathing.

Was such a man as this capable of hatching so rash a scheme as that described by Miss Carswell? Above all, for what reason had he hatched it? And how did he propose to achieve his aim?

In the features of the young woman I read only sincerity, zeal, determination. She did not *seem* to be lying, and failing any evidence to the contrary . . .

"I see your point. But why has the doctor done this? What is this 'better purpose' of which you speak? This wrong that so needed correcting he would embark upon such an enterprise — assuming all you have told me is true — to accomplish it?"

"Let us talk elsewhere," Miss Carswell suggested.

"Perhaps the study?"

"The very place."

She bent again over the doctor, to assure herself that his condition remained satisfactory. Little Figgie meanwhile had stirred at his post and was eyeing her drowsily. Her response was gentle, comforting — "Rest, little one," she said, "for you're not to worry now. For your friend the doctor has it all well in hand."

So hearing, the kitten settled himself again and resumed his nap. Shortly his watch over his friend was supplemented by the arrival of Annie, whom Miss Carswell had detailed to relieve her.

We made our way downstairs to the study and shut the door behind us. Going to the fireplace, I raked the embers together and tossed some wood on them. Miss Carswell meanwhile reached down a book from the shelves and handed it across to me.

It was a quarto volume of some age, privately published, and full of close print. I glanced at it curiously. *The Derivation of Man* it was titled, its author an unknown who had styled himself "Orkla of the Woldfolk", in all likelihood a *nom de plume*.

Miss Carswell explained that much of what the doctor had told her of the Woldfolk, and more, might be found in this book. Above all, however, it was the cordial, of which the Woldfolk are the guardians, that had most excited his interest. For the cordial induces something like a dream-state, one in which the dreamer is able to revisit certain key events in his life. The remarkable thing however is that the dreamer actually returns to the world of the dream, to the place and time of those events. In fact he is not dreaming of that bygone world, nor even is he remembering it — *he is living in it again.*

On very rare occasions, she went on, the dreamer's activities may proceed beyond the mere repetition of events, but may alter them — however minutely — and thereby influence their outcome. In such a case the dreamer would awaken to a world in which history had changed; although he himself would be insensible of the change, for the history which he had known had never happened.

You may imagine my response to this latest whopper.

Again Miss Carswell stood her ground. She was entirely serious, entirely in earnest, entirely assured.

Myself, I fumbled about. "This is — well, I don't know what this is. Magical charms and spells, and a potion you call a cordial! If such a thing as you describe is possible, it could be dangerous — it could be monstrous. For in the doctor's desire to do good, might he not do harm?"

"It is precisely for this reason that the cordial has remained under the jealous guard of the Woldfolk."

Miss Carswell added that it was difficult if not impossible to alter the train of circumstances within a dream. It required an exceptional strength of will, and concentration of the mind, to produce anything beyond a simple iteration of events.

"For history, you see, is possessed of a certain momentum, and is resistant to change. But despite this, the doctor has made the effort."

The whopper she had foisted on me was this: that the doctor, by means of the cordial, had traveled into the past — *his* past — to re-direct the flow of events towards a better outcome.

It was wild and fantastic, and reckless in the extreme. Who in his right mind would attempt it? Who in his right mind would believe it?

But what was it that the doctor was seeking to change? What was the terrible wrong he had gone to such lengths to correct? And how in heaven's name had he secured the cordial?

The last question I put to Miss Carswell.

"This I cannot say for certain, but he may have had dealings with — with a being known as Obadiah Outland," and at the sound of the name she shuddered.

Outland! Where had I heard of him before? Well, in the dream, of course. Obadiah Outland, the mythical old man of the waterways, the fiend of a bargee who plied the rivers and streams of Lingonshire taking select folk on impossible journeys. He was a name and a legend in the dales; indeed it was said he had roamed these waters since the birth of time. For a fee he would bear you in his craft to some distant, unimaginable shore, where for a spell you might walk again with those departed friends and family who resided there, for one last meeting this side of eternity. All kinds of wonderful and terrible and impossible things had been attributed to Obadiah Outland. Scholars in the colleges would have termed him a Charon figure, piloting his barge on the River Styx, or the Acheron, to the very gates of the underworld.

But this particular Charon figure, as it happened, was notoriously fussy in whom he chose to help, and in the fee he charged, and in the keeping of appointments. He might help you or he might not, as the fancy took him. It was rumored that he himself was of the Woldfolk or was in their employ. Perhaps this is how the doctor had obtained the cordial, through the intercession of Outland? Perhaps it had suited the old man's fancy to grant his request?

Then all in a moment it struck me — another absurdity. Obadiah Outland, the *mythical* old man of the waterways, was a figure of legend, an imaginary being. Obadiah Outland did not exist, never had existed. He was no more real than was Giant Eldritch or a piskie for that matter.

What was it then that Stinker's blade had gone whistling towards in the dark of the Cupboard? What was it that had come rattling after me and spun me about with such ferocity that I had screamed?

This was not going very well at all.

The rest aside, it had become rather clear that Miss Carswell held the doctor in great affection. It was she who had been superintending his care, for it was she to whom he had entrusted himself while under the spell of the cordial. She was doing this for him, at his request. Lying unconscious in his sick-room, dreaming his implausible dream, he was her charge and responsibility. In some sense he had placed his life in her hands. Certainly this spoke to her trustworthiness?

But of course I had only the young woman's word for it all, a whopper of a tall tale which might or might not have a basis in fact. From the doctor I had had not so much as a syllable.

As I paced up and down I felt the eyes of Miss Carswell studying me with an anxious scrutiny. It seemed that matters now had reached a crisis.

"The doctor will have dreamed the dream many times over since he first took the cordial," she explained, "and yet nothing has changed. This leads me to fear that something has gone wrong. When the doctor awoke for a moment, as I had been late in administering him his dose, he asked me — 'Is he here?' — before slipping back again into the dream. If he had achieved his goal he ought already to have awakened, fully and completely, on his own. This he has not done. For of course what he is attempting is supremely difficult."

"You believe he has failed, then?"

Miss Carswell's voice sank almost to a whisper.

"I know he has failed," she said simply.

## Chapter Sixteen

YET still I had no notion what it was the doctor was endeavoring to change.

"Do you know the house called the Moorings?" Miss Carswell asked.

"Yes. The great rambling place above the stream. It looks a sight now — ruined gates — shuttered windows — lichen — bramble — the approach choked up with grass and weeds — "

"It was not always so. It once was a happy place."

"Indeed I remember — in the dream — Squire Fetching and his leg that needed oiling — Miss Dora and her little 'whatsit from out of time', as she called the pocket glypt — "

But I remembered as well my earlier stroll past the house, the picture of sad decay its fabric had presented, and contrasted this with its rather livelier portrait in the dream.

"Stokes told me that Miss Dora passed away years ago, that it had left the Squire a broken man for the remainder of his days."

"So much is true," said Miss Carswell.

In her brief account of events she affirmed that Miss Dora Fetching had died young, that her death had blighted not only her father's life but the doctor's as well. The long, lonely years that ensued had told upon their spirits, the grieving for her loss — in short, her death had been a catastrophe for both of them.

"Yes, but how did it happen?" I asked.

"The doctor has never told me, except to say that he viewed it as having been entirely his own fault — a 'stupid accident', he called it, that easily might have been prevented. Once he discovered the cordial, he resolved to do all in his power to put things right, not only for the sake of Miss Fetching but for that of his friend the Squire as well."

"Perhaps Stokes knows something of it? For he was here in those days — 'Natty' they called him then. Or one of the neighbor-ladies?"

Miss Carswell shook her head.

"There is no one with any knowledge of it still living, save for the doctor himself, to whom it has remained a memory too painful to be spoken of. For it all was kept rather dark at the time; there were few who knew anything of it."

The legal tussling continued amongst the distant heirs, as the late Squire's son Robert was thought to have died at Newmarsh without issue. But there had been some question at the time whether he really had died, or had vanished, or had gone off of his own accord. There had been a rumor he had been traveling home to the Moorings, some weeks after his father's death, but had never arrived. At any rate he had not inherited, and it was this, amongst other complicating factors in the will, that had drawn out the case for so long. I recollect I had heard something about it from Mr. Trimmer, one of the more senior members at the firm.

And so all these years on the Moorings stood empty still, the case unresolved.

The tragedy of Miss Dora's loss had quite staggered the doctor. The two practically had grown up together, but then had taken their different paths in life. He had gone up to Penhaligon and had enjoyed success within the walls of Alma Mater. She had remained at the Moorings with her father; indeed she never could have left the Moorings, as she herself many times had stated. Each of them had come to inhabit a different world, and the distance between them had grown. But though their parting had not been entirely amicable, neither had forgotten the other.

"And the Squire knew nothing of it!" I marveled.

"What was that?" said Miss Carswell.

My thoughts snapped back to the present. For an instant it seemed I was there again — there at the Moorings with Squire Fetching and Dora and Dr. Hankey — in that happier time before disaster had struck.

In that happier time after Dr. Callander had returned home to the farm — and perhaps to Dora as well. How might it all have turned out if but given the chance? Turned out in the doctor's better world?

I let my gaze roam about the shelves bending under the weight of their ponderous volumes — the doctor's books, his father's books, his grandfather's. Beside me lay the quarto by "Orkla of the Woldfolk", which brought my thoughts round again to the cordial — the gift of the Woldfolk, and key to the mystery of the dream and the doctor's better world.

"Why did I not re-live my own past after drinking the cordial?" I asked.

"Because the cordial was prepared for the doctor, and he in turn prepared himself for the undertaking. By consuming a small measure of the cordial, you were introduced to the doctor's dream — shared it, as it were. Now I fear that something has gone awry, for had he succeeded the dream ought to have ended. But it is still going on."

"Perhaps the doctor *can't* succeed? Perhaps it's impossible to alter the flow of events? For you said it demands an extremity of effort."

"A grueling effort of will and concentration, yes."

"Perhaps then it is something beyond human attainment?"

Miss Carswell frowned. "I don't believe that. Nor did the doctor, or he should not have made the attempt. However . . ." She paused a moment in thought.

"Yes?"

Dr. Callander in the dream had returned to his past, she said, but not without a hitch. It turns out that the dreamer, once absorbed in the dream, loses all cognizance of future events. Thus the doctor himself, in his own dream, cannot know when the critical moment will arise; indeed he is unaware even that such a moment exists. How to prevent Dora's death, when he has no inkling how or when it will occur, or even that such a fate awaits her? His knowledge is limited to that he possessed at the time — knowledge of the present and past as they then existed; for only then might one truly "re-live" a prior experience.

*You will not know the minute, or the hour, or the fated day.*

How to put right a wrong, I asked myself, when one hasn't a clue when that wrong will occur, indeed has no knowledge even of the wrong itself?

No small wonder that it was difficult — if not impossible — to alter the train of events. For if a man could dream in the past with full knowledge of the future, he conceivably could visit destruction upon history. Then indeed might time's course be changed — to disastrous effect.

To influence the past, the dreamer had to rely on the vagaries of chance, *i.e.*, that some slight deviation from the record, however minuscule, however harmless, might lead to the desired result. The doctor likely had dreamed the dream over many times, and yet no such chance occurrence had arisen. In brief, there existed a flaw in the doctor's plan. The very resistance of history to change was its salvation, its momentum carrying events forward unaltered in every particular.

The springs, counterbalances, wheels, the whole internal machinery of it was stacked against the dreamer. For history, one might say, is a done thing.

There seemed little more to be gained in this area, which led me to ask —

"The doctor, when he awakened briefly, whispered to you 'Is he here?' What did he mean by that?"

"He wished to know if you had arrived."

"Yes, he'd instructed Stokes to send for me should he become ill. But his legal affairs are entirely in order. Of what other use might I be to him?"

"It was not his legal affairs the doctor was concerned over."

"Well, what then? In what way might I help him that Sir Lancelot cannot?"

"There is but one way remains, Mr. Earnscliff."

"Yes?"

"And that is to enter the dream yourself — *as* yourself — and help the doctor."

The resulting hush was so loud you could see it. In the shut and silent room I cast about for some reply, but no more sound than that made by a passing ghost escaped my lips.

I was shocked, to say the least of it.

"That," I managed at last, "would be the very height of folly — the height of madness," and sank down a weakling in my chair.

What was it Stokes had told me? "Belike, sir, he simply wished 'ee h'yur — *in case he had need of 'ee.*"

"Great sticks alive," I murmured.

Starting up, I turned to Miss Carswell and expressed myself in the highest degree sorry for the doctor's plight, and for the fate of Dora, and the Squire's sad decline, and the ruination of the Moorings; however —

"It's totally out of the question. Totally, absolutely, altogether out of the question."

"But not impossible?" said Miss Carswell.

"But altogether unconscionable. Moreover, what business is it of mine? I am the doctor's solicitor. What would he have me do?"

"He would have you help him. That is why he sent for you."

Her eyes, curiously luminous, refused to leave me. I imagine that any man may make a fool of himself for the sake of a pretty face; indeed it happens almost every day. But in this case the thought acted only to accentuate the unreality of the scene, the stagnant, closed-in atmosphere, the recollection of the dream I had shared . . . the Moorings, the Squire, the lovely Miss Dora whose allotted span had been cut tragically short . . . the stopped life, the broken threads of yesterday . . .

"The doctor was aware he might fail?" I asked.

"He regarded it as a possibility."

"And he wished me here in the event he had need of me — *in the dream?*"

Miss Carswell nodded.

"I see." I paused to think this over. "I suppose it might be so. But of what use can I be? I am unfamiliar with the events that took place. Why should my presence make any difference if the train of circumstances cannot be changed? If history is a done thing?"

"It is the very fact that you had no role in this history that is key. You may enter the dream as yourself, become an actor in it, and perhaps influence its outcome. You were not present when the events of interest occurred. Perhaps it is you who will save Miss Fetching, even if the doctor cannot, and thereby avert the catastrophe. It is because you are a new element, one which was not there before."

Again I thought over it hard. Unconscionable or no, the idea had the still small voice in my head thundering at me one moment "Yes, indeed!" and the next moment "Not on your life, Earnscliff!"

Miss Dora dead — the doctor blaming himself for the tragedy — the Squire a broken man for the remainder of his days. Had I not a duty of sorts to aid them, if it were in my power to do so? But was it even possible? Above all, was it *right?* What if some other variable were to be changed as a result? What consequences might ensue?

And how ludicrous was it even to be contemplating such a thing? How absurd to imagine one could undo the past simply by dreaming it differently?

"Recollect, Mr. Earnscliff, it was Dr. Callander himself who sent for you," Miss Carswell pointed out.

"And I came in all haste, did I not? Although in actual fact it was Stokes who sent for me." No sooner had I spoken, however, than a startling thought crossed my mind, one that caused me to regard my young companion in a different light. "Or was it you who sent for me perhaps — by suggesting it to the doctor?"

She returned no answer, but her eyes were eloquent.

"But why was I approached for the task? Why did he not ask you for the favor — you who are his friend? I am only his solicitor, and a junior to boot."

"True, I am his friend and confidante. I look after him now — for someone must — and no other here might be trusted with knowledge of his connection to the Woldfolk. For should it be made known the doctor would be branded a pariah by his neighbors — or worse."

Gently she closed her hand over mine. A wistful tenderness filled her glance, her voice softening as she made her appeal.

"Please, Mr. Earnscliff, will you not help him in this extremity? Will you at least pause awhile to consider it? Help him — help us — help Miss Dora and her father — for you are the only one who can."

The proposed mission was a risky endeavor to say the least, one with little expectation of success. What unintended mischief might result from such an intrusion into the past? Although the motive was admirable, suppose the altered outcome should instead make matters worse, owing to some unforeseen chance occurrence? For it seems to me that sometimes things are not meant to happen, and yet they do.

Perhaps it was the wiser course not to tamper.

The sighs of the frost wind as it passed along the casement further dulled my spirits. At the same time another small voice in my head seemed to whisper —

*It's an ill wind blows nobody good . . .*

## Chapter Seventeen

HAVING thought over her proposal awhile, I still had come to no decision regarding either its merits or my purposed role in the adventure.

Miss Carswell in the meantime had left me to my deliberations. Keen to know something more about these Woldfolk whose enigmatic cordial lay at the heart of my dilemma, I settled into a chair with *The Derivation of Man,* and soon was engrossed in its pages. With rapt interest I pored over them, aided by the notations in the margins made in the doctor's large, loose hand.

It was all there, or most of it — how, secure in their hilly fastnesses, the Woldfolk had exploited their discovery of the fern-seed to conceal their presence from mankind. Discouraged from mixing with human beings openly, they were *not* prohibited from observing them in secret; and it was for this that human folk despised them. Footfalls in the dead of night, the opening or closing of doors, vague murmurings where nobody was, and other like ghostly effects — from these had arisen the notion that commonly prevailed, that people were being spied upon by beings whom they could not see.

Too the Woldfolk were master illusionists, who could alter their appearance at will. Hence they need not wear fern-seed to be walking amongst us, so long as they simply observed and did not meddle. The Woldfolk were much connected to the natural world, and to animals especially, from whom their presence could not be hidden. For animals of every kind were able to see them and to hear them.

Some there were who viewed the Woldfolk as a branch of the human race, whereas others believed them to be something else entirely. Others thought it all nonsense, that there were no Woldfolk and never had been any, that it was just so much humbug born of a surfeit of alcohol.

The most curious item I ran across was this — that although immortal, the Woldfolk were without souls. Now why should this be, I asked myself, and what consequences might follow from it? The immortality of the Woldfolk was entirely earthly; an afterlife was quite beyond their reach. Might it be that they were envious of human beings as a result? For the Woldfolk, their existence lay entirely in the here and now. If this earth tomorrow were to explode, it would be the finish of them.

Interestingly, I found no reference whatever to the cordial. How then had the doctor learned of it? In whose charge was it, whose responsibility to superintend its use? And what had Obadiah Outland — if such a being existed — to do with it? Was it he who had given the cordial to the doctor, and if so, what had been his motivation? Why should the mythical old man of the waterways have approved its use in the doctor's case? Or perhaps there was not a grain of truth in any of this?

And what was Miss Carswell's own interested motive? By all reports she was an acquaintance of the doctor's of long standing. As for myself, I knew her not from Eve. Indeed what did I know of her, apart from her being a veterinary's daughter from St. Bees? And just where was St. Bees, by the by? For I had never heard of it.

The entire business was murky, and as I closed the book of Orkla and laid it by I felt as if I still were stumbling about in the dark. And perhaps that was the very point. It should not be so easy to change the course of history; the whole of creation ought to rebel against it.

The uncertainty of it all had begun to take its toll. I flung myself back in my chair, exhausted. In short, I was dead beat.

How many times must the dream be gone through before something changed? How many iterations were necessary ere that chance event arose? Or would my presence — the new element that had not been there — accelerate the process?

A gloomy dawn was filtering through the study windows when I awoke on the couch. A broken sleep, snatched by intervals in the night, had been my sole refreshment, and had little eased my concern over the decision this day would bring.

Sir Lancelot arrived promptly at nine, and did not at all like what he found. It seemed the doctor was looking very poorly — "Worse than yesterday, I grieve to say," he announced — whereupon Annie burst into tears and plunged her face into her handkerchief.

I can't describe how guilty I felt not telling Sir Lancelot there and then of the deception, even as Miss Carswell was staring at me in silent appeal not to give away the game. He questioned everyone as to the doctor's movements in the night — there had been none — but hardly knew what further steps to take. Although he did not speak it aloud, I could see that any residue of hope he may have entertained had all but evaporated. Nevertheless, he gave fresh instructions which were aimed at supporting his patient's comfort but that did nothing to alleviate his affliction.

He remained upstairs yet awhile after I returned to the study. After a time I felt myself weakening, however, and having plucked up a little mettle had resolved to tell him everything, only to find that he had gone. As well it had occurred to me that he might have some knowledge of Miss Dora's death, for he seemed acquainted with those past events at the Moorings. *A shame . . . a lovely girl she was . . . yes, another lamentable house.* But he had left to call on the vicar.

I paced round the study like a man who doesn't know what to do with himself. Then, unable to relieve the concerns that were pressing on me, I decided to take a walk into town.

The weather was dull, and the sky hung sulky and low over Dithering and the dales, when I strode in at the door of the Pack Horse Inn. I conjectured that perhaps the landlord might have some recollection of Miss Dora and the Moorings, for as everyone knows it is impossible to hold secrets from an innkeeper.

"Marnen to 'ee, Mr. Earnscliff," smiled a woman with a dishcloth who was wiping down a table.

I glanced round for her husband. "Mr. Readymoney — is he disengaged?"

The woman looked surprised and, putting her hands to her ample hips, turned eyes on me that were at once amused and quizzical.

"Readymoney? La me, Mr. Earnscliff — you'm some merry one,

right 'nough. For ould Jago Readymoney as did have the Pack Horse afore us be dead an' buried now these nine year. How quick the time does go, to be sure! But my husband bain't handy at present. Might I serve 'ee myself?"

All at once my brain seemed to see with different eyes, and what it saw now was not the Pack Horse Inn of years agone, but the Pack Horse Inn of today, and Mrs. Asa Mundey patiently awaiting my response.

I shook my head to clear it. It had seemed for a moment as if I'd slipped back into the doctor's dream. For of course there was no Mr. Readymoney; nevertheless . . .

"And no Gilbert the fat boy — er, the pot-boy?"

"Him? Aw, fie — no, sir," scoffed the landlady. "Cornelius there be our pot-boy now. But how do 'ee know o' Gilbert, sir? The poor, ha'f-baked loblolly! For my Asa did sack him but two days after we come into the business. It seems to me he did hie hisself to Dozmary to his mama's, as was Readymoney's sister."

"I see. And no Toad Henry the jowster, I suppose?"

"That ould Scotch cake? Hardly, sir. A great talker that one was, and a wheedler to boot, for his wee drap o' dripshan. Him was one as cud talk the hind leg off a donkey, out o' doubt. 'Ee may ask 'en dreckly, sir, ef 'ee like, ef 'ee plaise to step by Dithering churchyard. But no answer will he gi'e 'ee now."

"Like Mr. Readymoney, eh?"

The landlady nodded regretfully. "'Tis the way o' flesh, sir."

"And what of Cedar Jack? Old Jack o' the wolds as he styled himself? The forester with his wide-awake as big as the moon?"

"Jack Tregennis, him do 'ee mean? No more luck, sir, for Jack do be Jack *under* the wolds now." She glanced at me curiously. "La, an' what do 'ee be about, then, Mr. Earnscliff? Readymoney? Tregennis? Howe'er did 'ee hear of 'em? For by yer laive, sir, you'm scarcely of an age to have know'd the rascals personal."

"I thank you for the compliment, Mrs. Mundey — but it simply was some talk I overheard."

It turned out there was no Tristan Colley either. It was his sons

Quince and Kale now who managed the farm. One of their cows had dropped a calf yesterday, and where Mrs. Mundey and I were standing they themselves last evening had stood to inform the regulars and staff how pleased they were over the birthing.

"And how be Mr. Callander now? Some better?" the landlady inquired. "Tell 'en us do wish 'en well, my Asa an' me. For Mr. Callander he do be as fine a gentleman as ever I heard tell on in these dales."

"Not to worry, Mrs. Mundey. And we thank you for that."

"You'm kindly welcome, sir."

And smiling she gathered up her dishcloth and bustled off.

As I turned to go, my mind upon other concerns, I felt a sudden weight as of eyes upon me — or rather, of a single, goggle-eye — and discovered, just as I remembered it, the vizard-mask of pumpkin-wood — the so-called "Eye of Days" — leering at me from the wall.

*'Tis for safety's sake — a charm to protect the wearer* explained Mr. Readymoney.

*Protect him from what?* Stinker asked.

*Piskies! I knaws 'tis piskies! And I see'd one, too* said Gilbert.

Once clear of Dithering I made my way up the road towards the farm. A distance away to my right the moss-grown pile of the Moorings beckoned to me from amid its flanking firs and bramble. At one point I halted and stared at its gloomy frontage, at the shutters blanketing its windows that were like so many eyes closed in death. I was struck by the change that had come over the place, for it was not as I recollected it. There was the door at which I had been welcomed the afternoon of the dinner party; that same door through which I had handed Flounce in to Mattie, the day Stinker and I had met Bothack at the Cupboard. The door now was shut and boarded. When next might it be opened?

What a strange, melancholy scene it was, but one in which might still be traced the faint outline of happier times.

Had I really the ability to change all this, I wondered? To restore the Moorings to that happier state, in those days that were sweet? Could I change things *for the better*? Was it truly in my power to bring the Moorings to life — to roll back time those many years, to make the very grave yield up its dead?

The notion of it of a sudden enthused and inspired me, and mustering up my courage I challenged myself — could I do it?

*Oh, Dad,* Dora sighed, but in a smiling way, *whenever will you understand me?*

*Probably never,* her father grunted — also in a smiling way. *Daughters!*

*Fathers!*

*Dodgy business, daughters,* the Squire observed. *The prettiest girl in our dales, and she cares not a bean about it. Perhaps you might talk some sense into her, Mr. Callander, as you're old friends . . .*

Or was it all a humbug, like the doctor's apoplexy?

I quickened my pace and soon reached the farm. Inside, in the little rustic gallery, I felt another weight of eyes — those of the Callander ancestors, which seemed to track me as I strode by them. *The eyes of the house are upon me.* Did the Callanders of yore as well expect my help? All at once the gallery seemed a haunted place, and I myself but a shadow passing by.

The house was quiet. Annie was watching over the doctor, whose condition was unchanged. Stokes was somewhere about the grounds, and Miss Carswell too. So I returned to the study, which I had made my quarters, and sat there awhile thinking.

I thought of Miss Dora and the tragedy, its particulars unknown, which had thrown its shadow over her father's life, and over the doctor's too. Had I really the power to drive that shadow away?

Hang it, the entire business was ludicrous! To change the past by dreaming it differently? What might the Squire have said about that? *A lot o' damfool nonsense . . .*

Of all the yarns that ever had been spun out of human brains this of the cordial was the most laughable, the most absurd — too preposterous to be true. And yet, there was another part of me that was intrigued by it — that part which desired to aid these people who, but for the doctor, Stokes, and Miss Carswell, I had met only in the doctor's dream.

And how to explain the dream if the cordial was too preposterous to be true? What indeed *was* the truth? For the events of these past days had succeeded in shaking my sense of reality, my sense of what was fact and what was not.

*Have you no heart, Earnscliff? Do you not want to help these people? How can you doubt the reality of the doctor's dream, which you yourself have shared?*

Heretofore I had been feeling my way along slowly, inch by inch. But now with one bold cast — my intrusion into history by means of the cordial — I might resolve the problem at a single stroke.

Round this time Miss Carswell appeared.

"Should I proceed with this scheme of the doctor's," I began slowly, "how exactly would it be managed? And for how long should I be under the spell of the cordial?"

Miss Carswell gave a sudden, excited release of breath. Eyes sparkling, she smiled her joy, her gratitude — her relief, it seemed to me — and proceeded to explain that it was all rather simple and straightforward. Tonight, pleading weariness and asking that I not be disturbed, I should retire early to my couch in the study. There a dose of the cordial would be awaiting me. It would be a larger dose than that I had received previously. Ere I drank it, however, it would be necessary that I fortify my energies for at least an hour's time beforehand.

"You must bend your whole will to the task, for you must enter the dream not as the doctor, but as yourself. You must bring all your powers of concentration to bear upon it. You must say to yourself, repeating it many times over, that you are Mr. Philip Earnscliff of Hoggard, that you have commenced a traveling-tour of the dales and are stopping at the Pack Horse Inn, perhaps for the angling, or to sample the local color. You have heard something of this place called the Moorings, and of Squire Fetching and his daughter, and are keen to be introduced. You must hammer it into your mind — impress it with the force of iron upon your consciousness — that you are Philip Earnscliff of Hoggard, solicitor — *that you are not the doctor* — so that in the dream you will appear as yourself.

"In making ready you must as well keep your thoughts bent upon averting the catastrophe, for once under the spell of the cordial you will know nothing of the times that are to come. In the dream you will have no inkling that Miss Dora will die. You must prepare yourself in advance and afterwards be guided by circumstance, relying on your intuition, if you will, to direct you. For you'll not recall this conversation we are having."

As she spoke I had been pacing to and fro with thoughtful steps, head down and eyes on the carpet.

"And suppose the thing doesn't work? What then?"

"Indeed it may not work, but we must pray that it will. As you are swept along with the tide of history, you must rely upon that chance occurrence, that rare opportunity that may cast up suddenly; and for that your inner self, your intuition, must be prepared."

I hesitated, and a sigh escaped my lips. I still was debating in my mind what to do, my thoughts going round and round on the various points of her argument, which did not seem so convincing now. How was I to succeed when no plan of action was possible?

To erase the gloom from this household, to restore the Moorings, to put things right again for the doctor and his friend the Squire and above all for Miss Dora — such was the errand I proposed to undertake. Was it not a worthy one?

*Don't be a goose, Earnscliff. And for heaven's sake don't make a botch of it. Take up your task, yeoman-like and bravely.*

"My stars," I heard myself say, "but the time is getting on. I'll do it."

The face of Miss Carswell shone with a rapturous light. Hope and gladness radiated from her every feature.

"If you succeed, Mr. Earnscliff," said she, taking my hand in hers, "then we two shall never have met. I thank you from the bottom of my heart for what you are about to do — and bless you!"

Her eyes were moist and glistening, and there was an involuntary catch in her voice which betrayed more, perhaps, than she willingly would have expressed. She dashed a tear from each cheek; I returned her my wordless understanding.

## Where The Time Goes

*If you succeed, Mr. Earnscliff, then we two shall never have met.*

And so I advanced to the parapet. For that is how I viewed it, this task which I had assumed. A step — a sudden rush of breath — a leap in the air, like a spring from a dizzy battlement — and then . . .

## Chapter Eighteen

THE bumpings and joltings, the sound of wheels churning, the rattle of hooves and jingle of harness, the *gee-upping* of the postilion, the mixed aroma of straw and sawdust in the air —

With a mighty effort I broke the spell that bound me, and started awake. Through glazed eyes still half-asleep I blinked drowsily round. Next a stifled yawn and a stretch — a drawing-up more snugly of my rug and muffler — a squint at the blur of landscape passing by . . .

I seemed to have lost all count or cognizance of the hours. Unable to recall the events which had preceded my dozing off, I struggled to fill in the blank.

Where was I, and how had I gotten here? For I had lost not only the hours, but a sense of myself as well. I saw the trees flashing past, and realized that I was breezing down a country road, a passenger in a chaise — the voice of the postilion told me as much — swaying to and fro at speed as we dashed along.

Moments later I was aided in my efforts by a cheery voice, which broke in upon me with such abruptness that I jumped a little in my seat.

"Well, well! Thought you'd never wake up. You're not dead by any chance, are you?"

Before me sat a middle-aged gentleman, amply waisted, of smart appearance, who was regarding me with an air of jaunty nonchalance. He was buried up to his ears in a smother of wrappings, arms crossed and his hat tilted on his head at a rakish angle. His lips wore a jovial grin, and in the eyes under his hat twin gleams of amusement lurked.

"Whereabouts am I?" I mumbled.

"Capital! Still alive," he exclaimed. "Dead would be hard cheese. Dazed and shaken, are we? Chilled to the marrow?"

And so saying he bundled himself up still more, for it was rather cold in the chaise. Principally it was his twinkling eyes that showed amongst the wrappings, and his ruddy cheeks and genial temper.

A sudden lurch threw us against the side of the carriage, as a furry pine-snag went scraping past. My companion excavated a silver watch from somewhere and looked at it, announced we had half an hour to spare, then replaced the instrument where he had found it. A jolly-favored man, he glanced at me and inquired —

"Who are you, then? For I thought I'd engaged the chaise for myself. But as we're sharing the fare, and you look a decent sort, I'd be pleased to know your name."

"My name?" I echoed — for I had been struggling with that myself. Casting about for some response, I managed to stammer out — "Well, I — I — I'm Philip Earnscliff, of H-Hoggard."

"Hoggard — from the city, eh? The hum and press of business! And what is your line, Mr. Earnscliff? For you look a professional man."

"What is my line?"

"Yes, your line. Your profession. Certainly you know your profession? For it would be a singular fellow who didn't."

I don't well know why I said it, but I answered — "I'm a — er — a solicitor, I believe — er — yes, that's it — a solicitor — Earnscliff and Bodmin, Bagwash Square — or is it Bagwash and Bodmin — or — er —"

A hurrying stream glided into view beyond the roadside, against a backdrop of looming hills and lowering sky. The air was filled with a din of wheels, the plunging tread of the horses, the occasional shout from the post-boy.

"Well, well. A legal man? Come to hunt up a job, eh? Coach upsets, innkeeper murderings, general larceny — things of that delightful nature?" my companion said affably.

"Well, not exactly . . ."

"What brings you then to these wildways of Lingonshire? For the divine art and mystery of the law has ever been a mystery to *me*. No black marks against your name, I trust? Never been struck off? Jolly good. Deuced thing that — being struck off. Rather like getting the chop, I dare say."

"I — er — am on a traveling-tour of the dales, and am stopping at Dithering for the — er — for the angling. Yes. For the angling."

"Ah, so there's the connection. Same chaise, same destination — makes sense now. And for how long will you be stopping?"

"I have no fixed itinerary. For the space of a week or thereabouts, I expect."

"A gentleman of leisure, eh? Well, well. Jolly good. How wonderful for you. By the by, my name is Jarlcot — George Jarlcot, M.F.H., J.P., that sort of thing. I've a place called Littlegates. Probably you've heard of it. No? Well, quite a few people have done."

We continued on in like fashion for a time. Our road lay through a dreary yet romantic country of hill and dale, of meadowland and wold, of brawling waters and scattered, lonely farmsteads here and there. While I worked to clear my head, my new acquaintance entertained himself by sorting and counting the trees that filed past along the way.

Swiftly the miles dropped behind us. We had been following the stream for some while, when my companion rose a little in his seat and in a comfortable voice observed —

"There's nothing like a post-chaise, I dare say, as I'm all for traveling in privacy. Give me a post-chaise, and deuce take the expense! It's a scandal the way these newfangled coaches are overloaded. Sadly the trains — which ordinarily I prefer — no longer ply these backwaters, so distant from the main arteries of traffic. For you know, Dithering is on the road to very few places. From Hoggard, did you say, Mr. Earnscliff?"

"Er — that's correct."

"Acquainted with Mr. Burleigh Gut?"

I sifted the name through what passed for my memory, but it did not register.

"Does the gentleman reside at Hoggard?" I inquired.

"Indeed. It occurred to me you might be friends, and he's said to be a useful man to know. I thought you might introduce me."

"Sorry."

"Not at all. Think nothing of it, old man. Perhaps then you're acquainted with Fowey, my tailor? For like yourself he does a thriving trade in suits. Ha, ha!"

And chuckling Mr. Jarlcot returned his attention to the window, to the scenery passing by. Still struggling to remember, I settled back on the cushion and shut my eyes.

"These are indeed remote precincts," my companion remarked after a while. "The trains go no farther than Dozmary, so that amongst these outland hills one is obliged to — "

"Hallo! Outland? What do you know of Outland?" I exclaimed suddenly.

Interrupted in mid-flow, Mr. Jarlcot threw me a questioning look. "Eh? Outland? And what is that, Mr. Earnscliff?"

*Yes,* I asked myself, *what — or who — is Outland?*

I strove to recall. Outland. *Outland.* My stars, of a certainty that was a queer dream I had . . .

My new acquaintance, amiable fellow that he was, shrugged it off. His eyes tracked a milestone as it went gliding past.

"We have a seven-mile drive yet before us," he announced.

He then informed me that the town of Dithering afforded a very desirable little inn, one well-regarded for its angling, in the calm retirement of rural quiet. The best inns are noted for their comforts, he said, and this Pack Horse of Dithering was one of the most comfortable. Indeed he was rather familiar with it, having visited a score of times or more, and recommended it highly.

"My wife's aunt has a sort of distant relation living in the area — the local squire, name of Fetching. His place is called the Moorings. There's a lovely crib if ever I've seen one! Gorgeous spot. I make it a point to call round whenever I'm in the district."

"Why *are* you in the district, Mr. Jarlcot — that is, if you'll pardon my asking?" In truth I was curious, but as well it served to take my mind off my difficulties.

"Don't object in the least, old man. As I've said I'm the reigning M.F.H., in charge of the local hunt — meet at Littlegates, of course.

Well, there's a breeder of hounds, chap called Heeler, who lives some thirty miles t'other side of Dithering. Well, his are capital hounds — real, blooded goers, that can run like smoke — and as our kennel has endured some losses, I've come to replenish our stock. Meantime it gives me leave to hobnob awhile with our relations of a sort."

"Fetching, you said? Squire Fetching?" I asked, for the name had a familiar ring.

"Just so."

"Hasn't he a daughter who lives with him?"

"Indeed, a lively young woman. Unmarried — been waiting a long time. Are you acquainted with them?"

"And a son as well — a sort of banker, I think — name of Robert —"

"At Newmarsh. Hallo! You're a regular fount of knowledge, Mr. Earnscliff. How did you come by your info?"

How *had* I come by it, I wondered? Again I had no answer, but found myself prompted to inquire —

"Speaking of introductions, might you do me the service of introducing me to the Squire and his daughter? For I've heard of them in some connection, and of the Moorings. I should like very much to meet the leading gentry in these towns as I go, to broaden my circle of acquaintance."

Mr. Jarlcot smiled comfortably. "Let me put you at your ease on that score. Delighted to be of service, old man." Again his eyes were drawn to the scenery flowing by in the windows. "It's the 'other side of the moon' round these parts, a place where few people go — the back of beyond — and there's the joy of it! Meanwhile, let me tell you something of Littlegates . . ."

As we rumbled along Mr. Jarlcot proceeded to wax lyrical over his small holding, which was situated not far from Long Puddle, the town where his wife's aunt, a Mrs. Bunce, resided. One by one he described for me his home's many fine features, and the variety of improvements he had instituted in recent years: amongst them a refurbished chimney for his drawing-room, a handsome dinner set of Magma ware from Gloamshire for his dining-room table, a new five-bar gate for his pasture, and for his coach-house a nice little basket chaise for touring.

And he spoke of other, wider matters as well, for though he was a man not given much to traveling, in his position certain obligations arose from time to time which necessitated his resorting to the open road. Chiefly it was the various methods of transport, and the accommodations one met with on the journey, that stirred his interest, and which explained his familiarity with many of the old posting-houses and wayside inns.

There was the Duchy of Cornwall, for instance, at Chedder ("the taproom is like a hive after six o'clock, full of old servitors and clodbreakers"), the Quarter Moon at Threep (a village in the west of Lingonshire, where in spring the short-faced bears are as thick as flies), the New Inn, at Culliford ("my wife's cousin, Guy Henslowe, recommends it amazingly"), the Grub and Grinder at Tillington, in Fenshire, and, lastly, the Goat in Boots, nearer home, at Long Puddle ("simply tell them Jarlcot of Littlegates sends his compliments, you'll have no trouble") — to name but a few.

Fortunately he did not solicit my opinion of the inns of Hoggard, for in my present state I should have had some trouble responding.

As regards the means of travel, Mr. Jarlcot was entirely settled in his views, as he had earlier shown in his acclaim for the post-chaise, a vehicle he much preferred to a lumbering coach. Or what was infinitely worse —

"Have you gone much into Slopshire, Mr. Earnscliff? No? Well, you may account yourself lucky, for in Slopshire they have a sort of plodding beast of transport called a megalops — 'hammer-head' is another term for the creatures — will knock you for six. Delightful species, these megalops — dodgy old bone-shakers, and homely to boot. Really — the ride one is subjected to! For the passenger-cabs are slung from the backs of the creatures, one on either side, and the pitching and tossing one undergoes is quite beyond endurance. Upon one such journey — ordeal, I call it — my wife and I were never so pleased to see the Three Men o' Slops, our inn for the night, swing into view — I do mean swing — heralding our deliverance from the side-cab.

When in Slopshire one endeavors to avoid a megalops at all costs, or stand the consequences.[1] Fortunately the creatures have been banished from Lingonshire. When traveling my wife and I generally prefer a mastodon train. For there's no better way to see the country than from the shoulders of a thunder-beast, nor a more civilized."

My new acquaintance went on to relate some gossip he had heard, concerning "a weird-looking species of tramp fellow, or dwarf-hunchback," who it was said had been making his home in an old megalops side-cab on the outskirts of Dithering. The cab had been abandoned some years ago by megalops men, one of their hammer-heads having dropped dead in an adjacent meadow. Mr. Jarlcot recommended that had I an unencumbered afternoon it might prove an instructive outing.

I let my gaze wander to the distant hills beyond the stream, their lifting slopes cloaked in shaggy timber. Presently we rounded a thick stand of pine and descended into a level basin through which the waters were chattering merrily. At this juncture my companion rose a little and looked about him, for after what had seemed an age we at last were nearing our destination.

"Dithering ho!" he announced after a brief survey. "We're nearly there. Dear old Pack Horse — there she lies, Mr. Earnscliff, the metaphorical gold at the end of our rainbow. Well — all's well that inn's well, as the poet says, eh? Ha, ha!"

In its pleasant surroundings of dale, stream, and wooded hills the Pack Horse Inn hove in sight, swelled full large as it rolled up to us, then glided slowly by as the postilion turned his horses into the yard.

The Pack Horse at Dithering is an establishment of some antiquity and curiosity, as I would soon learn. A considerable degree of bustle attended our arrival. Straightway the landlord came forward, bowing and smiling, for Mr. Jarlcot was known there and was a relative by marriage of Squire Fetching's to boot. Our host, whose name was Readymoney, went up and down on his toes in a rapture of hospitality. On being introduced to him my scalp prickled, for I could have

---

[1] See *A Tangle in Slops* (2011) for further cautionary particulars. — *Ed.*

made oath that I'd met the man on some occasion or other, the details of which were hazy. Plainly I was confused, struggling as I was yet with Earnscliff and Bodmin, of Bagwash Square, Hoggard. Meanwhile the boots of the inn came to take my luggage, and went away with it somewhere.

A shilling for breakfast, half-a-crown for dinner, including a glass of Nantle port, eighteenpence for a snug supper — such, Mr. Readymoney informed me, were the charges of the inn. And as well a shilling, payable to the landlady his wife, for linen, fires, and candles.

Other things — other, vaguely familiar things — there in the taproom did not escape my notice. There was for example the long-case clock keeping cheerful watch in the corner, and the sporting gear on the walls, and the signboard extolling the local fishing-grounds, and the bizarre bit of doggerel concerning a piskie and a man in a cupboard who was no sluggard.

And there was the vizard-mask hanging from a peg on the wall, a grotesque artefact with a single, staring goggle-eye. Something told me that it had been carved from pumpkin-wood, and had some connection to the "piskie" of the doggerel.

Who but a cyclops might have fancied such a thing? It must have been a joke — I should need to learn the history behind it — or more likely a memento from the local production of some classical Greek drama.

In another part of the room, in a blue haze of smoke of his own making, a leathery forester held a circle of regulars in thrall with his account of a recent narrow squeak in the woods. He was a wild-looking figure, garbed in a fleecy jerkin strapped by a weathered baldric, with a cutlass at his belt and a wide-awake shading his head. In his hands he held a quarterstaff — a stout pole some eight feet in length — which he was wielding with considerable authority, as he demonstrated for his audience the various thrusts, parries, and other warlike maneuvers with which he had awed and amazed his assailant.

"I'll have 'ee knaw, naybors," he explained, in a further show of skill, "that piskie or no, 'tis a spankin' great dobeck wud dare trust hisself in close quarters with ould Jack o' the wolds — for he'd put ghosts to the rout, wud ould Jack, like so — sa-ha! — break heads like so — sa-ha! — rattle bones — like so — "

And brandishing his weapon he illustrated how he had dealt with the creature that had assaulted him from the air, its wings a-flutter with a noise like the droning of bees, by swatting at it with his staff, his thrusts aimed at its silvery cranium and ghastly, protruding orb. In so doing he seemed to mimic the vizard-mask on the wall, in the fierce show of his teeth, and by closing his left eye and rounding the other into a fixed stare, as though to paralyze his adversary with his glance. For no one and no thing, evidently — not even a goggle-eyed piskie — had the fortitude to withstand a bout at quarterstaff with Cedar Jack Tregennis.

Then he grounded his weapon and called for a pint, and tossed up another rank cloud of smoke from his old briar. His audience meanwhile stood round nodding in admiration of his derring-do.

Mr. Jarlcot chuckled. "There are always lots of stories going about places," he remarked, "and there's as loud a one as any I've heard. I'd not give you so much as a threepenny bit for that performance."

The innkeeper's wife eyed my friend skeptically from her place at the till. "La, sure 'ee don't say so, Mr. Jarlcot? Not Cedar Jack o' the wolds? For he bain't a man to spake foolishness, else the world do be turned all upsy-down like a burley-cake."

"But I do say so, Mrs. Readymoney. As for the world, methinks it will right itself in time," smiled Mr. Jarlcot. "Now, then, my good woman, if you could see your way clear to render me a small service . . ."

While he and the landlady spoke apart, the boots kindly showed me to my chambers where he had deposited my luggage. It was odd, I mused, my having luggage; for the more I looked at it there in my room the less I remembered it. Very odd indeed . . .

And why had the landlord, whom I had never before met, seemed so familiar? And Cedar Jack the forester — why had I a memory of his cloud of vile mundungus vapor and his wide-awake as big as the moon?

Later I was reunited with Mr. Jarlcot downstairs. He had dispensed with his wrappings and hat, revealing the plump, rosy gentleman that he was, with his fancy waistcoat, ruddy cheeks, and onion bald head.

Almost at once a domestic came up and placed a note in his hand. After reading it he passed it across to me, saying —

"Please to run your eye over this billet, Mr. Earnscliff."

Earlier he had had a servant sent round to the Moorings with a note and his card, and this was the reply.

"As you can see it's an invitation to dine, extended to Mr. Philip Earnscliff. Hallo! Introduction accomplished. And one never knows — the old gent may be in need of a sharp attorney, eh?"

Matters having been arranged to everyone's satisfaction, it lacked an hour yet before we were expected at the manse.

"Come, I'll hold you a hand at piquet while we await our chariot. For the manor is but a step off. Bring us coffee and cards, landlord."

We played a hand — I lost. We played another — same result. A third did not improve my position.

"Hard cheese, old man," commiserated my friend. "It would seem fortune has altogether deserted you. Belike it's the piskies in the air round these parts. Better luck at the Squire's." And so saying he tossed his hat on his head at a jaunty angle and announced — "We're for the Moorings, ho!"

## Chapter Nineteen

THE others paused and stared at me in surprise, and for a moment no one spoke.

I can't quite describe for you the odd sort of feeling which their looks communicated to me. What had I said? Something to offend them? *Proper job, Earnscliff, insulting your hosts at the first go.*

I simply had inquired where Dr. Hankey was, and hadn't he been invited to dine with us this evening? For I had quite forgotten to ask about him over the meal.

"How do you know of Hankey?" Dr. Callander asked.

His gaze I met with a sort of chill, with that particular qualm one feels at having been *found out* — the so-called mark of a guilty conscience. But of what had my conscience to be guilty over?

Then, stopping short, I asked myself — yes, how *had* I known of Dr. Hankey?

And who was Dr. Hankey, by the by?

"Well, it's true, he dines with us on occasion," said Squire Fetching. "Much obliged to him, too — not for the dining, but for sawing my leg off for me, once upon a time. Saved my life. Dodgy business it was. Would have kicked it were it not for Hankey."

"Oh, Dad," chided his daughter, "don't remind us of such things. Don't be morbid."

"But by thunder it's the truth, Dora."

Turning to me, his daughter — a lovely young woman with sparkling eyes, lustrous hair of a rich chestnut shade, and a smile like an April morning — suggested: "Likely someone at the inn mentioned Dr. Hankey to you, Mr. Earnscliff. Or perhaps it was George in the chaise?"

"Never," stated Mr. Jarlcot emphatically, "never, as I scarce know the sawbones myself. We may have raised a glass a time or two with Mine Host of the Pack Horse, but aside from this we're hardly acquainted."

"Dr. Hankey," Miss Dora informed me, "is our town physician. He is in fact our only medical man, save for the apothecary."

"Mixit," I blurted out.

"Eh?" returned the Squire, pricking up his ears.

"Mixit — the apothecary. I gather he and your Dr. Hankey don't get on. Apothecaries — always thinking of their money," I remarked, without knowing why. It was as though a voice was speaking inside my head, and I was merely repeating the words. I'll confess, I was as much startled to hear them tumble from my lips as were my hosts, who paused again to exchange glances.

"I'm damned! So you know Mixit as well?" said the Squire, stroking his mustaches.

Evidently I knew Mixit, but how or in what connection I scarcely could fathom. My brain seemed to be hurting me, and my nerves — well, there was an edge to them that had not been present earlier. I averted my glance and with an embarrassed shrug tried terribly hard to *think, Earnscliff, think*.

Dr. Callander in particular was regarding me closely.

The doctor — of philosophy, as it turned out — was a tall, slim, distinguished-looking man, with a head of dark hair already graying at the temples. He was the Squire's nearest neighbor, and a former University don, who had charge of a small holding he had inherited from his father. A graduate of Maunder College, Penhaligon, for several years he had been engaged in promising researches there, something having to do with "glacial theory", which had gained him a measure of renown amongst his colleagues. Then all unexpectedly, after his father's death, he had gathered up his books, washed his hands of Alma Mater, and retired to Dithering to become a farmer.

"On a tour of the dales you said, Mr. Earnscliff? You know, we're on the road to very few places here," he told me.

"Yes, Mr. Jarlcot's words almost exactly."

The play of the doctor's features was hard to interpret, but he did not seem overly troubled, merely curious, as if I were one of his intellectual mysteries to be solved. And yet there was something else as well . . .

"Have we met before, Mr. Earnscliff?" he asked.

"No, I don't believe so. No, I'm certain of it. How can we have done?"

"I haven't a clue, but you seem familiar to me. You're a fellow Haligonian — a graduate of which college, did you say?"

"That would be Cardigan." (It had popped into my head when we had been introduced earlier.)

"I was a Maunder man, as has been touched upon. Tell me — who was your tutor while at Cardigan? For I was acquainted with most of the leading men in the other colleges."

I gulped. "My tutor? Er — well, that is — "

*Come on, Earnscliff — rack your brains! If you attended Cardigan College, you will certainly have had a tutor. Now what was his name?*

While the others waited, I weltered.

"Hallo! Wasn't it Spendrift now? For you were telling me of it in the chaise," said Mr. Jarlcot, twinkling his gray eyes.

Old Spendrift — of course! That was it. I remembered now, it had occurred to me, betwixt some lazy dozes, as we were bumping along in the road.

Dr. Callander frowned. "Never heard of Spendrift. Was he a new man?"

"Oh, indeed — a new man — that's it exactly. Round sixtyish he was, but looked two hundred."

Here the doctor's innate good humor came to the fore. "Sixtyish? Well, your Spendrift sounds rather an old fellow to be a new Fellow," he chuckled.

Whereupon I endeavored to divert attention from myself by remarking in turn, again I don't know why —

"And your tutor's name was Vivian — Alastair Vivian — later Sir Alastair, Master of Maunder. And a fellow Cornishman."

The time ticked by — flowing drop by drop as it were, second by second. It was as though a heavy bar had fallen, but without making a noise, so profound — and so agonizing — was the quiet.

The cloth had been removed, after a very handsome dinner, and we'd been sitting round the table with our coffee and claret and some delightful Cornish cakes. The venison pasties and chine of beef had been superb, the dessert perfection itself. Now, gathered together as we were, the center of attention no longer was the cuisine but, unfortunately, myself.

"So you know of Sir Alastair Vivian?" said Dr. Callander, folding his hands.

Mr. Jarlcot turned to him in some surprise. "What! Do you mean it's true?"

"It is. Alastair Vivian, of Cornish descent, was my tutor at Maunder, and now is Master of the college and a knight of the sundered realm."

"Well, well! Methinks Mr. Earnscliff can't have picked that up at the inn."

"Most unlikely, I should think. Perhaps at Penhaligon, then? But Mr. Earnscliff, you remarked earlier you knew nothing of me," the doctor said.

I didn't know what to tell him, except that I must've heard of Sir Alastair and himself in some connection, as I had heard of Squire Fetching and the Moorings. I scoured my memory, what there was of it, and tried to ignore the looks in the others' faces. The answer, I concluded, most probably could be found in my legal work. Likely it was something I had run across in the performance of my duties, and which my mind had put away for later recall.

Said Dr. Callander, recollecting that my chambers were at Hoggard —

"It's a Mr. Junius Bladdergowl there who has the management of the deeds and leases pertaining to Callander farm, and who drew out my father's will and saw it proved. To my mind he is a worthy gentleman and a most competent. Our lawyer here had sunk into rather a feeble state, and was no longer effective. So some few years ago, to aid my father, I went up to Hoggard and engaged Mr. Bladdergowl, who had been recommended to me by Sir Alastair. And that is how Mr. Bladdergowl, of Battle, Bagwash and Bladdergowl, came to our notice. Perhaps you're acquainted with him? Perhaps he is the connection through whom you heard of Sir Alastair and myself?"

Mr. Jarlcot turned to me and said, "Hallo! By my reckoning you were Bagwash and Bodmin, Mr. Earnscliff. Or is it Bodmin and Bagwash?"

"Who? No, it's Earnscliff, of Earnscliff and Bodmin, in Bagwash Square. Er — no — " I stumbled.

"Don't you mean Bodmin Square?" Dr. Callander suggested.

Eyes regarded me expectantly. I strained my mind to remember, but no solution presented itself.

"Surely there can't be two Bagwashes, nor two Bodmins either? For that would be past believing," Miss Dora spoke up brightly. "But *I* believe you, Mr. Earnscliff, although I know you not from Adam. It's just a feeling I have. Yours seems to me a trustworthy face, I dare say."

"I thank you, Miss Fetching — f-for your good opinion of me," I managed to stammer out.

By now I expect they were thinking my entire story was past believing, and, frankly, so was I. But what was I to do? There was Dr. Callander studying me in his curious way, Miss Dora trying her best to reassure me, Mr. Jarlcot looking amused, and Squire Fetching, the master of the Moorings, calmly tamping his pipe in anticipation of further entertainment.

It was another awkward moment — but one of many. I took the remainder of my claret and drank it down.

It was precisely at this juncture that I was rescued by a maidservant who had appeared at the door. She stood quietly until our attention was gained, then begged pardon and curtsied, and asked whether Miss Dora might come with her? For she was having some trouble getting Clemendy to eat.

"Is she being fussy again, Mattie?" Dora asked.

"Ef 'ee plaise, miss, but Clemendy she no longer fancies her stewed tomato of a marnen', or of a tay-time either."

"I see. Well, I shouldn't wonder. I'm not overly fond of stewed tomatoes myself."

"Terrible stubborn she is, miss, an' won't eat her greens nor her carrots now less 'ee be present."

"Fie, Clemendy! Won't Cook do?"

"No good 'tall, miss, for Clemendy she'll take nowt from Cook but a nip o' celery betimes, or drop o' girty-milk. She do be a-waitin' for 'ee, miss, to fill 'er stummick."

"Very well. I see I must sit with her while she eats. Such sensitive natures these little creatures have! Come along, Mattie."

And so saying Dora excused herself, pledging to return once her errand had been accomplished.

"Who is Clemendy?" I asked.

The Squire gave a lazy whiff at his pipe. "Pocket glypt," he drawled. "Do you know of 'em, Mr. Earnscliff? Damnedest of these little creatures of Dora's as any you've seen. Like a turtle, but not a turtle. Plucky little thing, though — stood right up to Mr. Callander's cat there."

I nodded mechanically. "Ah, so they've got it right now. For *she* used to be Edmund, if I remember correctly. Her 'whatsit from out of time', Miss Dora called her."

The Squire's eyebrows jumped, each one so thick a brush of brow it looked painted on. A slender stream of smoke shot from his half-open lips and he blinked two or three times.

"By thunder," he murmured.

I glanced uneasily at his astonished countenance and at that of the doctor. Again that staring silence! What — had I offended again? Baffled, I placed a hand to my forehead, feeling the perspiration that had come out there. *It's a botch, Earnscliff —*

"Well, I myself am all in the dark," complained Mr. Jarlcot, looking round him for an explanation.

It turned out that Clemendy had at first been called Edmund, owing to a confusion of the sexes, and that Miss Fetching had dubbed her pet her "whatsit from out of time" because of the animal's possibly great age, a hallmark of the species.

The thoughts had been coming thick and fast into my brain. But from where had they been coming, and why? And who knew what might be next?

Out of the chaos a clear voice arose.

"Wh-h-e-e-e-w-w!" whistled Mr. Jarlcot, regarding me with amazement. "Deuce take it, Mr. Earnscliff, you're no fount of knowledge — you're a regular geyser!"

## Chapter Twenty

THE Squire's pipe well might have fallen from his lips, had the bowl of it not been cupped in his hand.

"By thunder!" had been his startled response to my words, and now "Great sticks alive!" his utterance as he thought over it more.

"You seem to know a good deal about us, Mr. Earnscliff. How can this be?" Dr. Callander asked. For even he had been taken aback by the extent of my knowledge of their private lives.

I offered a kind of rambling apology, expecting to be turned out of doors forthwith as a spy, sneak-thief, or worse. What could I say? How was I to defend myself? They had received me, a stranger, with hospitality and courtesy, and I had been treated to the bounty of the Squire's table. And how had I repaid them?

Perhaps I *was* a spy or sneak-thief, and not a solicitor from Hoggard as I believed. But from where had this secret knowledge of mine sprung? And in light of it, how was I to counter their suspicions? For I was insensible of any effort on my part to deceive them.

"I can't explain it," I said — it was the entire truth, so far as I understood it — "for it's as much a mystery to me as it is to you."

Dr. Callander had been observing me thoughtfully. *I feel I know you* his glance seemed to communicate. He did suspect me; the sense of it was palpable. *This chap is a lawyer, and a city man — ergo he may be up to something,* or so the reasoning went; I could see it in his eyes. And yet there was internal strife behind the mask. On some account he appeared hesitant to think ill of me, of this stranger who had appeared in their midst. *A lawyer — a city man — stamp him guilty.* But wasn't Mr. Bladdergowl, his worthy and competent solicitor, himself a lawyer and a city man?

This Dr. Callander was a gentleman of some presence, as befitted his history. Tall and stately these dons are, but easy and good-natured they are not, as a rule. Yet Dr. Callander was the very picture of the exception to the rule. In the main he appeared to take himself not all that seriously; and yet he was passionately devoted to his researches, which he was pursuing at leisure in his new life as a gentleman farmer.

It crossed my mind then that we likely had some common interests, being fellow Haligonians, and that perhaps this topic offered a way out of the present impasse. I approached it cautiously.

"A University education had been quite beyond my family's humble means," I recalled, "until my mother's brother, my Uncle Jory, passed away. A legacy left me in his will enabled me to attend Maunder College."

"Thought it was Cardigan, old man," said Mr. Jarlcot.

"Did I say Maunder? Well, naturally I meant Cardigan College."

"Odd," the doctor remarked, with a curious glint, "but it was an uncle of mine who helped me in much the same way. For he'd been a college man — Maunder College."

"Indeed?"

"A much-respected uncle. My mother's brother, in fact."

I felt a sudden stricture in my throat. Already I had an inkling of what was to come.

"Indeed?"

"His name too was Jory. My Uncle Jory."

More confusion! More embarrassment! I mopped my brow. In the name of reason, was the like coincidence ever heard?

The chilling thought struck me that perhaps I was going mad. Perhaps this was the explanation — that slowly, surely I was losing my mind. Even now, perhaps, a malignant growth was spreading its vile tentacles through the corridors of my brain, insinuating itself into the deepest reaches of my memory . . .

I turned with a start when the doctor observed —

"But one may be misled by the play of coincidence. Indeed it's a capital mistake, one to which few of us in the sciences pay sufficient heed."

His manner throughout remained calm and relaxed. Why was he not troubled by my seemingly inexplicable revelations? Why was he not more worried over the stranger in their midst?

"Tell me, did you know Ivinghoe? Or Tullibody? At Cardigan?" he asked.

Lest worse should follow, I denied any knowledge of such people, whoever they were. Again it was the whole truth, so far as I comprehended it. I knew no more of Ivinghoe or Tullibody than did the decanter on the table.

"Or old Middleton? The Professor of Paleology?"

Again I was at a loss.

"Surely Bouche-Fermé then, the college chaplain?"

Again I shook my head. All in all my responses seemed to please him.

"Good. I'm glad you haven't heard of them, for neither have I. If you had heard of them, I should have had grave concerns." And with a brisk chuckle he signaled that he had disposed of this little matter — meaning me.

Next it was my turn to indulge my curiosity concerning this unusual species of academician.

"Why did you choose to return to the dales?" I asked him.

"I live here in Dithering, you see, Mr. Earnscliff, because I like it. I like the country and I'm fond of the people. And because Dithering was the home of my fathers for generations untold. Here there's plenty of room to move about — rather different from rooms in college! I was bred and born on the farm that lies up the road — Callander farm."

"Some people say a farmer's is a bad trade."

"I'm sure that is what city folk in Hoggard may say. But I've not found it so, nor did my father James, nor my grandfather Hugh, for whom I was named. And you'll not find cleaner or better land than that we have here in the dales."

"But you changed the entire nature and current of your life in resigning your post and returning home."

It was at this juncture that Miss Dora reappeared, and it became clear to me at once, the way the doctor's glance lighted softly upon her, there was more than Callander farm and farming had entered into his calculation in his return to the dales.

The problem of Clemendy having been resolved, Dora resumed her seat.

"She refuses to eat unless I am present. She is becoming far too attached to me, my little whatsit. Even Mattie will not suffice, but she must have Dora, Dora!"

"As must we all," noted her father.

"I believe it's a characteristic of the species," the doctor remarked, "that these pocket glypts may become excessively fond and protective of their human guardians."

"And so as I understand it do calico cats," Dora observed, with a nod towards the lump of fur that was dozing by the doctor's chair.

"I expect it's the mark of a perceptive nature, and reflects well on her upbringing. Although Flounce can be adventurous at times, when it suits her."

A drowsy eye opened at the foot of the chair. A furry ear twitched, a contented voice purred its pleasure. *Bravo, Callander.*

"Alas, my little whatsit is not nearly so adventurous as is your Flounce. Although she does enjoy her rambles in the garden."

The drowsy eye closed. *Pity.*

"Speaking of adventures," said the doctor, leaning forward in his seat, "we have yet to work out the details of the proposed expedition to Eldritch's Cupboard. The 'poachers', you know."

"Don't you mean Sideboard?" I asked.

"Why, Mr. Earnscliff," returned Dora, in a voice of surprise, "that is just what *I* call it. For it's the place where the Giant Eldritch is believed to have laid out his luncheon. But Dad says it's poachers."

"Another coincidence, I dare say," the doctor suggested, "for Eldritch's 'Cupboard' is the more usual designation."

I confess to having had some obscure, ill-defined memory of this Cupboard of Eldritch's, but from where it originated I couldn't say; it was another puzzle. And where the deuce had that "Sideboard" bit come from? For like so many things, I had heard of it in some connection, in some circumstance, somewhere.

There followed some talk of a legend concerning a monster in this Cupboard, a creature the doctor claimed to have seen as a boy, in the company of a youthful playfellow, one Dickie Fish. But Dickie Fish had disappeared and never was heard of again. Such too had been the fate of certain others, over the years; but as time went by their memory had passed out of mind.

While an undergraduate, home for the Long Vacation, the doctor had pursued some of his geological researches in the Cupboard, and in the course of them had seen or heard nothing in the way of monsters. But then the "poachers" had not been active in those years; lately, however, it seemed they had returned to the neighborhood.

"There are some who believe the monster to be Eldritch himself," the doctor continued. "But of course there are no giants, and never have been any. They are fanciful, mythological creations — entire inventions of our ancestors. One might as easily leap a fifty-acre field as bump into the Giant Eldritch in his Cupboard. But there may be other things than giants . . ."

To me it sounded a trifle hazardous, this proposed adventure of theirs.

"Do you think the expedition wise, doctor?" I asked.

"Curious you should call me doctor," he remarked, "as most hereabouts do not. But then you're a college man, and a Haligonian, with experience of tutors and professors and the like. As regards the Cupboard, not to worry — we shall be fully prepared. My man Stinker is to have charge of arms."

"As I shall have charge of the provisions," Dora noted.

Her words took me by surprise. "You don't mean to say that you are going as well?"

That is precisely what she did mean, it turned out. Moreover her father the Squire was in complete accord with it. He himself set no store by monsters — his was another kind of poacher — and regretted that his leg prevented him from joining the expedition, or excursion, or outing, or whichever you choose. Picnic, I think, Dora called it.

"Blasted beggars — poachers — Cupboard — den o' thieves — rascally villains — smoke 'em out!" the Squire growled, drawing fiercely on his pipe.

As for our friend Jarlcot, he had begged off, and with good cause, as he was expected at Heeler's to select his stock.

"Perhaps another time," he said comfortably. "Funny thing, time. We've this tortoise in our garden at Littlegates, Madeleine and I. Alfred, we call him. Amiable chap — speaking of giants, a titan compared to your pocket whatsit — been larking about the family estates a jolly long while. Why, he already was ancient when I was a boy! To think that he may have taken roughage from the hand of my great-grandfather, Jasper Jarlcot, a man I never knew."

"Aye, time is a great feaster," the Squire nodded, levering himself up from his chair, "for in the end it consumes us all — damn and blast!" he muttered in rebuke of his creaking leg. "Keep meaning to oil it."

And on this note the meal was brought to a close.

It was late afternoon. A heavy shroud of sky hung over the dales, bearing down as if it would smother all life below. Across the stream the tumbled hills already had been swallowed up by it.

To my surprise — not to say shock — I was invited by the Squire to remain as his guest, as Mr. Jarlcot would be departing come dawn. It was suggested that I surrender my room at the inn — an apartment I had but barely occupied — and establish myself at the Moorings until such time as I should resume my tour of the dales.

"We'll have your things collected. Readymoney will understand," the Squire assured me.

I had a feeling that Dr. Callander had had a hand in this, and my impression was largely confirmed when he approached me and offered the services of his gig and his servant Stokes — also called Natty — in retrieving my luggage.

"For there my father's old two-wheeler stands conveniently in the drive," he remarked, as we were looking out at a window, "and the errand will serve to keep my man in trim."

"So how do you like us, Mr. Earnscliff?" Dora asked, all freshness and smiles. "I dare say we've donned our very best behavior for you. For we're not always such elegant and witty companions of an afternoon, if you must know."

To keep a watch of me, I fancied, lay behind her father's invitation. But who in his right senses would have turned it down? What a smasher Miss Dora Fetching was — her pretty eyes, her lively manner, her every feature radiating spirit and animation. What a topping young woman! What a splendid prize for any man!

"And you'll join us on the expedition, certainly?" she added.

It was clear that the doctor suspected me of something — but was Dora suspicious as well? Perhaps they thought me an impostor of a sort. I kept cudgeling my brains to remember, Earnscliff, remember! Somehow I understood that I was meant to be here in Dithering — at the Moorings — amongst these very people — to accomplish some task I had been sent to perform . . . sent by whom . . .? And why?

The doctor had summoned his servant Stokes from the kitchen, where he had been taking his dinner. A rumpled young chap, his face folded into a smile when he learned that his mission entailed a call at the inn, and he ambled off. Meantime I remained at the window, admiring the scenery. Some yards away in the drive waited the doctor's horse and gig. A girl stood at the horse's head, bridle in hand, stroking the animal's shoulder.

"You have a female groom?" I said.

"Stokes acts as my groom," the doctor replied.

"Who then is the young woman holding Bob Cob's head?"

The doctor returned to the window.

"I see no young woman. I see only Natty."

I looked again. There indeed was the rumpled Stokes, preparing to mount to the seat for his drive into town. Of the girl there was no trace.

"But I saw her as plainly as I see Bob and the gig," I insisted. "She was no household domestic, but was dressed like a groom, in cords and leather leggings and a cloth cap. I saw her there — just there — just now — "

"Perhaps your eyesight is going back on you," the doctor suggested.

"Or perhaps we've a brownie in our stable?" said Dora, who had joined us at the lattice.

I bit my lip, my eyes trained on the vacant space where the girl like a duteous page had stood. Was it possible I could have mistaken Stokes for . . .?

No, it was not possible — most decidedly not. Although the light was thin, I could not have been in error. I was not so far gone in my mind as to have mistaken a girl's shapely figure for the shapeless outline of Stokes.

More mystery! Perhaps it was not my eyes but my imagination that had played some juggler's trick with me.

"By the by, Mr. Earnscliff," the doctor remarked, "how did you know that my gelding's name was Bob Cob?"

## Chapter Twenty-one

**M**ISS Dora was saying "I think it will be a tremendous lark" when I came downstairs the morning of the expedition. The Squire's pair horse wagonette had been scrubbed and polished till it gleamed, and a couple of fine bays chosen from his string. Although the Squire himself would not be joining us on account of his disability — "wouldn't have a leg to stand on," he quipped — he had relished his time spent in the stables and coach-house superintending operations.

In the matter of the provisions, his daughter was in her element. "Already my gnomes are busily at their labors," she told me, in allusion to her staff in the kitchen, who were making ready the pasties, fairing biscuits, clotted cream, saffron cakes, and flasks of tea and cider for the picnic hamper.

Lastly there was that other matter — the business of the weapons. This responsibility had fallen to Stinker. This "Stinker" was a slight, grizzled little man with a bald head and a toothy grin, who had been Dr. Callander's servant while at Maunder and who appeared to enjoy the doctor's utmost confidence. It was Stinker who would select the arms that would guarantee our safety on the road.

At last all was in readiness for the outing, which was to include a tour of the marvels of Eldritch's Cupboard, to be conducted by the doctor himself. For Dr. Callander had been and remained a noted authority on the subject of geological processes, and had amassed a deal of experience in the way of field work. By comparison, today's expedition would constitute little more than a geological jaunt, amongst the hills a few miles from Dithering.

Dora had been undecided at first whether to bring her pet glypt along. But as Clemendy declined to eat now except in her presence, her leaving meant that the animal must forgo sustenance for the balance of the day. Still Dora hesitated, uncertain for the moment how to proceed.

"Perhaps the air will do her good," I suggested. "And Flounce will be there as well."

"You're a dear, Mr. Earnscliff, to be thinking of my dinky girl," she said, brightening. "Air — lunch — the healthy light of day — all while safely ensconced in her wire cottage — she shall do very nicely, I think. For there is only so much browsing can be done about the garden."

"I am happy to have been of assistance."

As for Flounce, she would be traveling in her usual way — in her club bag. As a result of her visits at the Moorings, she and Clemendy, under Dora's tutelage, had grown more accepting of one another, were less bellicose, more trusting, more peaceable than before. So it had been concluded no trouble would ensue if they were to share the outing.

The time for our departure arrived. The Squire, his leg creaking, stumped forth with his stick to see us off. The wagonette stood in the drive, the two fine bays in the traces. Dora was helped to a side-seat in the back, where she was given charge of Flounce. Mattie sat beside her with Clemendy's cage at their feet. I took my place on the opposite cushion. Up front Dr. Callander had command of the bays, with Stinker at his right hand.

"Gee-up, lads!" the doctor sang out, and with a flick of the ribands away we rattled down the drive and into the road.

At the inn we crossed the bridge and swung into an old cart-track running northeastwards into the hills. Our course led through a gully that bordered the stream, on the edge of a silent wood. All round us the tumbled hills rose like the backs of sleeping giants, their undulating steeps cloaked in a dusky verdure. Throughout we proceeded at a relaxed pace, as suited the occasion, but with eyes and ears alert and weapons at the ready.

Ordinarily few passed this way, for it was the way that led to the Cupboard. As well it was the way that led to the hovel of one Mawgan Bothack, the which was pointed out to us now by the doctor. It stood well back of the road, at a little height above the trees. Long and low, it retained here and there traces of a blackish-brown paint, where time and the elements had not scraped it bare. A range of windows stretched along one side of it. Years agone, the faces of travelers might have been seen peering in dismay from these windows, as their enormous, homely mount of a megalops, snorting and galumphing, had carried them down the road.

For this hovel of Bothack's was in actuality a side-cab — a sort of combined passenger-cab and freight platform, one of a pair that had hung on either side of a megalops. Damaged, it had been abandoned by the megalops men after one of their beasts had fallen down dead in a meadow near by. It was in such a cab, swaying wildly in answer to the megalops's violent, lurching gait, that its luckless passengers would have been tossed and shaken in their seats, and thumped and bumped, and otherwise flung about, like so many corns in a pepperpot. Such had been the state of overland transport in the boggy shire of Slops, and such it still was today. It was for this reason that megalops and their drivers had been banished from the highways and byways of Lingonshire.

The damage to the side-cab had been extensive, and had included a partial collapse of the roof. This had been stuffed with thatch. A few of the windows remained whole, the rest had been sealed with canvas. From the door a flight of steps reached to the ground.

It was the hermit Bothack — the "dwarf-hunchback" and "weird-looking species of tramp fellow" mentioned by Mr. Jarlcot — who was suspected by some in the recent spate of poaching.

"Look 'ee there, missy," Stinker called to Dora, "ain't that a plain fright now? It ain't a wonder his neighbors sent him packing."

We followed his glance and beheld a coarse-looking individual, thickset and heavy, who had emerged from the cab and was regarding us with unfriendly eyes from the top of the steps.

"Morgan Crookback," Stinker nodded ominously.

"Ah," I remarked, why I know not, "Mawgan Bothack — the bad lot who's been knocked about some — plaguy villain — with a clock on him as would stop time itself."

Frowning, Stinker screwed himself round and thrust me a glance over his seat-back.

"Here, now — what's this? And how d'ye know that, sir? For 'tis me own words I'm hearing."

How *had* I known that, I asked myself? For I knew this Bothack no more than I did the man in the moon. A wild, solitary creature he looked, who stood scowling upon us from afar, hard eyes glaring from under the brim of his tall, chimney-pot hat.

*For few come this way, lying as it does on the road to the Cupboard.*

Oddly proportioned, he had shoulders of a breadth, one of them markedly higher than the other, but stood only as tall as those shoulders were wide. It occurred to me that I had encountered his rough figure before, but when or where and in what connection was yet another puzzle.

Somewhat to my surprise — and I believe to that of the others as well — the doctor flung out a hand in greeting as we passed from the hermit's sight. The gesture struck me as ironical, and as if in confirmation of the fact Stinker was heard chuckling to himself as we rattled on.

Presently the doctor hauled in his team, whereupon he and Stinker alighted and led the horses into a narrow by-path. In some secluded ground farther along it we left the wagonette, and staked the bays out to browse. Then taking in hand Clemendy, Flounce, the blankets and hamper, we set off on foot.

The silence of this eerie wood was profound. On every side shaggy firs and cedars pushed their towering spires high into a glum gray heaven. The scenery was wild, alluring, and gravely mysterious, evoking as it did stories of ogres and antique giants sporting seven-league boots. In this latter particular we were to be disappointed, however, when no fearsome Gargantua arrived to grind our bones into bread.

*Most sane folk won't go a-nigh the place.*

At the foot of the Graystone Crags, in a natural amphitheater shaped by the crowding hills, a gaping hole in the rock face beckoned — the Cupboard of Eldritch.

One long survey to the right, another to the left, satisfied our caution that no one was near, though it abated our vigilance not a jot.

To ward off the chill we soon had a little fire going, round which we settled ourselves on the blankets. A big-trunked pine afforded a convenient shelter not far from the gloomy opening in the rock wall. There we unpacked the hamper and arranged before us the delicacies Dora's gnomes had supplied. Needing no urging to partake, we fell to with an appetite. Flounce and Clemendy as well were treated to tasty meals. Ours meanwhile was capped by a little surprise — three bottles of muddy brown ale, which someone had smuggled into the hamper.

Stinker's eyes lighted up when he saw them.

"Merry doings!" he exclaimed. "Here's to yer good health, sir" — and he drank down the toast — "and to yers, missy" — and drank another — "and yers as well, Mr. Earnscliff" — ditto — and so it went.

"This cider agrees with me charmingly," Dora said. She was not so certain as regards the ale, however, which she judged a trifle thick for her taste. Meanwhile her eyes roved comfortably about the scene and surroundings. "Really, I don't know why folks are so shy of this place. Eldritch's Sideboard seems a placid spot. What do you think, Mattie?"

"Oh, miss," the maid replied, "I'm sure I cudn' say, one way or t'other. Hows'ever . . ."

"Yes?"

The girl hesitated, glancing round uneasily. "Hows'ever . . . there do be somethin' cold h'yurabouts, miss. Ascuse my sayin'."

"Nothing more certain, Mattie, in view of our Lingonshire climate. I do wish the sun would show himself now and again in these dales of ours."

"No fear of that," I remarked, munching on a biscuit, "for I think it's odds we'll have no sight of him today."

"Over to Lakeside, by Bacon Hill, folks saw the sun once. I recall hearing of it, when I was about as high as this." And she indicated a height a child of five might have scoffed at.

"You jest, Miss Fetching. Surely it's not so bad as that? For you know at Hoggard . . ."

I stopped, suddenly at a loss how to continue.

"Yes, Mr. Earnscliff?" said the doctor. "And how is the weather at Hoggard?"

What was I to say? What did I know of the weather at Hoggard? No more than I knew of Cardigan College, I expect . . . or of Bodmin and Bagwash . . . or was it Bagwash and Bladdergowl?

Fortunately the topic of discussion was changed at this point, to nobody's greater relief than mine.

But any such relief was to be short-lived, for there had been growing upon my senses a vague impression of something monstrous and unspeakable connected with the object of the day's outing — with Eldritch's Cupboard. It may simply have been my imagination; or was it a memory perhaps, of something I had heard at one time or other? At present it was but a shapeless cloud, a specter of mist, which suddenly vanished before I could make anything of it.

The others had been chatting away for a while, talking of this and that, when I surfaced in time to hear Dora remark —

"And so the idea of it came to me — that of the expedition — that with Mr. Callander's help perhaps we could draw them out — Dad's poachers, I mean — entice them from their lair, if indeed the Sideboard is that place. Mr. Callander doesn't think it is — doesn't think there are any thieves or poachers — any real ones anyway — but he's been very patient and accommodating nonetheless."

"Then the excursion today was your idea, Miss Fetching?" I asked.

"Entirely. I think that if there are poachers, as my father believes, and if that rude being who makes his home in the side-cab has aught to do with them, then this is the place for them to have established their headquarters. What better spot than one having already a bad reputation?"

"I agree, it's a reasonable hypothesis."

"Do 'ee think the varmints be hid h'yurabouts, miss?" said Mattie.

"I think it a possibility. For we are not so far from the town and farms, as the cow flies."

"Don't you mean as the crow flies?" I asked.

"Ah, but Mr. Earnscliff, we *are* speaking of stock thieves here," Dora said with a twinkle. "Though admittedly Mr. Callander believes I am on the wrong scent. But I am a person of decided opinions — you may have heard something to this effect, I dare say, in your brief time with us. Oh, dear — I hope I haven't shocked you?"

"My dear Miss Fetching, I've heard no such thing" — it was a lie — "and you have not done."

"Dad is forever telling the young men of it, in the hopes it may pique their curiosity. But it never does; I believe it scares them right off. Don't you agree, Mr. Callander?" and she slanted a glance at the doctor.

She really was a splendid young woman, was Dora — witty, intelligent, good-natured, lovely to look upon — and as we talked together there under the big-trunked pine my regard for her grew by leaps and bounds. Indeed I seemed innately to be drawn to her. She was older than I, I judged, by some few years, and wiser perhaps too. For she had been brought up in the countryside amongst country people, whereas I had been raised — just where was it again, exactly?

"I dare say we all of us have some extravagant ideas when we are young," I heard her remarking, when I surfaced again.

"But Miss Fetching, you *are* young," I protested.

"I fear I must disappoint you there, Mr. Earnscliff. For ever since childhood I have felt that I was really a base old person at heart. Isn't it strange what tricks the mind is capable of?" And she smiled and shook her head in her waggish, delightful, thoroughly charming way.

*What a queer thing the mind is.* The words echoed in my memory, but who was it had spoken them? For Dora's ruminations had jostled something in my brain; and then almost as quickly, like the shapeless cloud, the specter of mist, it dissolved into nothing.

After the last drop had been drained and the last morsel consumed, we rose to our feet. It was to be Dr. Callander's task now, as our guide and cicerone, to illustrate for us the chief features of interest in the Cupboard. And who better for the job than he, who as an undergraduate had made a thorough study of its mysteries?

The doctor had brought with him his rucksack, which he made regular use of on field excursions. He slung it now on his back, and into it Flounce was placed. It was in the rucksack that she had gained some of her earliest experiences of traveling with the doctor, after she had come to him as a kitten. Being well used to it she snuggled comfortably into its folds, with only her furry head and ears showing.

A lantern was prepared and given to Mattie, who took her place at the doctor's side, that she might more easily direct the light where his narration dictated.

It was I who had suggested that Clemendy be added to the party, but when I offered to take charge of her Dora intervened, preferring to look after her pet herself. So wire cage in hand she joined Stinker and myself at the rear of the party. And thus arranged we strode into the cave mouth.

Indeed it looked very much like a mouth — like jaws spread wide to receive us, with jagged edges like teeth, and two immense boulders perched above it like eyes staring down.

Mattie's light sent a ghostly radiance into the chamber that opened up before us. At her post back of the doctor's shoulder, Flounce's head could be seen revolving first this way and then that, as her eyes alertly tracked the lantern's darting beams.

We had proceeded no more than a dozen paces, when the doctor suddenly lifted a hand and called for us to stop.

"Did anyone hear that?" he asked.

## Chapter Twenty-two

THERE was a pause of some seconds while we listened, but the noise, whatever it had been, was not repeated. One hears such strange things in a cave. Perhaps it was simply an echo of our footfalls which the doctor had heard; for even now as we were discussing it in low tones, echoes of our voices could be heard murmuring away into the distance.

As there seemed to be no imminent peril, we resumed our walk. Shadows sprang up and fled before the press of Mattie's light, its circle of radiance illuminating a broken ground of boulders and of chipped masses of rock that had crumbled from the walls and ceiling.

"Watch how you go," the doctor warned, "for it's rather a maze in here."

My eyes scanned the vaulted reaches, the pillars oozing slime, the sculpted shelves of stone, the fissures and recesses opening into mysterious, unknown depths. The shadows of the rocks lay like puddles of ink around leaking bottles, or loomed menacingly large upon the terraced slabs of earth.

"Seems a bit posh," Dora remarked. "I do hope they won't throw us out."

Through this labyrinth we took our careful way. But as there had been no return of the sound the doctor had heard, he saw fit to commence his narration.

"Mattie, your light here," "Mattie, your light there," he directed, and magically the yellow beam would flash over this geological curiosity or that, which the doctor then would describe for us. The beds of layered rock, in which might be read the long history of the dales, the overhanging courses, clusters of stalagmites, above all the shimmering deposits of flowstone — all were commented on with the doctor's experienced and very professional air.

Waxing poetic, he related how, in a distant era — "in the morning of the world" — the flow of river-water had helped to carve out this and other similar tunnels in the rock, which are so common a feature of the dales. But with the rise of the glaciers in a subsequent age, the waters had receded and become the hurrying stream all in Dithering knew so well. This all was in accord with the new glacial theories, which had excited the doctor's curiosity and fired his imagination when he had come to undertake his researches at Maunder.

It struck me while he was speaking that I had heard this talk of the doctor's before; indeed it seemed that I knew what he was about to say ere the words had left his lips. Now, how could this be? How had a solicitor from Hoggard come to know these things? When and under what circumstances had I gained this knowledge?

"For it was many years ago," the doctor went on, "that Mr. Lyell first proposed, incorrectly as it turns out, in his *Principles of Geology* that — "

We had advanced more deeply into the cave, having entered now a chamber much larger than any through which we had passed, when the doctor again called for a halt and stood a moment listening.

In the rucksack at his back Flounce had pricked up her ears and was listening too. *I heard it, Callander.*

A faint trickle and drip of unseen water. Was that all it had been, or had there been something more? Something stealthy and in motion beyond the trickle and drip?

"Who's there?" the doctor called.

Of a sudden I felt a creep at the nape of my neck. The passage in which we found ourselves had opened out into one of considerable height and depth, and in its arching vaults and craggy hollows sinister shadows dwelt.

Stinker glanced round with an uneasy and not very friendly curiosity. His hand closed about his sword-hilt. "Aye, 'tis the place, sir," he nodded, "but the pit it looks to be clean."

"This is the place?" Dora repeated. "And the pit? What place and pit are those, Mr. Callander?"

Mattie's redirection of the light threw the doctor's face into sharp relief. But ere he could respond I had answered for him.

"It's the place of the piskie. And the roasting-spit. And the — "

The doctor stayed me with a gesture.

"It is," he explained, "the place where Stinker and I had our skirmish with a creature of mythology and legend."

"Sure it bain't a piskie ye be a-meanin', sir?" Mattie asked.

Stinker jerked a nod. "Sure he do! Just along there it was, floatin' in air over our noggins like a horrid great beast-bug. Came for us it did, but the doctor he took a tumble over a boulder, backwards like, and down he went — "

The doctor felt the back of his head where the memory of it still lingered. "Knocked myself out," he said, in wry remembrance. "Fortunately Stinker managed to hurry the thing off with his blade."

This all was news to Dora.

"Then we must conclude," she said, "that a creature of mythology and legend the piskie is no longer?"

"The creature we encountered in this chamber was decidedly real. But whether it satisfies the definition of a piskie, or represents some other, altogether unknown species, is unclear to me. A capital bogey it is, though, to frighten folks with."

He went on to explain about the fire-pit, and the leavings of the meal he and Stinker had discovered there.

"The bones were those of a sheep and calf. Dr. Hankey was good enough to identify them for me."

"Then it be true, sir? This be the lair o' the poachers?" said Mattie.

"Possibly . . ."

"Well, there you are, then! Mr. Callander, you and I are in perfect agreement on that score," Dora said brightly. "What better headquarters than the Sideboard, unpleasant and inhospitable though it may be?"

"But I think as well it's no ordinary band of thieves who've chosen it. And there is something peculiar about the chamber itself."

He related that a general disturbance of the earth, signs of which were everywhere visible, at some time in the recent past had jarred this portion of the Cupboard. The cause of it, however, he had been unable to determine.

"But I don't believe it to have been a tremor, for its effects were limited to this single chamber."

A sudden growl of warning burst from the throat of Flounce, as a slight noise caught her attention — a bare breath of sound, which had alerted her keen ears and sent them swiveling about in search of the source.

*There it is again, so secret and sly! But where is it, Callander?*

Whiskers bristling, she gave a long, low-toned, drawn-out *miaow*, half-questioning, half-threatening, whose echoes reverberated through the chamber.

Stinker, fearing that some unseen horror might be readying itself for a pounce, drew his sword from its sheath. I followed his example. At the same time Mattie cast round her light. The doctor, observing that her hand trembled, gently took the lantern from her.

We strained our eyes in the gloom, but no danger rose up to meet us. Instead all was dead silence. The doctor swung the light here and there, before him and behind, but no bogey to frighten folks leapt at us from the chilly dark. The air reeked of slime and damp, but not a breath of it seemed to be stirring in this Cupboard of Eldritch's about which such evil things were whispered.

"What can it have been?" I asked.

The doctor, his eyes combing the dim recesses, made no answer.

"We must brace up our courage, then," Dora said at length, "and we'll soon thresh it out, I'm sure of it. Hallo, piskie? Piskie, are you there?"

The atmosphere in the room had become oppressive. The feeling of an intangible presence, stealthy, watchful, malevolent, was palpable to all.

"Stay behind me now," the doctor whispered to Dora and Mattie. Stinker by this time had taken Mattie's place at his elbow. Again the doctor flung round his light, his eyes scanning the deepmost pockets of the chamber.

Meanwhile Dora, more fascinated than afraid, had set down Clemendy's cage on a convenient shelf of stone.

At the doctor's back Flounce voiced a monitory howl. *It's here, Callander! It's right here!*

With a strange sense of foreboding — as if I had been through this same experience before — I glanced round and, revolving my cutlass, murmured — "Here it comes, I think . . ."

Scarcely had I spoken than, like an adder darting from its coil, a narrow ray of light, green and piercingly bright, shot forth from the darkness — from a blank rock wall, apparently — and grazed by me. For an instant, something like a cold mist seemed to probe my flesh. Then the light withdrew, only to flash forth again seconds later, on an altered trajectory, which sent it raking past Stinker's nose.

As one we sprang back in alarm, the doctor instructing us to seek cover behind the nearest fall of rock.

This way, that way — that way, this way — the light reached out again, and again — testing, probing, searching —

Incensed, Stinker demanded — "What's all this, then?" as if daring black-browed Eldritch himself to appear before us and explain it.

All at once the emerald ray darted over Clemendy in her cage on its shelf of stone. But this time it did not withdraw; instead it settled on her, spreading in a physical wave over her peculiar anatomy, from her furry snout and head-shield to her shell of bony scutes and the intimidating knob at her tail-tip.

Clemendy's ears twitched; her eyes, dazzled by the glare, peered curiously forth. She sniffed the air, as though sniffing the light, and swished her tail-armor to and fro. A moment later the light began to pulse, its brilliance alternately rising, falling, rising, falling.

What did it all mean?

With sudden decision Dora leaped to rescue her pet. But instead her arm was caught by the doctor, who drew her back to safety.

"Remain here," he said, speaking quietly.

"But Clemendy! She musn't be harmed, she musn't. Please, Mr. Callander — "

It was of no avail. The doctor would not release her.

"There is more here, Dora, than a beam of light," he said.

"'Tis true, missy," Stinker nodded. "A light be the least of it, 'out a doubt, in this damp hole."

We waited, hardly daring to breathe. In her cage Clemendy was heard fussing and squirming in her straw. Then, seconds later, the emerald ray vanished. The stillness returned, and for the present it seemed that our mysterious monitors, our band of poachers, might have fled the scene.

Band of poachers — band of villains! Who were they? Where were they? What sort of magic was it that could produce a ray of emerald light? For such a thing had never before been seen, except perhaps by the doctor and Dickie Fish.

"May I fetch her now?" Dora asked, a trifle impatiently.

The doctor gave her leave. In two shakes she was at the cage, and Mattie with her. But they were not quick enough.

Already I could hear it — a whirring noise like a droning of bees, the sound of wings beating lightning-fast, drawing swiftly nearer.

"See where it comes!" the doctor exclaimed.

From out of the dark there appeared a winged shape. Rapidly it descended towards us, before gliding to a stop in the air some few feet above our heads.

We drew back, half in surprise, half in horror. I felt the blood tingling in my veins; mechanically my hand tightened about my sword-hilt. I could feel my courage surging to the fore — now where had *that* come from?

And from where had come the thing that was hovering above us in the lantern-light?

It seemed to consist mostly of a head, a huge, egg-shaped cranium. Silvery, metallic, it was featureless but for a single, protruding goggle-eye, honeycombed and velvety like an insect's. This egg-head topped a minuscule body that was similarly hairless, and from which six delicate, crab-like limbs depended, whose fingered ends were less like claws than like tiny hands for grasping. At its back translucent wings were beating in such rapid motion they were little more than a blur in the light. It was from the wings that the droning arose.

No fluttery aireymouse this — no cave bat — but something more like an incarnate devil from the bottomless pit.

Flounce's hackles were up, as evidenced by the growling and hissing that issued from the doctor's rucksack.

"Body o' me — it *is* a piskie!" Dora exclaimed in amazement.

A moment later the thing abruptly swooped down, tiny limbs extended, their fingered ends making a grab at the wires of Clemendy's cage as though to bear it off.

In answer some forceful jettings of spittle like reflex sneezes came shooting from between the bars. Clemendy's timid little eyes erupted in flame; her tail, which she had been lashing restlessly in the straw, with exquisite precision thumped its bony knob against the cage just where the finger-ends of the piskie had snagged it, crushing them.

Dora voiced a shout as the cage, released from the piskie's hold, thudded to the ground. Straightway she and Mattie made a dash for the spot.

As the piskie swung about for another go, the doctor, his tall figure silhouetted against the light, commanded us to —

"*Up blades, and strike!*"

## Chapter Twenty-three

SWORDS uplifted, we closed on the piskie. Repeatedly, however, it swerved aside in the air, easily evading our thrusts and stabs. The height of the cave chamber enabled it to remain just out of reach, so that no hits were landed. The thing was vulnerable only when making a dive at Clemendy.

"Get along with ye — ye lunatic bugbear!" Stinker cried, after another pass with his blade had fallen short.

Burnished steel flashed in the lantern-light. The doctor hewed at the creature with broad, sweeping strokes, but like Stinker he found only empty space. My own experience was disappointingly similar. Attack after attack we essayed, lunge after lunge, each as ineffectual as the last. The piskie sprang here, sprang there, nimbly dodging our every blow. Meanwhile its huge goggle-eye remained fixed on Clemendy in her wire cage.

I was reminded of the savage vizard-mask hanging on a wall at the Pack Horse Inn.

*'Tis for safety's sake — a charm to protect the wearer.*
*Protect him from what?*
*Piskies! I knaws 'tis piskies! And I see'd one, too.*

"Deuce confound it, this is pointless," the doctor muttered. "We must give it Clemendy."

Dora, bent over the cage with Mattie, regarded him with dismay.

"You shan't," she protested. "Oh, Mr. Callander — you *mustn't!*"

"We must," the doctor explained, "or we'll have no chance of disabling the piskie — the term I use reservedly — so that we may learn what manner of thing it is."

"What manner of thing? But you called it a piskie."

"Yes — a convenient designation. But it's no more one of our 'piskies' of mythology and legend than I am. Look at it, Dora! That's no living, flesh-and-blooded creature. It's mechanical — made of metal."

"'Tis so, missie," nodded Stinker, breathing hard, "for when I did strike at the villain afore, after the doctor had his tumble, it rang like a bell."

"But why must we give it Clemendy?" Dora persisted. "And what can it want with her?"

"We must allow it another go at her," the doctor replied, "for only then will it be within reach of our weapons. So long as it remains aloft we are powerless to bring it down."

"I see. Do you suspect then what manner of thing it is?"

The doctor shook a spare negative. "Haven't a clue what it is. But unless we're able to subdue it we certainly shall learn nothing."

The indecision in Dora's face was evident — painfully so — as she struggled to make up her mind. Then her eyes of a sudden grew big as the piskie wheeled round again and with limbs outthrust made another dive for the cage.

At the last moment Dora hurled herself to one side, taking Mattie with her.

The finger-ends of the piskie closed on the cage and lifted it from the ground; seconds later the doctor and Stinker closed on the piskie.

Down came their whistling blades on its shiny egg-head and torso. Echoes of the crash and clank of steel on metal reverberated through the chamber. But no appendages were severed, and the piskie refused to yield up its prize. Instead it tugged the cage higher in the air. Jets of glypt-spittle came flying through the bars, bony tail-armor thudded against grasping finger-ends. But to no avail; the piskie's furiously-beating wings carried the cage away.

Peering forth, Dora exclaimed her alarm as Clemendy was borne off into the shadows.

The doctor whirled as if spun on a pivot.

"Stinker — the light!" he commanded.

Hurriedly Stinker took up the lantern and flung its beam piskiewards; at the same time the doctor shied a stone at the winged whatever-it-was, after the manner of his youth. Unfortunately he missed the whatever, but scored a hit on the cage bearing the whatsit. The shock jarred it free and it dropped with a crash.

As the piskie made another swoop to recover it, we sprang at the little monster with readied arms. Its egg-head snapped round with a jerk and was dealt a ringing blow by Stinker. With swift strokes we fell upon the thing, but it availed us little; a few scratches here and there were all that we managed to inflict. Plainly it was composed of sterner stuff than were our blades.

Meantime Dora had scooped up the cage and Clemendy and with Mattie was fleeing towards the outer chambers.

Alerted, the piskie halted in mid-flight and tracked them with its goggle-eye. This action brought another surprise, for when it faced round its wing-motion for a few moments ceased. Rather than fall to earth it remained suspended in the air, in seeming defiance of gravity. Then, seconds later, its wings commenced to beat again and it went racing after Clemendy.

Down it plunged, crab-like limbs outstretched, finger-ends poised for seizing. The collision caught Dora on the shoulder and she was thrown to the ground. Mattie shrieked and sought concealment behind a fall of rock. The cage, Clemendy, and Dora lay unprotected.

With a bound I sprang forward — I was closest — and threw myself Dora's way. Not knowing where the piskie was, I lashed out at it with my sword, praying I might land a hit. Speedily my prayer was answered. Straight up into the air shot my blade; straight down shot the piskie. However in groping for the cage the little monster was temporarily distracted, not heeding my weapon till the point of it had been driven deep into its goggle-eye.

The eye appeared to be made of softer material than was the head, my blade having pierced it to a depth of some six inches at least. The piskie made no cry, seemed not to feel pain; but that didn't mean it was not annoyed. In answer it rose up again, dislodged my cutlass, and fell upon me with a vengeance. Scarcely had it begun to pummel me with its finger-ends clenched into fists, than Stinker and the doctor bounded up and dealt the thing a veritable tempest of blows —

hewing, hacking, cracking blows — from which an answering storm of echoes was sent ringing through the Cupboard.

In the end it proved to be too much. Partly blinded perhaps, the piskie of a sudden vaulted into the air, hovered magically a moment with its wings stilled, then set them to beating again and in a burst of speed vanished in the gloom.

I took Dora's hand and lifted her up. Fortunately she was unhurt, and in excellent spirits. In characteristic Dora fashion she thanked me and the others for our aid, and remarked what a good job it was she had had the foresight to choose such manful gentlemen as escorts for the outing.

Having determined that the health of Clemendy was similarly unimpaired, she was brushing the cave-mire from her skirts when Mattie arose from her hiding-place. The maid's step was hesitating, uncertain, and her face wore a peculiar look.

Dora rushed to her at once. "Mattie — you're trembling!" she exclaimed.

The girl made no reply but, choking down her shame, broke into tears.

"Why, Mattie, what is the matter?"

"Oh, Miss Dora," she sobbed, "'tis a b-b-bad w-world — a terrible bad world — " and wrung her head in a despairing way. Then a shiver convulsed her slender frame, Dora managing to catch her as she swayed and nearly went down.

"Oh, miss," cried the maid, her eyes streaming, "forgi'e yer poor Mattie — for 'tis a coward I am — a spankin' great coward . . ."

"Mattie — dear Mattie — whatever do you mean?"

Her mild girl of a waiting-maid, her Mattie — so docile and neat, so prudent, so reliable, so entirely devoted — what can have wrought such a change in her?

She sat quivering on a stone shelf, her hands clutching it as if for dear life, like a limpet on a rock. Slowly, gradually, her grip on it eased, and with a handkerchief she began wiping the tears from her cheeks.

"Ascuse, miss," she sniffled, averting her glance — bereft she was, unable to meet her mistress's eye — "but cruel ashamed o' yer Mattie ye must be. For I did abandon 'ee, miss, when the danger 'twas upon us — oh, forgi'e yer Mattie — plaise do — "

Then she broke into sobs again and buried herself in Dora's arms, imploring her forgiveness.

Next it was Dora's turn to speak, and this she did in such kindly tones, so sympathetic yet so encouraging, it quite melted my heart to hear.

"Chin up, my girl! Come, you must shake off this mood of yours now. You mustn't give way to fantasies. Whatever do you mean — ashamed of my Mattie? You are my dear, sweet girl, and have been faithful to me ever since the day your poor mother placed you with us. And have I not always treated you in kind? Now push it from your thoughts, this little adventure of ours. For that's what one must do, or one surely must go mad. One must be doughty — not doughy! There is no cowardice when faced with a thing so unnatural as that we faced here today. Moreover, it was all my very own idea, and you and the others gamely went along. If any blame is to be attached, attach it to me. Do you hear? To *me*. For you're a sensible girl, Mattie, and always have been. Indeed it was for this reason I chose you."

There was a hush of some seconds; then, slowly, the maid lifted her eyes, having found courage enough to look her mistress again in the face.

"Oh, miss," she sniffled, gazing at her fondly, "thank 'ee — thank 'ee, miss — God bless 'ee! For yer Mattie she did go clean mazed today, I b'lieve . . ."

It hadn't escaped my notice that her mistress was a plucky young woman, as well as a pretty. In the brief time I had known her, I dare say I had come to admire Miss Dora Fetching. Her nerves and constitution appeared to be made of a stouter texture, like her father's. She had seemed without fear — indeed she seemed to have relished the day's adventure, caring little that she might have been injured by the piskie so long as the rest of us were unscathed.

Decided opinions notwithstanding, she was a woman of character, with an affectionate disposition, and had a well-developed sense of duty — again like her father. And, like her Mattie, she too was very sensible.

There is a kind of woman who never loses her presence of mind, even in moments of dire predicament, and who generally, even when stressed, sees and does instinctively, and with decision, what needs to be done. Miss Dora Fetching was that kind of woman.

*She's a peach, Callander* — or so I imagine is how Flounce might have expressed it. *Why, she has the pluck of ten men, I dare say!*

As it happened Flounce's head at that moment popped out of the doctor's rucksack, which had served as her snuggery for the duration.

*Well done! Taken care of the unpleasantness, have we? Put 'em to the rout, I see.*

"Well, we have had a proper time of it," Dora remarked, adding, with only a hint of irony — "What a dreadful place this Sideboard of yours is, Mr. Callander."

"Unless I'm greatly mistaken," I said, "this piskie is the same creature that a certain 'Cedar Jack', a woodsman I met at the Pack Horse Inn, was boasting he had driven off with his quarterstaff. It's too bad we were unable to snare the thing. But what did it want with Clemendy, do you think?"

"I fear it remains a puzzle, Mr. Earnscliff," said the doctor.

"And where did it come from? For it's like a thing from another world," Dora put in.

"Don't you mean a whatsit?" I asked.

Stinker threw out a stubborn jaw. "Whatsit? Nasty beggar, more like. A pox on't!"

We had collected Clemendy and the lantern and had turned our backs on the inner chamber, when a faint stirring in the dark behind us prompted us to arrest our steps.

An orange light had begun flowing up from behind a slab of rock on the far side of the chamber. It was as if a door in the ground had opened, disclosing the fires of the underworld. From below, noises of a skittery, rattling movement caught my ear.

A feeling of dread rolled over me in a wave. I hardly could move, so horrid was the sensation the orange light had evoked in my mind. There was a palpable menace to it, an impression of lurking evil, arising as if from the deepest depths of hell.

"What is it, Mr. Earnscliff? Is it further danger?" Dora asked, for she had seen the look in my face and it had startled her.

Coincidentally the same look had sprung into the face of the doctor.

"Let us cut this matter very short," he urged, and putting an arm each about Dora and Mattie he hurried the two of them along in the direction of the cave entrance.

Stinker and I followed at their heels. I had charge of the light, and Stinker of his small-sword, which he was brandishing in a most warlike manner as we beat our hasty retreat from the Cupboard.

## Chapter Twenty-four

A FTER retracing our way we lost no time in collecting our things, for we were in rather a hurry to be gone. Still it seemed to take an age, and many were the uneasy glances we cast behind us as we worked.

Upon reaching the secluded ground where we had left the wagonette, Stinker and I put in the bays while the doctor prepared the vehicle. Mattie, who had braced up her courage some, had been given charge of Clemendy and Flounce and resumed her seat in the back. I occupied the place next to hers, and Stinker the side-seat opposite. For the return journey Dora had asked if she might sit up front with the doctor.

And so arranged we took again to the road, the doctor lifting his team to a brisker pace that far outmatched that of the morning.

Morning! I could scarcely believe the afternoon was half gone, so far had we lost track of the time. But it was good to be clear of the Cupboard and at liberty again under Lingonshire skies, dismal and lowering though they might be. For the events of the past hour had cast a certain damp over our spirits.

While keeping a wary lookout, now and again I managed to overhear snatches of conversation between the doctor and Dora, as my place was directly back of theirs.

"My father will be disappointed," Dora remarked at one point, "as we found no poachers."

"There's no reason for him to be," said the doctor, "as I don't believe there are any poachers of the kind your father envisions."

"I never saw Mattie so shaken before. It's my doing — I shouldn't have brought her. She's sensible, but sensitive. She's the best-hearted girl I ever knew."

"I know. I like her too. We must make it up to her."

Dora glanced round her at the looming steeps that rose on our every side. The very trees themselves seemed watchful, she reflected, as though hiding many eyes.

"What is it that haunts these highlands, I wonder? It's a feeling I have. Or is it a memory perhaps? For the Woldfolk — "

"Do you still believe in these Woldfolk?"

"I can't say, really. I *think* I believe in them. For we live in such remote country, at times it seems that almost anything could be true. Still, I find it comforting in a way . . ."

We drove on in silence for a while, and then Dora asked —

"Mr. Callander, what was that orange glow?"

The doctor shrugged, not taking his eyes from the way ahead. But it did not satisfy Dora; and so —

"Poachers, and no poachers," he offered.

"What does that mean?"

"Truly, Dora, I don't know what it all means — not yet, at any rate. I expect it's not unlike your thoughts on these wolds. It's more a feeling than it is real knowledge, real proof. But there *is* something here . . ."

"And the light which fastened itself on Clemendy — what did *that* mean? And how is such a thing possible? For I never saw the like in my life."

The doctor cleared his voice, and was about to remark that almost certainly he had seen the same emerald ray — he and Dickie Fish — but then thought better of it.

"Is Clemendy in some danger, do you believe?" Dora asked.

"I think it likely — perhaps even probable. We shall need to keep a guard over her."

"But what should anyone want with my Clemendy?"

Again the doctor shrugged, and said he did not know.

She stole a sidelong glance at him. "For a college man, Mr. Callander," she smiled, "you appear singularly uninformed on a number of topics."

"As a college man one is forever striving after new knowledge, or should be; otherwise one never advances. To settle for 'received opinion' in any field of endeavor is a capital mistake. As for Clemendy, I'm in perfect agreement with you. I am singularly uninformed what it is they can want with her."

"They?"

"There are two of them at least — probably three — and only one of them is human. Yes, there is something here that does not belong . . . something of old . . ."

Broke in Dora, with that air of authority she could so whimsically assume —

"Pray, might you explain yourself a little better, Mr. Callander? After all it is my Clemendy who is in some danger, as you say."

"I can only conjecture at present," the doctor said, his eyes on the road yet lost in thought, "but I suspect they've lain hidden here for a very long time, these two — this so-called piskie and its master. The third is a newcomer."

"I see."

"What brought the two here is a mystery, but from my studies of the disturbed ground in the Cupboard, I believe their arrival to have been coincident with the — "

He glanced at Dora and saw that she was not listening, her attention having been drawn to something a distance off the road.

"Mr. Callander," she said, touching his sleeve, "now what do you suppose a gargoyle can be doing on the roof of that man Bothack's hovel?"

The doctor's glance traveled to the ruined side-cab on the hill, and there, perching in its thatch, he beheld the goggle-eyed piskie of the Cupboard. It appeared to be tracking our progress in the road, damaged ocular or no. As for Mawgan Bothack, he was not in evidence.

*For a hellish scrape do await 'ee ef 'ee durst challenge the Cupboard.*

"Is it following us, do you think?" Dora asked.

"I shouldn't doubt it."

"Mattie is facing the other way. I'm happy she can't see it."

"We shan't ask her to turn around."

Across my shoulder I had caught a glimpse of the "gargoyle"; and now Stinker had risen a little in his seat and was eyeing it fixedly, at which point the doctor shot him a look, alerting him to be less conspicuous.

And so we rattled along, the piskie keeping watch of us from the thatch, till we got round the turn in the cart-track and passed out of its view.

A wind had come up that was stirring the trees, and as it was at our backs had we hoisted a square of sail we might have doubled our pace. As it was we drove on without appreciable loss of time, or further sight of the piskie.

By day-down we were comfortably ensconced again in the parlor. There was a lovely fire roaring up the chimney, and with the wind scraping rough hands along the walls and windows, making doleful music, it was a very snug parlor indeed.

"I believe I shall long remember this little excursion of yours, Mr. Callander," Dora remarked from her place on the sofa. In her lap Flounce lay drowsing. This drowsing is a special form of cat-alertness having nothing to do with sleep — so I am told — in which the eyes remain watchful under heavy lids, the ears, though still, are open to every sound, and the lips are curled into a smile whose secrets only others of the cat-kind are privy to.

"Excursion of mine?" said the doctor, lifting his brows. "How do you mean? For as I recollect the idea was entirely yours."

"La you there, now! Excursion of mine? Did you hear the gentleman, Flounce? Why, whatever do persons such as *we* know of 'diluvium' or 'flowstone draperies' or 'terminal moraines'? What are 'convulsed strata' to us? That is what a guide is for."

Her caressing fingers, passing over Flounce's coat, had set in motion a rhythmic thumping of the calico's showy plume on the sofa-cushion.

"And as it is for the guide to do the guiding, and the guided to be guided," Dora went on smoothly, "however can the excursion have been mine? Why to follow your logic, Mr. Callander, it just as likely was Flounce's idea."

The doctor, knowing what awaited him, averted his head to hide a grin.

"I hope I shall not fall into so great a mistake again," he conceded.

It was the old familiar kind and playful despotism for which Dora was known, the same affectionate, ironical banter which the two had shared since they were children.

Dora's father meanwhile had endured a perfectly dreadful day. He had played host to the vicar, an occasion that never failed to staunch the free and easy flow of his spirits. The vicar for his part considered it a ministerial obligation to break bread as often as possible with the leading members of his flock. And of those leading members, Squire Fetching of the Moorings was the leadingest by far.

So it had come as a relief to the old dalesman when we ran over for him the particulars of our rather more eventful hours of the afternoon. He listened with alert attention, the little puffs of smoke rising from his lips like gray ghosts, that one by one went spiraling up into the ceiling. Needless to say he was amazed by it all, but sorely disappointed, as Dora had foretold, that not a one of the "blasted beggars" had been collared.

Our tale concluded, he levered himself up and stumped across to the bar, where he took wine and water, mixed himself a gobletful, and drank it off. Then, leg creaking, he returned to the sofa.

"By thunder, I wish I'd been there to see it, and to have lent you chaps a hand," he exclaimed, easing himself down again and resuming his pipe, "instead of wasting my time here with a glib young fellow in gaiters who spouts a lot o' damfool nonsense."

"Dad!" Dora cried. "That's a wicked thing to say of the vicar. It's most uncharitable of you."

"And it's most uncharitable of him to burden me with his nonsense," her father retorted, "and to drink the last of my port while doing it. Fellow thinks he's entitled to give counsel to every being he meets. I dare say he has a fancy for you, Dora — mark me. Ah, well. Anyhow I wish I'd been there, for we might've given the rascals a damned good thrashing. But there's nothing for it — blighter won't allow it," he sighed, with a disgusted rap at his leg. "Made of cork, you know. Well, they should have felt my supple-jack were I some twenty years to the younger."

"Not to worry, sir — it wouldn't have helped," the doctor assured him, "for our steel barely nicked it a scratch."

The Squire frowned. "How can that be? What sort of a thing is it, this piskie?"

"I believe only Mawgan Bothack can answer that."

The Squire made a disagreeable noise. "I'm obliged to you, Mr. Callander, for affording me proof for certain ill thoughts I've had of that blackguard. Surly as a butcher's dog, always looking out curses at people from under his brows! This 'ill-usage' he claims to have received at the hands of Dithering folk is all so much humbug. Keeping bad company is *that* scoundrel's trouble."

"I tend to agree with you."

"And what role, do you think, has Bothack in the matter of the Sideboard?" Dora asked. "Or was it coincidence the piskie was on his roof?"

"I think not."

The Squire laughed shortly. "The villain's in a fair way of being hanged — unconscionable rascal! Let him go to the devil, if he hasn't done so already. Let an indictment for calf-lifting be brought before the Bench, it stands to be the swiftest proceeding in the annals of the county — great sticks alive!"

"He can neither read, write, nor cipher, as I hear it," Dora said.

"In a ruder age," her father went on, "a cow-lifter and thief should have been — "

"Dad!" his daughter protested.

The Squire barked out another laugh and narrowed his eyes at the fire, grimly working his pipe in his teeth.

"He would certainly be a newcomer to this poaching. For these thefts, as I understand it, can be traced back many years before Bothack," I said.

"Correct," the Squire nodded between puffs.

"There has occurred in these dales, every six years or so, an 'outbreak' of this thievery — did you know that, Mr. Earnscliff?" Dora asked.

I answered that I did know it.

"Every six years — as regular almost as clockwork," the doctor added.

"I hadn't given it so much thought ere this. I wonder why I have not done so?" Dora mused. She looked at Flounce, who was purring contentedly in her lap, fan-tail dusting the cushion with its rhythmic swishes. From Flounce her thoughts turned rather naturally to Clemendy.

"Certainly the piskie is not consuming these animals," she reasoned, "for if it's a mechanical thingummy it has no need of digestion. And it can't have any relation to the Woldfolk — "

Her father raised his eyes to the ceiling. "Not her Woldfolk again — Obadiah Outland next — heaven save us from daughters reading books!" quoth the lord of the manor.

"As I was about to say," Dora flowed on smoothly, "these Woldfolk have no need or want to be poaching, for they are much in tune with animals. It would be entirely unlike them. Mr. Callander, you don't suppose it's Mawgan Bothack who is angling to eat my Clemendy? For I think she would be a tough nut to swallow."

The doctor was regarding his folded hands in thought, and did not immediately answer.

"Perhaps this thievery is in retaliation for the perceived slights at the hands of his neighbors in Hog Gut Lane?" Dora ventured.

"Now there's a sensible suggestion," her father said. "For the beggar has a history of hurling back offered kindness. He's funny in the head that way. And there's not a man jack in Dithering knows his means of income. Mark me, he's bent on mischief."

"Stealing to support himself, do you mean, sir — under cover of superstition?" I asked.

"But Colley and his sons found nothing at the hovel," the doctor pointed out.

"Could it have been Bothack coming up from below there in the Sideboard?" Dora said. "Perhaps there's another chamber underneath where he hides his spoils?"

The doctor's headshake was firm. "It wasn't Bothack," he replied, "although he is tarred with the same stick."

As for myself I shivered inwardly at the recollection of the orange light — and yet could scarcely tell you why.

"Such a mechanism as this piskie," I speculated, "must be a secret of some arcane science that lies entirely beyond our understanding."

"I wish *I* understood what the orange light signified, and the emerald ray too. I believe Mr. Callander knows more about them than he cares to tell," Dora hinted, "and for that matter I believe so do you, Mr. Earnscliff."

"Miss Fetching," I returned, a trifle surprised, "I can assure you categorically that I do not!"

It was the truth, as best I knew it. Yet still unexplained was the feeling of dread that had washed over me in the Cupboard, the sense of some unspeakable horror which the orange glow had evoked in my mind.

But Dora well saw where it all was pointing. *And only one of them is human.* The celebrated doggerel next moment she called up from memory —

> *Hickory, dickory, dare.*
> *The piskie flew up in the air.*
> *The man in the Cupboard*
> *Hisself is no sluggard.*
> *Hickory, dickory, dare.*

Was it a man — or a monster — whose approach had been signaled by the orange light flowing up from below?

"It isn't as if we ourselves are in imminent danger of extinction," Dora went on, "but every six years or thereabout it seems that livestock round here mysteriously go trotting off — and sometimes people do, too. It's as though this monster every six years is roused for a spell from its slumber to gorge, before returning to its lair for another doze of some half-dozen years."

"Like a cave bear or short-face in hibernation?" I suggested.

"Perhaps our hibernator is the Giant Eldritch himself?"

Her father's bushy eyebrows hoisted. "Good Lord, now it's giants in cupboards," he exclaimed.

As for Dr. Callander, he had lapsed into a thoughtful silence. I could see that he still was trying to work it out, trying to make sense of it all in his mind.

What then of that other light — the piercing green ray which had darted searchingly round the Cupboard?

"It was chilly cold when it grazed you, Mr. Earnscliff," said Dora, "and Stinker felt the same. I've never heard of anything like it in connection with poachers, or in any way whatever. Have you, Dad? No? Well, we'll not blame it on the Woldfolk then, though it's very convenient to blame things on folks who can't be seen. But why was it drawn to Clemendy?"

"Apart from the light, perhaps there is a more mundane explanation," I suggested.

"What is that, Mr. Earnscliff?"

"Well, pocket glypts as a species are rare and valuable items, certainly in these parts. Clemendy was the one specimen your shopman in Medlow had on offer, and his asking price was rather dear. Surely most everyone in Dithering must know of her by now."

"Do you mean someone is looking to steal her — in order to sell her? Who could it be but that rude fellow Bothack? For certainly not the piskie . . ." Dora considered a moment, exchanging glances with her father and myself.

The doctor meantime unfolded his long figure from his chair.

"For the present your 'whatsit' will bear close watching," he reminded her.

"I shall guard her myself, of course. Do you know, Mr. Callander, it never occurred to me that anyone should have such wicked designs on my poor Clemendy."

## Chapter Twenty-five

CLEMENDY twitched an ear as a sudden gust of wind blew by the window and rattled the panes behind the curtain.

The rich wainscot oak on the walls glimmered up to the ceiling-beams, and in its glossy panels weird shadows cowered and quivered.

Then the wood-fire was raked out, as Dora made her preparations for bed. She folded back the covers, smoothed her pillow, then sat down to her dressing-table for a last inspection. On her *toilette* stood a little old-fashioned sort of mirror, in a filigree frame, and in its glass Dora saw reflected a little, old-fashioned sort of person, which is how she often viewed herself. Old-fashioned, out of style perhaps — like her dad and the Moorings. And that was just the way she liked it; for father and daughter, despite their differences, had much in common.

Her hair fell like silky rain to her shoulders. Of course it was not half so long as it had been in times gone by, but it pleased her now that it was shorter — it was easier to manage — and as the years passed she fancied its length became her better. Having shaken down her tresses, she gathered them in her slender fingers and began to brush them.

The rising wind sent another gust scurrying along the casement. Again the noise drew the attention of Clemendy, her nostrils quivering as she sniffed the air. Mattie already had retired to her sleeping-apartment, which was *en suite* with Dora's. So too had Clemendy retired — to her little cushioned bed in a box, which lay at the foot of Dora's four-poster. The little bed had been made for her by young Stokes at Callander farm, who was handy that way.

Seeing her now Dora of a sudden rose and, joyfully snatching her up, lifted her high into the air. Instinct caused the glypt to curl itself zow-bug-like into a ball, her squat little feet drawn into her shell and her clubbed tail gone limp.

"My dinky girl — my whatsit — such a roly-poly you are!" Dora exclaimed, gazing upon her fondly as if she had been the most ordinary kitten or puppy-dog. Then down again she plunged and restored Clemendy to her nest at the foot of the four-poster, before resuming her seat at the dressing-table.

No more than a minute had passed, ere Dora became conscious of a vague stir that had grown upon the quiet. Swiftly it rose in volume on the night air — a chorus of hounds — the hounds of her father's kennels, alerted to the presence of an intruder.

Dora put by her brush and listened. Above the din she could hear her father's voice calling for lights, lights, and instructing the men — trusty lads, every one — to redouble their watch on the barns.

*Poachers!*

For a moment she contemplated donning her clothes and rushing forth to give aid. Then, upon reflection, she instead tucked her dressing-gown more closely about her and resumed her brush.

Hist! What was that?

A slight sound, nearer at hand, caused her to start.

There it was again!

She rose to immediate and alert attention, and felt something cold tickle her down the length of her spine. Her late grandmother, she recalled, used to tell her it was an omen from her guardian spirit that some danger impended.

Time slowed its pace to a crawl. Dora cocked an ear, listened to the baying of the hounds, the scraping of the wind, the voices of the lads . . . and something more?

Directly, she knew not why, her attention became focused on the window — the shut casement and drawn curtain. Moments later she heard something that was *not* the wind scamper across the bars, stop, and then . . .

Along the window there stole a furtive, rustling sort of touch, as of someone feeling uncertainly for the way in.

Alarmed, Dora summoned her energies — but did not act, not

wishing at first to open the curtain, not wanting to see what might be there.

Came a faint *tap-tap-tapping* on the glass.

It was the terror of the unknown. Even Dora's considerable nerve for the moment seemed in danger of failing her. She felt the hair stir upon her head, the dampness spring out upon her brow.

*Tap-tap-tap!*

In her little box Clemendy had risen up and was swishing her tail-club to and fro, in a posture of defiance. Her ears were twitching, her eyes were two glowing spots of flame, the spittle was gathering in her gorge; in brief, she looked ready and able to take on all comers.

Seeing this, Dora's innate strength of heart reasserted itself. Every last drop of fear she cast from her, like a spaniel wringing the water from its coat.

*Tap-tap-tap!*

Having regained her courage, Dora stole lightly to the casement. Her hand reached for the curtain, then paused — and there she stood awhile, hesitating.

Behind her she caught the steady swish-swish of Clemendy's tail.

*No, no, this won't do . . .*

I believe ultimately it was Dora's curiosity which spurred her to act — this, and her desire to keep safe her little whatsit from out of time.

At a stroke she flicked the curtain aside, and stared through the leaded panes at the shiny egg-head and glaring goggle-eye of the piskie.

Walking slightly crabwise, its claws gripping the iron fencing of the casement, the little monster peered at her through the bars. Seconds later one of its grotesquely-sharpened finger-ends reached in and made contact with the glass.

*Tap-tap-tap!*

Riveted by the sight — by the irresistible fascination of nightmare — Dora found she could not take her eyes from it.

Was it the piskie that had brought the hounds out?

But almost at once another thought struck her. Was it she herself the piskie's gaze had fastened on — or was it looking beyond her at Clemendy in her little cushioned bed?

*Is it following us, do you think?*

Not only had it followed them, it knew now where to find the glypt.

The idea of it — the monstrous, unholy injustice of it, the sheer inexplicability of it — produced a sudden upswelling of anger and resentment in the breast of Dora.

"Hateful thing!" she snarled, and with a jerk of her hand she flung shut the curtain.

## Chapter Twenty-six

"MARNEN' to 'ee, Miss Dora!"

"Good morning, boys."

"And a fine marnen' it be, too. 'Tis kind of 'ee to make so free."

The "boys" were graybeards, mostly — farmers, retired dalesmen, superannuated retainers and the like, past their working time of life and with little now to occupy their hours. From their musings they had been roused by our arrival — or more correctly by Dora's arrival, which never failed to produce a stir amongst their numbers.

They rose at her approach, old men but hale, though the weight of innumerable winters lay on their heads. But those heads were unbowed, save in deference to Dora as she passed by them, the rest of us following in her wake. Eyes peering from whiskered faces turned their admiring gaze on her; she in her turn delighted them with her lively fashionable stare, with its hint of impudence and sprightly dash of spirit.

"Go on now about your business, boys, and don't you in the least mind us," was her amiable directive.

Obligingly they resumed their seats. It was remarkable, however, how far their posture had improved, how nicely their hair and beards had been smoothed down, their coats and collars tidied. Several enterprising gallants went so far even as to remove their hats. Although leathery old dalesmen all, they turned green as gourds in the presence of so handsome and popular a damsel as Miss Dora Fetching of the Moorings.

"You have many acolytes," I observed, as we sat down to a table there in the coffee-room.

"The boys are old friends of my father's and of our family," Dora explained. "I've known them since I was no higher than this."

Whether beaming contentedly at each other, or chuckling in their beards over some new jest, or venting the latest gossip that had come their way, the boys found their hearts lightened, their day brightened simply by Dora's presence amongst them. And taking in hand their cups again they went on about their business.

"Pasty was capital."

"Fine dish o' tay, this."

"What the jiminy? Coffee at tay-time? Why, what's up with 'ee, Tomas?"

"I dunnaw — 'tis quignogs, I'spose. But 'tis a coffee-room, an't it?"

"'Tidn' in nature for mortal to go widout tay at tay-time . . ."

This coffee-room of the Pack Horse Inn looked much the same as it had done in the days when the boys' grandparents had been little boys and girls. Generations in Dithering had come and gone, been born and buried, and still the coffee-room was the coffee-room, and so it would remain. Times and the world might pass by and change, but the Pack Horse Inn was immutable.

Warm and welcoming, a snug retreat with a cheery bay window overlooking the road, was the coffee-room. Its woodwork, like most of that in the house, had been buffed and polished to the tint of old ale until it gleamed. Colored prints of pack-horses and angling scenes hung upon the walls, as did a man-sized map of the sundered realm illustrating the extent of the long coast and its varied towns and cities. A fieldstone hearth, a deal dresser loaded with plates and dishes, a high-backed settle, sideboard, and other accessories completed the picture.

It had been a few minutes shy of eleven when we reined up in the courtyard. We had driven to town on some errands of business related to the Moorings and Callander farm. These accomplished, we had swung round to the inn for some light refreshment, the coffee-room, which lies opposite the taproom, opening conveniently off the yard.

As we sat down to our table Flounce sprang from her club bag. Nonchalantly, her plume waving in the air, she sauntered to the fireside, investigated the rug a spell with inquisitive nostrils, then threw herself down and commenced her grooming.

*Call me if you need me. If you have rodents in the house, I am your mouser — remember the old days, Callander?*

A waiter came in response to the bell, and not far behind him was Mr. Readymoney, when he learned that Miss Dora Fetching was of our party.

The landlord greeted us with his usual excess of courtesy, in particular where Dora was concerned. Seeing her, his spirits rose considerably; in fact he was quite beside himself. He asked how our wants this morning might be addressed, but as our wants were few — some ginger tea, coffee, a few sundries — he left us in the capable hands of the waiter. Bowing, he inquired then if there was aught else he might do for us, and accepted, in his capacity as postmaster, some letters from the Squire and Callander farm to be sent off.

"You'm welcome, Miss Dora, you'm kindly welcome. And Mr. Callander, too. Mail coach she'll be 'long dreckly now, never 'ee fear."

And so saying he bowed again, and smiled, and bowed again, and smiled, and bowed again, until he had bowed himself right out at the door. For in the eyes of the proprietor, as in those of the boys, "the like o' Miss Dora for beauty ne'er stepped in these dales," it being always an especial event whenever she graced his establishment with her lovely self.

The whole of the next hour we spent discussing a certain plan we had in mind concerning the pocket glypt and the piskie. More correctly it was the doctor's plan, which he described for us now in full. It was a plan in which Clemendy was to be taken to Callander farm, secretly, that we might fool the piskie and Bothack into believing her still to be in Dora's apartment. At the farm she would be safely secured behind bolts and bars, and under the constant watch of Stinker and Natty. At the same time a trap would be laid for Bothack at the Moorings. For now that the piskie had traced Clemendy to that place — so the doctor reasoned — it was Bothack who might be delegated to collect her.

His scheme met with instant favor. The seizure of Bothack in the act would be compelling evidence of his role in the business of the stock thefts, and Eldritch's Cupboard. Perhaps then the mystery of the disappearances might at long last be solved, and the truth behind it revealed.

"For I intend to learn what has been afoot in the Cupboard," the doctor said — "the how, the why, and by whom. All this Bothack knows, I believe, and will tell us when he understands that the game is up."

"Are you certain of that? Perhaps he'll refuse to speak," I suggested.

"I believe he'll speak once the facts have been made clear to him, and his support has been removed. He is no fool."

The plan sufficed for our purpose. We could see no flaw in it, so long as the removal of Clemendy to the farm went unobserved. At the Moorings the dogs would be kenneled, and a cellar door left unlatched — accidentally on purpose — through which the villain might gain entry. Inside, in the kitchen, our forces would be awaiting him with weapons drawn.

Even now — indeed since last night — Clemendy remained under guard. In our absence she had been left in the care of Mattie, Stokes having ridden over from the farm to assist her. Certain of the stablehands had been posted round the house, at tactical intervals, should Bothack or the piskie elect to show themselves in daylight.

Without a doubt the events of yesterday had thrown a scare into Mattie. The world had taken a wrong turning, in her view; but in the interval she had braced up her nerve marvelous well. Now there was a growing belief that the capture and interrogation of Bothack would bring a speedy end to the trouble, and provide an answer to that question we found especially baffling —

Whatever did Bothack and the piskie want with so indigestible an item as Clemendy?

## Chapter Twenty-seven

R OUND about this time it came to my notice that we were being watched. It was not so much by the boys — who largely had resumed their business as Dora had requested — but by a couple of others, whose grinning faces one moment peeped in at the door, the next darted back, then peeped in again, like two children at play.

And how like children they were: the plump, apron-bellied youth, he of the shock-top of curly red hair; and his companion, the moldy-looking little man with fluffy side-whiskers and a battered Scots tam. The shock-top belonged to Gilbert, the nephew of Mr. Readymoney, and resident pot-boy — an awkward, unmannered dowdy — and the tam to Toad Henry, feckless, and forever short of funds.

Such were the innocents who had bolted from the taproom for a glimpse of Dora.

Gilbert, like many another swain in the neighborhood, had long admired her from afar. The sad-dog sort of feeling came strongly upon him now as he ogled her from the passage.

"An't she a chicky-sweets," he drooled, in a rapture of affection. His eyes were round and watery, and his cheeks quivered like blancmange.

His companion respectfully doffed his tam. Fonder of refreshment than of feelings, he had been treading on thin ice of late. Those few friends of his upon whom he relied to "stand treat" had become less giving of their coin. As a result he had been forced to go without, as he himself hadn't a ducat to his name. His daily flow of grog — his *wee drap o' dripshan* — had diminished to a trickle.

Now leaning in, tam in hand, a smile on his blubber-lips and an air of ingratiation in his eye, he was hoping to attract Dora's notice, and by this means her sympathy. Nonetheless he would take his drap o' dripshan from most anyone — Dr. Callander for instance, or even myself, the stranger Sassenach from Hoggard. For "broadclaith or tartan, 'tis a' the same tae Henry."

As for Dora — light-filled, charming Dora, lively and alert — well, Dora simply was Dora. Not one of your grim, prim, secret-looking girls was the daughter of Squire Fetching of the Moorings. She and the rest of us understood that if a hint was worth a dram, then Toad Henry must be thirsting aplenty today. And so we ignored him, and his drooling playfellow too. Until —

"H'yur's a stale ould yarn," sounded an ominous voice behind the gawkers.

Mr. Readymoney, frowning his annoyance, stood with feet wide apart and arms akimbo, eyeing the infants who had fled his taproom. He had seen this game before.

"Wasson, now? What be doin'? For Miss Dora she bain't no giglet to be a-geekin' at."

"Blimey nuncle," complained Gilbert, "but I likes a pretty chicky-sweets, I do."

"Chicky-sweets?" flung back the landlord, aghast. "Chicky-sweets? I'll chicky-sweets *you*, my lad, see ef I don't. I'll send 'ee home to yer mama, sarten sure, ye great loblolly. Chicky, is't? Cheeky more like! For you'm talkin' downright foolish. Chicky-sweets? Miss Dora? The Squire's own daughter? You'm potty, y'are."

"'Tis pot-boy, nuncle," corrected Gilbert.

"*Cheeky swats* — off with 'ee!" said Mr. Readymoney, a flick of his dishcloth sending his nephew scurrying to the taproom.

Never had there been such a backsliding generation. The landlord turned to his other nursery charge.

"An' what of 'ee, Henry? 'Tis mischief agen, I s'pose?"

"Dinna fash," the Scot answered mildly, "for I do forgie ye, Maister Raidymoney, for yer unkind words, the whilk do pain me tae the quick tae hear. Speer me nae questions, and I'll tell ye nae lies — 'tis ma thirst, sir. Deil a drap hae I tasted the day, an' mysel' famishin' the noo for ma pickle dram. Aweel, 'tis a wicked warld, sir, wicked. Howandever, mebbe by the kindness o' the braw bonny maid — "

"'Tis house rules — no beggars in the coffee-room," said the landlord, firmly.

"Guid save us! Fie for shame, sir — an' can it be sae? Juist 'cause a body craves a wee keek at the lassie there?"

"So 'tis. No beggars. And no keeks."

The sometime jowster wrung his head dolefully. "Tae think — 'tis come tae this, an' mysel wi' no a drap o' dripshan in ma wame. No e'en ma pickle dram, sir, tae haud ma auld heart up?"

"No coin," said the landlord, "no drink," and with a stern finger he pointed the loiterer in the direction of the street-door.

"Ma heart is sair to see't. Get hame wi' ye — is't wha' ye be sayin', Maister Raidymoney? Sheer off an' be gane? Away wi' ye?"

"Ef 'ee plaise, Henry," smiled Mine Host.

"I canna see wha' for I should. Mickle gude may it do ye! Aweel," he sighed, "'tis the waeful luck o't. Ony gate, I'm fair amazed at ye. 'Tis twenty years hae I ken'd ye, an' no sae muckle as a wrang word hae I droppit in passin'. Dooms me, 'tis a wicked warld indeed." And having screwed himself sufficiently down into his trousers he strode away, shaking his head.

"The ould sinner's some thirsty today, right 'nough," the landlord grumbled. But order had been restored. His eyes scanned the coffee-room, to see that all was well.

*Still the prettiest girl in our dales, I'll bet a biscuit. Better Mr. Callander had married her when the stars was favorable. Though I bain't one to gossipy . . .*

By this time we had finished our discussion, and the doctor having paid the reckoning — he insisted — he collected Flounce and her club bag and we took our leave.

The door to the taproom lay across the corridor, and as we were passing it Stinker halted, his attention drawn to a thing he saw hanging on a far wall of the room. It was the goggle-eyed vizard-mask — the so-called "Eye of Days."

His curiosity renewed, he asked whether he might be allowed another peer at the relic. For a full minute he stood before it, examining it again in all its particulars. Then he stretched hesitating fingers towards it, as if he were half afraid the nasty little thing might bite them off.

"Did ye ever see such a clock in yer life? Ooh, it's awful."

"S'posed to be," said the landlord. "For 'ee see, Mr. Stinker, as my auntie Elva Blossom did tell it, 'tis to be worn on the face, the vizard is, so the piskies won't trouble 'ee. 'Tis to doodle 'em, by makin' 'ee out to be one o' their own. H'yur — have 'ee a go at it."

Stinker reached it down from the wall, then gingerly set it to his grizzled countenance, fitting one eye to its single eye-hole. Through the opening he gazed wonderingly out, as through a window onto another world.

From her club bag Flounce regarded him with interest, as if she were comparing the one visage to the other, Stinker's to the mask's. *It's a remarkable likeness — absolutely bang on.*

"And 'twas old folks as made it?" Stinker asked.

"Woldfolk," Dora said, "or so it's believed. However, there's no one who knows for certain who made it."

"Don't see it," Stinker sniffed, taking the object from his face. He looked at it again and grimaced. "Still don't care for it at all."

The landlord returned the mask to its place. Stinker, hanging his hat on his head at a cocky angle, shot it a parting glance that might have stared it out of all countenance.

"Piskies? Crikey, what a clock. *Shoo!*" he muttered, and promptly dismissed it from his thoughts.

There was another sort of clock, the gruff old giant of a long-case in the corner, was marking dutifully the passing seconds as we stepped by it towards the street-door. The doctor had requested that the shay-cart be brought round from the yard, and already we could hear the *trit-trot* of Bob's shoes and rattle of wheels on the paving.

"Hallo! There she is again," I exclaimed.

The others glanced at me in some confusion. I had observed that Bob was being led from the yard by a female groom, whom I recognized instantly as that same young woman I had spied at the Moorings, but of whom the doctor and Dora had claimed no knowledge. I brought this curious fact to their notice, and inquired of the landlord who this female groom of his might be.

He seemed puzzled. "No such groom h'yur, sir," he said, scratching his chin.

I looked again, and saw that indeed there was no female groom. There was only the ostler, standing quietly at Bob's head.

This was getting to be too much. I searched around and under the cart — no girl there. I turned and hurried back to the yard and looked up and down it — no girl there either. I looked to the left, to the right, from the coffee-room door to the range of timber stabling. I did not see the girl.

Perhaps she had escaped by the postern gate? I questioned a servant lad who happened by. He knew of no girl, he said; and as for the postern gate — "There bain't one," he informed me, and shuffled off.

Up the yard a chaise was being readied by the helpers. I spied the postilion approaching on his jockey's little legs, buttoning his waistcoat in preparation for departure. I interrogated him as I had the lad. He considered a moment, then slanted a keen look one way, then another way; then he glanced my way and, settling the chin-strap of his shiny white hat, replied that he had seen no female groom, sir — that indeed he had never before heard of such a being, sir.

*Where can she have gone?*

I gestured vaguely. "But she must have run past you. Surely you saw her."

No, sir, he told me, she had not done so, nor had he done so, for no such person had come within miles of him. But upon his return, he confided to me with a nod and a wink, he would be much obliged if I might introduce her to him. Then grinning he touched a parting hand to his hat, swarmed astride his mount, and off went he and the chaise with a clatter into the road.

I still was by no means satisfied. But what else was there to do?

With a thoughtful tread I returned to the cart and mounted to my seat. Bob Cob lifted his ears, and the others, already in their places, regarded me sympathetically.

"My wits," I explained, "must be on holiday."

"Ah, but Mr. Earnscliff," Dora said brightly, "we had understood you *were* on holiday?"

## Chapter Twenty-eight

WE had traversed the little cobbled lane which serves as the chief thoroughfare of Dithering, and climbed into the road that led to the Moorings and Callander farm, when the doctor abruptly reined in Bob and brought him to a stand.

"Is there something amiss?" I asked.

"Not at all, Mr. Earnscliff. Stinker, has Natty collected the paddles and eel-basket we spoke of, do you know?"

"Ain't had a smell of 'em yet," was the reply.

"Do you mean those from the skiff?" Dora said.

"Yes. You'll recall — Natty had offered to varnish the paddles for you, and to mend the door of the trap," the doctor explained. "For he enjoys such tasks and is an apt hand at them."

"Yes, he made Clemendy's bed for her as well. Did you think to collect them now?"

"As good a time as any, as it's just along the path there. And you can show Mr. Earnscliff how the Moorings got its name."

"That's a jolly idea," Dora agreed. "Come along, Mr. Earnscliff — and prepare yourself for a shock."

I had no notion what she and the doctor had in mind, but as they already had clambered down from their places I followed their example. Stinker meanwhile had been detailed to remain with Bob and the cart.

We set off on the winding path that runs above the stream, a little below the Moorings. On our left a broad sweep of ground ascended to the house; on our right the bank rolled steeply down to the waters as they flowed curling and rushing between two shores. As we trod along it the path described a bend round the foot of the slope, so that after some minutes Stinker and the cart were lost to view.

In time we arrived at the quay, which was of fieldstone and brick. Alongside it a small skiff had been drawn up on the shingle.

"Behold," Dora announced with a lordly wave, "there before you, Mr. Earnscliff, lie the far-famed 'moorings' to which our house owes its title. Tell me — the truth now — are you shocked?"

Moss-grown and moldering, these far-famed moorings of hers with their single mooring-post unquestionably were in a dismal state. An open railing some four feet high, made of deal boards, guarded much of the perimeter. Weather-worn steps led down to the skiff.

"The waters are not in spate at present," Dora explained, as she and I took places at the rail, "otherwise our bark there should be gaily afloat. I'm afraid it's rather a crumbly old thing, this quay of ours — been this way for years. Its history goes back centuries. In days of yore there used to be many more of us Fetchings, and those who remain are not of such sailorly stock as were our ancestors. In times past these moorings were rather more extensive — three, four posts even — and a fleet of skiffs graced the line. This was before the sundering, of course, when the stream waters were more robust — but then Mr. Callander has told you about that. Suffice it that *tempora mutantur*, etc., etc."

It was a delightful spot, and I allowed my eyes to roam about the varied scene. Meantime the doctor had ambled down the steps to collect the paddles and basket-trap from the skiff. The stream murmuring through the firs, the quiet plashing upon the shingle, the wooded slopes, the occasional note of a bird ringing distantly like a dropped coin — a delightful picture it was indeed.

"It isn't so shocking," I remarked at length, "indeed it's a wholly natural evolution, I should think. I expect brethren of the angle have found inspiration at this railing as well. And perhaps a philosopher or two? For peace and solitude always have been conducive to deeper thoughts. The rush and chatter of the waters, the chiming brook, the eddying pool, the tangy scents of spruce and pine drifting down from the wolds — "

"Are you by chance a philosopher yourself, Mr. Earnscliff? Or is Mr. Izaak Walton your chief inspiration?"

"Neither I'm afraid, Miss Fetching. Only a humble solicitor from Hoggard."

"Who is on holiday?"

"Who is on holiday."

We were standing side by side at the rail, watching the doctor as he took the paddles and eel-trap from the skiff.

"Why did Dr. Callander leave Maunder College?" I asked — a trifle boldly, perhaps.

"But Mr. Earnscliff, surely we have been over this? He wished to return home and become a farmer, like his fathers before him."

"But was this his sole reason for so doing? For abandoning his career?"

Dora lifted her eyes to me. At the same instant a stray sunbeam pierced the mist, flooding her face with light.

"Why, Mr. Earnscliff," she inquired, "what other reason can there have been? Besides, he hasn't abandoned his career — not entirely, at any rate. He has his researches he carries out, when the opportunity is afforded him. For farming is no easy work, you know, requiring long hours and with not much chance for laying by. Although the farm remains on troubled waters, as he says, he is at least rowing now with the tide. For to crop, stock, clean, and manure fifty acres is — "

The next moment the eyes of Dora spun away from me, as I felt the ground give a little under my feet. A piece of the crumbly quay, along its edge where the years had gnawed it, had broken loose. Just where Dora was standing it had broken, and the fragments sent crashing to the shingle below. The railing-boards had been severed as well and, splintering, trailed the fragments into space.

Time seemed to stop and lose its meaning as I wavered dizzily on the brink. At my elbow I saw Dora stagger forward, unable to arrest her tumble from the precipice.

Mechanically — as if by a reflex, without resort to thought — my hand shot out, catching Dora as she fell. For an instant we tottered there, the pair of us, on the edge. Gripping her by the wrist, I held her and did not let her go; for without the support she would have plunged headlong.

But it did not last, for I had not the strength. The yawning space over the shingle beckoned and I felt us toppling.

From the corner of my eye I saw the doctor frozen in breathless, horrified silence in the skiff. What could he do, the poor man, other than listen and look? He gave an anguished cry, that was all; he had no power to help; he never can have reached us in time.

It was then the miracle happened. As we were about to be hurled onto the rocks my free hand, flailing backwards, slapped against the mooring-post — the single mooring-post, sole survivor of the many. Hungrily my fingers coiled round it; I lofted a prayer; and the post, planted in firmer ground, held. With a mighty heave I willed myself back from the brink, from the abyss, from sure oblivion, bringing Dora with me.

Dimly I heard boots crunching the gravel of the stone steps as the doctor mounted them, two by two, in feverish haste.

A terribly long moment passed. Dora's face had turned a deathly, ghostly white. The near-disaster had left her in a world of confusion, of amazement — confusion as to its cause, amazement that we had been spared a lethal drop to the shingle below. Indeed it left both of us gasping for air, as in a fit of exhaustion we stumbled back from the precipice.

"Body o' me," quavered Dora's small voice, "my heart seemed almost to leap from my throat . . ."

Then the doctor came hurrying up, fear starting out of his soft, quiet eyes.

"In the name of twenty devils," he exclaimed, "how did this happen?"

I shrugged in a vague sort of way. Having ascertained that Dora was well and had not been hurt materially, I was content. She stood trembling at my side, clinging to me with both her hands.

"Bless you, Mr. Earnscliff," she murmured. "Bless you. What a sinister and a dreadful thing it would have been . . ."

She found it difficult to take her eyes from the precipice — from the sinister and dreadful thing that might have been — and was staring at it with a kind of fascinated terror. Then a qualm of panic came over her and she might have swooned, had not the doctor and I been there to catch her. Almost at once, however, she recovered herself. She set her teeth, as if willing the color to return to her cheeks. But though she maintained an outward ease I think she still was fighting off the idea of the precipice.

Ensued the sort of reverent hush that follows any such wondrous escape from catastrophe. I disengaged myself from Dora's grip and delivered her into the doctor's arms. In his relief he drew her to him with an almost exaggerated gentleness, as though she were the most delicate china and the slightest jolt might have finished her. She pillowed her cheek against him, at about the level of his top waistcoat-button; for you know the doctor was rather taller than she. Both of them were breathing easier — as indeed was I — now that the danger had passed. She raised fond eyes to him — eyes that were big and starlike, that did not leave him — and smiled. Such a world of meaning in her glance!

It shamed me that even for a second I might have viewed the doctor as a sort of rival for her affection. For rivals the doctor had none — so spoke the world of meaning in Dora's eyes. Her lips quivered with words she could not express; then suddenly she flung her arms about him and embraced him all the more. The feelings of these two old, old friends for each other had no need of speech.

Meanwhile I had removed myself to the precipice and with a cautious scrutiny was glancing over the trouble there.

The lip of the quay had collapsed, just where we had been standing. The mortar was loose, and as we leaned against the rail the splintered boards had given way, disintegrating the brickwork at our feet.

So commonplace, so ordinary, so matter-of-fact an explanation for a sinister and dreadful event that might have been. Even now disaster seemed still to hang in the dark clouds. It was strange, I hadn't noticed them before. How cheerless they looked — such gloomy colors — a sky like a dirty ceiling, empty and drear.

With Dora resting against him, the doctor extended his hand to me in gratitude for my timely intervention. For had I not been there to draw Dora back from the edge, he might well have held himself to blame for what transpired.

"It was a miracle," he said.

"What matters most is that Dora is alive and unharmed."

"Most assuredly. Thank you, Mr. Earnscliff — thank you. We are forever in your debt."

"I could scarcely have helped it. It was — it was — as if some instinct . . ."

For it had flashed into my mind then that I had seemed to know, somehow, that a thing like this had been waiting to happen — indeed had been destined to happen. The thought of it sent a queer, prickly sensation crawling over my scalp and down my neck.

"An accident, easily prevented — a proper blunder of mine not to have foreseen it," said the doctor, with considerable emotion. And a twinge of conscience, perhaps?

"Not a whit," Dora said gently. "It was no one's fault, except my own. For 'erring mortals are we all'. This is my family's property. If it had been kept in better trim — " She raised her head as a sudden thought struck her. "Not a word of this to Dad," she warned, with an eye to us both, "for you know how liable he is to his fits of melancholy. I shall myself send a workman round to effect repairs, and my father shall know nothing of it."

The doctor offered her his arm, which she accepted with a lightness much more akin to her usual self. My heart was gladdened to see it.

Then abruptly she turned to me with a thoughtful air.

"Thank heavens your wits were *not* on holiday," she said. "There are some things in life, I find, that are past all understanding. Thank you, dear Mr. Earnscliff — and God bless you — for without you I might have died today."

## Chapter Twenty-nine

"I FEEL that behind our every action there is a guiding hand, to see we come to no harm, or to keep us from harming. I have felt this all my life — a sense of something lighting the way ahead, past a difficulty, or reining up on the verge of disaster . . ."

Though Dora still trembled slightly, she concealed it well. She — as well as I — had passed through a trying experience, however brief it may have been. It would seem that mine today had been the very literal hand of which she spoke.

Glancing at my watch I saw that the time was getting on. My eye happening then to fall on the mooring-post, it occurred to me upon what unassuming objects do the significant events of our lives sometimes depend. *Lives!* For it had not been lost on me — nor on Dora — that but for this slender post I too might have died today.

But we were neglecting that for which we had come this way — the eel-trap and paddles from the skiff. It was the job of but a minute for the doctor and I to collect them and return to the quay. The three of us then retraced our steps along the path to the cart. There, at Dora's request, not a word was said to Stinker about the incident. The trap and paddles were deposited in the box, and we resumed our seats as if nothing unusual had occurred.

We proceeded at a brisk trot up to the road to the Moorings, and there Dora and I were set down in the gravel drive. The doctor then continued on to the farm.

It was later in the afternoon, round half-past three, that a dog-cart drawn by a buckskin mare was seen approaching the Moorings from town. As it swung onto the gravel the driver took out his watch and looked at it, then flicked his horse round behind to the stables. No citizen of Dithering was there who would not have recognized this particular dog-cart, or this mare, both of which belonged to Dr. Hankey; nor failed to recognize the driver as Dr. Hankey himself.

Some half-hour the physician passed at the Moorings ere the dog-cart emerged again from behind the house. It then proceeded a little farther up the road, where it turned into the drive leading to Callander farm. There, once more, the dog-cart disappeared for a time, back of the farmhouse. On this second call of his the physician expended perhaps a quarter of an hour, no more; then the dog-cart rattled off down the hill and into town.

As the somber day waned and the hour of dining drew near, Dr. Callander was seen leaving the farm in his weathered gig, that which had belonged to his late father. Down the road a space he reined up on the gravel sweep before the Moorings, and there was received at the door by Mattie.

In such wise had been effected the removal of Clemendy to Callander farm. Upon secrecy had its success depended, and speedy accomplishment; and on both scores the parties concerned accounted themselves in luck. They found it difficult to perceive any flaw in their scheme which might have led to its discovery by spies.

There had been no illness at either house requiring the physician's attendance. Earlier in the day, while paying the reckoning at the inn, Dr. Callander had slipped into landlord Readymoney's hand a letter, which he had requested be delivered to Dr. Hankey straightway. The letter offered no explanation other than to ask that the physician call round at the Moorings — specifically, that he come to the stable-yard — at half-past three that afternoon.

Upon his arrival, Clemendy in her wire cage had been transferred to the boot of his dog-cart — out of sight, behind the house — after which he had proceeded to Callander farm, where she had been passed along to Stinker and Natty. The physician had then returned to Dithering. Later, at an appropriate hour, Dr. Callander arrived at the Moorings as though in answer to an invitation to supper.

Thus so far, so good.

Instead of supper, however, it was a trap that had been laid on at the Moorings — a trap to snare a "poacher" by the name of Bothack.

As evening approached a cellar door strategically was left unfastened in the area, beneath a range of windows well-fenced with iron bars. Inside this door a flight of steps led up to the kitchen. And it was in the kitchen that Dr. Callander, the Squire, and I, and two trusty stable-lads, would be waiting. In pursuance of the doctor's scheme we had taken up positions there, that we might intercept Bothack on his errand.

As a magistrate it was important that the Squire be present at the capture of the miscreant, so that the evidence of his own eyes might be entered into the record. The Squire himself bore no weapon aside from his stick (and perhaps his wooden leg). The doctor and I, however, were well provided with bladed steel, and the lads with switches and with lengths of rope with which the prisoner was to be secured.

In addition to these, others of the staff had been posted as sentries in obscure corners of the house. Another was keeping an eye on the cellar door from without, from the boughs of a clumber pine, that he might fasten shut the door once the hermit had passed through it. The villain thus would find himself trapped without means of retreat.

Presently night dropped into the dales, town and country vanishing under a thick cloud-coverlet of sable. No star shone out, nor sliver of moon, through the overcast. In the kitchen we settled down to our task, eyes glued to the door that led to the cellar, ears alert for the stealthy creak of stairs being mounted.

Meanwhile, to further appearances, Dora and Mattie had retired, and after a while put out their lights. Soon the entire house was still and dark. To Bothack, observing from a distance, all would seem as it should be, with Clemendy in her place — for he had no cause to believe otherwise.

In the kitchen too all was quiet — tranquil as a cloister. Our sole illumination arose from a chamber-candle kept partly shaded, its pale flame casting only a feeble light but sufficient to see one another by. Still we were little more than shapeless masses in the gloom.

The Squire had eased himself down onto the tall-backed settle by the hearth, his stick planted on the floor. Every now and again came a faint squeak from his leg when he shifted it. The doctor and I occupied chairs placed at an angle to the shut door of the cellar. The doctor's expression was firm and set, for he was determined this night to get at the bottom of a great mystery. Our cutlasses hung in readiness at our sides; the lads, switches in hand, hunkered near by.

In suchlike fashion we waited, mute and still as mummies. And waited.

The air in the kitchen was cold, but pleasant for all that with its blend of aromas from the apple-scented pantry. Mostly we waited in silence; when we conversed it was in hushed tones or whispers. Every now and then a ceiling-beam would yield a little and groan, or a wall would crack. But in the main all was quiet, save for the noise of the blood beating in my ears.

We awaited Bothack's arrival with a mix of impatience and calm resolve, each of us filling in the time in his own way. I strained my ears for a hint that Bothack had taken the bait, and kept my eyes on the shut door in anticipation of the tread of feet on the cellar-stairs.

The hands of the clock crept slowly round, and still we waited. Shrouded as we were in the near-dark, and in view of the growing lateness of the hour, it was not an exercise calculated to stimulate the mind. And there was the sense of confinement as well. With nothing to disturb the monotony, it was inevitable that boredom should set in. One of the lads, struggling to keep awake, sat with his head down and pulled like a turtle's into his collar. The other yawned and adopted an air of casual unconcern, *i.e.,* he was dozing with open eyes.

The empty hours dragged. The Squire's leg creaked, then creaked again. I stole a glance at the doctor, and found him rubbing his jaw in sober reflection. The time passed, and still no intruder. We chafed our hands and shivered inside our coats.

Appropriately, a chilling thought crossed my mind. Can we have been mistaken? Was it possible that Bothack somehow had tumbled to our plot, and had made his way instead to the farm? Might Stinker and Natty even now be engaged in battle? Might Clemendy already have been lost?

The doctor, still meditating, inched his chair forward — uneasily, it seemed to me. Likely the tenor of his thoughts was not far removed from my own. He squinted at his watch. "It should not be much longer," he whispered.

Minutes later I heard the Squire prize himself from his seat. Leaning on his stick, he confessed that he found the vigil hard going — his leg was troubling him — and announced his intention to retire to the parlor. It was clear he missed his pipe and glass. He sighed regretfully.

"I think it is odds we are bilked. Damn the fellow! May he go to the devil."

And he limped creaking to the kitchen door and into the passage, and shortly was heard mounting the stairs.

Perhaps our plan had turned out a botch — a failure. Perhaps our reasoning had been in error. Or perhaps *tomorrow* night . . .

The doctor stirred, murmuring under his breath, "I don't care for the feel of things. Something's gone awry. Bothack should have come by now."

Was he secretly wishing he had remained at the farm with Stinker and Natty? Were the two at this moment in danger from Bothack — from the piskie — or from worse? How much longer to wait before hastening to their aid?

More minutes passed, and I couldn't escape the growing conviction that we had been duped, as the Squire had suggested — had been outmaneuvered by a low ruffian. Where had we gone wrong? Where lay the flaw in our plan?

I had only begun rolling it over in my mind, when a distant shout broke the stillness — the words sounding very much like "What the blazes!" and the voice sounding very much like the Squire's.

We sprang up. Already hoarse cries of alarm could be heard filling the air. Heavy steps pounded on the floor over our heads.

The doctor and I whipped out our blades. The lads, stirred to action, readied their switches. We expected the cellar door at any moment to be flung open and Bothack to come charging through it. But it did not happen.

A confused din of voices sounded throughout the house — everywhere, indeed, but in the cellar. Steps thudded this way, thudded that way. Chairs were pushed about, doors slammed. A heavy bar dropped with a thunderous crash. More shouting followed, more noises of stir and alarm, more evidence of the hasty and disorderly scramble that had broken out on the floor above.

"My stars," I cried, "what is that rumpus?"

All at once a bell in the kitchen jangled at the end of its bracket, ringing out like a siren.

*Someone was calling to us for help.*

Next instant a woman's voice joined the chorus of distant cries.

"Dora!" the doctor exclaimed.

As one we broke for the kitchen door, the doctor in the lead, all thought of the cellar forgotten as we made for the staircase at the end of the passage. On the landing above we turned with a start as a door opened and a figure like a gust of wind blew in.

It was the chief gardener — he too had been assigned a sentry position — and when he spied us he sent up a jubilee shout.

"Mr. Callander, sir," he exulted, "'tis Bothack, the shammick — he've been took, sir, bless me ef he bain't!"

## Chapter Thirty

"**D**EVIL confound the man!"

And having so spoken, Squire Fetching, in his office as a magistrate, pronounced sentence of a kind on the ruffian who had invaded his parlor, and whom he had surprised in the semi-dark in the act of drinking his gin.

Sentence the Squire delivered with a taut voice and a stern aspect, his iron countenance and formidable mustaches a bulwark against villainy.

Disheveled but triumphant, the gardener waved an accusing finger at Bothack. "The shammick he be hid i' the house half the afternoon, by the look o't — I'll be bleddy bound!"

As it turned out he was not far wrong. To this point however the shammick had refused to admit a thing. Instead he glowered at us in wrathful silence, furious at having been subdued so easily, and perhaps at having had the Squire's gin removed from him in the act of guzzling it.

Several of the lads posted about the house had responded to the Squire's shout, and scuffled with the villain — and quite the scuffle it had been. Directly more had come to join the fray — the pounding of feet we had heard — amongst them the gardener, whose name was Briar. How sorry and disordered he looked now, and so too the lads, from the extremity of effort they had expended on Bothack! For the hermit, despite his stature, was exceedingly powerful, with brawny, muscular limbs, and substantial shoulders which, although uneven, measured almost as wide as he was tall.

He'd led them a proper chase. From room to room the lads had pursued him, up staircase and down, brawling here, brawling there, exchanging buffets and blows, till cornering him in the parlor where it all had begun. For it was there that the Squire, having quitted the kitchen in search of his pipe and a glass, had seen a light in the parlor — a light where no light should have been — and discovered the intruder imbibing some his best geneva.

And there it was that the lads had at last managed to collar him. Meanwhile Dora, alerted by the fracas, had come racing downstairs to urge them on. It was not until they had stumbled wearily into the parlor, the intruder in tow but battling to the end, that he had submitted. Perhaps it was Dora's method of wielding a chimney-poker, and threatening him with a rap on the costard, that had brought him round.

The Squire had lost no time in congratulating his daughter and his servants on their successful defense of life and property. His indignation had been mightily roused, and his bile stirred in no small degree, by this invasion of his family's space. It was worse even than poaching; it was impudence of a sort he had never before heard of in Dithering.

Turning to his captive, the Squire's mustaches fairly bristled.

*He looks a right dog. But this broken-down old horse-jockey can still turn a corner with any man in the sundered realm, even a villain such as this one is.* And yet at the same time the Squire was asking himself — *What! is he one of these Woldfolk of Dora's, that he wears fern-seed and walks into my house invisible?*

But the villain despite threats refused to enlighten him, refused to tell him how he'd contrived to elude the sentries and enter the house undetected; for of the unlatched cellar door so carefully prepared for him he had made no use. In his harsh expression was read naught but bitterness and contempt.

It later was discovered that since early morning Bothack had been looking out his chance, and when it had come he had taken it, in the full — albeit gray — light of day. A laundress going in and out at the wash-house door had vacated her post long enough for Bothack to have slipped inside. The wash-house was joined to the still room by a passage, and the still room to the scullery; so that the villain, finding these apartments unoccupied, had succeeded in making his way to a secluded staircase, and there had hidden himself in a closet under the stairs.

Only after the house had gone dark and quiet had he emerged. Intending to effect his mischief while the inmates slept, he had moled his way along, inch by careful inch; for he was unfamiliar with the layout. Moreover it was pitch black, and he dared not strike a light. But he knew the casement-window the piskie had marked out — for he had been observing from the shrubberies — and so it was in that direction he had bent his steps.

Passing the parlor and thinking himself lost, he at last gave in and scraped a match into flame. Its light had flashed and sparkled on the glassware and decanters at the drinks station there; and in that moment of revelation, the outcast — Bothack the rude, Bothack the unsociable, Bothack the resentful — had felt himself in need of a little Dutch courage. For even Bothack had understood his mission was a perilous one.

But even had he succeeded he would have found no Clemendy, though Dora likely would have given him a scalding had she discovered him in her chamber. For by concealing himself in a remote corner of the house he had overheard nothing of the doctor's plan, and so had remained in ignorance of the removal of Clemendy to Callander farm. Indeed he had no idea even that Dr. Hankey had visited.

As to what use Clemendy may have been to the piskie, and why such an effort had been made to abduct her, Bothack had offered not a word. And as the villain on principle had refused to answer this or any of his questions, Squire Fetching, in his authority as a magistrate, had no alternative but to take him in charge and order him confined to the kennels.

*Proper lodgings for a right dog.*

"The law, sir, is not to be trifled with," the old dalesman thundered at him, "and as you have willfully clothed your behavior in all the color and livery of guilt, it's the kennels for you — damned thieving beggar!"

In tiny Dithering there is no such official as a constable, and no such office as a gaol or lock-up; and so it is the responsibility of the magistrate to find accommodation for any prisoner he may take in charge, till such time as the case is heard before the Bench. Ergo, the kennels.

It was the Squire's hope that an inquiry into his prisoner's rascally activities might bring to light the names of the fellows with whom he had allied himself, others of his ilk who were addicted to thievery and who showed such utter contempt for the law. But thus far the villain had only hardened his resolve to reveal nothing, to admit to nothing, indeed to say nothing. His sullen exterior appeared proof against all interrogation.

"The beggar's a greater fool than I took him for. Well, at least the calf-lifting may cease for a time. Colley for one will be pleased, and Sweezy and Kneebone as well," the Squire reflected.

An information would be lodged against the prisoner in connection with his activities of this night. Failing any evidence to the contrary, the wheels of justice would deal with him summarily; for there could be no assaults and battery upon innocent citizens of Dithering without consequence.

"Miserable object!"

"Unconscionable villain!"

"Nurly creature!"

"Rank poison!"

The prisoner had been called worse before; still he returned these barbs from the stable-hands with black looks and eyes flashing fire. But no word escaped his lips.

Unfortunately, the mystery connected with him remained, that which the doctor had been in hopes of solving tonight. With no admission forthcoming, we were at a loss what the intended theft of Clemendy signified. If not for money, why should anyone go to such lengths to obtain a pocket glypt? And what had been the meaning of the emerald ray that had fastened on her in the Cupboard?

So to the kennels the villain was led, but it softened him not an iota. The same menacing expression, the same vengeful scowl on his massive bulge of brow, the same sneer on his lips and frightful show of fangs — the same Bothack. His huge fists, roped together, clenched and unclenched themselves at his back like breathing things.

"We bain't afeard o' nurly creatures — nor o' piskies neither," was the challenge of those who met his glance.

The prisoner, relenting nothing of his rudeness, spat on the floor. It was clear he despised the lot of us. Daggers flashed from his eyes; then of a sudden he squared round and looked us all full in the face, with so aggressive an attitude that it quite took our breath away.

"I bain't a creature! And it bain't piskies nor Bothacks as 'ee shud be afeard of, friends, in time coming," were the only words he deigned to speak, ere he was taken from us.

Still Dr. Callander made a final appeal. "Can't you throw the least light on this mystery? What did you want with the glypt?"

But the villain only laughed him to scorn — a ghastly, dry, creaking laugh, bitterly contemptuous.

"A finer gentleman, sir," the Squire shot back, his gorge rising, "than Mr. Hugh Callander of Callander farm never drew breath, unless it were his own father. If you only had acted as you would be done by, you should have had no trouble in Dithering."

The prisoner, defiant to the last, tossed up his chin with its stubble of beard, his smile communicating clearly that he knew more of the affair of the glypt than we realized, and that to spite us he would tell us — absolutely nothing.

"Get along with you — beggarly lot!" the Squire commanded. "I'd thrash you myself if I were the man I once was. My five-times great-grandfather knew how to deal with your ilk, sir. Now you may go to the devil for what I care."

Still firing from his eyes, the prisoner was led off to the kennels, where a guard was placed over him.

"Not to worry — we shall get to the bottom of the business," the Squire assured us.

But I was not so certain as he, for there was something abroad in the air that had given me serious pause. But of it I, on Bothack's example, said nothing.

As it had been an exhausting vigil for all concerned, we retired at last for the evening, grateful that the outcome had been so favorable. The doctor had reasoned correctly, and as a result Bothack had been taken.

In the morning the doctor drove to Callander farm and gave all there the good news. A few hours later he returned with Clemendy and restored her to her valued place at the Moorings.

That night after supper there were cards in the parlor. We'd spent a comfortable hour at whist, the four of us — Squire Fetching, the doctor, Dora and I — when our play was interrupted by noises of a disturbance upstairs. First came a loud crash — the rending of metal and splintering of wood, and shattering of glass panes — then a woman sent up a piercing shriek and a door was flung shut with a bang.

We started up — all of us but the Squire, who had to struggle on account of his leg. Down the stairs Mattie came flying, her face like chalk and her eyes glassy with fear. Trembling in every limb, she cried out to Dora —

"'Tis Clemendy, miss!"

There was no time to be lost. Up the stairs raced the doctor, with myself and Dora at his heels, and Mattie, vainly urging caution, trailing behind. When we arrived at Dora's apartment we found the door closed.

"Who is it? Who's in there?" the doctor demanded, beating on the panel.

To our surprise the door was unlocked; and though Mattie's cries imploring him not to venture within rang in his ears, the doctor ignored them and threw the door wide.

Mattie started and nearly fainted, and as the door swung open she shrank back in horror.

An icy draft struck us face on. Freezing cold filled the room, as if the casement-window had been left open to the night air. Warily my eyes circled the apartment, which was in darkness but for a faint glow from Mattie's bedchamber.

The casement indeed was open to the air. To be entirely accurate, there no longer was a casement. A tangle of lattice-work and shattered panes covered the floor. The curtain had been torn from its rod and was lying nearby. The exterior iron that had guarded the window was nowhere in evidence. Instead, a black rectangle where bars and casement had been was looking out onto the night, and through it a chill wind was blowing.

Where was Clemendy? Sadly, like the bars, she too was nowhere to be found. Her little cushioned bed, made for her by Stokes, had been overturned and thrust under Dora's four-poster. But Clemendy herself was gone.

In a fit of remorse Mattie sank onto Dora's bed, tears streaming from her eyes. Again her nerve had failed her — again *she* had failed! It served only to compound her sense of guilt.

We had saved Clemendy from Bothack, only to lose her the very next day. Nor could the hermit be blamed for it, for he remained under watch in the kennels.

The doctor stepped to the window — or rather, to where the window had been — and with a light examined the evidence there. What he found spurred him to quick action.

"There is not a moment to waste. Mr. Earnscliff, will you accompany me?"

"Of course."

"For the thief is not in the house. Dora, please stay with Mattie. Mr. Earnscliff and I will do all that we can."

We met the Squire and two of the domestics on the staircase, and asked that they go to Dora and Mattie. We ourselves hied to the parlor, where we took down a brace of cutlasses and, so provided, rushed forth into the night.

The hounds could be heard yelping — I wondered what Bothack was making of it all — as we were joined by several of the lads with lights, and proceeded to the stretch of ground under Dora's window. Near the base of the wall we found the grating that had secured the casement. And hard by it, plainly visible in the soft earth, were the telltale footprints — large, three-toed marks, each with a fourth, smaller toe showing behind — which led up to the house and away again.

What the doctor had deduced, in examining Dora's window, was that its frame of iron bars had been wrenched loose *from the outside* and tossed to the ground. Before us lay the proof of it. And before us too lay the tracks of the thief who had made off with Clemendy.

The picture it presented to us was one of matchless strength. For the thief to have scaled a sheer wall — no trees were near enough to have been of use — ripped the grating from its fastenings, snatched Clemendy from her box, and clambered down again, before vanishing into the night . . .

"Well, the thing seems impossible," said the doctor, "but there it is."

"Can 'ee tell us, sir, what manner o' thief 'e be?" queried one of the lads. Wide wonder was in his eyes, as he stared first at the bars, then at the trail leading off into the dark.

Slowly the beginnings of an awful awareness had been growing inside me, conjuring up scenes and visions that came from I knew not where. The shapeless cloud, the specter of mist, the something monstrous and unspeakable. A shudder passed from my scalp to my heel, freezing me to silent horror; for the source of the evil, I recognized, was not a misanthrope and outcast called Bothack, was not a faceless piskie, but was a nightmare called —

*Eldritch's Cupboard.*

It was strange, for the doctor and I, almost as one, each had blurted out the words. We glanced at one another in surprise.

*There's a chill not of night which steals upon me, and a cold creeps down my spine, as if my bones had been reduced to jelly.*

There flashed into my mind then the lines inscribed on a certain signboard in the taproom of the Pack Horse Inn —

> *The man in the Cupboard*
> *Hisself is no sluggard.*
> *Hickory, dickory, dare . . .*

A short time later an account of what had passed in Dora's room was received from Mattie.

It seemed that Mattie had been in her sleeping-apartment, *en suite* with Dora's, and Clemendy in her box-bed, when a tremendous crash had shattered the quiet — first a metallic wrenching, as the bars over Dora's casement were torn free, then a splintering of lattice-work and smashing of diamonded panes. Had followed then a heavy thud, as of an awful weight dropping to the carpet.

Shaken almost beyond endurance, Mattie had taken up her candle and stolen to the door. Her ears caught the sound of movement — swift, furtive, purposeful movement — and a skittery sort of rattling or crackling noise, as of some jointed thing moving stealthily in the dark of Dora's apartment.

She peered in with her light, and in its flicker stirred by the wind blotches of shadow writhed and danced. A reek of slime, as had filled the air of Eldritch's Cupboard, enveloped her like a shroud. She staggered back, sickened to her stomach by it, or very nearly so.

Recovering herself, she peered in again, in time to see an ungainly shadow-mass dart through a patch of light. She had but a transient glimpse of it, enough to see that it moved with a hideous speed, but jerkily, its foul, lurching gait like nothing human. She had an impression of elongated, stalk-like limbs, of knobbed joints that rattled, of fingers like claws flexing. Next moment the vision, startling and horrible, was gone again in the dark.

Mattie's hand wavered, and the candle with it, for she was on the very knife-edge of panic. More furtive movement in the gloom; then suddenly the thing heaved round its shadow and darted again into the light. There was a sharp hiss of venomous breath, which shocked and terrified her, and for an instant a ghastly, swollen head, grotesquely outlined, with a single large, goggle-eye protruding from it, loomed above her.

Involuntarily Mattie put out a hand, as if to push the thing back from her. It was then she dropped her candle, gave a piercing shriek and fled the apartment. As she did so a claw-like hand swept out and shut the door behind her.

"What a dreadful thing was here in my room . . . threatening my Mattie . . . and now it has our poor Clemendy," Dora murmured.

"Oh, miss — forgi'e yer Mattie — plaise, miss, plaise do," implored her maid, heartbroken and trembling.

"Dear Mattie, there was nothing you could have done."

The monster — how else to call it? — had gone out not at a door, but by the way it had come — through the window — and had taken Clemendy with it.

How uneasily my thoughts were running! For I recalled the hermit's threat of consequences to come that boded no good. How the flesh of my arms crawled at Mattie's picture of the unholy, misshapen caliban that had prowled the dark of Dora's chamber, rattling as it went . . .

All at once there came over me a dizziness — a queer sort of light-headedness, as oft results from exhaustion. It was as though all of my internal resources suddenly had been drained from me. A veiling mist swam before my eyes. Then the world round me dimmed and faded, and the next I knew I was alone.

## Chapter Thirty-one

UNACCOUNTABLY I found myself buried in a dull gray fog, so murky it prevented me from seeing more than a yard in any direction. It was as if a cloud had descended to earth and was smothering it in a blanket of gloom.

The cloud must have invaded my brain as well. Still half asleep, like the fog I felt dull and thick. A fog of the mind, a fog of the soul, an actual fog — it was difficult to tell which it was. But even as I was trying to work it out, it started to lift.

Not that it went away entirely — it did not. But its denser tiers began to disperse, its opacity waned, and soon my eyes were able to penetrate the veiling mist.

Where was I? In a wainscoted apartment, by the look of it. But an apartment at the Moorings, at the inn, or elsewhere?

There seemed to be no one about — that is until my glance settled on the bed in the room. An older gentleman lay stretched beneath the covers. His face was pale and still, and his eyes were closed. Had it not been for the slight, rhythmic rise and fall of his breathing, one might have thought he was dead.

It took me a minute to recognize him. The intelligent lines of the face, the handsome, distinguished brow, the flowing hair gone silver — it could be no other than Dr. Callander.

How strange it seemed that the doctor should be old. For was it not but moments ago that I had stood beside him and Dora as we listened to Mattie's horrific tale? Plainly I was no longer at the Moorings, but in the doctor's sick-room at Callander farm.

In an instant it came back to me. The sight of the doctor unconscious in his bed had recalled me to myself, and to my mission in entering the dream.

Miss Carswell was not at his side, nor was Annie. It was most unusual, for someone always was watching. Even little Figgie had abandoned him. What had become of them?

I glanced at my watch. It seemed as if an eternity had passed since I had drunk the cordial of the Woldfolk. I took it as a positive sign that I *did* recall drinking it; now everything was returning to me.

I had succeeded in my errand. Dora Fetching's death — the "stupid accident" for which the doctor had blamed himself — had been averted. She had not tumbled from the quay and broken her head on the shingle. I was the element which had not been there before; I had been at her side when the ground collapsed under her feet. My presence had altered the chain of events, just as Miss Carswell and the doctor had hoped it would.

So that what I found now in the doctor's shut and silent room came as rather a surprise.

Why had he not awakened, now that all had been accomplished? Where was everyone? What was this murky gray gloom that *would* persist and not entirely leave me? I call it a mist or a fog but in truth it was neither, as it had no feel to it, was neither damp nor cold.

I strode to the head of the stairs and called aloud, but no one answered. So I went and had myself a look around. There was no Annie. There was no Stokes, no Mrs. Stokes. There was no Sir Lancelot Wale. There was no one.

Where the deuce at least was Stinker?

Oh, yes — remember it now — dead. Where was Flounce? She too was gone. Illusions of shadow and light, products of the cordial, she and Stinker were no more now that I had exited the dream. Both belonged to an era gone by, to a period before my own birth . . . in Hoggard, wasn't it?

Well, yes, of course. Philip Earnscliff, bred and born in Hoggard. There I had made some progress; I remembered who I was. Philip Earnscliff, solicitor, a junior in the firm of Bagwash and Bladdergowl, Bodmin Square. For I had had some trouble with that.

I made a thorough search of the premises, but found nothing. The veiling mist, though not so heavy as before, was everywhere; everything round me was bathed in its dulling influence. It felt like another kind of dream.

It was as if the doctor and I suddenly were alone in the universe, exiled, shut away. It was as if I had stepped outside of myself, had removed myself from the realm of the living and were seeing as a ghost might see. There existed only myself and the doctor, he still unconscious and in a coma after his attack of apoplexy —

Hold on! There had been no apoplexy. There had been no coma, only the cordial. The doctor himself had induced the sleep-state by partaking of the dark liquid, the gift of the Woldfolk.

The pervasive mist, the feeling that something was awry, must be a result of my having drunk much more of the cordial than previously, so much more than the few drops Miss Carswell had placed in my sherry. There it was — there was the answer — it had to be — *I had not yet fully awakened from the dream.*

It occurred to me then that I ought not to have left the side of the doctor. And yet . . . till I was more certain of my ground, was I not simply musing on possibilities? One possibility, which I greatly feared, was that something had gone wrong in the dream. But what can it have been?

I passed a window and happened to glance outside. It was late — nearly dark — but out of doors too the mist held sway. A sea of vapor — the term "gray" scarcely sufficed — pervaded all. It was as if all color, all life, had been drained away.

I was about to return to the sick-room when a gleam of light, dim and wavering, caught my eye in the leaded panes. Peering out I descried a cloaked figure trudging away from the house. Slow-footed, head bent, a lantern swaying limply in its hand, it looked a dejected object — for all the world like a lost soul setting forth to meet its doom.

Of course this was sheer fancy on my part, as I hadn't a clue who it was or what the person's errand might be. I knew only that he or she did not seem too happy about it.

The figure was slight in stature, and mantled from head to foot; but from its gait and appearance I took it to be a woman's. I opened the casement and called to her, but she made no answer. Indeed she gave not the least sign that she had heard me. So I donned my coat and hat and went outside.

Already she had gained the road and was descending towards the town. Her lantern dimly illumined the way before her, as if lighting her path to the gallows; or so my imagination made out. For a more dismal-appearing creature never walked.

Silently I followed, matching my pace to hers. I had some trouble in doing so, however, as I still was a bit groggy and my legs felt sluggish. And that deuced mist was everywhere! The ground was thick with rime, cloud-monsters of fog were crawling over the fields, the trees had all lost their limbs in the gloom.

I quickened my pace, trailing as closely as I dared. I did not wish to disturb the woman in her errand; I wanted to see for myself what that errand was. I wanted to see for myself what the deuce was going on here.

Who could she be? She certainly was not Mrs. Stokes. An image of the invalid's white head and dazed, frightened expression passed before me. I pictured her again at her casement in the sitting-room, gazing helplessly out. Helpless she was indeed, but for the love and attention bestowed upon her by her husband. No, the trudging figure hardly could be that of poor Mrs. Stokes.

Annie, perhaps? As a dejected-looking object the maid certainly qualified, endlessly weeping in a corner of the sick-room. But no — Annie was taller, it seemed to me, and bonier — as lean as a rail. I doubted that the figure was Annie's.

And so the woman I was following could only be Miss Carswell. But where was she going, and why? Why had she left the doctor in the care of no one? And where was everybody else? What was going on?

*If you succeed, Mr. Earnscliff, then we two shall never have met.*

Plainly I hadn't succeeded. I had rescued Dora Fetching, true; yet I remembered Miss Carswell, as I remembered my mission. Saving Dora had not altered the flow of events. Miss Carswell had said that history was resistant to change, that it was difficult if not impossible to re-direct its course within the dream. But Dora had lived; so what was the trouble?

We were by this time in Dithering, and not once had the woman glanced behind her. A silence deep and strange lay all about us, as if the very air were saturated with sleep. The mist hung thickly over town and inn and stream. It was nearly dark, yet there was seen no thread of smoke from any chimney, no trace of light in any lattice. In foot-path and horse-road a dull quiet prevailed. Somber streets, empty and forlorn — nothing more.

Where *was* everyone?

It was as if the entire world had closed down, put up its shutters, and gone away. For of living thing, apart from the trees climbing into the murk, I saw none. I strained to catch a glimpse of anyone, of a single face in a single window, but there was nobody.

The woman's path was leading her away from town, away from the inn and towards the stream. Glancing round her with watchful concern — watchful, as she seemed to be looking for something, or waiting for something, and with concern, as she did not appear at all anxious to find it — she bent her steps towards the shore.

What can have called her from the doctor's side, called her down here in the mist and gloom, called everyone else away?

Presently she came to what appeared to be a crossing-place a distance from the bridge-end, an area of shingly beach not unlike that round the quay at the Moorings. Here the woman rested her light on the ground and, folding her arms, settled in to wait. After a time a faint noise reached my ears — a rhythmic plashing, that seemed more than merely waves on the shingle. It sounded for all the world like an oar or pole being dipped in the water.

I had approached as near to the cloaked figure as I dared, and like her I stood in wait of — something. Still she had not once looked behind to see if anyone had followed her. Perhaps she didn't care.

Then, as I watched, something began to grow upon my sight in the gloom. A vague shape had appeared on the water, one that by gradual degrees resolved itself into that of a narrow barge or punt. It was being poled easily along by the tall, bent figure of a bargeman.

A nervous thrill swept over me, shot across my scalp and down my spine.

What was this — another dream? Another nightmare? Or was the bargee in the approaching craft the man, the creature, the legend — call him what you like — I suspected him of being?

The sight of his tall figure as it emerged from the gloom threw all the hairs up on the back of my neck. Gaunt in the extreme, he was draped in a sort of monk's habit which hung in ample folds from his shoulders, like rags from a specter. The hands showing at the sleeves were skeletal, the nails untended and overgrown. A peaked cowl hid his features from me, save for the long white beard that spilled from its depths, signaling that his years were many.

With slow, deliberate strokes he drew his craft in to shore, where waited the mantled form I took to be Miss Carswell's. Shadowy, impossible, bargeman and barge wavered before my eyes like the apparitions they simply had to be, arisen it seemed as though from the very fog-stuff itself.

Directly commenced a low growling, not from the bargeman but from the animal crouching at his feet. Stout-built and thickly furred, on seeing Miss Carswell it rose up on its hind legs, flung out its ears, and fixed her with a menacing gaze. Its limbs were thick, short, and powerful, and equipped with massive claws for digging. Striped markings lined its head and snout; quivering nostrils sniffed the air as it scrutinized the newcomer.

The bargee quelled the growling with an outthrust hand.

"Hast naught to fear from him, girl," he assured the woman, in tones near as low and savage as the badger's, "so long as thou art true to thy vow."

His craft rested upon the shingle, but despite its proximity to the lantern his features were cloaked in darkness, a darkness as of other than night. He had no illumination of his own aboard that I could discern, and I wondered how he found his way in the gloom.

I scarcely could believe it. Was I in the presence of Obadiah Outland, the mystic ferryman? Was this gaunt figure indeed the mythical old man of the waterways?

Obadiah Outland and Miss Carswell — they were in league! This too I could hardly believe.

Had she played square with me, or had she played me for a fool? Had she and Obadiah Outland concocted between themselves some design — dare I call it outlandish — that I couldn't begin to fathom? If so, to what end? And what was the doctor's role in it?

My mind flew from one wild conjecture to another. It galled me that my clumsy male wit had been no match for this young woman's scheming. For we men, who pretend to wisdom, are never so wise as when we proclaim our ignorance of the sex.

But the next exchange put rather a different slant on the matter.

The woman tilted her chin defiantly. "I have done as you and the folk have commanded. Now do with me as you will, for I scorn you, as I scorn the charge."

It was Miss Carswell's voice, and Miss Carswell who stood before me. But her entire manner had changed. Her shoulders were thrown back and there was a prideful set to her head. Her words were hard-edged, her tone ripe with bitterness — disdain — not a hint of dejection.

The ferryman responded —

"Dost think perhaps thou hast been done an injustice? But 'tis not thy province to think — or else suffer the consequences."

The badger, prepared to rush upon Miss Carswell at an instant's notice, bared its fangs and growled.

"Steady on, cousin," the ferryman cautioned the animal, "for this one ashore won't harm me." Then to Miss Carswell — "Cousin Bolingbrock," he explained, indicating the badger, "is easily ruffled, and anxious for my safety. Come, girl — didst think to escape thy fate? Didst think thy machinations would remain unknown to the folk? Thy offense go unperceived? Thou knowest full well our laws; thou knowest the violation. Now shalt thou have much time to think over it." He extended a skeletal hand, with the grim air of a turnkey welcoming a prisoner into his keeping. "Come — let us be on our way. 'Tis not far."

Mindful of the badger — a surly character if ever there was one

— Miss Carswell stepped aboard the barge. The animal obediently kept its distance, but this did not prevent it from slavering and snapping its jaws at her. Disdainful to the last, Miss Carswell proceeded as if in a trance. Tight-lipped, perfectly self-contained, perfectly controlled, perfectly resolute, she would meet her fate — whatever it was — gladly, and with no show of regret. For was it not Miss Carswell who had spoken of a noble purpose, a better purpose, in the matter of the doctor's endeavor?

So what the deuce did it all mean?

At last I managed to kick open my mouth, as the ferryman was readying his craft for departure.

"Miss Carswell — don't go!" I cried.

Surely she could hear me? I had advanced till I was no more than a few feet from the barge, yet she had given not the slightest hint she was sensible of my presence. Either she could not reply, or she chose not to do so. I saw her clench one hand into a fist, tightly, and push the knuckles against her lips. Her cheeks, drained of their color, were as ashen as the fog.

Having been invited into the barge, she had acquiesced with only a faint, subtle inclination of her head, nothing more. Then, drawing herself up, she had gone aboard.

Meanwhile I had been casting about for some remedy, to no avail. Having settled herself on a thwart, one as far from Outland and the badger as possible, at last Miss Carswell turned her face my way. To my surprise I saw eyes of glass staring impassively, with not so much as a flicker of expression. She seemed unconscious of everyone and everything about her. It was if she had willfully emptied herself of all emotion and made her thoughts a blank.

*You shall not drive me from my purpose.*

Implacably determined, she had accepted her lot with a stoic calm designed to give her enemies no iota of satisfaction. Transformed by her resolve, by her righteous resistance, she sat stone-faced and silent. Then she drew down her veil and was alone.

The bargee too had ignored me, and yet I was standing so near his craft I might have touched him. Only the badger, Bolingbrock, took any notice of me. Bracing his legs, he flung out his ears of a sudden and raked me with his savage glance. Then his jaws opened and I was startled to hear him say —

"Churling — amble off with thee!"

Next I knew the bargee had pushed off and settled his craft in the stream. The lantern sat on the shingle where Miss Carswell had left it. I picked it up and held it out before me. But already the ferryman was beyond the range of its light; he and his barge had become one with the mist and the waters, and I saw them no more.

Given the eerie, unreal atmosphere, the stream upon which bargee and barge had floated off might well have marked the boundary line between earth and eternity. But wasn't Obadiah Outland no more than a legend — a creature of imagination, of superstition — an impossible being?

I took out my watch and looked at it, to see how much time had elapsed since I had come to in the doctor's sick-room. But the hands had not moved.

## Chapter Thirty-two

**W**ITH a shudder and a jolt I wrenched open my eyes. Where was I?

The gloom of the stream-side had vanished; instead I saw round me the doctor's small study. I was within doors, no longer out. In the space of an instant I had been transported from the shingle to Callander farm.

I swung down my feet and sat up on the couch. The mist had entirely fled; all the color of life had returned. On the table, beside my papers, lay the glass from which I had drunk the cordial of the Wold-folk. It was on the couch that I had then reposed myself and joined the doctor's dream.

I shook my head to clear it. So the gloom of the stream-side *had* been another nightmare, another illusion! There was little doubt but that I was myself once more — fully conscious, fully alert, fully alive in the waking world.

It was mid-morning, and as I was feeling much better I arose, slipped on my coat, and left the study.

As I was passing the sitting-room my attention was drawn to the feeble-looking little woman who sat there alone before the casement-lattice. It was her hair, stunningly white as a ghost's, that had caught my eye. Adrift in her world of lonely contemplation, Mrs. Stokes did not notice me. What was she looking at, I wondered? Whatever did she see out there on the fields, and what did she think about all day? What a horror it must be to be imprisoned in one's own mind, like a criminal in a lock-up.

I felt sorry for her, and for her husband too. The terrible whiteness of her hair, like some fantastic clown's-wig, was extraordinary. I wondered again what disease had brought it on and made of her so pathetic a figure. For Sir Lancelot hadn't said.

I proceeded to the kitchen and found Annie at her chores there.

"Marnen' to 'ee, Mr. Earnscliff, sir. Did 'ee have 'ee a proper rest, sir?"

"Very proper," I told her. "Very refreshing. And how is the doctor, do you know?"

"No better, sir," sighed the housemaid, who in expectation of sorrow always was ready with tears to shed.

I had thought I should awaken to better news. Indeed something *had* gone awry! But for the present I swallowed my disappointment.

"Would 'ee care for a dish o' tay, sir, and a bite o' food?" Annie asked.

I declined the invitation. I didn't feel so hungry now; perhaps the disappointment I had swallowed had dulled my appetite. I needed to talk over my concerns with Miss Carswell. Upon inquiring, I learned that Annie had not seen her this morning.

I decided that I should look in on the doctor. It was Stokes who was with him now.

As I paced thoughtfully by the sitting-room, trying not to disturb Mrs. Stokes, I saw her straighten of a sudden in her chair. Slowly her head swung towards me, and her sad eyes with it. Still they were gentle eyes too, but the long years of care had dug deep graves for them and buried them in place.

*Where am I? What has become of me?* they seemed to ask.

Then her expression changed and assumed that peculiar look that Sir Lancelot had remarked upon — that of a frightened hare, frightened almost to death. It was as though fear had sucked the very blood from her flesh, the color from her hair. Her eyes in their deep graves seemed to regard me as if I were the Gorgon itself, the sight of which would turn an ordinary mortal to stone.

*A lamentable case. There's no help for it; she is as mute as a fish. Try as hard as you might, you cannot make her speak.*

"Oh, I'm very sorry, Mrs. Stokes. I didn't mean to startle you. I didn't mean to — "

Abruptly I stopped short, struck by something in her glance that had awakened a curious echo in my brain. It crossed my mind that

I had seen those gentle eyes of hers before. There was a light in them I recognized, but the connection eluded me.

I approached her chair. She viewed me with apprehension, but did not cringe. I knelt and looked into her pale, frightened countenance, searching for the answer. Long and closely I scanned it, much as Sir Lancelot had done. It was then the flood of memories came rushing back to me.

*What a dreadful thing was here in my room,* Dora murmured.

*Oh, miss,* implored her maid, *forgi'e yer Mattie — plaise, miss, plaise do . . .*

Those eyes for which care had dug such deep graves were the very same — the very same with which she had pleaded with her mistress to forgive her for the loss of Clemendy. There could be no mistaking it; I could not doubt the evidence of my own senses.

"My stars! Mattie?" I whispered.

At the sound of her name she flinched. Behind her pupils the feeblest glimmer of recognition gleamed. Her lips quivered in mute entreaty.

"Mattie? Mattie, is it you? What has happened to you?" I said.

She touched a hand, pale and trembling, to her breast, and stammered out the single identifier —

"M-Mat-tie."

It was I instead who cringed, for her voice was a sorry thing, one that age and infirmity had reduced to a guttural croak. But it was the first I had heard her speak — the first anyone had heard her speak.

*Mute as a fish,* Sir Lancelot had pronounced her.

From across the bridge of years her glance reached for mine. Smiling, she dabbed a tear from her eye. Then all at once she caught herself and withdrew, shrank back again into her chair, like a shocked snail into its shell. Her gaze returned to the casement, to the view in its leaded panes, and she to the petrified silence in which she so long had dwelt.

What horrid illness had done this to her? And why hadn't I tumbled to it earlier that she was Mattie?

I reflected on the mild, dark girl she had been, so docile and neat, so devoted to her mistress. How Dora had loved her! As faithful as steel had been Dora's very sensible girl, her own dear Mattie. *She's the best-hearted girl I ever knew . . .*

"Poor Mattie," I thought, "how changed you are! That your life should have come to this. How terrible a thing time is . . ."

This illness of hers was something I wished to know more about, but for that I should have to speak to Sir Lancelot. For the present it made me all the more determined to discover what had gone awry in the dream. I needed to find Miss Carswell, and soon.

"I shall see it through," I told Mattie, although whether she understood me I couldn't say. Her unmeaning stare had returned; vacant and alone, she noticed me no more.

I mounted to the sick-room and there found the doctor asleep as before. But who was the rumpled chap sitting by him? For the briefest instant it puzzled me, until the man looked up and his face folded into a familiar smile.

*How strange that the doctor should be old . . . and Natty, too . . .*

I searched his eyes a moment for a sign he recognized me — that is, that he recognized me from those days that were gone — but no trace did I find.

*How strange that I still should be young, and these two grown old.*

"How is he?" I asked, although it was plain to any eye there had been no measurable change. "Is he any better?"

"Sir Lancelot he was h'yur, sir," Stokes replied, "but he gives little hope."

I nodded sympathetically.

On the doctor's pillow little Figgie had opened a drowsy eye. His nostrils sniffed the air a moment; then he yawned and, nestling closer, resumed his nap.

"Did 'ee sleep well, sir?" Stokes asked me.

"Yes, quite well, thank you. I'll sit with the doctor now, if you'd like," I offered.

"As 'ee will, sir."

As he rose to leave, a sudden inspiration struck me.

"I saw Mrs. Stokes downstairs a moment ago, in the sitting-room. She spoke to me."

He paused, not knowing at first how to take this.

"My ould woman — she did *spake* to 'ee, sir?"

"She did. Stokes, why didn't you tell me she was Mattie?"

His face crumpled into an odd expression.

"And how wud 'ee knaw that, sir? That my ould woman's name be Martha — or Mattie, as we called her?"

I had no proper answer for him, but mumbled that it likely was something I had overheard somewhere. Perhaps Miss Carswell had told me.

"By the by, where is Miss Carswell? Have you seen her?"

He responded that he had not done, that he did not know where she was. An unpleasant feeling began to steal over me concerning this absence of hers.

"Stokes," I said, not through with the poor fellow yet, "has Miss Dora been here, by any chance?"

His eyes fixed me with a very queer look indeed.

"Miss Dora, sir? Do 'ee mean — Miss Dora Fetching, sir?"

"Yes."

"My ivers," he exclaimed, "ef that don't beat everythin'. What! Miss Dora o' the Moorings h'yur? Not since all these long years, sir, that's sure. Whyever do 'ee ax?"

"Because I dreamed of her last night," I told him, "and of her father the old Squire, and of Dr. Callander, and of Mattie too. And of the Moorings of days past, and of Eldritch's Cupboard. Or was it Eldritch's Sideboard? And what's more I know how Miss Dora met her death — or didn't meet it."

The poor fellow seemed utterly confused, and left the room shaking his head. Likely he thought I had gone quite mad.

## Chapter Thirty-three

WHILE watching at the doctor's bedside, I had leisure to review how matters stood at present.

Plainly I had failed in my errand. There had been no change in the doctor's state, no change at the farm. Yet Dora had been saved — or had she been?

Perhaps there had been another mishap — a later one? Perhaps the later had been the "stupid accident" of which the doctor had spoken?

No, I reflected, that couldn't be it — it simply couldn't. But what other possibility remained? What other "stupid accident" can the doctor have had in mind?

I sat awhile thinking over the problem, but ultimately my brains failed me. So what was I to do now? Casting about for a solution, I even approached little Figgie on the topic; but like the doctor, he was oblivious.

What was it I had seen down there at the stream? Had it been but a trick of my imagination — or had it been real? For there had been a grim finality to that rendezvous on the shingle. A prisoner bound over for sentence — that was how Miss Carswell had appeared.

But why a prisoner? For what crime had she been convicted, and by whom?

An hour passed by, but the doctor did not stir; he remained fast locked in the dream. Unsure what my next step ought to be, I turned the watch over to Annie and retired to the study. Significantly, neither Annie nor Stokes had been successful in finding Miss Carswell.

On the couch I dozed for a time — without dreaming — then was jarred awake when an idea suddenly intruded itself upon me. Leaving the room I sought out a particular casement which gave a view down the road in the direction of the Moorings.

Beyond the lower wood, under the glum gaze of the Lingonshire sky, the Moorings stood abandoned to forgetfulness and decay. Moss-grown tiles, lichened walls, gables and chimney-stacks like blighted timber in a wilderness of fir and bramble — I found it transcendently dismal, depressing in the last degree. The evidence was irrefutable — I had failed. All was as it had been before; my rescue of Dora on the quay had changed nothing.

I paced the room slowly, turning it all over in my mind. Out of curiosity I went and found Stokes, and asked him what had become of Robert Fetching, Dora's brother, who, being no farmer, had left for a position in a banker's house in Newmarsh. Why had he not inherited after the Squire's death?

Stokes replied that he knew nothing of the matter, except that for years there had been suits at law challenging the will, but that naught had come of them, apart from an enrichment of the attorneys in the case. Scarcely had he said this than he checked himself, recollecting my profession, and told me he was sorry, sir, for his last remark, that concerning the enrichment of counsel. I told him not to worry, that it didn't signify. He then reiterated that he knew nothing of Robert Fetching or his inheritance, except that he never had come into it.

Miss Carswell had been absent now for some hours. No one had seen her go, and of her possessions only her cloak and hat were missing. Stokes had discovered that a lantern as well had been removed from the barn.

All this served to confirm my worst fear — that the veiling mist had been no dream. It had been the antediluvian Outland I had seen there at the stream-side, and he had taken Miss Carswell away with him.

Returning to the study I threw myself into a chair and debated how far now to pursue my errand. Perhaps I had it wrong; perhaps I actually had succeeded. Perhaps the doctor would awaken shortly and all would be changed. But it did not happen.

Sir Lancelot Wale arrived, and his prognosis was dire. He gave the doctor no chance now whatever, explaining that there simply was nothing he or anyone else could do for his old friend. Moreover his practice was calling him back to Medlow, for he had received an urgent summons from one of his oldest and loftiest patients, a gentleman very high up in the halls of governance.

"I grieve to say it," he explained, with clear regret, "but we medical men can't always choose . . ."

I was on the point of inquiring about Mrs. Stokes's illness — that is, Mattie's illness — but the presence of her husband led me to reconsider. I didn't wish to cause the poor fellow undue distress by intruding into a private matter that, in all honesty, did not concern me; so I held my tongue and returned to the study.

For how much longer might the doctor remain asleep, I wondered, without Miss Carswell to give him his dose of the cordial? Would he be plucked from the dream as I had been, once the cordial's effects had worn off?

Immersed in thought, I was idly turning over the papers on the table when I perceived an unfamiliar document lying among the rest. I drew it out. It consisted of a sealed envelope addressed to me, and enclosed a letter written in a small, neat hand. Its contents ran:

"DEAR MR. EARNSCLIFF — On reading this likely you will have discovered that I have gone. It was not my wish to go; it was a thing that could not be helped. I am indeed sorry to have left you at such an unfortunate pass. Please, Mr. Earnscliff — you must carry on.

"You must help the doctor. You must see that justice is done. The doctor is a dear man and deserves nothing less for the great chance he has taken.

"You will find sufficient of the cordial for your needs behind the volume of Orkla, which I have restored to its place on the shelves. You must guard it for the precious gift that it is.

"I wish that I could have done more to help the doctor, but I myself am unable to enter the dream. When you come to understand my meaning, you will understand all. For you shall not see me again.

"I shall be forever grateful to you for your devotion to the doctor, and remain

"Yours sincerely,
"VIOLET CARSWELL."

Thus had she taken her kind farewell of me. *You shall not see me again.* It sounded as though she had left the world. Well, perhaps she had done — she and Obadiah Outland. I might as well have shot at a sunbeam as understood her meaning at present; clearly there was rather more for me to learn. It all made me feel like a dog in a wheel — always moving but never advancing.

As matters seemed to stand, the only course open to me now was to rejoin the doctor. For there was something more that remained to be done — something still undreamed of, so to speak, that the doctor had yet to accomplish. And until he had accomplished it the dream would go on. It seemed there was more to the mystery of Dora than I had been made privy to, but I was baffled what it could be. Something which had been kept back? Some deeper, more secret intrigue?

I rolled it over *pro* and *con* for a time, but it was useless — the die had been cast. The only choice left to me was to return, to ride out one final tilt with fate before the darkness descended.

And yet still I hesitated, pacing awhile up and down, my eyes on the carpet but my thoughts on figures and shadows from days that had passed.

*Don't be a goose, Earnscliff. You know the proper course. It's all that is left to you.*

The doctor had not achieved his aim; that was why he still slept. There was something more that needed to be done back there, something beyond the rescue of Dora on the quay. What could it be? And what would he have me do now but help him? Why else had he sent for me? Would he have wanted me to shrink at the last?

*No, by twenty devils — to stick at nothing was more the ticket!*

The scene at the shingle and Miss Carswell's letter had stimulated me to renewed action. I had not failed; I simply had not yet finished the job. I had succeeded once before, in saving Dora; I would succeed again. I would not betray Miss Carswell's faith in me. What was it she had said to Annie, when the maid had expressed doubt as to the doctor's recovery?

*We musn't throw up the cards while we have a chance of the game.*

After a hasty meal I took the cordial from the shelf and repaired to the sick-room. I asked Annie to fetch another blanket for the doctor, as the night promised to be chilly. While she was about this, and with Figgie watching from the pillow, I approached the bed and gave the doctor his dose of the cordial, as I'd seen Miss Carswell do. Once Annie returned I made my way to the study, after informing her that I intended to have another lie-in.

I secured the door, then went to the table. There stood the empty glass from which I had drunk of the cordial. Into it I poured a fresh measure. Then I retired to the couch to meditate for a while on my errand, as I had done previously. But I was an old hand at it now, and excited over the prospect of returning to the field. It was an opportunity which, like the cordial itself, had been a pure gift of fortune.

I was resolved that tomorrow should be a new and a happier day for all concerned — even for Miss Carswell, wherever she was. Indeed it was she, even in her absence, who seemed to be spurring me on.

I drew a deep breath and took up the cordial. As I was about to pour it down I was struck by a sudden thought. I paused a moment and held the glass before me, gazing at its magical dark contents.

"So this," I mused, "is where the time goes . . ."

Then I tilted it and drank it off, and composed myself for another leap from the battlements.

## Chapter Thirty-four

AFTER the turmoil and confusion of the evening had passed, after the hounds had been returned to the kennels and a barricade of sturdy boards applied to Dora's casement, and after all the clocks in the house had testified to the extreme lateness of the hour, quiet descended at last on the Moorings. But it was to be an uneasy quiet, and a nervous one.

It had been decided that no advantage would be gained by pursuing the creature and Clemendy in the black dark. It was too difficult, the doctor pointed out, not to mention dangerous; and the rest of us, Dora included, had reluctantly agreed. He and the Squire then sent us all to our beds. Unfortunately the stable-lad who had been detailed to check on the prisoner, finding himself yawning and nodding, had gone to his bed as well. So that it was not until morning, as the first faint traces of dawn were painting the overcast, that Bothack's escape was discovered.

His flight, to be precise; and what was more, he had had help in the accomplishment of it.

The door to his small cell had been broken open — literally had been torn from its hinges — and replaced in a semblance of normalcy, so that no chance eye should note the damage. The help Bothack had received was manifest not only in this, but in the footprints left by his accomplice in the soft earth round the kennels. Large, bird-like prints they were, each with three toes directed forwards, and a fourth toe behind.

No sooner had we thrown our horses into motion and taken up the trail, than it became rather plain where that trail led — to the old cart-track winding northeastward into the hills. It was the way to Bothack's hovel, on the road to the Cupboard.

We pounded along at a rapid clip, the doctor and Stinker in the lead and Natty and I following with three of the trustier lads. The double track of Bothack and the creature, we found, veered sharply off at a spot opposite the hovel — the sometime side-cab, abandoned by the megalops men — and crossed the fields directly towards the abode of the recluse.

A freezing mist was blowing over the road, and through it we glimpsed, dimly, at a little height above the trees, the long, low-built structure of the cab, and the small spinney behind it.

We approached stealthily and quietly. I noted that the steps of the cab were down, but aside from this there was no hint of recent activity about the place. There was no sign of either Bothack or the creature, nothing to disturb the silence as we drew near but the muffled tramp of the horses and the creak of saddle leather.

At an appropriate distance we swung down and advanced on foot, all eyes hunting for the recluse. From the windows of his abode no brooding countenance glowered forth, no vocal challenge was thrown out. If Bothack was here and aware of our presence, he did not show it.

"Can he be asleep?" I wondered.

Swords in hand, the doctor and Stinker mounted cautiously to the door. Natty and the lads and I held back, circling round and taking up positions at intervals, to intercept Bothack should he seek to flee.

On the landing the doctor knocked on the jamb, but no answer was received. Carefully he pushed the door open and looked inside.

Together he and Stinker made a rapid search of the premises, but no Bothack was found. The hermit may have been there in the night, but he was not there now. Perhaps he had been alerted to our arrival, gone round to the spinney and was watching us as from a blind.

Next moment there came a shout from behind the cab, where one of the lads had stationed himself. Tingling with anticipation we raced to join him.

Over the broad, flat surface of a hoary tree-stump was smeared a quantity of what looked to be dried blood. As well there were sinister darkish drops, plentiful as blackberries, staining the ground adjacent, and there were footprints too. A trail of drops led to the side-cab where a line of buckets stood ranged, some with covers, some without.

The doctor blanched as his glance settled first on the stump, then on the buckets. One of them, which was covered, was spotted with bloodstains. The doctor did not hesitate, but removed the lid of the bucket, disclosing a bloody mass.

We grouped round him and peered inside. A breathless hush fell over us, the hearts of each recoiling at what was revealed there. Frozen in stares of disbelief, two of the lads murmured uneasily —

"Is't Clemendy, do 'ee think, Alan?"

"Ess, 'tis Clemendy, right 'nough — or 'twas she. Butchered, by the looks of 'un."

"You'm right. But there be so little of 'er, sure. Where be the rest of 'er?"

"Dunnaw. Eaten, most like."

"Ess, Alan, but these be the soft parts h'yur. Where ha' her shell parts got to?"

"Whatever are 'ee gettin' at, Nicholas?"

"Well . . ."

The doctor, having had his fill of the gruesome picture, started to say something, then held his breath and was silent. As for myself I nearly had turned ill at the discovery, for indeed it was Clemendy — Dora's little whatsit from out of time — reduced to a mess of offal in the bucket.

It was a cruel, ugly thing that had been done here. But Nicholas's observation was spot-on. Where *had* her shell parts got to?

We glanced uncomfortably at one another, and like the doctor said nothing for a time.

Then the doctor's face, having at first paled, suddenly grew black, as he struggled to find the words. Such savagery as this he saw before him sent a charge through his flesh, and a blaze of fire into his eyes. It was he himself who broke the quiet.

"Bloody jackals!" he gritted out.

Why had they done this to Clemendy? What possible cause can they have had?

Enraged, the doctor in his impotence shied a clod at the side-cab, saw it splatter there like the pumpkin-head of Bothack.

"I should have followed in the night. *Imbecile!*" he cried, choking down his disgust — disgust as much at himself as at the perpetrators. Then he stalked heatedly away.

All of us were feeling the same sick repugnance. Anger darkened every brow, for little Clemendy had been a favorite of most everyone at the Moorings and at Callander farm. Even Flounce had come to tolerate her.

It was decided to call on Dr. Hankey. Perhaps a study of Clemendy's remains might bring to light something that would be of assistance, that might explain what it was Bothack and his accomplice had wanted with her. It was Dr. Callander himself who took charge of the bucket, slinging it from his saddle-horn. Then we struck out for Dithering.

Grimly purposeful and silent we pushed our horses along. Slanting a glance at the doctor, I saw that the lines of his face were drawn and hard — immobile as a granite block. Of the chill wind that assailed us he took no notice, his eyes staring rigidly ahead under his hat-brim.

Fortunately Dr. Hankey was at home, having just had his lunch. We explained to him that we had found Clemendy — Dr. Callander related the particulars — and asked if he might make an examination of her, and give us his professional opinion.

The remains were laid out for him in his surgery. The physician clucked his tongue at the sight, and fitting on his spectacles he pored over the evidence with a meticulous scrutiny. We hung back as he went about his task. At length, after some hour's effort, he put down his instruments and stepped to the wash-stand.

"You saw no one round the place where they did this?" he asked, drying his hands on a towel.

"No one," said Dr. Callander. "So what is your conclusion?"

The physician blew his nose in a single, noisy burst, and blinked his eyes very rapidly.

"What you have here," he stated, with a little chuck of his head, "is an anatomical dissection."

"How do you mean that?"

"Exactly as I meant it. This animal was not slaughtered for food. The body cavities were not opened, the internal organs are intact and in place, as are the four limbs and the musculature. What the villains took from her," he concluded, "are her scutes. Now why should anybody want scutes?"

"Her bony shell, do you mean?"

"And the bony rings or sheath that encircled the tail, and the tail-knob as well. Even the head-shield has been removed — peeled right back from the skull. Someone wanted every last scute, and by jiminy," the physician nodded with a cluck and a snort, "he got it too."

"The scutes, and nothing more?"

"Not a sausage more."

"But why? They're unique to the species, true. But of what value can these bony plates be to anyone?"

Dr. Hankey shrugged and clucked his ignorance. Then he looked at his watch and murmured something about a call he had to make.

"It's for some foul purpose, no doubt," I ventured.

The medic glanced at me sharply.

"Well, I doubt that very much, young man. It's simply a case of a physician doing his job," he retorted.

"Sorry — didn't mean that — "

"A foul purpose, one which remains decidedly murky," said Dr. Callander, taking up my thought. Then he groaned and looked away, repulsed by the spectacle of Clemendy laid out before us like a carcass on a butcher's block. "What a proper blunder — I blame myself for it. I shouldn't have waited till the morning. Monstrous and abominable! This is the dirtiest piece of work that I ever heard of. They're playing some deep game they are, these three. *Idiot!*" he suddenly exploded, and smote himself on the temple for a fool.

There could be little doubt but that the three of them — Bothack, the piskie, and the creature in the Cupboard — were behind the present thefts. But of what use to them were the scutes of a pocket glypt? Where was the value? Certainly the bony armor was not digestible; meanwhile the few edible parts had been discarded in a bucket.

*Who amongst us is safe?* was the question that had been circulating of late in the taproom of the Pack Horse Inn.

Indeed who amongst us was safe, in view of Clemendy's fate? No one of us could rest secure until it was learned why scutes and nothing else had been taken from her. What indeed was this deep game the jackals were playing?

"But it avails us little now, for Clemendy is gone. In future I must use my head for something besides putting my hat on it," the doctor ground out. He clenched his hands into fists, his expression hardening the more his indignation rose. "It won't do — the man's in every way a scoundrel — ill usage, he claims — ha! — well, he's not seen ill usage until I've paid him his deserts — contemptible lout — worm — I'll make it deuced hot for him round these parts . . ."

"Better and better! For there's some low dogs," enthused Stinker, nodding his approval, "as deserves to be roasted. A pox on him, and a figo for his usage!"

As we worked to shake off the clouds that had gathered since the discovery of Clemendy, we began turning over in our minds the sundry means of vengeance at our dispose. Altogether though it seemed to me a poor deed to crush a worm, one who was, after all, not the real source of the evil; for that lay in the Cupboard.

Then the doctor drew himself up, slowly and deliberately, having prepared as best he might for the unenviable task that awaited him.

"For someone," he reminded us, "must tell Dora the news."

## Chapter Thirty-five

THREE days on, and still no Bothack.
In groups, searchers had scoured the vicinity of the hovel, the spinney, the road to the Cupboard. Sentries had been posted against his return, but the villain had not shown himself. He had disappeared, as if the very earth had swallowed him. Ordinary folk in Dithering wondered whether — nay, hoped, prayed — he had cut his lucky and fled the dales. Perhaps he had done so; or perhaps he had not done. Perhaps he had cause to remain. Perhaps he had more eggs on the spit, as the saying is.

At the Moorings the news of Clemendy had been received rather hard. But Dora, as became her, took it as well as could be expected. She had lost numbers of these little creatures of hers in her lifetime, for it was in the way of nature. But it was *not* in the way of nature to be treacherously abducted and flayed alive for the sake of bony scutes.

The villain Bothack had set at defiance the justice of the county, and that of Dithering in particular. As a result the Squire had taken pen and ink and lodged an information against him. As well he had dispatched a letter by express messenger to the sheriff's office at Medlow, that they be on watch for the scoundrel who was sought in connection with a variety of offenses, inclusive of housebreaking, assault and battery, theft of property, etc., etc. In his capacity as a magistrate the Squire intended to deal summarily with the beggar, once he had found him.

But three days had passed and no reports of Bothack had been received, in Dithering or elsewhere. It did not look promising.

Meanwhile a small service had been conducted for Clemendy and her remains laid to rest in a snug corner of the garden, that which in life she had particularly favored.

It was a melancholy scene. Grieving over the loss we stood round Clemendy's tiny plot, giving ear to the vicar's message of hope and consolation.

The vicar was that same young man — that "glib young fellow in gaiters" — who regularly was received at dinner at the Moorings, and whose spouting of "a lot o' damfool nonsense" did much to staunch the flow of the Squire's spirits. But the clergyman's words were received rather differently today by the sad little group in the garden, so that even the Squire, contrary to habit, had been moved by them.

The vicar was all grace, sympathy, and gentleness. He related how such misfortunes of the Lord's sending did but serve to strengthen us in our faith, to test us, to nourish us. At the close he presented Dora with a small spray of flowers, which she placed on Clemendy's grave beside her own and Mattie's offering there.

"A hundred joyful recollections," he observed, "of the brief time granted us with our pets — a gift of the Lord's — needs must suffice to comfort us in future and forever more. For remember that animals, even those beloved of us as pets, have not eternal souls; and so we and they shall never meet again, not even in heaven. Days together in this earthly life are all that is afforded us, so let us cherish them and their memory, and give thanks to God."

*It seems a terrible long time, forever more,* I reflected.

"Remember too, and be heartened by it," the clergyman went on, "that these our animal friends have been accorded a special place in our Maker's eyes. That is because Jesus was born in a stable, and so the animals know all about Him . . ."

*And so why give such special creatures no immortal souls? Is this not a hard and merciless judgment? Is this meant to pass for hope and consolation?*

I could not help musing over these things, there by Clemendy's grave, especially as it was the vicar himself — he of the damfool nonsense — who had brought them up.

At the conclusion of the service the Squire shook the vicar's hand and thanked him for his words of solace, and reminded him that he was welcome to dinner at the Moorings most any day of the week.

This was something of a departure for the old dalesman; but then, having thought over it a little, and recalling how the "glib young fellow" had drained the last of his port, almost at once he regretted the offer.

The days passed uneasily. There had been no further showing of the creature — no further bird-like tracks — and of course no sign of Bothack. Owing to this latest incursion all the livestock were under heavy guard now at the farms, and the hounds and horses too. Tristan Colley, Sweezy, Kneebone, and the others met often at the Pack Horse Inn, where Mr. Readymoney and his staff listened with interest to their complaints, as did Dr. Callander, Natty, Stinker, and I.

The discontent amongst the farmers was like the turbid gush from the sluice of a mill-pond. One afternoon there was a heated debate in which the dalesmen had inveighed against Bothack each in his turn. But it produced little result, for Bothack had gone to ground. A courageous few there were who recommended that they gather *en masse* at the Cupboard and search it; though most advised against any such rash action, saying they didn't know what might be stirred up there. Even Cedar Jack, one of the most knowledgeable on the subject, did not favor it.

"Not to be thought on," he solemnly intoned from his cloud of mundungus, "nor looked into . . ."

As for Bothack, going to ground had been a wise precaution. For had he chosen to show himself within a stone's throw of Dithering, odds were his neck would not have been worth a penny's purchase.

One morning the doctor awoke at the farm, and was apprized by Stokes that a gift had been left for him on the mat outside the door to the stable-yard. The doctor went to claim it, and discovered there a slaughtered mouse.

"A present from Flounce," he nodded genially.

In her youth Flounce had been a tremendous mouser with an admirable reputation. But in the years succeeding, her activities in this area gradually had diminished. In fact so far as the doctor could recollect this was perhaps only the third or fourth such trophy she had presented him with since the return to Callander farm.

"Very pleased with herself this morning, I expect," he chuckled.

And when shortly Flounce appeared, striding into the room with her chest outflung and her plume aloft, she was lavishly admired and congratulated, garnering almost an entire day's budget of praise for her fine work of the early hours.

Not long afterwards the doctor, Natty, Stinker, and Flounce were received at the Moorings, where they had been invited to breakfast. Flounce adroitly hopped from her club bag, and with a gracious air waited for her dish to be placed before her by Mattie. The rest of us, too, waited while the breakfast was laid on, then commenced our enjoyment of it with gusto.

Later, after the table had been cleared, we retired to the parlor and spent there a quiet morning reading and chatting. The Squire, his leg thrust stiffly out, occupied his usual place on the sofa, where he sat smoking his pipe and scowling at the paper, and muttering under his breath about the damnable enormities which the world had unleashed upon dalesmen in these times of ours.

"I wonder where Mattie has gotten to?" Dora said presently, raising her eyes from her book. "For I have not seen her since breakfast . . ."

She saw that her father had sunk into one of his moods, one that well matched the gloomy day in the windows.

Flinging aside his paper, the Squire wrung his head sadly. "I don't know about this world any more. Shocking state it's in. My world, certainly — that which I knew as a young man — has passed. All of it — gone and passed. It was a different time then, certainly. It was a time when people and things and ways were other than they are today. People were more intelligent, I believe. People showed the proper respect. But there's precious few left now who remember. Most of my school already have set off on the long vacation. Soon they'll be packing me off, too . . ."

"Oh, Dad," Dora cried, rising and kissing him on the cheek, "do banish that long face of yours! You musn't let George Jarlcot when he returns hear you talk so. For he's a jolly man and hasn't the time for it."

"You've had a difficult few days, haven't you, dear?"

"As have we all. Especially my poor Mattie. She's taken it rather hard. She blames herself, you know."

A housemaid who happened to be passing made a curtsy and nodded to the squire.

"Beg 'ee pardon, sir, eff 'ee plaise. An' did Mattie find 'ee in the garden, miss?" she inquired, addressing Dora.

"In the garden, Jenna? Well, I have not been in the garden. I have been here in the parlor since breakfast. I haven't seen Mattie; indeed I have myself been wondering what mischief she's gotten into. When was it she was looking for me? Is there something the matter, Jenna?"

## Chapter Thirty-six

THE housemaid seemed puzzled.

"'Twas earlier — an hour agone at the laist, mebbe two. Well, 'tis strange, so 'tis. Didn' she find 'ee there, miss?"

I shifted uneasily in my chair. A feeling had come over me, as of some ill news impending.

Plainly Dora knew nothing of this business of the garden — why should she have done? For as she had explained, she had been in our company since breakfast. She had not been near the garden.

She questioned the maid further. The doctor and I listened attentively. Even the Squire, having shrugged off his mood, champed his pipe and awaited the outcome with seeming interest.

The housemaid related that she and Mattie had heard a voice calling in the garden, not long after breakfast.

"Mattie, Mattie," had been the summons, firmly but softly delivered, "come 'ee h'yur, Mattie . . ."

"'Twas axin' her to come to the garden, miss," the maid explained.

"I never was in the garden," Dora reiterated.

"But 'twas yer own dear voice a-callin' to 'er — axin' pardon, miss — through the kitchen lattice. We did hear it ourselfs."

"I never was in the garden, nor did I call for Mattie. Did either of you see me there?"

A crease furrowed the maid's brow. "Well, no, miss — well, not azackly. Ef 'ee plaise, miss, we didn' knaw better, for 'e did sound so like 'ee, out o' doubt. We s'posed 'twas summat to do wi' little Clemendy's grave . . . the flowers . . ."

"Where is she now? Where is Mattie?"

The girl's face was a blank. "Dunnaw, miss — for I've not see'd her since she went out. Oh, where can she be, miss? Didn' she come in?"

My premonition had given rise to an ugly fear that something was not right. Likewise I saw a shadow darken the doctor's face, saw the look of concern in Dora's.

Further questioning of the maid produced a more complete record of what had transpired. It seemed that Mattie had left in response to the summons, that she had passed by the old thorn hedge at the bottom of the garden, where Jenna had had a transient glimpse of someone — she had thought it was Dora — who had stepped out to meet her. Just there the path bent sharply, and the two had disappeared from sight.

"It was not I who met her. Who can it have been?" Dora said.

A pendulum clock in the room began chiming the hour. I felt a sudden tingle as if an icy hand had been laid on my neck.

The housemaid added that Flounce too had been in the kitchen at the time, enjoying the company there, and that when Mattie had gone out she had risen and followed her.

The doctor, looking round, observed that Flounce was not in her customary seat of luxury on the hearthrug. Now that he thought of it, he had not seen her for some while — not, indeed, since breakfast.

Perhaps she had become absorbed in the stalking of a mouse in the garden? Perhaps her success at the farm had encouraged her to further endeavors?

The housemaid, thinking over it, recalled that she had seen something like a bird or aireymouse — a bat — dart by the kitchen lattice, moments before she and Mattie had heard the voice calling. But was it not a curious time of day for an aireymouse to be abroad?

The doctor sat motionless, his face a mask of thought.

"What can have happened?" Dora said. "Where is Mattie? Where is Flounce?"

I glanced at the pendulum clock. At least an hour and a half must have passed since the events recounted by Jenna.

Directly we went outside and commenced a search. We arrived at the bottom of the garden, beside the hedge, and there, clearly outlined in the moist earth, was a trail — the neat little footprints of Mattie — leading away.

And there too, shown emerging from the hedge, were the tracks of a man, made by a broad, flat-soled boot.

"It needs no crystal-gazer to see what has happened here," the doctor said. "Bothack has lured her away."

Bothack in the garden!

But it can't have been the hermit's surly rasp of a voice that Mattie and Jenna had heard calling, certainly?

The shadow of a bird or bat, darting past the lattice . . .

*Piskie!*

There exists, among the many folk traditions of the dales, another of those superstitions which can be traced to our Cornish ancestors — the notion of being "piskie-led". Travelers who have gone astray, become confused or lost; ordinary townspeople who report having heard a voice calling to them, then are found wandering in seeming loss of their senses, as if bewitched; such as these are said to have been piskie-led — enticed away by one of these prankish illusions of legend.

But our piskie was no illusion, and its enticements no prank, but a contrivance of the enemy.

Mattie had been lured into the garden through the piskie's dissemblance — by its counterfeiting of Dora's voice. Once there, evil eyes had watched her from the thorn hedge, where she had fallen neatly into the trap.

The doctor exclaimed his disgust. "The man must be half-crazed to have essayed this — another incursion!"

"Or been pushed to it," I suggested.

The housemaid, too, scarcely could believe it.

"Oh, oh," she quavered, "'twas a mean trick, miss, so 'twas — a downright cheat. But what be it about? Where be they gone? What be the use o' Mattie to a shammick like Bothack?"

"They still may be near. Dora — call for Stinker and Natty," the doctor directed.

Meanwhile he and I had begun hunting through the brush for the double trail of Mattie and her abductor. It was easily discerned — the villain seemed to have made no effort to conceal it — then moments later the doctor gave a shout.

From his fingers hung a ragged square of cloth, probably a handkerchief. It was of coarse material and was spotted with bright dabs of blood.

"Eveydence!" Stinker exclaimed, as he and Natty joined us.

The cloth had been lying on the ground, full in the doctor's view. It did not belong to Mattie and was presumed to be Bothack's. The evidence of the blood, however, was open to question.

Two pairs of eyes met: the doctor's and my own. Hadn't Flounce followed her friend Mattie out into the garden? And wasn't Flounce, that notable mouser, an adept in the employment of her claws and teeth? But where was she now? We called for her and for Mattie, but no one appeared.

The trail took the direction of the lower wood, towards Dithering and the stream. Side by side the tracks of Bothack and Mattie stretched ahead. He had led her off, and she had gone — to all appearances willingly. But the pair had stolen a march on us, certainly, of some two hours now.

It was a fair assumption that Bothack had threatened her, or had threatened to harm Dora, if she did not go with him. It seemed the only explanation for the evidence of the tracks leading away side by side.

But why seize Mattie? To exact a measure of revenge? And where had Flounce gotten to? Perhaps she was trailing them as well, if the bloodied cloth was a result of her activities.

The doctor made a swift appraisal of the situation. Proceeding on foot our progress necessarily would be hindered by the lead our quarry had gained. If we were to catch them we should need horses from the Squire's string.

We returned to the house. The despair in Jenna's voice was manifest as we entered. If only she had sounded the alarm, she lamented, wringing her hands . . . if only, if only . . .

Stoutly Dora set her teeth and declared —

"She'll brave it out she will, my Mattie. We must keep up heart, for there's no alternative. We'll take her from Bothack."

Perhaps he had removed her to his skulking-place, to his hovel of a side-cab on the road to the Cupboard? Or perhaps he had not done — for would it not be the first place searchers would look?

The doctor was pacing impatient strides up and down the floor, as we waited for the horses.

"By thunder," vowed the Squire, "the beggar shall account for her or be thrashed on the spot. This Bothack is one of the greatest blackguards yet unhanged. We'll send him to the rightabouts."

"Plaguy villain, I've a figo for him at the ready," Stinker growled, fingering the hilt of his sword. "A pox on him! Did ye ever see such a clock in yer life, and on such a head? Miserable creature!"

The doctor's complexion had been changing rapidly into various shades as he paced the room. For he had been thinking hard, and the thoughts he had been thinking were not pleasant thoughts. Then suddenly he halted, his eyes darkening and dilating as though stirred by a shiversome wind.

"In the name of twenty devils," he exclaimed, "it can't be . . . it *must* not be . . ."

He flashed me a look. A shudder passed through me as a horrid possibility crashed home.

Fanny Meadows, Bridgit Gooderly, Jocund Josie the little milkmaid from Sweezy's — all had vanished mysteriously. And of course there had been Dickie Fish, Harry Smelt . . .

*In the name of twenty devils, it cannot be . . . it simply cannot . . .*

Fighting off the thought, I glanced at the doctor, then at Stinker. Each in his turn nodded grim assent — for all of us, it seemed, had reached the same monstrous conclusion. All at once it struck me that there was no need to be hunting up footprints.

The set of the doctor's chin and his clenched fists were more eloquent than words. *There is an unspeakable evil here. Let us to horse and make for the Cupboard.*

There was not a moment to spare. The doctor whisked round and hastened off towards the stables. The rest of us followed — even the

Squire, whose leg today would be no impediment, given the circumstances.

"Time to pluck up a little mettle," he declared, fiercely adjusting his hat on his head, "and for every man jack of us to be counted."

The horses had been dressed and saddled as speedily as possible — the Squire's favorite, Dapple, for the old dalesman, Bob Cob for Dr. Callander, and some sturdy trail-ponies for Stinker, Natty, and myself. Over her father's objections, Dora had insisted that she too must be of the party. The Squire looked his astonishment, as she tossed up her chin and pronounced herself as ready as the next man jack of us to fly to the aid of Mattie. Knowing his daughter as he did, this had been sufficient to persuade him, and a palfrey and side-saddle quickly were obtained.

It was a surly kind of day. The light had a weird, unearthly cast to it. Everywhere, great tumbling masses of cloudstuff hung sinister and lowering over a doomed earth below. The very air crackled with tension and unease.

Riding in lead of the party was Dr. Callander, with Stinker and myself behind him, followed by Dora and her father, and in the rear Stokes and three others with a led horse for Mattie.

By means of the bloodstained cloth the hounds had been put on the trail — as a precaution lest we were wrong — and now the whipper-in gave them their heads.

The doctor shoved Bob Cob into motion, and duly armed and accoutered the party thundered into the road trailing the hounds, who already had the scent and were filling the air with their eager cries.

## Chapter Thirty-seven

THERE was a jitteriness had come over me, and as we pounded along I had an eerie sense that the brooding steeps on either side of us were watchful, that invisible eyes were tracking us from on high.

Was it the Woldfolk, or was it only my nervous imagination? Or was it all so much nonsense as the Squire believed?

At one point the way dipped between rising turf-banks. A shadow of the frowning hills would have lain upon us there, had there been sun to cast it. As it was, it was a metaphorical shadow that darkened our road and fell heavily upon our souls.

Then the turf-banks dropped away, their place taken by stretches of broken country between the cart-track and the gloom-shrouded swells. The hounds meanwhile had been coursing along with splendor and dash. They had the scent and were leading us in the anticipated direction. Already Bothack's hovel had been passed, and now it was on to the Cupboard.

The doctor had not held it expedient to divide our forces. It had been his view that Bothack would make straight for the Cupboard, taking Mattie with him. The trail of footprints had vanished — our quarry had left the cart-track — but the eager running of the hounds had all but confirmed the doctor's belief.

Ere we knew it, or so it seemed, the lofty sweep of the Graystone Crags had risen up before us. Higher they climbed, and still higher, above the timber-tops, and crowded in close, and then we were there.

As we swung down the whipper-in hurriedly called in his charges. The springy mat of moss and pine needles was like a cushion under our feet as we made our way towards the Cupboard. Straining against their collars, the hounds barked vociferously.

All at once a pungent odor other than of pines was in the air, and suddenly, as if from nowhere, a man was standing before us, in the loom of a giant clumber. A fleecy jerkin, much muddied, corduroys and knee-boots, a weathered baldric from which a cutlass depended — such were the accouterments of the man.

The hounds, startled too, momentarily ceased their yowling. We all of us gazed in surprise at the newcomer. He, having had warning of our approach, met our glances without remark. He stood leaning against the tree with his arms folded, calmly smoking. Eyes like black beads set in a familiar leathery visage, in the shadow of a wide-awake as big as the moon, regarded us through a turbulent haze of mundungus.

"Tregennis!" the Squire exclaimed.

The woodsman inclined his head in grave acknowledgment.

"Yer worship," he drawled. "Callander . . . Earnscliff . . ."

"Mr. Jack," nodded the doctor.

The veteran arched his brows as his glance lighted on Dora.

"Miss Fetching," said he, with a courteous tug at his hat-brim.

"Mr. Tregennis," Dora said.

Stinker, Natty, the lads — all of them known to the woodsman — were acknowledged in their turn.

His quarterstaff stood within arm's reach; like its owner it was inclining easily against the bole of the clumber pine. On the ground at his feet sat a tall, high-crowned hat, of the chimney-pot variety.

We recognized the hat instantly as Bothack's.

The Squire was blunt and to the point.

"Have you seen the blackguard?" he demanded.

The woodsman nodded. Clearly he understood who was meant, as we all were eyeing the hat.

"Where is he, then? For we have business with him."

The veteran gave a sidewise chuck of his head, indicating the Cupboard.

"But one way in," he stated matter-of-factly, "but one way out."

"Had he a young girl with him? Miss Fetching's maid?" the doctor asked.

"The abigail? Dessay he had."

"Where is she? Where is Mattie?" Dora demanded.

"Gone," said Jack.

"Gone?"

"Or . . . not gone."

"Gone, or not gone? Whatever does that mean?"

The woodsman shrugged. His manner, while entertaining perhaps in the atmosphere of the inn, was a trifle exasperating in the loom of the clumber pine.

"Tell us all you know," the doctor urged. "Bothack has fled into the Cupboard. You say he had our Mattie with him. He forcibly removed her from us, and we have come to take her back."

The veteran, squaring his shoulders, threw a wary glance at the Cupboard, over which he had been keeping a diligent watch. Then he swung back again and looked us all hard from head to foot, as if appraising our mettle. Gradually his features unbent.

"I'll acquaint 'ee, then," he said deliberately, between puffs, "wi' the partic'lars."

The volume of smoke that rolled from him was prodigious, as if an entire chimney had set up housekeeping in his guts. A solitary individual by nature and by vocation, he was in the habit of using few words. Few words were what he delivered, but they were sufficient to sketch out the tale.

By an accident of fortune the woodsman had been patrolling near Bothack's hovel, where from a distance he had spied the recluse and Mattie on the march in the cart-track. From the first it was evident that the girl was a reluctant companion, for her eyes were cast down and she walked with a dragging step, so that several times Bothack was obliged to shove her roughly on. In his experience the veteran had found this an odd picture, and sensing evil he had taken it upon himself to follow them.

It rapidly became clear where their destination lay. This too the woodsman found suspicious, and knowing as he did the reputation of the place — "a bad nayborhood, naybors" — and that of Bothack, he had made his stand and confronted the hermit.

No sooner had Bothack's ire been drawn, than Mattie's clenched fist struck at him — it held a knitting-needle — and she made a dash for liberty. Blood spurted from the jowls of Bothack. He caught hold of the object impaled in his throat and wrenched it free, then hoisted his club and engaged the woodsman and his staff.

As they closed, the forester from a corner of eye saw something sleekly metallic launch itself from a pine-snag near at hand, and go winging off in the direction Mattie had taken.

*Not to be thought on, nor looked into. Piskies — not human — not right!*

It was an affair of rough-and-tumble, the clash there in the glade. For a time the combatants successfully parried each other's strokes, crab-tree club versus quarterstaff. Bothack had seemed in an especially vicious humor, one made even uglier and more menacing by the injuries he had received, and he fought like a wild thing. The blood surged in his veins; his face glowed like a beetroot, his hard eyes flashed under his massive bulge of brow. The clatter of their weapons rang like hailstones on a latticed casement. Twice the woodsman dealt his opponent a buffet that might have felled an ox, and twice Bothack stood to it stoutly and returned it in kind.

But ultimately his crab-tree and sinews proved no match for the forester's skill. They had had a proper time of it, but Jack had pummeled him well enough. The hermit had been on the verge of surrender, when a blur of wings came droning overhead. At this new threat he took alarm and bolted. Round and round his head the piskie swooped, dove, darted, driving him forward — shepherding him along, as it were — and he fleeing from it in a panic. Cedar Jack had followed — stealthily, craftily, for piskies were not to be thought on — and had seen Bothack, brawny arms failing, disappear inside the Cupboard, the piskie harrying him to the last.

"'Twas his tall chimney-pot there he did lose i' the scuffle," Jack explained, nudging the hat with his boot.

"Sounds a bully good scrap. Wish I'd had me a sight of it," Stinker said. "Proper time, eh?"

Proper indeed. The villain had been in an exceedingly desperate state — desperate to escape from Jack, desperate to recover his lost captive, desperate in the end to be spared the Cupboard. But his hasty and disorderly flight had been for naught, the piskie having steered him dead straight into the lair of Eldritch. What had been abundantly clear was that he had not wanted to go.

*For a hellish scrape do await 'ee ef 'ee durst challenge the Cupboard.*

The woodsman pushed his chest against his fleecy tunic and strutted up and down, blowing clouds from his pipe. It was the chilly air on the wolds, he explained, that encouraged his smoking. Then, returning to Bothack, he nodded confidently — "He'll come to grief, I dessay. Clean mazed he must be, when 'ee think of't."

And there at the foot of the clumber he had retired to watch, his interest piqued by the singular events of the day.

So far then as we knew, Bothack was in the Cupboard. But what of Mattie?

It was the piskie that had driven Bothack into the den of Eldritch. Earlier, it was the piskie that had chased after Mattie in the woods.

*Had she too been driven into the Cupboard?*

Gone, or not gone — now we understood the forester's meaning. For he knew not whether Mattie had escaped, or whether she was in the Cupboard with Bothack. She, who had wounded and enraged the desperate villain . . .

Before us the jagged face of the Crags lifted like a wall, and at its base the gloomy opening so like a gullet seemed to be daring us to enter. Taunting us, even.

Where to search for Mattie? How to search for Mattie?

Gone, or not gone? In the Cupboard, or out of it?

## Chapter Thirty-eight

FOR a long minute no one spoke. Squire Fetching, his stick punctuating his steps, paced up and down, mind working, leg creaking. Meanwhile Cedar Jack had resumed his pipe, his head in a haze and his eyes on the Cupboard. The doctor stroked his chin in thought, trading glances with Dora and myself.

At length a decision was reached — we spread out a distance and called aloud for Mattie. Our hope was that she had eluded the piskie, and was in hiding somewhere within earshot. We called and called, our voices echoing through the timber, but without result. Reluctantly we gave it up.

"She may be in the Cupboard with Bothack — or she may not be in the Cupboard. Perhaps now we ought to divide our forces," the doctor suggested.

"I see no alternative," I agreed.

Came the dragging sizzle of the woodsman's pipe. His head rolled slowly from side to side, and his hat with it, a sober cast of doubt on his countenance. Gravely he informed us that we should need all our strength of numbers for the Cupboard — that is, assuming we meant to challenge it, as Bothack had phrased it.

"What do you know of Bothack, by the by? And what do you know of the Cupboard?" the doctor asked him.

Dora, impatient of delay, walked right up to him and demanded — "What do you know of my Mattie?"

The forester shook his head again, denying any knowledge of the abigail, as he called her, beyond that which he already had disclosed. But Mawgan Bothack, it turned out, was another story.

"Proper villain, *that* one," he drawled, with a long roll of his eyes. "And ould Jack shud knaw 'un, for Jack has seen an' heard plenty."

"Do you know something of Bothack?" I asked. "Is he a friend of yours?"

The veteran laughed shortly. "Friend? What friend be there o' Bothack in these dales but Bothack hisself? Like ould Helyer, him that won't be comin' back h'yur-along no more, as he was gibbeted on a post — 'twas but a step off there — years agone in the Christmas."

"I remember Helyer — damned bad lot," nodded the Squire, who as a magistrate had had some concern in the affair.

It turned out that the forester knew rather more about Mawgan Bothack than he liked to admit. For his vocation took him oft round these shadowy precincts, where he had run across Bothack more than a few times, had been invited even to share a bottle and some bread and cheese at the hermit's table.

"He did receive me cordially 'nough," he recalled, knocking back his head. "'Twasn't drink alone, hows'ever, but some fine talk he did foist on ould Jack. Sim me the gawkum done it a-purpose, too — terrible mean-spirited, *that* one is. 'I bain't a creature,' says he. 'For this misshapen figger, 'twas not o' my doin'. This poor trunk o' mine — this crooked back — this hideous lump of a carcass — 'twas bequeathed me by my mother. Look on me, friend — 'ee do not shrink from me as do the rest. The rest! By all the many wrongs I've sustained, I wish 'em naught but ill, the bleddy fools — I spurn 'em all — dash 'em to atoms, every one! Wretched outcast and miserable though I be, drabbet it — *I bain't a creature!*' Sure this Bothack be 'bout the sourest dog ould Jack ever did sup with."

It appeared the forester was not one of those Ditheringites with whom the hermit was at perpetual odds, like Bothack's sometime neighbors in Hog Gut Lane, or any of the miserly clod-breakers who viewed him with such suspicion.

"'For 'ee be such a one, Jack,' says he, wi' rare candor, 'as I looks on wi' least loathing.'"

It was for this reason that Bothack at times, when in his cups, had confided in the woodsman.

"And what," the doctor pursued, "has he told you of the real creature? Of the monster in the Cupboard? Of the 'great, long, gangly, ghastly' sort of thing, with the 'queer, creepin' manner o' gait' that you told us of at the inn? What is Bothack to this monster?"

The brow of the veteran dimmed and darkened under the canopy of his wide-awake.

"Mounster," he echoed, the smoke billowing in odorous waves from his lips. His eyes were heavy, his tone was grim.

"Is it Eldritch?"

"Not Eldritch," said Jack, shaking his head — "not Eldritch — not human — *not right!*"

"But what has Bothack told you of it? Surely he has told you of it?" the doctor persisted. "It is in there now, is it not? Inside the Cupboard with Bothack — and for all we know with our Mattie as well?"

He felt the urgent press of Dora's hand. Although she kept silent her touch communicated to him the fear that dogged us all.

"Ess, 'tis in there, I dessay — a-prowlin' and a-skulkin' — unholy devil!" spat out Jack.

"What is Bothack to it?"

"Dunnaw. As much a slave as anything, I dessay. A slave — an instrument o' the creature — an' so too the piskie."

From what the veteran had been able to winkle out, Bothack had been chosen by this monster to do its bidding, as in times past it had chosen others.

"Harry Smelt, the old tinker," the doctor said, "must've been one of these. For he lived out this way, during a stretch of years when the thieves were active. And then afterwards he vanished."

As for the monster, Jack related, long now had it dwelt in its den, since far back in time. For during one of their table discussions the hermit had let fall a remark that 'the mounster, it did come in wi' the sundering'."

*The sundering!* The cataclysmic event that had shattered the world some two hundred years ago, when nearly all of mankind had been obliterated, and the few survivors plunged into a new and even deeper Ice Age. All commerce, all communication beyond the long coast had ceased; the tall ships came and went no more. To almost everyone the wider world, if it still existed, in whatever form, had lost its meaning. No one gave a thought to it any more.

The doctor was like a man who, after a long journey, sees an old, familiar place with new eyes. He revealed to us then that the peculiar geology he had identified in the Cupboard's inner chamber — signs of a general disturbance of the ground, which were restricted to that space — he believed to correspond in time with the sundering.

What the woodsman had next to tell us was of even greater interest.

If he understood Bothack aright, said Jack, the creature had been trapped here since its arrival, and was unable to leave. Its sole objective now was to free itself and return to its own kind. But it was impossible — the monster was itself a prisoner of sorts — although the forester knew not why. Nor did Bothack, evidently. Or perhaps he was not telling.

Needless to say, this goblin tale all sounded rather fantastic. What had Bothack meant by 'its own kind'? Where were they? *What* were they? And were we really to believe that any sort of flesh-and-blood being can have survived in the Cupboard for two hundred years?

"Great sticks alive," the Squire mumbled, "whoever heard such a story? Damfool nonsense!"

The doctor recalled a vision from his childhood, the memory of it rising before him now like a bubble. A memory of two small boys, neither very well washed, setting out from town on their ponies for Eldritch's Cupboard. It was the morning he and Dickie Fish had set off to beard the monster in its den. The doctor remembered it well — the inner chamber, the roasting-spit, the remains of the braggaty calf. The emerald ray darting about, the *whirr* of wings in the black dark. The orange light flowing up from below, and emerging from it a scarecrow riding on spidery stalks and quick, bird-like feet, with knobbed joints that rattled, and forelimbs with grasping claws poised to seize him.

And later, Dickie Fish had disappeared.

The experience had made a vivid impression on the doctor at the time. A creature — monster — demon, if you will — risen from the infernal depths, where agelong it had dwelt . . .

Continuing his story, the woodsman had learned that the creature of needs passed nearly all of its life asleep — whole years at a stretch, six to be precise — before waking for a short spell, during which it must have nourishment, and then relapsing again into its hibernative state for another half-dozen years. It was this cycle which had enabled it to sustain itself in the Cupboard for the two centuries since it had *come in with the sundering.*

Every six years, regular as clockwork . . .

It was the creature that was the source of the thievery, it being Bothack's task to obtain for it the food it required. And what it required was meat, and in abundance. Only rarely did the creature itself venture abroad. Instead it dispatched its slave Bothack, for whom the smaller livestock were the easiest and simplest to procure.

For make no mistake: this creature in the Cupboard was the master and Bothack the slave. In the span of its two hundred years it had had many slaves, most of them pariahs — outcasts — friendless, isolated, alone — persons very like the monster itself.

Old Harry Smelt the tinker had been that sort of person; and yet Harry Smelt had gone missing. And what of the others who had vanished? Dickie Fish, little Fanny Meadows, Bridgit Gooderly, Josie the milkmaid from Sweezy's? Surely they were not slaves? What of Davy Zoze, Dr. Hankey's lad, who had sought shelter in a tree on account of something that had frightened him in the road, and who had then annihilated himself in a leap from his mother's window?

Why should Bothack have consented to this slavery of a sorts? It was as though a mystic spell had been laid on him. Well, perhaps one had been. Perhaps the persuasive forces of this creature were impervious to resistance.

"Funny in the head — always said he was," was the Squire's view of it.

Not formed as other men, solitary, resentful, driven before a gale of circumstance, Bothack had been confronted with a power he was incapable of opposing.

Perhaps this monster was of the Woldfolk? Perhaps it was to the Woldfolk it was seeking to return? Perhaps, being one of them, it had cast an actual spell on Bothack? For it was rumored that the folk were adepts in such witchery.

But Cedar Jack's headshake was emphatic. "Nowt to do with the folk," he intoned. "Nowt it knows of 'em — not its kind."

As for the piskie, the creature's other instrument — well, it was no living, breathing thing, but was a mechanism of some type. How then was it animated, and what manner of evil science, of black and secret arts, can have produced such a monstrosity?

And what the devil had Bothack's master wanted with the scutes from poor Clemendy? Had wanted so badly that it would itself steal forth from its den and tear the iron grating from Dora's casement to obtain them?

What was this deep game it was playing? Who were its kind, and where were they? How and why had it come to be marooned here?

All at once the Squire drew himself up, a sudden thought having struck him, and with some irritation demanded of the forester —

"And you did nothing about it? You told no one this man Bothack was the poacher? You deliberately withheld your knowledge of it? For by thunder . . . the blasted beggar . . . no respect . . ."

"And what of Mattie?" Dora said impatiently. "For why else are we here but to recover her?"

If she had managed to elude the piskie and conceal herself in the woods, so much the better; for the moment she ought to be safe. The rub was that we could scarcely proceed on such an assumption. For while the forester had been contending with Bothack, the piskie well might have chased her into the Cupboard.

There was but one course open to us — to assume the worst. And how the minutes were ticking by . . .

"The man is sought," said the Squire, disregarding the pain his leg was causing him, "and we must do all in our power to bring him to book. And I dare say it's odds our girl is in there with him."

No one particularly relished such an assignment, least of all Mr. Cedar Jack Tregennis. But where Mattie was concerned there was not a one amongst us to waver. The woodsman had his quarterstaff and cutlass, and we our bladed steel. As for Dora, she scorned her father's injunction that she remain with the hounds and the whipper-in. Instead she drew her own sword — a slender walking rapier, razor-keen — and declared herself as prepared as the next man jack of us for the challenge.

There was an evil feeling abroad in the air. Before us loomed the opening to the realm of Eldritch, and for a moment I reflected on the curious train of circumstances that had brought us to this pass.

With a sigh the forester knocked out his briar, took his quarterstaff in hand, shoved his wide-awake firmly down on his head. Stinker pulled his small-sword from its sheath, the rest of us our cutlasses. Two of the lads crowded up behind.

The doctor, leading the party, took a deep, long breath; and there being nothing else for it, we strode into the Cupboard.

## Chapter Thirty-nine

"CAREFUL how you go, Dad."
The Squire had found it hard slogging negotiating the maze of fallen rock that was the Cupboard. He hobbled and creaked his way along, guided by the feel of his stick and by the rays of the doctor's light. The lantern's beam flickered over the debris piles, the sculpted terraces, the shimmering deposits of flowstone. But no leisure had we for sightseeing today, as we were bent on a more pressing errand.

We crept forward stealthily.

"Mattie? Mattie, are you here?"

Our calls were answered by a silence so deep our voices seemed to trace concentric circles in it, like pebbles in water, the walls flinging back uncanny echoes.

As we neared the inner chamber we still had found no one, and no evidence that either Mattie or anybody else was present.

That is until a smoky aroma was wafted to our nostrils, as that of an ox being roasted. But the whiff given off was not so ox-like, I reflected, having a flavor of savagery to it, a hint of sinister doings. All at once I felt that creeping sort of uneasiness which often seems like the touch of something from another world.

Then the chamber opened up before us, and in the dark splash of shadow at the center of it a glow of embers stood out — the remains of a cook-fire. Tendrils of smoke streamed from it, suggesting it had not been long abandoned.

Already as we drew near it a hideous thought had arisen in my mind, so chilling as to freeze the air in my lungs and the blood in my veins.

The doctor's light played over the makeshift hearth and the charred mass impaled on the spit.

Revealed there was a half-finished meal. Had there been a further loss? For I knew not of one, the dalesmen having taken extraordinary measures of late to safeguard their stock.

Cedar Jack, a man in the know, stated there had been none — no animals gone missing.

He and the doctor and I stepped nearer to inspect the smoldering husk. The woodsman eyed it suspiciously, poking at it with his staff. A chunk of flesh, loosened from the main mass, fell black and sizzling to the ground. A fragment of bone was seen protruding from it, and some of the flesh looked to be invested in burnt cloth.

A prickly feeling spread itself all over the top of my scalp.

"That bain't a calf," said Jack.

The meal had been only partly devoured, a sizable hunk of it remaining on the spit. Scraps and discards were strewn about the area. Someone had dined here recently, very hastily, and very messily.

I stood frozen with horror, the truth dawning on me in a rush.

*"My stars . . ."*

What had been skewered on the spit lay almost beyond the power of human brains to conceive. It made the sweat come out all over my face and raised a tide of nausea in my middle.

I heard a low growl as of some animal beside me, and was surprised to find it was the doctor.

"Monstrous! Unspeakable!"

We stared aghast, scarcely able to credit our senses.

"Surely such an abomination is impossible," said the Squire, choking down his disgust. "What kind of world is this? What manner of people have we become? May God pity us . . ."

"What is it? What's there?" Dora demanded, pushing forward.

"See here, missy," Stinker cut in, attempting to arrest her passage, "'tain't a thing as yer dear eyes ought look upon . . ."

The doctor's hand shot out and clasped Dora by the arm, gently but firmly.

"You musn't look — really, you musn't," he said, affecting a composure which he himself, perhaps, did not entirely feel.

"Damned filthy savages!" the Squire exploded suddenly.

"I *shall* see it, Mr. Callander," Dora insisted, wriggling free of the doctor's grip.

Still he and Stinker tried to shield her from it, but as you know Miss Dora Fetching is a woman of some resolve, and would not be denied.

A startled intake of breath gave token she had comprehended the horror. She gasped, shrank back, uttered a long, low, piteous wail. A fit of trembling seized her; she blanched, staggered, and was about to faint. In her distress she cast about for the doctor — he was there instantly — and clung to him as for dear life. Her heart sank like lead in her breast, the tears pouring from her eyes in a relentless flood.

"*Mattie — oh, not my Mattie — not my poor girl —* "

Another anguished cry escaped her lips. Only afterwards did she recognize the miserable groaning as her own.

Gulping back her sobs, she turned from one to another of us with a desolate, pleading glance, hoping against hope that someone, anyone, might tell her that it definitely, distinctly, most assuredly wasn't so. But no one told her — no one could. Pangs of grief, of conscience wracked her delicate frame, in spasms so violent it seemed her heart must break. No, not so — it already had broken.

Her father, quivering with rage, smote the ground with his stick.

"Unnatural band of villains — reprobates — *damned blasted cannibals!*"

The well of my courage had very nearly run dry; but, as it proved for the Squire, wrath and fury had all but filled it up again.

It was then I noticed — as did the others — the orange light that was flowing up from back of the level slab on the far side of the chamber. It was as if a door had been thrown open, disclosing the fires of the underworld. For where else were we now, with the horror of the spit before us, if not at the doorstep of hell?

We froze, heard a noise as of clawed feet mounting treads, a sinister crackling of joints, a hissing as of venomous breath. From behind the level slab a scarecrow figure arose — a tall, ungainly shadow-mass, silhouetted against the hell-light. In one leap it sprang from the slab and came rattling towards us.

That blind unthinking terror, which often grips less sophisticated people than are we, gripped us now, every one. We stood as if rooted — could not move, could not cry out, could do nothing indeed but stare in horrified fascination. In part it was fascination which held us; but chiefly it was rage and anger at the spit that kept us from fleeing.

Startling and horrible were the contours of its loping frame as the creature bounded towards us. Seven feet high at a minimum, and lean and wiry save for its great, knobbed joints, it projected an unmistakable aura of strength. Its forelimbs, spiny and mantis-like, it held upraised before it, their ends furnished with powerful claws as for the grasping of prey. In its appearance and movement it seemed at once part insect, part spider, part bird, part human being — and yet none of these.

Although ungainly, the creature was swift — deadly swift and purposeful. The wreckage of some vanished race, a fragment of another world than ours, or denizen of Hades it must be. For where on earth could such an abomination possibly have arisen? Nowhere.

*Its sole objective now was to free itself and return to its own kind.*
Where indeed on earth to find another such as this?

Dora alone amongst us was too distraught to be terrified by it — the cause of all the trouble — the *damned blasted cannibal*. The revulsion of feeling, the contempt, the utter and complete loathing she felt for it trumped every other emotion. In her despair at the loss of Mattie, she jabbed fiercely at the tears that *would* persist in raining from her eyes. Then of a sudden she lifted her rapier and brandished it before the approaching abomination. Through and despite her tears she glowered her hatred of it, every ounce of fear having been squeezed out of her by the horror of the spit. It was as if she meant to annihilate this offspring of evil simply by the power of her look.

"'Tis the gangly devil hisself," murmured Cedar Jack, readying his staff.

It was then he and the rest of us noticed that the devil was carrying something in its forelimbs. It was a peculiarly-shaped wand of a sort, the tip of which was glowing a brilliant green.

The looming shadow-mass halted just out of reach of the doctor's light. Aggressively it thrust out the wand, directing its tip at the carcass on the spit.

Next instant the charred flesh shuddered, as if from a discharge of lightning, and the head, which until then had hung limply down and out of view, was jerked back as by the scruff of the neck.

Eyelids fluttered; glassy, unseeing orbs stared from under a bulge of brow.

This sudden, unexpected liveliness on the part of a corpse was one surprise. Another was the face on it.

No, not Mattie's face.

The face was Bothack's.

## Chapter Forty

A GUTTURAL gurgling from a lifeless throat, a vacant stare from lifeless eyes — so much proceeded from the smoldering husk that had been Bothack, skewered on the spit.

Again the wand was thrust at the carcass, again the carcass jumped. Dead lips pried themselves apart and a strangled groan was heard. Two words emerged —

"LEAVE — NOW."

In forming each syllable a violent effort was expended, a kind of spastic heaving and straining of the sinews, as the wand delivered the necessary jolt to compel the dead flesh to speak.

Really, what was one to say to this? What possible response could there be to such an exhibition?

We stood silent and aghast; then, when we had not complied by *leaving now*, a second *communiqué* was summoned from Bothack, in the same tones of strangulation —

"NOT — BELONG — HERE."

Again no reaction, save for the chilling of our blood and prickling of our skin. A third time the carcass heaved and disgorged its warning —

"REMOVE — YOURSELVES — BEFORE — TOO — LATE."

This horror from the bowels of the earth, this abomination, this cannibal of the Cupboard doubtless had slaughtered many over the years, as today it had slaughtered Bothack. Its distaste, so to speak, of human kind was manifest from its behavior — its devouring of its own slaves and others like them. The livestock had not been enough; necessity, it seemed, knew no law.

So this had been the fate of old Harry Smelt, Dickie Fish, little Fanny Meadows, and who knew how many others. A calf — a sheep

— Josie the milkmaid from Sweezy's — Bridgit Gooderly — all were one and the same to this ravenous beast of prey.

The doctor's eyes flashed with a vengeful light.

"I should very much like to roast this creature alive, here in its own den," he said quietly. "It would be a form of justice, to pay it back in its own coin. What do you think, sir?"

The Squire's tone was grim. "Pay it home to the beggar, is that it? Touch match to its nest? By thunder!"

"But one way in," nodded Cedar Jack, "but one way out."

Set the chamber alight? Begin with the horror on the spit, pile it over with brush . . . set it ablaze with lantern oil . . .

"You are a brave lot of people in these parts, I must say," was my first reaction. "But surely this creature will do all in its power to stop us?"

It was an unassailable point, an objection not easily countered.

"I believe," the Squire conceded, after a little thinking on it, "it's odds we ourselves would be cooked by the nasty devil, should we attempt to pay it home. Damn and blast it all!"

How then to confine the danger? How to keep this abomination from menacing the people of Dithering every half-dozen years when it awoke to gorge? How to imprison it here for good and all, and put an end to its depredations?

The beast, observing us from the gloom, seemed to be reading our thoughts. Indeed I had the distinct and rather uncomfortable impression that it was so, for the story Cedar Jack had pieced together from Bothack had given hint of it.

"ON — PERIL — OF — YOUR — LIVES — GO."

Another warning, and still we did not *go*.

Growing impatient, the monster scuttled nearer, its back bent low and its spiny forelimbs carrying the wand before it. With a disagreeable clatter of feet and rattling of joints it bore down upon us. Then, rearing up again onto its hind stalks, it stepped into the circle of the doctor's light.

The picture of it there in all its horrid magnificence, over which the lantern's flicker was shedding a ghastly brilliance, is one forever etched upon my brain.

Before us loomed as fearful and loathsome a vision as human eyes ever had beheld, one more hideous than any horror in an evil dream. Flesh drawn taut as canvas, and grotesquely mottled — a patchwork of ugly blotches. A torso supported by twin spidery stalks with their great knobbed joints that crackled and rattled, resting on thickly-clad, bird-like feet, each with three toes before and a fourth behind. Claws on spiny forelimbs flexing like fingers. Worst was the grisly, swollen cranium: a caliban head possessed of but a single eye, and this a huge, projecting bulb that glistened in the light, above slavering jaws armed with files of conical teeth.

There was a distinct aroma of slime arising, perhaps not unexpected in a being that for upwards of two hundred years had called the Cupboard home. Bestial, yet filled with intelligence, malice, purpose, it was a truly frightening horror. Where, where on earth were others of a kind such as this? Nowhere. Only in hell, surely.

A nice pickle we had landed ourselves in.

Regarding us evilly with its single orb, and thinking perhaps that this close view of its anatomy might spur us to flee, the abomination thrust its wand again at Bothack.

"CLEAR — OFF."

So transfixed was I by the spectacle that I did not at first pay heed to noises of a commotion that had arisen behind me. Indeed the stir barely registered, until —

"Squire, sir — Miss Dora — h'yur she be — you'm need go no step furrer — "

It was the voice of Bailey, the whipper-in. In his hand he held a makeshift torch, with which he had blazed a path through the dark of the outer chambers.

"What is it, Bailey?" the Squire said, his attention for the moment directed elsewhere.

"By yer laive, sir, 'tis Mattie — look 'ee — ef 'ee plaise, Miss Dora — 'tis Mattie, God be praised! She did hear us a-callin' to 'er, miss, but did wait a time to show 'erself, as she were distrustin' 'twas some sly trick o' the piskie's — "

Our heads snapped round and we stared in blank amazement, for there at Bailey's side Mattie stood. And a sight she was, too, with her garments awry, and her hair fallen in elf-locks about her shoulders, and her cheeks stained and smeared, and her eyes red from much crying. In brief, she looked fit to drop.

"So 'tis! 'Tis our Mattie!" young Stokes exclaimed.

"Great sticks alive," erupted the Squire.

Dora's heart gave a leap in her throat. Her first, faint gasp on seeing Mattie was like a prayer — an answered prayer. Her joy at the girl's safe recovery was overwhelming and unbounded.

Mattie had eluded capture, and so the monster had taken Bothack in her place — had taken him when he had failed to deliver her.

Small wonder the villain had fought so desperately against Cedar Jack! Small wonder it had taken the piskie to bring him in!

For her part Mattie scarce could contain herself, for she had news to relay — dreadful, terrible news.

"Oh, miss, forgi'e yer Mattie — Mr. Callander — 'tis cruel sick I b-be over it," she stammered out. "She be gone, Mr. Callander, sir — she be dead — God rest her little soul — 'twas murder — 'twas *vile* murder — the mounster Bothack, sir — Flounce — he did smite her wi' his club — struck her down, sir — killed her, out o' doubt — the mounster Bothack — Flounce — the m-m-mounster — "

All at once she stopped short, her eyes looking past us in dazed surprise. We saw the blood drain from her face, saw her brows form themselves into a haunting expression of terror, a bewildered, uncomprehending look, as her mind struggled to make sense of what her eyes had conveyed to it.

"Mounster . . . ?" she murmured faintly.

In that instant something came over me, as of a memory long lost or a dream perhaps, welling up from deep inside my consciousness. Before me passed a vision of a head turned ghostly white, of eyes like a frightened hare's; and it struck me then — I know not how or why — that some awful consequence might result should Mattie look full upon the caliban and the spit, as though upon the Gorgon — might be turned to stone, or made mute like Davy Zoze —

But ere Mattie's grasp of the horror had progressed sufficient to signify, Dora, knowing her girl as she did, sprang to her aid.

"Mattie, don't look! Look away, Mattie," she cried, thrusting herself between the maid and the shock that impended. Then as one she and Bailey and Stokes swept her up and conducted her in haste from the inner chamber, and through the dark and out of it again into the light of day, and so to safety.

From the charred mass that had been Bothack a final warning was received —

"GO — NOW!"

The corpse shuddered one last time; a ghastly, dry, creaking laugh dribbled out of the dead throat, before sinking into an unintelligible groan. Then the head fell limply down and was still.

The caliban spun on its heel and leaped away. A series of bounds returned it to the level slab, and there it descended again into the earth. A drone of wings went whirring overhead as the piskie followed after it; then the hell-light went out, attended by a metallic *clang* as of a door swung shut.

Came a low rumbling from underground that quickly throbbed into vibrations. I could sense a vague and immense stirring under my feet, as of some hidden power deep within the Cupboard.

An earth tremor was my first instinct, but the doctor was of another opinion.

"No tremor. There is some further devilry here. Come!"

Swiftly we crossed the chamber, the doctor lighting the way. To our astonishment we found that the level slab had vanished — that indeed that entire portion of the chamber had disappeared. The solid rock wall which but minutes ago had stood there had melted away, while at our feet, where had lain the slab, a sizable cavity had opened in the earth.

Resting inside it was as curious and enigmatic an object as any my imagination might have conjured up. A silvery, shiny, sculptured object it was that lay there, metallic and rounded and hard. At the top of it, just below us, was a circular aperture resembling a closed hatch. It was through this portal, I suspected, that the caliban and its minion had retreated.

There arose then a sudden surge in the throbbing underfoot, and in that moment I understood it was the curious object that was the source of the hidden power. Seconds later the object began lifting into the air. Startled by its sudden movement, we withdrew to what we judged to be a safe distance.

For a time the object hung motionless over the pit. If you have toured the Natural History Museum at Hoggard, you will have seen fossils of an exotic marine creature, now believed to be extinct, called a nautilus. If you have done, you will have some idea of the appearance of the strange craft that was hovering before us. The nautilus's elaborately-chambered shell, when stood upright, was the first image that had come to my mind on seeing the caliban's extraordinary vessel. For a vessel it surely was, one which, behind its illusion of terraced rock walls, had lain buried in the Cupboard since the sundering.

Directly the ship glided towards us. We had to scramble to avoid being crushed by it, hurling ourselves behind some debris at the periphery of the chamber. As it floated past us it swung far over onto its side, that it might slip through the low opening; for the dimensions of the Cupboard's outer chambers are more restricted. As it departed we rose from our places and followed.

Soon the gray daylight showed ahead. We could see Dora and the others crouching in the brush beyond the cave mouth, could hear the frenzied yelping of the hounds, as the craft of the caliban, after its long years of imprisonment, emerged rumbling and throbbing from the Cupboard.

The next instant — in less time than it takes to tell it — it gathered speed — impossible speed — and vaulted into the sky, and in seconds dwindled to a speck there and was gone.

## Chapter Forty-one

AGAIN that eerie sense of detachment from the world came over me, as the veiling mist descended.

Round me all was still, all was quiet. The mist lay everywhere about, as once more I was plunged into that dream-world of fog and dark that was no dream. On this occasion, however, there was a light glowing through it.

It was a distant light, streaming yellow and warm from casement windows.

Streaming *yellow* . . .

As the fog began to lift, an outline of the edifice housing the casement became more distinct, as though materializing from out of the gloom. It was the Pack Horse Inn.

I was on the other side of the stream, not far from the bridge-end. Crossing the bridge I hurried round to the street side of the inn, and saw there the door standing open, the glow of a fire in the big hearth pouring from it and from the deep bay windows. A *yellow* glow.

Color! Color showing through the fog!

All about me was a dreary gray save for that blaze of color flowing from the inn. How different from the last time!

Cautiously I entered. The veiling mist, it seemed, dared not enter with me, but remained without, barred from the threshold. Meanwhile inside the colors radiated in all their vivid splendor.

Drawing on my earlier experience, I wondered who if anyone I should find here. Might it be the proprietor, Mr. Readymoney? His nephew Gilbert, the pot-boy? Mrs. Readymoney . . . ?

Hold on — hold on! Stop a minute, Earnscliff. For these three belonged to the Pack Horse Inn of years agone. Wasn't it landlord Asa Mundey or Mrs. Mundey I should expect to find?

But I found none of these. Instead I found a stranger — a slight, insignificant-looking little man, whose dress and appearance put me in mind of an assistant in a haberdasher's.

He had drawn up a stool to the old long-case clock in the corner and was at work upon something there. The case-door of the clock was ajar, the pendulum stilled. As well the face of the gruff old giant had been opened and the dial mechanism removed. It was this mechanism with which the little man was busied.

From a pocket of his coat he took an oddly-shaped instrument resembling a two-pronged fork. From another pocket he extracted a silver watch as big as a saucer. Deftly he applied the prongs of the fork to the dial mechanism of the clock; the instrument answered by giving forth a musical tone. His eyes traveled repeatedly from the mechanism to the silver watch and back again as, guided by the watch, he made slow, stepwise adjustments to the dial with the fork. Each small change caused a different tone or note to be sounded.

Bent over the mechanism at rest on his knees, the little man was absorbed in his task, so much so that he failed to notice me until I had come within arm's length of him.

The instant his gaze encountered mine he was on his feet, his work laid by. A pair of startled eyes scrutinized me through round glass spectacles. The lenses of these spectacles were as thick as bottle-bottoms, and magnified his eyes to such an absurd degree that I nearly burst out laughing.

He was a clean-shaven, trim, very neat little man, with smoothly-slicked hair. He could have been a very young man or a very old, it was difficult to tell. Clearly he was surprised to see me.

"Who are you? How did you get here? For you nearly scared the pants off me," he exclaimed.

"The door was open. I walked in."

His eyes through their bottle-bottoms studied me for the space of several seconds more.

"What are you doing here?" he demanded. "Where did you come from? Who are you? Can't you see I'm busy? For it's very delicate work."

"Do you always wind clocks at" — I consulted my own watch —

"half-past three in the morning? Oh, hang it — it seems to have stopped . . ."

The little man appeared to resent the question.

"I'm not winding it. I'm not a clock-winder; I'm a clock-*minder*. There's rather a world of difference there," he said peevishly.

"I see."

"All the clocks in this sector have stopped."

"This sector? What do you mean by that? Well, when will you have them going again?"

The stranger frowned his annoyance.

"You don't understand. All the clocks have stopped because I've stopped them, so that the sector clock can be mended. Who are you, I say?" He regarded me skeptically. "For I don't recognize you, you know. You're not supposed to be here, whoever you are. In fact you can't be here."

"Well, nonetheless I am here."

His suspicious glance measured me narrowly. "You're not one of *them*, are you?" he said.

"Them?"

"Meddlers . . . tricksters . . . Woldfolk . . ."

"Ah," said I, understanding him a little now — a very little.

"So you are one of them," he snapped.

"I am not one of them. In fact I've never see one of these — these Woldfolk. But I've heard quite a lot about them, too much in fact. It seems that long ago in the past — "

A muscle flickered in his cheek.

"The past! The past!" he exclaimed in his dry, testy way. "What do you know of the past? Or of the present for that matter, or of the future? Are you a minder?"

"And what do *you* know of them? For I know a little."

"Then you know you can't be here. No one can be here, excepting the chief or myself."

"The chief? Who is that? And why is that?"

"Well, I'm the clock-minder for this sector. I've leave to be here. It's my job."

"It's your job to mend a long-case in the middle of the night?"

"It isn't the middle of the night."

"And where is the landlord? Does he know you've been tampering with his clock?"

The rest of the house was silent — dead quiet. There had been no hint of anyone stirring.

"He's unaware, as is everyone else — yourself excepted — and will remain so until I've done with my work. It's very important work. You musn't interrupt me again," said the little man.

"Just what is your work?"

"Mending sector clocks. This one has become woefully inaccurate of late, for there has been a massive displacement in this sector. You can't muck about with a thing like that."

"I see." (Actually I didn't.)

"As a consequence it was reported to my chief, and he dispatched me to effect repairs. And a proper job it's turning out to be, too. But you haven't answered *my* questions. Who are you, and how can you be here?"

I made a baffled gesture. "You keep asking me that. What do you mean, how can I be here? I came here after — "

Exasperation flooded his face.

"Well, how *can* you be here? For you're outside of time. How did you come to be outside of time?"

"And what does that mean? And by the by, so must you be too — outside of time, as you call it."

"Well, of course I'm outside of time! It's my job. How else am I to mend a sector clock?"

"I don't follow you. A sector clock? I took it for a simple long-case."

"A long-case it is, simple it is not. There's nothing simple, young man, about a sector clock. If there were, we clock-minders would be out of business."

"Still don't follow. Oh, by the way, my name is Philip Earnscliff, to answer one of your questions."

"You can call me Arthur — most everyone does. I'm big-hearted that way."

"You do resemble an Arthur, now I think of it."

"Well, there you are, then." He extended a genial hand. "Call me Arthur."

"But Arthur isn't your real name?"

"Er — no." He considered a moment, then shook his head. "No, it wouldn't make sense to you. Arthur will do. It does for most everyone."

"So what is this about a sector clock? And just what is a sector clock?"

The little man proceeded to explain that it concerned me rather vitally, and everyone else as well.

"To put the matter in a nutshell, every sector must have its clock. If it didn't, we should all be coming and going at different rates and times, in relation to one another. We should each be slightly out of tune, as it were, and getting worse with each passing second. Every now and again it happens, as it's happened now. That's where I come in, and others like me — clock-minders — in other sectors."

"Still don't follow you. In fact, I don't know what you're talking about."

"You'd be surprised how much you don't know. I know I was, before I acquired a sufficient background of experience. Young man, don't you know that time, aside from being fleeting, is fluid as well? That it sloshes this way, sloshes that way? That it speeds up, slows down, turns this way, turns that way, in response to local conditions and in keeping with the state of the observer? This really is quite elementary. Well, it's sector clocks that keep time steady and on flow."

I stared at him a moment, trying hard to take in what he was saying.

Was this a rib? Was he pulling my leg? Or was this strange little man touched in his upper story?

"But a clock only measures time. It doesn't regulate it," I said.

"Now there's where you're wrong — in this instance. You say a clock only measures time. Well, for ninety-nine point nine-nine-nine-nine percent of clocks, it's true. But a sector clock is a different beast altogether. It regulates the flow of time in a sector — keeps it aligned — keeps it from slowing down or speeding up, sloshing this way or that way, in answer to passing influences. Or did you think that time was a constant?"

"Well, isn't it?" I asked.

"Hardly."

"But surely a minute is a minute, an hour an hour — "

"Nonsense. O ye of little insight! Though it's no easy subject, not by a long way — I'll grant you that. A sector clock keeps time flowing smoothly in its sector, and in relation to other sectors. This inn and all within its sphere presently are outside of time. It's absolutely essential so that I may effect repairs. Sector clocks must function in harmony, or conditions in the different sectors would deteriorate. Suppose time in this sector were to stop altogether and for good? Do you know what the result would be?"

"People would . . . hmmm . . . live forever?" I suggested.

The clock-minder gave a tolerant sigh.

"Ah, but the human span is short. Young man — people like you, animals, insects, would know absolutely nothing about it. The lot of you would be frozen in time, frozen in the moment, all unconscious of the stoppage."

"Well, you have stopped time now — you have stopped the clocks in this sector, or so you tell me. I don't feel frozen, and I'm certainly not unconscious, I don't believe."

"That's because we're outside of it — *we're outside of time.* We're in a kind of bubble; time's little, er, peculiarities don't affect us here. Otherwise I couldn't do my job."

Suddenly he stopped and his scrutiny of me sharpened. His eyes in their round glass settings bored into mine.

"And so I'll ask you again, young man. How did you get here, and just what have you been up to?"

## Chapter Forty-two

I MUMBLED something about a cordial, the gift of the Woldfolk, Dr. Callander, and putting things right.

The clock-minder's brows hoisted sharply.

"The Woldfolk, you say! Not one of them, you said! You're in league, aren't you? I see it now — perfectly clear — you are the cause of the displacement in this sector. I should report you to my chief."

"What do you mean by a displacement?" I asked.

"A shaking of the sand-glass, as it were. Somebody in this sector has been meddling with the flow of time, and that person is you, I'll be bound. The cordial of the Woldfolk, you said — "

"But I'm not of the Woldfolk, nor am I helping them. I have no connection with them."

His gaze, ludicrously magnified, was slighting.

"You spoke of the cordial — the gift of the Woldfolk. If you're not of the folk, who gave it to you then? Was it Outland?"

"Outland? Obadiah Outland?"

"You know of Outland — I thought you might! These Woldfolk — meddlers — are guardians of the cordial. It's their 'gift to give', as they call it. I've made a study of them since I was assigned to this sector. Most are sober, quiet folk. But others are busybodies — meddlers — malcontents. This cordial of theirs, well it's a scandal and a nuisance. I've had a complete report from my chief . . ."

He proceeded to explain that the Woldfolk had charge of the cordial precisely because they themselves could not make use of it.

"For they haven't souls, you see. They're earthbound. And with the cordial, it's a journey of the soul that's undertaken. Rather like a dream, isn't it — this experience of the cordial?"

I told him that that was exactly what it was like. The little man knew rather more about the subject than I had given him credit; but then I expect it was all part of his job.

"The Woldfolk, they're immortal, but they're earthly immortals; they're born without souls. Without a soul, one can't participate in a journey of the soul; and so they can't participate in the dream of the cordial. But they may offer it as a gift to others — to humans, for example — when the need is particularly strong. They view it as a responsibility of theirs, part and parcel of their custodianship.

"For no Woldfolk can share in an afterlife. No soul — no afterlife. It's for this reason they are discouraged from mixing with *churlings*, which is their term for you humans. Loss of the soul was the cost the folk paid for earthly immortality. In the eyes of some I suppose they're a race to be feared — but pitied too, perhaps."

"What do you mean, 'you humans'?" I inquired, troubled by the phrase. "For what are you, then?"

"I'm a clock-minder," he replied, as if that alone explained it. He stroked the angle of his jaw thoughtfully. "Haven't you noticed how swiftly time passes on certain occasions, how it drags on others? You believe it's all in your mind, don't you? A trick of the imagination? Well, it's no trick — it's your sector clock. A celestial body, gravity well, dimensional rift, or other passing phenomenon has thrown it out of joint. That's where we clock-minders come in. We return the settings to normal. Otherwise time, over time, would spiral out of all connection to reality. Why, you wouldn't know if it was Tuesday week or a million years from now. Then of course there are the meddlers . . ."

It still was difficult to follow him.

He regarded me critically for a moment. "What do you know of the time-space fabric? Gravity and mass? The speed of light in a vacuum? Dark fields? Dunstan's constant? Wormholes? Twister functions? Ransom's paradox? Not a glimmer, eh?"

I shook my head. Inside it my brain was whirling. Again it seemed like another dream.

He waved a tolerant hand. "Not your fault. My chief has a first-class mind and understands it all better than I do. But I know enough to get by. For these are no easy subjects, believe me."

"I do believe you."

"Well, well," Arthur said, glancing round him at the dial mechanism and the tools of his trade he had laid by, "I expect the work can be put off for a bit — only just a bit — as we're outside of time. Fancy a cuppa — some tick-tock tea, as I call it — and a scone? For I've more than enough. Then we may resume our discussion."

"I'd like that."

The tea was excellent — there was a hint of chamomile, sassafras, and something else, tempered with an infusion of milk and sugar — as was the scone, the two complementing one another nicely. For an interlude outside of time, it was an invigorating one.

My host meanwhile had snugged himself down into a cozy wingchair, and I had done likewise, and for a spell we sipped our tea and enjoyed the fire and chatted over indifferent matters, before returning in time — as it were — to the subject at hand.

"It's perhaps easier to grasp if you think of time as a sort of vapor pervading all of space. The faster you travel through a given region of space, the less vapor you inhale; thus less time is consumed. That is to say, time passes more slowly the faster you go. Hence it follows that the more leisurely your course, the more vapor you will take in. Thus more time is consumed. In other words, time goes by faster the slower you go."

"That hardly seems likely," said I, scratching my head — "or even possible."

"Nonetheless it's true."

"It still is difficult to fathom."

He nodded patiently. "I know it's difficult, but still it's the way it is — you can ask my chief. His knowledge of the subject far exceeds mine, but this is the way he likes to explain it. That's why he's the chief and I'm a minder."

"You've handed me quite a jolt with all this. However, it would seem to be a timely — if I may so phrase it — opportunity . . ."

Now that we were outside of time, there was plenty of time — so to speak — for the clock-minder to hear my story, for it had occurred to me that here was a person of knowledge who might help me to understand it all better.

We drew our chairs nearer the fire. Arthur raked the embers and tossed some more wood on them. Then he sat down and, easing himself back against the cushion, fell into a listening attitude, with his legs stretched out before him and his hands behind his head. After I had completed my narrative he was silent for a while, as he thought over all I had told him.

"It's a curious yarn," he remarked.

"It's perfectly true in every particular, I can assure you."

"Oh, I don't doubt your word. On the contrary. I'm happy you had no dealings with Outland. It's he no doubt who supplied the cordial. For you know there's this legend of his taking the sorrowful on board his barge for a journey to the other side, for one last conversation with the dear departed. But he's Woldfolk, of course — no soul, no other side. It isn't his barge that transports them, it's a nip o' the cordial. But the fellow has a legend to uphold."

"So it was Outland who gave it to Dr. Callander?"

The clock-minder's headshake was a tolerant one.

"This Miss Violet Carswell — an odd girl, in her way. A 'very singular young person', I believe you called her."

"To be precise it was Miss Bingham who so described her."

"Well, this Miss Carswell of yours — she too must be Woldfolk, don't you think? For it stands to reason. It wasn't your Dr. Callander who finagled the cordial; it was she. She obtained it for him from Outland, no doubt explaining it was for one of those sorrowful journeys across the Styx. When Outland discovered her true purpose, he summoned her and took her back. That was the bit of business you witnessed on the shingle. Now she'll receive judgment from the folk. All for love, eh?" and he shook his head wonderingly.

Miss Carswell one of the Woldfolk! *That very singular young person.* Not so young she, nor so human — Miss Carswell an immortal on earth!

"All for love?"

"It's as plain as a pikestaff," Arthur nodded confidently. "She — a Woldfolk — has been enamored of this doctor for ages. Didn't you tell me you'd spied a young woman in your dream, and that she had seemed familiar to you?"

A startling thought crossed my mind. Recognition dawned.

"The girl dressed as a groom, holding Bob Cob's head . . . no one else had seen her . . . yet it seemed she always was round the doctor . . ."

Those glimpses I had had of the female groom — one moment she was there, the next not — had puzzled me no end. It was Miss Carswell I had seen all those years ago in the dream. Devoted to the doctor — a Woldfolk in love with a churling — yet she could do naught, would do naught, but admire from afar; for the doctor himself loved another. Miss Carswell must have known there was a chance I would see her, perhaps recognize her. And still she had gone forward with her plan.

"All for love . . ." I mused.

"All for love? All for bunk," scoffed Arthur.

It seemed that members of the folk on occasion had fallen in love with churlings, but such attachments were discouraged. Because the Woldfolk were without souls, their love was doomed to be earthly only; they never could rejoin a loved one who had crossed over. Nor could any of them participate in the dream of the cordial, as it involved a journey of the soul.

What was it Miss Carswell had written in her note?

*I wish that I could have done more to help the doctor, but I myself am unable to enter the dream. When you come to understand my meaning, you will understand all.*

There in the letter was her admission to me — that she was of the Woldfolk. It was for this reason that someone else had been needed to aid the doctor. She could not herself enter the dream — could not help him in that way — because she had no immortal soul to dream with.

This love of hers was a kind of love unfathomable to me, and to most people I dare say — an utterly impossible kind of love. Out of love for the doctor she had obtained the cordial, that he might save the young woman he himself loved. For the loss of Dora — a lamp too early quenched — had scarred the doctor as much as it had the Squire.

Miss Carswell had sacrificed herself and her hopeless kind of love that Dora might live, that the long years of sorrow — sorrow for the doctor, sorrow that had left the Squire a broken man, sorrow for Mattie, for all indeed who had known Dora — might be blotted from the record.

"What," I asked, "will they do with Miss Carswell, do you think? What judgment will they render?"

The clock-minder shrugged. "It's their business. In my view," he confided to me with a roll of his eyes, "she sounds a bit of a nut. But then these meddlers oft are unstable. A bad case. Young man, you're better off without her!"

## Chapter Forty-three

B UT love a crime? Surely not.
But why then should Outland have summoned her back? Had he not himself given her the cordial? Why the change of heart? Why a judgment?

"Well, because it *is* a crime — using the cordial in that manner — one punishable by the Woldfolk themselves," Arthur explained. "The cordial is intended for use but sparingly, and only to experience again pleasanter, happier times — not to change them. Change is expressly forbidden. It's there your Miss Carswell went wrong. Altering the flow of time is clean against the law, and inimical to the natural order. Why, it's little short of insanity! Take my word for it, for time is my job. No safety-firster it sounds, this Miss Carswell of yours."

"But I was under the impression it had been the doctor's idea," I told him, "and that it was he who had suggested it to her, this notion of introducing a new element — namely myself — which hadn't been there before. For it was this new element they were banking on to produce a favorable outcome. So it was Miss Carswell all along?"

"And it looks very much as if they succeeded. But in saving Miss Fetching and sparing her maidservant a life of incapacitation, a crime was perpetrated, for which Miss Carswell will pay the cost. Amazingly, it seems she was entirely prepared to pay it." And he rolled his eyes again and shook his head at the foolishness of Woldfolk — and perhaps of human folk as well.

"The people round these dales seem to be afraid of them — afraid of the Woldfolk, what with their being invisible and all. This notion of their spying on people when no one can see them — "

"Stuff and nonsense," snorted Arthur, with a Hankey-like clucking of his tongue. "It's true, they do wear fern-seed — have done for ages. But it's chiefly to keep you people from spying on *them*. All in all they'd rather not mix, most of them. And the legends, well — it seems to me they're more to keep your kind from seeking them out. They aren't overly sociable, as I've found, and most are wholly content to mind their own affairs. But a few are meddlers — busybodies — unhappy with the old ways. Or like your Miss Carswell, just plain unhappy."

The discussion's turn caused me to reflect upon the events I had altered in the dream, those which had been changed because of my presence — the element that hadn't been there. Had I not saved Dora on the quay, she would not have lived to have spared Mattie the horror of the caliban and the spit. Because of me, Dora herself had become an element that had not been there. Nor would Clemendy have been with us on the excursion to the Cupboard, when the emerald ray in the inner chamber had fastened on her —

"A *questor beam*," Arthur explained. "A jet of intelligent particles, released to gather information concerning one's environment. It's use has been widespread for some time. My chief has one at his dispose."

"Questor beam," I repeated, accustoming my ears to the sound of it.

Had I not suggested to Dora that she bring Clemendy on the outing, the glypt would not have been detected by the beam. As a result the caliban would have had no knowledge of her, and wouldn't have taken her from Dora's room. Clemendy would have lived.

But if Clemendy had lived, then the train of events leading to the confrontation in the Cupboard might not have happened. Like as not there would have been no confrontation; thus Mattie would not have seen the caliban, or seen Bothack on the spit — there may have been no spit, and no dead Bothack — and so she would not have needed sparing by Dora . . .

But what of Mrs. Stokes — Mattie of the ghostly white hair? Did she not exist in the Dithering of the present? Plainly she *had* seen the caliban . . . or had seen something at one time or other, something which had so frightened her that . . . or had she done . . . or hadn't she . . . ?

I felt the eyes of Arthur, whose glance was knowing.

"Ransom's paradox," he smiled. "Do you see what happens when you meddle? Do you see what happens when you create a displacement? You produce more work for us minders."

The emerald ray — the questor beam — had scanned all of us in the inner chamber, but it was poor Clemendy its jet of particles had settled on. Why?

"Pocket glypts," Arthur informed me, "have a unique material in their armor, chiefly in their scutes. It's an organic crystal, unlike any other in earthly nature. Even the big glypts haven't got it, only the pockets. Elsewhere — by this I mean on other worlds — it's rather common, being found in the bark of certain trees. Under proper conditions the raw crystal can substitute for the more refined arrays, like that in the dial mechanism of the sector clock. Its chief use, however, is in celestial navigation. Without it you're as blind as a mole if you mean to ride the spaceways. As well it has a function in extradimensional transceiving — "

I raised a hand in surrender. My host's explanation was getting far too advanced for my poor earthly brain to follow. And so he simplified it for me, saying it was likely the caliban's navigation or possibly his communication system had been damaged in the crash of his ship. Without fresh crystals the pilot would have had little prospect of seeing home again.

"For the species isn't of this sector," he went on, "and would have no knowledge of glypt crystals, or *gontiomers,* as they're termed. It was lucky for him your small pet came within the range of his beam. For glypt crystals are the only earthly source, and discovering them meant the pilot had a chance of escape, or at the very least of signaling others of his kind."

Still it was not entirely clear to me. Where for instance was the caliban's home, and what was the monster doing here? How had it "come in with the sundering"?

"They call themselves *esculonds,*" Arthur related, "although they're not of this sector, as I've said. Don't know much about them, really. Some two hundred of your earthly years or more ago — it's relative — a colony vessel of esculonds entered this sector. For centuries it had roamed the heavens, inoperative and adrift. It had suffered a catastrophic failure of its life-sustaining machinery, and most of the colonists had perished. A few — a very few — perhaps no more than this single pilot — may have gained the safety of one or more small, one-man scout ships aboard. There they would have placed themselves in *torpor* — a kind of perpetual sleep state, or dormant condition, which would have enabled them to weather the long journey amongst the stars. In time the colony vessel, which was of tremendous size, its dimensions rivaling those of a minor moon, was hurled into your star system. By a sublime accident of fate, its trajectory carried it straight to your world, where it went down over a southern ocean.

"Through a fortunate alarm, one scout ship at least must've been released as the colony vessel was entering the atmosphere. The vessel then broke apart, flinging debris and whole chunks of itself over the entire globe. This was the event known to you as the sundering.[1] The scout ship, too, fell to earth, but the esculond pilot, revived from his long sleep, succeeded in guiding his damaged craft to safe harborage in the place you call Eldritch's Cupboard. And there he has remained, his ship disabled, with only limited energy reserves for torpor, and he in hiding, for these two centuries."

*It had come in with the sundering . . . its sole objective now was to free itself and return to its own kind . . . its name not Eldritch, but esculond . . .*

I pondered awhile all that Arthur had told me. It seemed fantastic, improbable, incredible. And yet, I had heard whispers of the like before. Most thought the sundering had been caused by a shooting star or comet that had struck the earth, or perhaps by a cataclysmic volcanic eruption. But there had been rumors . . . rumors of an evil science that had existed since untold ages, since before the first speck of intelligence had gleamed in the mind of man . . . an evil science mastered, I knew now, by a race of esculonds . . . by a race of *damned blasted cannibals* . . .

"In fact they're not cannibals, strictly speaking," Arthur pointed

---

[1] See *Strange Cargo* (2004), ch. 34, for another's perspective. — *Ed.*

out, "for they're not dining on members of their own species, but on those of another. Why, it's little different from your drooling over a beefsteak or a fat capon."

"Frankly I don't like the sound of that," I told him.

"Well, we can't help being what we are."

"And moreover there is a difference, a most decided difference. A man can't have an intelligent conversation with a beefsteak or a fat capon."

"And you released him — you and your friends — and let him take his ship into space. Myself, I don't like the sound of *that*." His smile had faded and his eyes were showing concern behind their bottle-lenses.

"It was trapped. It needed to return to its own kind. At any rate, we didn't mean to do it. The doctor was all for burning the hellish thing alive there in the Cupboard."

My companion was silent for a time, drumming softly with his fingers on the arm of his chair.

"We're treading on a thin crust here," he remarked at length. "Esculonds are colonial, and this one never was released, so far as I am aware. This has now been changed — *you* have changed it. You and your friends have meddled. Let's hope it wasn't a botch . . ."

"Where is its home?"

"Haven't a clue, really. Some distant estuary amongst the stars. As I've mentioned they're not of this sector, but one hears of them occasionally."

*Not too often, I trust.*

Had I not saved Dora, she would not have lived to spare Mattie. But in saving Dora, what else might have been changed? Still the doctor's plan had served to —

The doctor's plan? Miss Carswell's plan! For it was apparent it all had sprung from her hopeless love for him.

All for love? All for bunk! But the doctor —

That's right, blame the doctor. Blame Miss Carswell. Blame the Woldfolk. Blame everyone but yourself, Earnscliff, for having been talked into so foolhardy a scheme. *You could have refused.*

Had I not considered as much before embarking on my leap from the battlements?

*That would be the very height of folly . . . the height of madness . . . it's totally out of the question . . . totally, absolutely, altogether out of the question . . .*

But no, Earnscliff, you convinced yourself of the rightness of the cause, had the presumption to suppose that you alone were the man for the job . . .

*Had I really the ability to change all this? Was it truly in my power to roll back time those many years, to make the very grave yield up its dead?*

Aye, just fling the helve after the hatchet! One intrusion was not enough. Two were needed to *change things for the better*.

Of course it had all been for a good and noble purpose — to save Dora Fetching from a tragic death, the Squire from despair, Mattie from a life of imprisonment — but what else might have been changed as a result? What might the doctor and I find once we had awakened from the dream?

"Bit of a nosy lot you humans are, meddling in affairs that don't concern you. Ah, but human nature is odd," Arthur nodded complacently. "To pursue your own, right course headlong, regardless of the consequences. But it requires wisdom to refrain, and that isn't a thing in your line, as I've found . . ." and he broke off shaking his head and sighing.

Indeed! What business had I interfering in the lives of these people of the dales? What were they to me, a junior in the employ of Bagwash and Bladdergowl, Bodmin Square? The very idea of it seemed so preposterous now, so . . . so . . .

Indeed what right had I to meddle?

Frankly, I was amazed by all that I had learned from my new acquaintance. I had never before in my life met anyone like this clock-minder, and I told him so.

"You are *sui generis*, sir," I said.

"No need to call me names, young man," he retorted.

"Names?"

"'Big-hearted swine', I believe you called me."

"No, no — you misunderstand — nothing like that! *Sui generis.* It's a Latin phrase, meaning, loosely, 'one of a kind'."

"Oh, it's a posh term."

"Well, not so much — "

"Let me put you up to a wrinkle, young man," said Arthur. "The next time you're summoned to these dales and a pretty girl invites you in for a cordial and asks you to play the hero — don't."

"I take your point. I wonder now what will become of her father, the old veterinary at St. Bees? For someone will have to tell him that his daughter — why, that means that he himself is a — "

"There is no veterinary at St. Bees," Arthur said.

I saw his eyes stray to the dial mechanism of the long-case, heard him mumble something about getting back to his work, that the displacement in this sector might be rectified. I glanced at the inn-door in which the gray mist was standing. I fancied that the mist was like the vapor of time, unable to enter here; that its presence marked my current condition as a sort of transitory state between the dream and wakefulness. As well it suggested that I, too, must be getting back to work — back to the waking world, once the effects of the cordial had left me.

The magnified eyes of my host had grown pensive behind their bottle-lenses. It struck me that they were rather like two lamps, these eyes of his, illuminating processes and mysteries invisible to me and quite beyond my grasp. Then all at once a strange sort of weariness came over me, and I felt myself drifting slowly down, and down, as though onto a bed of softness and dark. It was not an unpleasant feeling, but I didn't understand it. For it seemed I should be coming out of the dream, not sinking back into it . . .

"Well, no matter," I heard Arthur say — his voice was faint, as if from a distance off, and growing fainter — "for you'll not remember this talk we've had. Sorry — a precaution — a little something I placed in your tea. Awfully nice to have met you, though. I enjoyed our little chat. And good luck to you. I believe you'll need it."

# Epilogue
## Flounce's Dream

*- i -*

THE small party grouped round the dewy plot of earth behind the farmhouse looked a sad little bunch. Their figures, dark in mourning weed, stood like silhouettes against the shrubberies. Barnyard aromas, tempered by the sweeter scents of balsam and evergreen, flavored the air. Distantly hens could be heard chattering, and overhead the rustle of an icy wind in the trees. A few yards off, Bob Cob was idly cropping grass and musing.

It was a somber affair. The party included Dr. Callander, and beside him Dora and Mattie, then Stinker, young Stokes, the cook and housekeeper Mrs. Peters, and the maid-of-all-work. All were muffled tightly against the chill, and with bowed heads were giving ear to the clergyman who was reading aloud from a book. The women, dusky veils shading their faces, were communing regularly with their handkerchiefs, and drying their eyes and sniffling. Everyone seemed much affected by the ceremony, particularly the doctor.

Flounce's keen glance swept the scene, touching on all the people there and on the patch of ground at their feet. It was edged with tiny stones, each of them meticulously placed, and the soil had been freshly turned. Snatches of the clergyman's speech drifted to her on the breeze and to her three companions who were looking on.

"Well, this is superlative. Isn't he that same holy Joe who preached at Clemendy's service that we have no souls?" sniffed a handsome old gentleman of a cat, a long-haired gray with festive ear-tufts. "The idea of it! Why, one would think we were Woldfolk. Now, there — there *is* a sad bunch for you."

"Still, we're rather like Woldfolk, in a way," remarked another of the lookers-on, a spotted tabby. "For there's not a one of 'em can see or hear us."

"It's the same chap," nodded the third. She was a dainty little ginger female, with bright blue eyes and a barred tail. "Croakstone he's called. He's the one who drank off the last of the Squire's port."

"Well, he's a priest and must have wine."

"And quite a talker as well," said the handsome longhair, plainly the graybeard of the trio. "He's like an exuberant puppy, that can't help but trample all he happens on."

"What does a fellow like that know of our souls? Are you allowed in law to spread such misinformation?"

"Yes, unfortunately. But people are strange creatures. What humbug is he feeding them now, I wonder? For I can barely hear him."

"The same line, no doubt," sighed the little ginger female.

Flounce and the three were observing from a small rise of ground only a step off from where the service was being conducted. Cracks gaped in the shivery skies above, where low-flung clouds borne along by the wind were streaming over Dithering and the farm.

"By the by, what's going on here? For I can't remember much of what took place," spoke up Flounce, who had been silent until now. "I followed Mattie into the garden at the Moorings — scampered out after her — as I had had a sense things weren't right. I had heard the voice of the piskie, and knew it wasn't Dora calling. But everything afterwards is hazy. When Bothack pounced from behind the hedge, I knew something was up. Of course I didn't trust him — never had done. So I went after him tooth and nail. He cursed me something fierce, and thrust a ragged handkerchief to his chin where I'd caught him. Next I knew I saw his club looming dark against the sky, and felt a heavy blow that staggered me. I crawled off into the brush. By and by the strangest feeling came over me. There was a weird thrumming in my ears, then I seemed to go all limp and melted down into the grass. And that's the last of it I recall."

"He clobbered you — that Bothack brute," said the spotted tabby. "That's you now they're mourning over."

Flounce's ears went up and she scanned the scene with rising interest. "Really? Mourning over me?" She seemed genuinely surprised. "Then I'm . . .?"

"As a doornail. Cold as a key. Stiff as a cat's whisker — "

"Hallo! I get the picture. It's not a pretty one."

"It seems you were quite the favorite round here," observed the venerable gentleman in gray.

Flounce paused a minute to reflect, for the news had touched her deeply. Then, as it began coming back to her, she resumed her story.

"Hmmm. Well, then a very extraordinary thing happened, after Bothack — after I — er, well — you know. It still seems like a dream to me. Perhaps I'm dreaming now? For there are some who say that all life's a dream. Well, next there came a change, after the darkness. It felt as if a giant's hand had plucked me right out of myself. And then I saw the hand! For there was a golden light, dazzlingly bright and clear, that grew and grew before me. I couldn't imagine what it was, or where I was. I could see nothing and no one apart from the light. Well, it threw a scare into me, I can tell you. Then a vision began to form in the light — a vision that *became* the light, and it was the hand that had plucked me — and the next I knew I was riding easily in the palm of it. It was so very warm and comforting there. It was a light warmer and brighter than any sunbeam, before which the sunlight itself should be as night.

"Next I heard a voice, deep as a bell, calling to me as though from the deepest deeps of time. I felt the light weighing me in its hand, as if taking the measure of me. 'My, my,' exclaimed the voice deep as a bell, 'aren't we the hefty one?' And so we chatted awhile about this and that, and the voice asked me what I had learned from this adventure, and what I'd learned from that one. All the time, bygone scenes and memories were passing before me as if in a pageant. It seemed we talked together for ages and ages; or perhaps it was no longer than an eye-blink — it's difficult to know. But at last the hand unfolded and out I tumbled.

"What I heard then was this — 'You've made a decent job of it. Off you go then, Flounce my girl.' The next I knew the light faded, and I heard the voice no more. Instead there was a tremendous rush of wind, and an instant later I was here with you fellows." Flounce looked the three over curiously, as if she were seeing them all for the first time. "By the by," she remarked, "who *are* you fellows?"

It turned out that they, like Flounce herself, were Callander farm cats, who had been valued members of the household in days gone by.

The handsome gray was Solomon Tater — a wise old gentleman. James Callander, the doctor's father, had adopted him "away back in the years." He was a person of considerable sagacity and experience, with impressive jowls to match his ear-tufts.

The spotted tabby had been the doctor's chief companion while growing up on the farm. His name was Pliny, and he was something of an historian. In his lifetime he had been exceedingly well-regarded in cat circles in the neighborhood on account of his learning.

Tig Tig was the name of the dainty little ginger girl, and she had been much attached to the doctor's late mother.

"I was her favorite," Tig Tig recalled with a sigh. "She was more beautiful than they make them today, I believe; although Miss Dora may be nearest her equal. Her portrait hangs in the family gallery in the house — perhaps you've seen it. Old James Callander would gaze at it for hours on end after she left us. My one regret," she confessed, with a sad little droop of her ears, "is that I never thanked her properly for her care of me. She passed away quite unexpectedly, late one evening, and no one told me for hours."

Flounce nodded thoughtfully. "I know what you mean. I had an inkling of a sort on that last day, an eerie feeling that something terrible was about to happen. I don't know why, but it came to me that I hadn't thanked my guardian in such a long while for his good care of me over the years. More times than I can reckon up he fed me; he sheltered me, and he took me with him almost everywhere he went. He made an adventurer out of me! For I was orphaned in college — Maunder College — and he adopted me, like Sol there and old James Callander. He really is a fine fellow, my guardian. I call him my guardian, but he prefers simply 'Callander'. He has looked after me wonderfully. Although truth be told it was he who needed the looking after — he and Stinker. What a pair they made! And so on that last day I caught a mouse and left it for him, in thanks for his many kindnesses to me. Then together we set off for the Moorings. And that was the last I saw of him. How sad he looks, poor man . . ."

"So what are you now? A five? A six?" Pliny inquired. "For you look a six to me."

"Eh?"

"Lives — life-passages. How many is it? Five? Six? What's your number?"

"Oh, I see — follow you now. Well, the voice in the light told me I was a five. Five lives down, four remaining."

"So you're not done with your chances yet."

Flounce's smile was comfortable. "Heavens, no — not by a long chalk. So," she purred, lounging easily on her forepaws and swishing her tail, "what have you chaps been up to?"

"Pretty much anything we care to get up to — resting, mostly," said Pliny, "or drowsing. I call it that, for it really isn't sleep. And watching. And observing. We do a lot of watching and observing."

"You're master of your own affairs here — or mistress, as the case may be," explained Solomon, scratching at a furry jowl with a hind foot and yawning.

"How do you like it?" Flounce asked.

"I'll admit, it was a bit peculiar at first," said Tig Tig, "and required some getting used to. For instance, you're never hungry here — and yet I do so miss eating! Fish wild-caught in the stream, chicken livers, turkey breast. Mrs. Callander, she did prepare such lovely dinners."

"And I can't sniff as well as I once did. In fact," Pliny confessed, "I can't smell at all. None of us can."

"How I miss my fishy aromas!" Tig Tig sighed.

"And you'll never freeze in winter — that's a good thing."

Flounce glanced at her tail swishing to and fro, and was startled to observe no movement on the part of the grass. Curious, she made a grab at some pine needles that were lying nearby, without result.

"How odd," she said. "Yes, I expect it will take some getting used to..."

"Well, that's the picture," finished old Solomon. As the graybeard of the group he had long since gotten used to things. For he was an eight — eight life-passages behind him — and had long since gotten philosophy as well.

"But they haven't a clue we're present," Flounce observed, meaning the mourners gathered round the little plot of earth edged with stones. "What's the good of that?"

"Isn't being here with them sufficient for you?"

"Well..."

Flounce cleared her voice and was silent for a time, while pondering over the matter. Meanwhile her new friends kept a lazy watch on the service.

"So what's next?" Flounce said at length, after no solution to the dilemma had presented itself.

"Pretty much whatever you'd like," said Pliny. "Myself, I've been brushing up a little on my historical researches. For instance, do you know that not a single Dithering cat in recorded memory ever has bested Sol in the hunting field — birds and rodents category? Old James Callander was mighty proud of that, I can tell you."

This compliment the venerable Solomon accepted with a gracious nod, and a little throaty murmur of satisfaction. For an accomplished eight he really was a very modest and kindly old gentleman.

"But enough about us," he proceeded, smoothly taking charge of the discussion. "So what are your plans, do you think, Flounce?"

"I've nothing definite at the moment. I'm still 'getting used to' the situation," she replied.

"Some prefer to laze about and enjoy themselves. Rest and recuperation from the hard business of living. Free from worry, from responsibilities. A carefree existence. Liberty Hall. Easy Street. But all within limits, of course. No loaves and no fishes..."

"I do miss my fishes," Tig Tig sighed, licking her lips with a dainty tongue.

"Others become bored and look out for a chance at another go."

"Oh, yes, I'd forgotten about that," Flounce said, perking up her ears. "Do I have a choice? That is — who is it decides?"

"As for a choice, well — yes and no. It's you yourself who decides when and if you return. It really depends how much leisure you can stand. As for *how* you return — that is, what your circumstances will be in your next life-passage — that is for a higher authority to decide, though you'll have a voice in the matter. You may plead your case, as it were."

"I see. That is if I choose to advance from a five to a six?"

"Exactly."

"And if I choose to return to Callander farm as a six?"

"Your wish may be granted. Or it may not be."

"Or I may remain here as a five? Remain as I am now? As we all are? Seeing and hearing, but unseen and unheard?"

Solomon nodded. "It is entirely at your discretion. Do you strain for pastures new? Are you keen to learn, to enlarge your circle of acquaintance, your fund of knowledge? *Do you yearn for life to be poured back into you?* Or are you content with the present? Content to remain as yourself — as Flounce, a five — and progress no further? Are you satisfied with the breadth of your acquired wisdom?"

Flounce was thoughtful. "These are momentous questions," she nodded soberly.

"Indeed it is a decision of moment," the old gentleman concurred, "and not to be made lightly. It requires great discernment, and a deal of serious study."

"That I can see. However at present I'm uncertain of my course. For this is all so new."

"New? Well, yes and no — for you are a five, after all. *You have trod this path before.* You have faced this same decision and have made it, more than a couple of times; it's simply that you don't recall having done so. None of us does — it is a sad, but necessary truth. It required many passages for me to appreciate this.

"We're all of us bound in the same direction, however some of us are more keen to get there than are others. We each must go his own gait and blunder along in his own way. But when the time comes to balance the ledger . . ."

Flounce didn't care for the sound of that.

"The golden light . . . the palm . . . the voice deep as a bell . . ." hinted Solomon.

A light of another sort dawned. "Oh, I see," said Flounce, brightening. "It wasn't as horrible as all that."

"Then comes the decision of moment."

Flounce's ears fell again. "Of course," she murmured. "The decision of moment. So that is how the ledger is balanced, is it?"

"That is how it is balanced — in the next life-passage. Who knows what the future may hold for you as a six? For we little dream of the experiences and challenges in store with each new turn of the wheel."

Flounce looked at Pliny and Tig Tig, who nodded in glum assent.

"Well . . . I'm sure you're right, Sol . . . for yours is an older, wiser head than mine . . ."

Followed a silence heavy with thought. At the end of it Flounce rose, yawned, arched her back as high as it could go, ruffled her tail, and adroitly changed the subject.

"Well," she said, stretching her forelegs luxuriously, "now I think on't, I could do with a bit of a holiday. Yes, indeed. This Bothack affair has been awfully trying. Do you think he'll miss me while I'm away? Callander, I mean? For I believe he needs me. And I do miss our adventures together."

"But dear," Tig Tig pointed out gently, "he can't see you, and he can't hear you. He doesn't know you're alive — er, well, he doesn't know you're *here*. He doesn't know any of us are here. Although it's rather apparent he misses you . . . just look at his face . . ."

"Why not take your holiday, then come back and stay with us for a while — just as you are?" suggested Pliny. "For we love these dales and Callander farm, and having our friends about us."

"Yes, do," Tig Tig urged.

"Of course, there are others who have gone on and not returned. Do you remember Dr. Dee, Tig?" To Flounce he explained, "We called him 'Doctor' Dee because of his great knowledge of the medicinal shrubs and plants of the district. A regular herb-wife he was. And he had divers other interests as well, for his tastes were very cat-holic." Here Pliny's whiskers lifted and a sly grin spread to his ears. He was not only an historian, but something of a humorist as well.

"You're probably right. I don't believe I'd be happy elsewhere," Flounce reflected. "But I'd not mind taking a little holiday for a spell. I shall go adventuring! Where shall I be off to? Some exotic place, I'll be bound. I'll travel, see something of the world . . ."

Tig Tig heaved a sigh. "What there is left of it," she reminded.

Flounce's expression sank. "Oh, yes, there's that. I'd forgotten — the sundering. But still, there's plenty that remains . . ."

"And remember, apart from others like ourselves the world won't see you — can't see you."

"So," smiled Solomon, curling his forepaws in comfortably under his chest, "where will you go, do you think?"

Flounce pondered a minute or two. "What say you to Hoggard? For I've heard rather a lot about it."

"Hoggard? Hoggard exotic?" returned the old gentleman in some surprise.

"And Fenshire is charming — particularly northwards of Marley Wood. For isn't that where Miss Dora's brother has settled? Or perhaps the islands in the channel — or Nantle — a seaside holiday — there, that's the ticket! Or perhaps I'll go down to Bogminster . . ."

"Bogminster!" echoed Pliny, with half a shudder. "You're not serious? Slopshire? The abode of megalops and mylodons? Half-wild fenslodgers? Flat-head boars? Slopshire? For a holiday? Man, man — I'd rather have the distemper than go down into Slopshire. Why, the stories I could tell you — "

"Well, where would you suggest I go?" queried Flounce.

"I've heard Medlow is lovely this time of year."

"Medlow? I'm not so sure about that. The place I hear is crawling with medical men and superannuated pensioners and fogeys. Where's the pleasure in that?" Flounce returned.

Abruptly she broke off on hearing a familiar voice, one that gained her instant attention. It was the doctor, her guardian, speaking in hushed notes over the little plot of earth edged with stones. The vicar had concluded his reading, and it had been given to the doctor to say a few words in memory of his friend and companion since Maunder days.

Heads were bent in sober reflection. The domestics sniffled and dried their eyes. Flounce and her companions listened as the doctor's words were wafted towards them on the chilly air.

" . . . life's work is done . . . best of cats . . . a child of mystery, as you came to us, so have you left us . . . never again to meet . . . let us pray that some good comes from the sad events of these past days . . ."

*Amen.*

A solemn hush followed, punctuated by the sniffling of the women. The vicar sprinkled sod over the freshly-turned earth, and Dora and Mattie laid flowers there.

"They'll miss you, Flounce, have no doubt of that," Tig Tig whispered. "Your guardian loved you. They all loved you. Indeed you are blessed."

"I can't help but feel that I let him down, somehow. I failed him in that Bothack business. However did I relax my guard and permit that brute to clobber me?"

"Failed him? Why Flounce, what more could you have done? For there is only so much one cat can accomplish on this earth. And now you're one of us here on the farm — sure there's no grief in that?"

"I believe you worry too much," was the verdict of Solomon, given once the service was over and the mourners had dispersed. "But it was your time, Flounce. It was an unfortunate combination of circumstances, true. But it was your time."

"You know what they say — care killed the cat," Pliny advised.

"Well," said Flounce, recovering herself anon, "I'll have my little holiday, that's certain. And then I'll think it all over — everything. Perhaps I'll go back, if the opportunity presents. For I do believe my guardian needs me."

"He needed me as well," Pliny reminded her.

"Besides, he has Miss Dora now," Tig Tig pointed out, "and she's a right one if ever there was one."

"She's a charmer, indeed — a trump," Flounce agreed, with a little swish of her plume.

"And I know a right one, for I was the favorite of Mrs. Callander — your guardian's mother. There was a charmer! But she left us too soon."

"And remember this, Flounce," added the wise voice of Solomon, "that you'll recollect nothing of this interlude once you've returned as a six. Your soul will be as a blank tablet. Oh, you'll carry with you your principles and guiding truths, those lessons which you have mastered along the way. But otherwise the slate must be clean, so that upon it may be inscribed the new knowledge acquired on your next journey. For to tread the identical course as in an earlier life-passage would be unavailing."

Thoughtfully Flounce scratched her cheek, and brushed up her whiskers. "Yes," she said, nodding slowly, "yes, more of it is coming back to me now . . ."

Meanwhile Solomon resumed his counsel.

"Your memory will return again during the next interlude — that is, in this state in which we presently reside — but only those recollections concerning the life-passage just ended. This condition of ours here I call the 'happy meanwhile'. It's a way-station of sorts, a halting-place between two lives. Most of your earlier lives have been retired to the past; this side of eternity you'll not recall them. Your memory will extend only from one life-passage to the next. Don't ask me why it is, for I'm sure I don't know. I suspect, however, it's so one may review and reflect upon the passage just completed, thoroughly and in full, in readiness for the next go. For tomorrow is a new life."

"And so what of you chaps?" Flounce asked, after a suitable pause for reflection. "Why are you still here? Aren't you going back?"

"I myself am an eight," Solomon explained, "and so have but one life-passage remaining. It thus represents for me the gravest of grave decisions, one that I have yet to ponder fully. And this happy meanwhile of Callander farm, I think you will agree, is a capital spot for pondering."

"Pliny?"

The historian shrugged. "I haven't given it so much thought. The doctor was my guardian as well, you'll recall, and like Sol I'm rather comfortable here. And I'm only a four — I have lots of time. I'll go back some day, I expect."

Then it was Tig Tig's turn. The dainty girl hesitated a minute. "Well, you know," she said slowly, "I'm only a three, and so I hardly count. But Callander farm has been my 'meanwhile' for so very long, that it has made me something of a homebody."

"I see. What you all are saying," Flounce concluded, "is that you are undecided about going on — that you take greater pleasure in a happy meanwhile here on the farm than in risking your necks in an uncertain future."

"Spot-on. That's it exactly," nodded Pliny. "No need to rush into things, particularly a thing as serious as that."

"The decision of moment. Balancing the ledger."

"That's the ticket."

Flounce spent some time thinking over all she had learned from these new friends of hers, and what already in her own mind had begun returning to her. Meanwhile the breeze had stiffened, chilling the air all about her; though of course Flounce and her companions felt nothing of this.

One who did feel it was Bob Cob, who unnoticed had left off his quiet cropping of the grass. Of a sudden he threw up his ears, opened wide his eyes, and stared in the direction of Flounce and her fellows. He sniffed the wind, snorted, flicked his tail, and snorted again, and pawed the earth with a forefoot. Then he bobbed his head and whinnied an eager greeting.

"There are times, chaps, I'm positively certain he can see us. For horses are quite sensitive," Pliny remarked. "Bob may not be able to clear a five-barred gate, but I dare say he knows we're here."

"We're here, and Bob is here," said Flounce, "but there's one who hasn't turned up. I wonder what's become of him?"

"Who's that?" Tig Tig asked.

"That Mr. Earnscliff. You know — the young man on a traveling-tour of the dales. The lawyer chap from Hoggard."

"Oh, him. Well, no, we haven't seen him of late — have we?"

The others echoed her observation. Young Mr. Earnscliff had disappeared as if time itself had swallowed him.

"Perhaps he had business which called him home," Pliny offered.

Flounce gave a sigh. "I hope you're right, and that it explains his absence today. For I always thought he liked me."

- ii -

"My dear, here is the young man from Bodmin Square, the conveyancer who is to amend the leases and draw up the title-deeds. For you know, old Mr. Bladdergowl's health is not of the best, and as a result he has dispatched his junior to us to arrange for the needed papers here and at Callander farm."

Dr. Callander having so introduced him, the newcomer — cordial, clear-eyed — entered with a brisk step.

"Mr. Bladdergowl assures me his young representative is an able solicitor, with a good deal of experience in these matters," the doctor added.

The doctor, a tall, impressive-looking man, had been a University don when, some years back now, he had resigned his post, upon the death of his father, and returned home to Callander farm to assume charge of the family holdings.

"I told you, dear, that I had a surprise for you," he remarked to his wife, as the young visitor presented himself.

Mrs. Callander's lively eyes looked their astonishment.

"Didn't I tell you the likeness was exceptional?" her husband said, folding his arms and smiling.

Mrs. Callander, gazing on the newcomer, scarce was able to credit her senses.

"Exceptional is hardly the word, dear," she answered.

Mrs. Callander and her husband had been married now for some years. She was an heiress, she and her brother having inherited this house and estate of the Moorings from their late father. A short distance up the road lay Callander farm, her husband's property, which had been home to the Callanders of Dithering for generations.

"Your face, Mr. Earnscliff, is familiar to me," Mrs. Callander said, "as is your name. But how can this be? For we can't possibly have met."

Their visitor too was puzzled. "And as this is my first experience of the dales, I must agree with you. That is, unless we may have met in Hoggard . . .?"

"I have never been to Hoggard. Although my husband has been, of course."

"Yes, he has seen Mr. Bladdergowl a number of times on affairs of business." For the firm of Bagwash and Bladdergowl, in Bodmin Square, had long been the Callanders' legal advisers in the metropolis.

"Perhaps I remind you of someone?" Mr. Earnscliff suggested.

"Indeed you do," said Mrs. Callander, "for your resemblance to another young man from Hoggard, who was our guest here at one time, is striking. But that was long ago, before my husband and I were married. The young man's name as well was Earnscliff, and he too was a lawyer."

"From Hoggard?"

"From Hoggard. From the city."

It seemed quite inexplicable. The visitor's brows were knit, before suddenly relaxing.

"It could have been my father, now I think on it. I understand he indulged in a bit of rambling in his youth. His wild oats, you know. That was before he met my mother, of course."

"The likeness is remarkable," the doctor said.

The young man was a trifle self-conscious over the scrutiny. "But probably you wouldn't recognize him now, as he has changed rather a lot."

"As have we too, I fear," Mrs. Callander agreed. "But it was long years agone. Wherever does the time go?"

On his arrival in Dithering Mr. Earnscliff had secured for himself a room at the Pack Horse Inn, the chief hostelry in the town. But no sooner had he moved in than he'd been prevailed upon to move out — that is, he had accepted an invitation from Dr. Callander to establish his headquarters at the Moorings for the duration. This was his first interview with Mrs. Callander, here in the snug parlor of the great house.

"Your father, Mr. Earnscliff — assuming that it was he," the doctor went on, crossing to the fireside and posting himself there, "did my wife — indeed did all of us — an incalculable service when he was with us all those years ago."

The young man regarded him with curiosity. "Sir?"

"In point of fact, he saved Dora's life."

It was briefly recounted how Mr. Earnscliff's father had come to the aid of Mrs. Callander one day — one all-too-nearly tragic day — when she had been in grave peril of death.

"But for his swift action," Mrs. Callander recalled, "I should have tumbled from the quay and in all likelihood would have been killed."

It was the young man's turn to show surprise.

"I've heard nothing of this from my father; indeed it's a complete revelation to me. For of course I wasn't alive then. My father wasn't yet married, and would not be for several years more."

"I expect that is the answer."

"My father has never been a man for telling us tales of any sort, in particular those concerning himself. I believe he has kept this admirable deed of his a secret all these years. But that is his way."

"Of course I was immeasurably grateful to him for saving me, for he well could have lost his own life in the attempt. A short while afterwards he vanished — simply disappeared. He was gone from our midst without a word to anyone, as if he had never been here. Whatever came over him? For we never discovered."

"I'm sure I don't know, Mrs. Callander, for as I've said he hasn't spoken of his adventure here. Indeed till today I was unaware he ever had seen these dales."

The doctor, I had observed, had been regarding the young man through narrowed lids, but the significance of his scrutiny was lost on me.

"Well," he concluded presently, with a brisk rub of his hands — "we'll have a go at it then, shall we? For we have some few hours remaining before dinner — time and light enough to survey the lands in question. Then tomorrow we may commence work on the papers, at least in draft."

"As you wish, sir."

As the doctor had explained it, there first were some small matters to be addressed related to the Moorings — "tenants who had suffered reverses of late, all of them friends of long standing of my wife's family. It is her intent that the leases should be amended, to allow for an easing of the terms going forward."

"Readily accomplished, sir."

However the chief of the work awaiting Mr. Earnscliff concerned Callander farm. Some years ago, old James Callander, the doctor's father, being pressed for funds, had sold off entire tracts of land to his neighbors, that certain claims against him might be paid. At his demise there had remained a number of debts still outstanding, which his son had been obliged to settle. As a consequence of these actions of the old man's, the estate had been greatly diminished. But now, all these years on, opportunities had arisen, and it had become possible that the Callander property might be put together again. The freeholds of certain of the tracts lately had changed hands, and there existed a willingness to sell back the acres and restore them to the farm.

"I see no cause why the business can't be transacted to the satisfaction of all parties," stated Mr. Earnscliff. "About Callander farm — who is it now who is in charge there? Have you an agent or overseer for the property?"

"A man named Stokes, an old retainer of mine," the doctor said, "and his wife, who was Dora's waiting-maid, have had stewardship of the farm for many years."

"I see. And Mrs. Stokes — is she better now?" the lawyer asked.

Bewildered looks greeted his query, so that it was a few moments ere any answer was made.

"Mrs. Stokes is in excellent health, to the best of our knowledge. Why do you ask?" the doctor said.

Confusion showed in the young man's face, which had turned a dusky red. He quickly apologized, stammering out that he had absolutely no idea what he had meant by the question, as he had not met either Mrs. Stokes or her husband, nor had he ever before heard their names.

Shortly afterwards he and the doctor went off in the doctor's gig, to make a survey of the acres for which the deeds were to be prepared and the purchases completed. They returned to find that another member of the family had joined her mother in the parlor. This was Miss Lolly, the Callanders' young daughter. An affectionate child of some twelve or thirteen, her bright eyes and eloquent smile were the very spit and image of Mrs. Callander's. Her hair, richly brown as her mother's once had been, spilled about her dimpled cheeks in tiny curls, a single, stubborn cow-lick falling aslant her brow. She and her mother were almost of a height, although Lolly in her youthful lankiness gave promise of emulating her father's taller frame in years to come.

The Callanders were justifiably proud of their children. "We have as well twin sons, James and Jory," the doctor related. "Both are up at Maunder, though both are interested in farming. For my wife and I believe strongly in the advantages a University education affords — scholarship, athletics, the society of a fine, gentlemanly set of men, and the stamp of a college degree. Having once acquired said stamp, both are free to return home if they so desire. We think that Callander farm, particularly with its extensive acreage restored, will be a fine challenge for them. Lately we've had the farmhouse enlarged, and it really is quite an airy place now. In the old days it was rather cramped."

"Yes, I remem — "

The visitor stopped short. Whatever had he been about to say? Remember what, he wondered? For till this afternoon he had never laid eyes on either the farmhouse or Callander farm.

The mystified glances of the others prompted him to explain — "I remember . . . your telling me of the improvements."

The doctor frowned. "While riding in the gig, do you mean? Well perhaps I did — offhand I can't recall. There has been so much bustle of late, what with the activity at the farm, and the talks over the freeholds all at once. It has been a strenuous few months. This is why we are so happy you have come, Mr. Earnscliff! We shall have the deeds at last and the leases revised. For these tenants are old friends and acquaintances, and my wife is anxious that their interests be properly addressed."

"You shall have no cause for disappointment on that score," the young man assured him.

Throughout the meal they chatted easily and comfortably. Miss Lolly, bless her, did not forget me, having seen to it that my regular dish of milk and pastry was laid at the foot of her chair, that I might dine with her and the others.

Mr. Earnscliff, whose place was beside Lolly's, scarce could help remarking upon the arrangement, and on the meal which Cook had prepared for me.

"Yes, it's figgie hobbin," Mrs. Callander smiled. "Everyone asks."

"He adores it," Lolly said, "and has done ever since he was a kitten at the farm. Dad found him one day there in the barn."

It seemed that the doctor had a particular fondness for cats, having had several such companions over the years.

"Curious thing about Figgie," he mused, smoothing his chin.

"Figgie?" repeated Mr. Earnscliff.

"Figgie — for that's his name," Mrs. Callander explained, "owing to his partiality for the dish."

"That is not so usual in a cat, is it?"

"Not in my experience," the doctor agreed — "save for one other who had something of a taste for sweets. You remember Flounce — don't you, my dear?"

"Of course," his wife replied.

"Flounce was a beautiful, big calico I adopted while at Maunder.

She was a kitten and sorely in want when I discovered her one day on our staircase. She became very popular with our set, being a tremendous mouser, and for years was my companion on walking-tours and on surveys." He leaned across and eyed me speculatively. "Figgie reminds me often of Flounce, in his likes and dislikes, and in some other aspects as well. Indeed there are times I feel as if . . ."

"As if what, dear?" said Mrs. Callander.

"I'm not entirely sure. Certainly it is imagination on my part, but there are times I feel as if it were Flounce there behind Figgie's eyes. For there are a hundred little mannerisms and ways of his that are similar . . ."

Wine was taken after dinner by the doctor and Mr. Earnscliff, and then everyone retired to the parlor where the coffee was laid on. All shared in the fragrant, dark beverage — all but myself, of course, as I preferred the lazy warmth of the hearthrug after a good tuck-in.

Night was coming on apace. Unusually for the time of year, the clouds all had scudded off, giving hope of a starlit evening. Silence seemed to have enfolded the world, but for the distant rush of water from the murmuring stream below.

Meantime Lolly had gone to the window and was peering curiously out. Likely she had been drawn to it by the clearness of the skies. But then —

"Why, what can that be?"

"What is it, dear?" her mother called from the sofa.

Lolly craned to look. "Oh, I see it now — a shooting star! Or is it? For how can it be a shooting star when it has slowed down?"

Seconds ticked by. I had been enjoying the warmth of the fireside, but now a disagreeable feeling had come over me that something was amiss. For do they not say that a shooting star is a bad omen?

"Oh, there's another — and another," Lolly sang out, "and now they've slowed down, too. How beautiful they look! What can they be?"

She glanced questioningly at her parents and Mr. Earnscliff. This and their innate curiosity drew them to the lattice.

"See — there are still more of them," Lolly exclaimed. "What are they, Mother? Dad, what can they be?"

They followed her gaze. The next moment Mrs. Callander started to say something, but caught her breath audibly and was silent.

Multiple points of light were glowing in the night sky over Dithering. Some looked to be hovering and were nearly motionless, while others were describing long, lazy arcs through the darkening heaven. One by one they had appeared, and still were appearing, as if coming from out of space.

Fascinated, Lolly was caught up in the mystery and the spectacle of it. The lights in the sky were very beautiful indeed. And still more were arriving . . . and more . . . and more . . .

Glancing at her parents, she was startled to see that her mother's face had turned a ghostly white, that her father's lips had thinned to a stern, resolute line. Something was wrong — very wrong. An ominous chill sliced through her like a knife.

"Mother, what is it? Dad? What's wrong?"

Beautiful though the lights may have been, they were menacing too; for beauty and evil often are sides of the same coin. The dread they seemed to have inspired in her mother and father was palpable.

The tingle and shiver of fright was upon Mrs. Callander — a sudden, very nasty sort of fright. Anxiously she turned to her husband.

"Dear," she whispered, "oh, dear, can it be — ?"

But already he had divined her meaning. The shadow of far-reaching thought lay across his brow. The lines of his face were hard, his pupils wide and staring as he studied the sky.

The points of light had grown more numerous and were circling about now in queer convolutions, an entire fleet of them thronging the heavens.

"They are the oddest things, these stars," Lolly remarked.

Her father's tone was grim. "They are not stars, Lolly."

Vague outlines of the trees beneath the house were only just discernible in the gloom. Beyond them, the mysterious lights had settled into a pattern of wheeling and diving over the town and countryside.

Everywhere they could be seen descending and dropping to earth like a fiery rain.

Mr. Earnscliff, peering through the lattice, was heard to mumble something under his breath, although he seemed scarcely conscious of it.

Mrs. Callander flashed him a sudden look. "Esculonds?" she echoed. "What are esculonds?"

He returned her glance, much perplexed. "I've absolutely no idea, I'm sure. The word — well, it just came into my head. But it's no good word, I don't believe . . . no good word at all . . ."

He peered out at the window again, alarmed by the malevolent spectacle — could it be anything else — that was unfolding in the skies over the dales.

Mrs. Callander's inmost thoughts meanwhile had found their own expression.

"The man in the Cupboard," she murmured, "hisself is no sluggard . . ." Her words trailed off with a shudder.

"There is a board bears that legend, or something like it," said Mr. Earnscliff, "at the Pack Horse Inn."

"Yes. 'Mordaunt's Refrain' it's called."

"Who was Mordaunt? And what does it mean?"

"I'm afraid it doesn't matter now. Oh, what have we done?" she said to her husband. "This ghastly trouble — have we not brought it down upon ourselves?"

The doctor, his scrutiny of the lights done, squared his shoulders, his plan of action — hopeless though it might be — having crystallized into clarity.

"I greatly feared this time would come," he said, and striding to the wall he reached down a pair of cutlasses. One of them he tossed to the young man from Hoggard and, slanting him a glance, challenged him — "Are you a fair swordsman, Mr. Earnscliff? For we shall need every man jack of you."

As well he took down a long-bow and quiver of arrows, to complement the bladed steel. "These will be useful too, if we are to brave the tempest. For it's a mighty storm awaits," he declared, anger hardening his every syllable. "We must spread the alarm — alert the lads to gather in the stock — put up the shutters — secure the entryways with bolts and bars. And someone must ride to the farm and instruct Stokes and the others. For if we are to have any hope of averting the catastrophe — "

At this last word a bond seemed to snap in his wife's heart.

"Come to me, Lolly," she cried, her voice faltering — shrinking — and drew her daughter close. Again and again she kissed her, caressed her, as though for the last time. The flesh of her arms had begun to crawl and she was shivering, a terrible fear having taken possession of her.

Lolly, uncomprehending, with frightened eyes implored her — "Mother, Mother, what *is* it? Mother, what is happening?"

"Something unholy," was her mother's reply, to explain the chaos which had erupted so suddenly and from out of the air.

For Dora recognized only too well the nature of the storm that awaited. The world was closing in; here, with these lights in the sky, was proof in full. Already she felt the creeping coldness of it, the unspeakable horror of it, the approach of things monstrous and abominable . . .

A grim scene took vivid shape in her memory — surely as fearful and loathsome a scene as ever human eyes had beheld. It had seemed like a nightmare, all those years ago.

Oh, would that it were but a nightmare now!

"I am happy," Dora breathed, "my poor father did not live to see this day."

*"Numquam non paratus,"* said her husband, belting on his sword. "Never unprepared — never, by twenty thousand devils! This eventuality I have long anticipated and guarded against, Mr. Earnscliff. By night and by day it has haunted me, in waking and in sleep, the possibility of this time. Would that Stinker were here! But he, too, has gone the way of the Squire. Ah, better as well for him, I expect . . ."

Noises of a growing commotion sounded through the house — a clamor of confused voices calling, hoarse shouts, shrieks and cries, the slamming of doors, the thudding of boots.

"A fortuitous omen perhaps, your being here, Mr. Earnscliff," the doctor noted, "for your father before you performed for us a gallant service. Perhaps now we may return the favor."

Would only that it might be so!

Was it to be a brief, unequal struggle? Or was it to be a lengthy siege — an ordeal of survival?

Had we any real hope of defeating an evil science from its outpost beyond the stars? Any hope at all of forestalling its minions in their brutal purpose?

Nothing else for it now, as the die had been cast.

"Mother! Oh, Mother! What is it? Tell me! Tell me!" Lolly cried, gulping back her sobs.

Fervently Dora clasped her daughter to her heart, as if indeed for the very last time.

"They have come, dear Lolly," she whispered, "and now we must be brave."

"For we still live," the doctor reminded them — reminded all of us — the flame of a magnificent courage blazing in his eye.

Indeed, all else failing what remained to us *but* courage? To everyone?

I believe I never saw anything finer than my guardian, cutlass in hand, standing at the ready between his family and the onslaught that any moment was expected.

Came then a strangled cry from without.

"Mr. Callander, sir! They'm h'yur! Mr. Callander! They'm in the yard, sir — God save us — freaks an' mounsters — !"

The which was, very possibly

### THE END

ABOUT THE AUTHOR

Jeffrey E. Barlough was born in 1953, and holds a Doctor of Veterinary Medicine degree from the University of California, Davis, and a Ph.D. from Cornell. He has published some seventy research and review articles in scientific journals, and has edited several small-press publications of minor and archaic English works. His "Western Lights" series of fantasy-mysteries, begun in 2000 with the renowned *Dark Sleeper*, has been widely acclaimed for its imaginative setting, eccentric characters, droll humor, and unconventional storylines. *Where The Time Goes* is his sixth Western Lights book for Gresham & Doyle.

To learn more about Jeffrey E. Barlough and
the Western Lights series visit

www.westernlightsbooks.com

## ABOUT THE SERIES

Imagine a world in which the last Ice Age never ended.

With much of her territory locked up with ice, medieval England was forced to seek a more habitable clime for her growing population. From every port, merchant-adventurers in their tall ships set sail to scour the earth for a new home. Amongst the places they came to was the land we know as North America. There they found a vast continent untouched by man — a wild, mysterious realm, teeming with saber-cats and their kin, mastodons ("thunder-beasts"), short-faced bears, ground sloths ("megatheres" and "mylodons"), glyptodonts, flat-head boars, megalops, and other Pleistocene giants. Huge, vulture-like birds ("teratorns") roamed the skies, and predatory, toothed whales ("zeugs") the seas.

The shores of the continent were the most amenable to settlement, and there new cities were raised. On the long western coast, cities like Crow's-end and Saxbridge, Foghampton and Fishmouth, Goforth and Nantle quickly gained prominence, and there two great universities were founded, one at Salthead in the north and another at Penhaligon in the south.

Imagine a world where shaggy red mastodons in silver harness serve as proud beasts of transport, and where their southern cousins, the steel-gray shovel-tuskers, are employed in the building of roads for long-distance coach travel. Imagine a world where guns and gunpowder never were invented, where bow and blade alone are the measure of man's ferocity.

Then, in the year 1839, everything changed. It was the year of the "sundering", a cataclysmic event which some attributed to a comet or meteor fall, or to a volcanic eruption of unprecedented violence — or was it perhaps something else? Irrespective of the cause, most life on earth was obliterated, and the world plunged into an even deeper Ice Age. In the words of Mr. Kibble in *Dark Sleeper* — "The sky was filled with clouds of smoke and grew very dark, and remained that way for months and months. Then the great ice sheets came down from the north and froze up the world."

By an accident of geography the cities in the west of the continent were spared, only to find themselves deprived of all contact with the outside — if, indeed, the outside still existed. For no one who had set out for England had returned, and no one had come from there ever since.

It has been some two centuries now since the sundering, and up and down the long coast life goes on. Marooned and alone, Victorian society, little altered since 1839, abides in her sundered realm with its gallery of fearsome monsters, and a prey to powers even mightier than those of the wilderness that surrounds her — the powers of magic and the supernatural.

But why the "Western Lights" series? The author explains —

"The series title is derived from the sundering. For since that dread event the sole place on earth where lights still shine at night is in the west."

*Also in the Western Lights series*

## Dark Sleeper
(2000)

"Are you pleased with your station in life, man?"

So asks the dancing sailor, before unscrewing his own head and handing it over to a very startled Mr. John Rime, the cat's-meat man, one foggy night.

Mocking laughter pierces the dark sky. An enormous brindled mastiff is seen in the streets, walking upright like a human being. A little lame boy with red hair and a green face haunts the corridors of the Blue Pelican public house — eighty years after he died there. A sunken ship rises from the ocean bottom and comes sailing into the harbor. A manlike creature with great leathery wings is seen clinging to the spire of St. Skiffin's Church.

Such are a few of the mysterious apparitions afflicting the ancient city of Salthead. What do they mean? Who is responsible for them? And what of the marvelous glowing metal that looks like gold but isn't, and the exploded statue in a remote chapel crypt?

In a frigid world shattered by a cometary collision, where saber-cats prowl the mountain meadows and the old mastodon trains are fast disappearing from the land, something wicked has been released. Join Professor Tiggs and Dr. Dampe as they search for answers and uncover a 2,000-year-old menace threatening all that remains of earth.

# The House in the High Wood
(2001)

It looked to have been once a very picturesque little market town, but had fallen into decay. Signs of neglect and disuse were everywhere evident, in the general disrepair of the houses, in the tattered casement-windows and tottering chimneys, the disarticulated doors, the extensive overgrowth in the churchyard and gardens and village green. Over everything lay a ghostly pall of silence.

"Driver," I called out, "what is this place? This hamlet below us?"

"Shilston Upcot," replied the coachman, then added, slowly and enigmatically — "or more rightly *was*."

"Who lives there?"

"None what has a decent brain, sir," answered the guard. "Though there might be some — some folk as yet at the great hall, up there in the wood. But none takes to the village now, sir, unlessen they be off the latch. Crackers I mean, sir. Daft!"

What frightful secret lies hidden in the dismal ruined village high in the mountains of Talbotshire? Where have the inhabitants gone, and why have they gone there? Who — or what — lives now in the old mansion-house atop Skylingden point?

"There's deviltry here," said the guard. "The village, the mansion-house, the woods, the black waters — mischief — devil's work — "

"Aye," nodded the coachman. "The kind as don't bear thinking of!"

Discover for yourself the startling answer to the mystery of Shilston Upcot, in this second volume of the Western Lights series.

# Strange Cargo
## (2004)

She opened the case and from one of its compartments removed a lady's hand-mirror. The mirror itself was not of glass but of polished bronze, which reflected but poorly.

She turned the mirror over in her hands, examining every aspect of it with a mixture of fascination and dread. But nothing untoward happened, and so she returned the mirror to the dressing-case. She was about to close the lid when she heard it.

It was a noise like a hissing whisper, and it came from the mirror. A slithery, slippery thing it was, that whisper, dark and sinuous, like an evil vapor rising from a caldron.

"Djhana," it said.

A cold breath of fear raced up her spine, chilling her to the marrow.

"Djhana of Kaftor," said the mirror.

"I do not hear you," she answered, "no, no, I do not hear you — "

"Djhana of Kaftor," said the mirror again.

"No, no," she said, her head turning slowly from side to side and her eyes shut tight. "No, no, no!"

"Our mighty lord the earth-shaker commands you. Return — *or beware the Triametes!*"

# Bertram of Butter Cross
## (2007)

Something stirred back of the nearest tree. There was a rush of movement, and a face leaped into the gap between the branches. It was an ugly face, as faces go. It was a face with two angry, staring eyes in it, and a pair of lips drawn back in a hideous scowl, teeth bared and nostrils blown wide, the whole of it pasted onto a human head and framed by a tumbling mass of orange hair.

But there all resemblance to humanity ended, for the head was perched atop a grotesquely long, sinewy, and altogether unhuman kind of neck, round which the orange hair streamed down like a waterfall.

Jemma saw the head snake its way towards her through the branches, saw it push its face right up to hers; and stopping there, its eyes mere inches from her own, it glared at her and growled . . .

Return now to the Ice Age world of the sundering, and join Jemma Hathaway and her brother Richard, Ada Henslowe, Sir Hector MacHector and their friends in deepest Fenshire, as they struggle to solve the unsolvable — the mystery of Marley Wood.

# Anchorwick
(2008)

It is hard to say just what sort of noise it was.

I swung the lamp round and scanned the darkened chamber. I saw no one, of course, and nothing. It was then that my ears caught hold of it — a faint, energetic whispering, as of a voice struggling to make itself heard.

My scalp tingled with a sudden sense of impending danger.

"Who is it?" I demanded. "Who is there?"

All in an instant I spied a glimmer of movement, and was struck cold to see a strange, ghostly shape swimming in the air before me. The words it was whispering were but two, louder now, and repeated several times over in a desperate, pleading tone —

*"Help me!"*

In *Anchorwick* author Jeffrey E. Barlough returns to the scene of the first book in the Western Lights series, the renowned *Dark Sleeper*. The time, however, is some thirty years before the events recounted there, with certain of the characters from the earlier novel returning in the new work as their younger selves. But they are not the chief focus of the story — that belongs to the narrator, Eugene Stanley, who has come up to Salthead and its fabled university to help his uncle, Professor Christopher Greenshields, in the drafting of the professor's latest scholarly tome. Little hint has young Stanley of the mystery and danger that await him there . . .

# A Tangle in Slops
## (2011)

Round a corner of the house it came — a huge, ungainly form, shambling along on its four oddly-curved, paddle-like limbs. A deep-voiced growl could be heard rumbling in its throat.

The moon's silvered beams were shining full upon it, when of a suddenty the monster reared up onto its haunches and stood awhile observing us.

"We must have our revenge!" sang out Stroppy, who of the lads appeared the more inebriated. "For the Foud's sake, have a taste o' this, ye brute!"

In a fit of courage he drew an object from his pocket and hurled it at the beast — a large, well-aimed object, which sailed like a shot from his hand and struck the looming giant square in the face . . .

When *Bertram of Butter Cross's* Ada Henslowe found herself called to distant Plumley down in Slopshire to aid her little orphaned cousin Mary Trefoil, she had no inkling of the strange adventures that were to follow. Why had the creature that had slain Mary's father returned? Was its goal, as many feared, to eliminate, one by one, the Trefoils of Orkney Farm? And what of the enigmatic green woman — the apparition in the mossy-green mantle — who had been frightening the citizens of Plumley? Was she indeed the ghost of Tronda Quickensbog, wise woman and soothsayer, on a mission to avenge the desecration of her relics at the farm? These and other mysteries will need to be resolved if Ada and her friends are to thwart a looming danger from centuries past.

Also included in this volume is *Ebenezer Crackernut* — the delightful tale of a very bad squirrel, and the author's first Western Lights story for children.

# What I Found at Hoole
(2012)

To all appearances the room was unoccupied.

Moments later a feeling as of doom impending swept over me with a chill. Whose house was this, I wondered? And how had I come to be here?

Hanging from a peg was a tiny silver call, such as might be used to summon a domestic. It was a curious little thing, of a peculiar and antique workmanship. I saw at once that it was valuable. Much intrigued I was about to apply it to my lips, to test the sound, when I became aware of a stealthy movement in the room.

A figure — that of an elderly man with grave features, craggy and deep-seamed — sprang up from behind one of the wing-chairs on the hearthrug. He eyed me uneasily. "What do you mean to do?" he asked.

As I raised the call to my lips he flung a warning hand at me.

"No, sir, no! Do not sound the call!" he cried, in a tone of stifled horror. "Take heed, sir — *lest the devils be unchained!*"

# The Cobbler of Ridingham
## (2014)

"Hallo! Who's in my kitchen?" the cook demanded.

For no reason that she could divine, a feeling as of some looming evil had taken hold of her. Warily she eased her eyes round the arm of the high-backed settle, to see who was there. What she found acted only to magnify her dread.

There was nobody.

Mrs. Flitch fell back a step, certain that there had been a presence there only seconds before, that now was gone. Afraid that some specter was readying itself to leap upon her unawares, she flashed her light round the chimney-corner, the open hearth, the brick walling, the rush-bottomed chairs.

All in a moment the looming evil closed about her like a shroud. Steadily, stealthily, like a misshapen giant, it rose up before her, bigger and blacker than any shadow had any cause to be, flowing upwards and outwards as it spread itself over the bricks and mortar from sanded floor to beamed ceiling.

Then, detaching itself from the wall, the phantom swung round to face her, more like an angry cloud than a solid substance.

The cook shrank back in alarm. A qualm of panic set her heart to racing. "By the powers," she managed to gasp out, "by the powers, what devil is this . . .?"